No words were needed.

His arms drew her tightly to him, his mouth, firm and strong, touched hers. Her soft lips parted and she tasted him. The ground shook beneath her feet, so she clung to him. Their figures meshed in the hot afternoon sun. The cold, swift water raced around their ankles.

Colly's hand brushed across Lone Wolf's broad back. She wanted to know every part of him. Each touch, each new discovery, cried for more—until she feared she might never be satisfied again without his presence. The kiss ended and she bowed her head against his shoulder, trembling with unfamiliar emotions. That she, old maid Colly Mead, should feel this way was a wonder to her. She gave no thought to anything else, only the moment and the man who held her. . . .

CHEYENNE DREAMS

Peggy Hanchar

FAWCETT GOLD MEDAL • NEW YORK

A Fawcett Gold Medal Book
Published by Ballantine Books
Copyright © 1993 by Peggy Hanchar

All rights reserved under International and Pan-American Copyright Conventions. Published in the United States by Ballantine Books, a division of Random House, Inc., New York, and simultaneously in Canada by Random House of Canada Limited, Toronto.

Library of Congress Catalog Card Number: 92-97254

ISBN 0-449-14769-X

Manufactured in the United States of America

First Edition: April 1993

Chapter 1

SHE WAS ALONE!

Abandoned in a great flatland, adrift in a vast, lonely silence. The wind moved across the gold-tipped prairie grass like surging ocean waves, then died away without a sound. Insects, burrowing beneath the hot, thick roots to the cool, black soil, were mute. Even the brown-feathered field sparrows had ceased their slurred whistles. There was no sound!

Kneeling beside her parents' common grave, Colly Mead raised her head and peered at the cloudless sky, as unending as the prairie itself, and strained to hear some sound, some evidence that another living being besides herself actually existed on these unending plains. There was nothing.

Her pale gray eyes were wide and slightly wild as she swiveled her head this way and that with increasing tempo until her single thick braid whipped from side to side along her shoulder blades and finally *thunk*ed against her cheek painfully. She didn't feel it. Wisps of red hair straggled across her round, freckled brow and clung to her sweat-dampened temples and neck.

A cry built, forcing itself from her empty, bilious stomach, past rigid throat muscles, pouring itself into the ugly silence of the prairie. She gave vent to her terror and grief until she had no breath left and collapsed forward onto the grass roots she'd wrested from the soil with her bare hands to cover her

1

parents. She swooned for a moment, not wanting to draw breath, not wanting to continue the weary struggle for life. But even here, fate tricked her. With a will of its own her body shuddered, her muscles quivered, and she drew a great gulping breath that filled her lungs with earth-scented air and, once begun, the acts of breathing and thinking couldn't be stopped.

She lay crumpled across the mound, her cheek pressed against the black earth, her torn and bleeding hands curled beside her, and remembered another time and place.

Spring on their Tennessee farm, with the dew-misted morning grass cool beneath her bare feet, the cluck of hens as they gobbled the grain she flung them, her mother's voice raised in a hymn, her father's deep growl as he harnessed the team and plow, the call of geese overhead. The sounds like music, the beauty, the contentment.

Once she'd dreamed that a man would come along who would look beneath the plain exterior and find the true worth of her, a man who would love the farm as she did and lend his hand, but none had done so. The work had been hard, but she hadn't minded. She'd trudged behind the plow, pressing with all her slight weight so the steel blade cut deep into the red clay soil. She'd cut wood, hauled hay, and tended the animals better than Papa even, but it hadn't been enough. In the end they'd lost the farm.

Brother Davey had brought them a new dream. Coming to sit out on the porch in the evening, he'd spread his maps and books in the lamp glow while Papa and Mama had bent their heads to study the trails. Brother Davey had his own dream—of leading a congregation to Oregon Territory, where they would start a new community and prosper as they never could in Tennessee.

But Brother Davey was not qualified to lead them all into unknown territory. Once they'd reached Independence, he'd listened to reason and hired a wagon master who'd been reluctant to go so late into the season—until an offer of more money overcame his caution. They were the last train to leave

Missouri for the Oregon Trail this summer of 1848. Jim Farley had driven them hard. They had to reach the mountain passes before the first snowfall or perish there.

But a different killer had stalked the emigrants. Sadie Mead was the first to fall victim to cholera, quickly followed by Andrew Mead. Brother Davey had made only a token protest when Jim Farley decreed they be left behind on the prairie.

"As soon as you're well, Brother Andrew, you catch up with us," he'd said, thus salving his conscience. He hadn't even looked back as the train rolled away, leaving only Colly behind to tend her parents.

That task was done, and now she must choose to claim her share of the dream in a dirt grave beside her parents here on the trail . . . or rise and begin anew the struggle for survival. She rested, seriously considering both options and, finally, with a sigh, rose and looked around. During the past moments, when she'd teetered between choosing life or death, her world had changed shape and dimension, yet the prairie had remained the same beneath the unwavering sky.

She was exhausted and light-headed. A sharp pain in her flat stomach reminded her she'd eaten little while she'd tended her parents. Now, clasping her aching stomach, she twisted prairie grass into knots, then knelt to light a cooking fire. If she intended to live, she must eat something to maintain her strength. She mixed a handful of cornmeal with the brackish warm water from the barrel until it formed a thick paste, then dropped spoonfuls into a skillet. When the corn cakes were half-done, she removed them from the pan and ate them, washing them down with more of the brackish water. Feeling stronger, she turned her attention to the problem of survival.

The trail stretched away through the tall grass as far as the eye could see, the unceasing flat plains halted only by a smudge of mountains on the distant western horizon. Brother Davey's wagon train was three days ahead on that narrow trail. She could never catch up with them driving the wagon, but she might if she rode the mules and traveled day and night.

Resolved, she climbed into the wagon and went through the supplies and mementoes brought from Tennessee. There was her father's fine leather saddle. He'd kept it, expecting one day to have a riding horse again. She tossed her mother's fine quilt onto the ground and added packets of cornmeal, a hunting knife, a frying pan, and the last of the salt pork. Digging through their clothes, she chose an extra dress, some clean underwear, her father's heavy coat, his felt hat, and his clean pair of woolen trousers. Finally she took his rifle from under the seat, along with the box of ammunition.

Taking down the white canvas awning from the wagon ribbing, she threw it over the back of the mule she deemed most cooperative and fashioned pockets on either side, which she then filled with the gear she'd chosen. Then she saddled a second mule and turned the rest free. Climbing into the saddle, she looked back at her parents' grave. It already seemed forlorn and forgotten. The day was waning. She needed to leave. Every moment that passed Brother Davey and the others traveled farther away from her.

Yet some memory of the happiness she and her parents had once known made her step down from the mule. Cutting hanks of prairie grass, she fashioned a cross of sorts and placed it on their grave. Taking a sheet of the precious writing paper Sadie Mead had brought, she wrote, "Here lie Sadie and Andrew Mead, dead of cholera this year of our Lord, 1848." Without looking back she rode away, heading west toward Oregon, toward a dream that had never been hers.

She followed the wheel ruts cutting a narrow path through the prairie grass, urging the stubborn mules forward in a vain hope of catching up to the train. As long as she could see the thin ribbon of track in the moonlight, she pressed on, and slept and rose again at first light. The trail wound back to the river as she'd known it would, for they'd followed the meandering course of the muddy Platte all the way across the prairies. Now the flatland gave way to rolling ridges and foothills. Late on the second day, a cold, driving rain blurred the trail ahead. Colly kicked the mule's belly and pressed on. Jim Farley wasn't likely to let the train halt because it was raining. No sense to stop, anyway; she had no place to take shelter from the downpour.

The sky had grown black, darkening the prairie to an eerie dusk. Thunder, deep and ominous, rumbled in the distance. Shivering, Colly pulled her father's felt hat lower over her eyes and wished she'd brought the wagon after all. She could have crawled underneath and been warm and dry.

The rain seemed to intensify, falling in gray sheets before her, until finally she was forced to stop. Stepping down from the saddle, she felt the cold mud ooze beneath her feet and fill her boot tops. The rain beat against her face and shoulders as if it meant to bury her in the prairie mud. The sound of it pounding against the earth was menacing and unpleasant.

Shivering with cold, Colly dug out her father's coat and slung it around her shoulders. It would protect her for a while. She had to get dry or she'd take a chill and come down with a fever. Dragging the heavy canvas bag off the pack mule, she fumbled with the knots, stopping often to sluice the rain away from her face. Her hat was useless and lay in a sodden heap on the ground. At last the knots gave way and Colly crawled underneath, making room for herself among the supplies. For a moment the comfort of the canvas was heavenly—until she began to feel the cold, wet mud beneath her.

One of the mules neighed a protest at something and took off at a gallop. Colly flung back the canvas, prepared to sprint after the mule, but he had already disappeared into the gray shroud of rain. Only the pack mule remained. Quickly Colly grabbed hold of his reins, scolding herself for not having thought to do so earlier. She had no way to hobble the animal. She hadn't thought to bring wooden pegs and a hammer.

Pulling the frightened beast back toward the canvas, Colly huddled down again, the short reins wrapped tightly around her hand, while she assessed her loss. Her father's saddle was gone . . . and the rifle and ammunition. She still had the food supplies and a change of clothes. She'd have little need of the rifle if she reached the wagon train soon, but she mourned its loss.

Andrew Mead had set great store by the piece. She could remember him cleaning it lovingly before taking it out to the hills to shoot squirrels and rabbits for their supper. Mama had always made the best rabbit stew, and they'd sat around the fire on a cold, rainy day listening to Papa talk about how he'd spotted the rabbit and shot it.

Colly's stomach contracted painfully as she thought of her mother's stew. She hadn't eaten decently in more than a week. She could feel her ribs poking out of her sides.

The rain paused as abruptly as it had begun, but the sky was still black and threatening. Something thudded to the ground nearby. Clutching the canvas around her head and shoulders, Colly swiveled to see what had caused the sound. The noise was repeated and became a staccato. A fat pellet of ice struck her in the face, and she quickly ducked beneath the canvas.

The mule whinnied and reared, trying to break loose, but Colly held on for dear life. In the struggle, the canvas fell away, leaving her hand and wrist exposed to the fiery sting of the hailstones.

The mule pulled at the reins, dragging Colly with him down the path. The canvas belled around her, dropping her meager belongings along the way. She was forced to let go of the canvas and use both hands to subdue the frightened mule, but to no avail. His strength was greater than hers. The reins slid from her hands and the whinnying animal galloped away, leaving her wallowing amid the white hailstones on the muddy ground.

Colly curled into a ball, wrapping her arms around her unprotected head, and rocked herself in misery. The thunder of hail against the earth slowed and faded altogether.

She stayed where she was for a long time, until she felt the heat of the sun on her wet back; then slowly she raised her head and peered around, marveling at the quick moods of this land. Her mules were gone, her supplies scattered hither and yon along the trail, but somehow she took hope in that warm light pouring down on her.

Wearily she got to her feet and walked back along the path the mule had dragged her, picking up and discarding items as she went. The cornmeal was wet through with muddy water, her mother's quilt a sodden, muddy rag, its bright colors obscured forever. Colly retrieved a frying pan and a knife. The extra clothes she'd brought were muddy and wet—and looked worse than what she wore, if that was possible.

She stepped into her father's woolen trousers and, tearing the muddy skirts of her dress away from the waist, she discarded them. She made a small bundle of food and drinking water and turned resolutely up the trail. She couldn't think of what would happen if she didn't reach the wagon train. She had to, that was all.

She found the runaway pack mule on the swollen riverbank, standing with his head down, reins trailing, looking as miserable as she felt. She hurried to take hold of the reins and pet its neck, pulling handfuls of grass to wipe down its coat, crooning to it as she worked, wooing it to some semblance of loyalty that might keep it from bolting again.

The river was too flooded to cross, even with the mule, so she gathered wood for a fire and mixed flat cakes from the muddied cornmeal. Even with the grit of sand and dirt between her teeth, the warm food soothed her aching stomach. Carefully she wrapped the remaining cakes and stored them, then set some dried beans to boiling in a meager supply of water. She was nearly out. Soon she'd be reduced to drinking from the muddy river.

She made a bed on the still damp ground and watched the moon rise over the horizon, its golden light glinting on the river in a way that reminded her of home and the pond down by the pasture. She'd have to cross the river tomorrow, no matter how high it was. She couldn't risk a further delay.

The wagon train would pull too far ahead for her to find it in this vast land.

Knowing she'd done all she could for the day, Colly tried to sleep. The mule was tied to a scrawny tree branch along the riverbank. With half a mind, he could no doubt uproot the pitiful plant and be on his way again. She dozed, jerking awake throughout the night to assure herself he was still there.

By morning the river had receded a little. Colly climbed onto the back of the mule without benefit of saddle or blanket. Her long feet dangled awkwardly and, as she kneed the animal into the muddy water, she drew up her legs to keep her boots from getting wet again. On the other side, she looked back longingly, thinking of all she'd left behind, then turned up the trail. Back that way lay her past, ahead lay her future . . . if she was to have one.

At midday she noticed large black birds circling up ahead. At first she didn't recognize them as vultures, but as she drew nearer, she drew in her breath with dread. Surely nothing had happened to the train, she thought. The birds must have found a dead animal, perhaps the other mule, but she knew in her heart the mule would never cross the river without someone there to prod him across. For the next hour she worked her way along the trail, mulling over what she might find on the trail ahead. The mule turned difficult long before she topped a hill and looked down on the valley, where the wagons sat in a circle.

Colly felt the blood drain from her face as she looked at the charred wagon frames and bloated bodies. Birds had already been at work, their dark wings spread like a malevolent spirit as they alighted near a body and cautiously pecked at it with their curving, sharp beaks. Colly felt the bile rise in her throat and turned away, gasping for air. The mule pranced to one side, whickering uneasily. He had no liking for this place. Slowly Colly regained her resolve and looked again at the devastation. She had little doubt what had brought about the death of the wagon train. Arrows pierced some of the bodies of the fallen, and even from the ridge she could see the smudged red wounds of those who'd been scalped.

Tears streamed down her face as her head fell forward, her mind a blank.

So much death!

So much silence!

The shadows had grown long, the sunlight lying in streaks along the curve of the valley before she could stir herself to go down to the mayhem below. Only the mule's hooves striking the rocky ground and the flap and screech of the vultures as they fought over disputed territory broke the grip of silence.

The stench was overpowering, making her clamp her hand to her mouth and pause to retch. She tried not to see the mutilated bodies, tried not to recognize the bloated faces with the sightless eyes. Only the desperation of her own plight drove her here to this valley of death. Steeling herself, she paused at the first burned-out wagon shell. The fire had done its work so thoroughly, she couldn't even recognize the outfit.

Sliding off the mule's back, she searched among the charred remains for some remnant of food and water. There was none. She moved on to the next wagon and the next, systematically searching for anything that would help her stay alive. There was little to be found. Everything had been taken by the Indians, from the pots on the campfires to the barrels of salt pork and chests of clothes and guns and ammunition. Even the mules had been driven away, the oxen slaughtered and left to bloat in the sunlight.

Scattered over a grassy knoll was a white pile of flour. The wind caught it, whirling it into little peaks and eddies. Colly scraped as much of it as she could into a cloth bag and tied a string around it.

Finally there was nothing more to be done, nothing to find, nothing left to search except the pitiful bodies, and she couldn't bear to look at them, except one. Her sorrowful gaze lit on Brother Davey.

He'd fallen against a burned wagon wheel, one side of his face charred by the fire, one arm outflung as if in a last desperate appeal to his attackers. A feathered axe was driven deep into his chest. At the open neck of his shirt a paper fluttered, catching Colly's attention. Brother Davey's maps! Jim Farley had laughed at his eastern maps for their inaccuracies, but they might help her find one of the forts scattered along the trail.

Colly forced herself to kneel beside the preacher's body and tug at the maps. They wouldn't budge, wedged as they were by the tomahawk. Colly reached for the rough axe and jerked her hand away, unable to touch it. For a long moment she gave way to the squeamishness, then, gritting her teeth, seized the handle and pulled. The flint blade grated against bone, then broke loose.

Colly pulled the map free and carried it away from the bodies. She was unaware she'd brought the blood-covered axe with her until she dropped it on the ground. Sliding to the ground she sat holding her head and breathing deeply. The tomahawk, with its painted handle and trailing feathers, lay within her field of view and, slowly, she reached for it and wiped the blood away on the dirt and grass. She might need it to protect herself. She might even be able to procure food with it, a rabbit or deer. She put it aside and opened the map.

One corner bore the stain of Brother Davey's blood, but she wiped it away and fell to studying the trail. The lines and curlicues meant little to her, but near a mountain peak, written in Brother Davey's neat script, was the name Fort Laramie. How many miles away was it? she wondered. Could she make it? She looked beyond the hills to the mountains. They looked steep and formidable. Could she, a woman alone, find her way through their maze? She had to. Either that or die. She was too far away from Independence to return.

Carefully folding the map, Colly gathered up the tomahawk and her small bag of flour and mounted the mule. She thought of the bodies left unattended. She couldn't bury them all. It was impossible. Next year a wagon train would come along and find the charred remains and the bleached bones. She had no room for proprieties now. Surviving would take every ounce of skill and perserverance she possessed. She kicked the mule's sides and turned him toward the mountains. If a body could survive here in this flat, hostile land, then she was determined she would. She'd never been a quitter. She surely wouldn't start now.

High in the foothills, Lone Wolf peered over the rocky ledge at the carnage below. His dark eyes were fierce in his painted face and the muscles along his shoulders bunched as he gripped his rifle and scanned the distant ridges for signs of the white soldiers from Fort Laramie. He had little doubt they would appear once the train failed to reach its destination.

Beside him, Little Bear and Doll Man motioned to each other and waited for his command. Their expressions were grim, for they knew this attack would bring the swift and deadly retaliation of the white guns. Regardless of their innocence, the *Tsitsitis* would be blamed, for this was known to be Cheyenne Territory.

Lone Wolf's eyes narrowed as he watched a solitary horseman approach the burned-out wagons. The rider carried no gear or weapon, nor did he even have the leather saddles the white men used on their mounts. Puzzled, Lone Wolf watched as the pale rider halted. He heard the wounded cry, sharp and womanlike, and shivered at the wild loneliness of it. How had this man managed to live when his comrades had fallen in battle? Had he run away? Lone Wolf had little doubt the rider was with the wagon train. The men who roamed these mountains were well equipped, their appearance wild and unkempt, their faces covered by great flowing beards. This youth's face was clean-shaven, although his attire was motley enough. His clothes were covered with mud and filth, his head covered by a floppy felt hat. He was tall,

Lone Wolf judged, for his long legs hung nearly to the ground
on either side of the mule. His thin shoulders and lanky body
were lean and hard-muscled, as if used to hard physical labor
and spare subsistence.

Patiently Lone Wolf waited as the figure registered shock,
then huddled on the mule, unable to move forward. At last
the horseman rode down to the wagons and, alighting,
searched among the charred remains. Only when the tall,
thin figure knelt beside the patch of white powder and began
to scoop it into a bag did Lone Wolf perceive the desperation
of the survivor. Silently he watched as the youth drew the
tomahawk from a body and staggered away.

Sagging to the ground, the youth swept the battered hat
aside and bowed his head against his bent knees, his body
convulsing. Lone Wolf drew in his breath sharply.

"It is a woman!" Doll Man exclaimed beside him.

"Silence," Lone Wolf ordered, and continued to stare at
the huddled figure. Many times he had seen the white man's
fair hair and had long since ceased to be amazed by it, but
never had he seen such a fiery color, like a sunset before a
rainstorm, like the fiery plants of the prairie during the time
of the freezing moon. A braid, fat and long like a rope, lay
against her shoulder.

Recovered from her shock, the woman opened some pa-
pers and bent over them for a long time. Finally she folded
them and tucked them into her shirt. Rising, she slung one
long leg over the mule and guided it toward the western
mountains.

"The Woman With Fire On Her Head will not live long
in the mountains," Doll Man observed. "She has no lodge
or food."

"She will perish," Little Bear said, with satisfaction. "She
deserves to die for her foolishness."

"She cannot help that her countrymen have been killed by
the Sioux," Lone Wolf answered. "Did you not see how she
searched among her dead for the things she needed to survive?"

"And rode away to leave them unburied," Little Bear answered. "Our people would not so dishonor our dead."

"That is true," Doll Man answered, for of them all he was the most diplomatic.

Little Bear was quick to anger and mount his war horse, yet they both, diplomat and warrior, looked to Lone Wolf for leadership. He was a war chief and had already counted many coups. Even now, just over the hill, a herd of horses that had once belonged to the Arapaho awaited their return. Lone Wolf had led them well, riding directly at an armed enemy warrior. The enemy's arrows could not touch him, so great were his powers. Such a man would one day sit on the council with all the other great chiefs, and they would relate stories of how they once had ridden with him.

Now they fell silent and waited for Lone Wolf to speak.

"Go back to the herd," he said. "Wait for me three days, and if I do not return go on without me."

"Where does Lone Wolf go?" Little Bear asked mutinously. He had no liking to be a herder when another battle might be had.

"I will follow the white woman and see if she meets with others of her kind," Lone Wolf answered.

"Why do you care? She is the white man's woman. She will perish long before she reaches the fort. It will be spring before the wagon train is discovered."

"I will follow her. She is brave and resourceful for a white woman. If she needs my help, I will give it."

"Too many times you've given aid to the white man and what good has it done?" Doll Man asked. "They take our goodwill and turn it against us. Look how their wagons have cut a trail across our prairies. And now, when they have met with misfortune, the Cheyenne will be blamed."

"That is true," Lone Wolf answered. "Still, I will follow after this woman for a while. She alone has survived the attack by the Sioux. Her spirits must be strong."

"Perhaps she is protected by evil spirits. Remember the

warning of our prophet, Motsiiu. He told us the white people have much evil magic that will harm the *Tsitsitis*.''

"If that is true, then I, Lone Wolf, will see for myself. If her magic tries to harm me, I will kill her.''

Lone Wolf sprang into his saddle and, with a final salute to his warriors, spurred his pony up the trail the white woman had taken. Soon he slowed his mount, though, for he had no wish for the white woman to know he was following her.

She was thirsty and hungry. The river was far behind her now and the steep mountain passes sported no streams. She'd traveled two days since leaving the wagon train. The flour she'd so painstakingly scraped from the earth was half-gone, but there was no water to mix the rest. Little good it did her now. She must find water and soon.

She pressed on, urging the stubborn mule up steep paths and along narrow ledges. Rounding a boulder, she came upon a trickle of water dripping from the granite mountain walls. It evaporated almost before it reached the rust-colored stones below. Scrambling up the rocks, she placed her tongue against the rough surface in a vain attempt to take in water. Smelling the water, the mule whinnied and tried to climb the steep rocks.

"No, go back," Colly cried, leaping to her feet and hurrying down the shale slope. The thirst-crazed beast whinnied again and renewed its efforts, slipping backward. In the rattle of rocks, she heard the scream of pain and the mule lay still, one hind leg bent to the side.

"No!" Colly slid down the slope and examined the broken leg. A jagged shard of white bone was exposed. Guiltily she looked into the dark, pain-filled eyes. They'd become more than master and beast of burden over the past few days. They'd depended on each other, instinctively understanding that without the other they might not survive. Now she'd led this dumb, trusting animal to this, a painful, lingering death, for she had no bullet with which to end its misery.

She cursed in frustration, her hand groping for the tomahawk at her waist. Could she deal it a blow hard enough to end its suffering? Growing up in the harsh, sparse reality of a Tennessee scrub farm, she understood the inevitability of the mule's fate. But now she shivered, reminded that her own death was as likely. She could never traverse these mountains alone and on foot.

Beside herself with rage, she paced, giving full rein to her anger, for it masked her real feelings of terror. She had escaped the horror of cholera and scalping—only to die here on this mountain trail of thirst and starvation. Some part of her rebelled at the thought. She wouldn't give in so easily.

The mule made a small whicker of pain, and Colly turned to regard him, a desperate thought taking shape. She'd heard of men being stranded without food and water and of the outlandish things they'd done to stay alive. Could she go through with such an act? She had to if she was to live.

Crouching beside the mule she patted its neck, crooning to it, thanking it for carrying her so far. Then, steeling herself, she rose to her feet, pulled the tomahawk high above her head, and brought it down with all her might against the mule's neck. She'd aimed for the pulsing vein beneath the satiny coat, but her aim wasn't true. The mule screamed, thrashing wildly.

Colly leaped to one side, sobs escaping her tight throat, and raised the axe again. This time it struck deep into the neck, cutting off the mule's horrible scream. Blood oozed about the axe blade. Breathing deeply to quiet her revulsion, Colly withdrew the axe and cupped her hands to catch the spurting blood. Slowly she brought it to her mouth. The smell of it, strong and warm from the mule, made her gag. She drank, drawing the liquid into her mouth; then revulsion overcame her and she spat it out, shuddering with disgust, wiping at her mouth with bloodied hands. The mule was still, his life-giving blood seeping into the shale beneath him, but she could make no move to catch it, to use it to preserve her own life.

She'd gone mad! She was sure of it. She, Colly Mead, was

a mad, spinsterish woman, left alone on a mountainside to
drink mule blood. She was no longer fit for human company!
It was best she die. Rising to her feet, she staggered down
the slope, half falling, half sliding, until she regained the
trail and began to run blindly.

Lone Wolf watched as the woman struck the injured mule
and caught its blood to drink. These things his people did,
but he'd never seen a woman drink fresh blood before. This
was the act of a warrior. He was puzzled that she had not cut
away parts of the mule to roast over the fire. But she was,
after all, a white woman, and the white eyes did not respect
the ways of survival here in the mountains and prairies.
Slowly he made his way to the fallen animal and cut away
flanks of meat, wrapped them in his parfleche, and continued
after the strange white woman.

For a third day he tracked her, knowing that Little Bear
and Doll Man would be gathering the herd to move on. Still,
he felt compelled to follow this strange creature. He'd seen
no white women behave as she did. If not for the long braid,
he would still believe her a warrior. Perhaps she was a spirit.

When she collapsed on the trail and lay unmoving, Lone
Wolf sat for a long time regarding her from a distance, trying
to decide what he must do. She sprawled across the trail, her
long legs flopping as if no bones or muscles existed. She
made no move to protect herself from the burning rays of the
sun. Now and then he heard wild laughter and muttered ex-
clamations. Sometimes she pointed one wavery hand to the
sky and uttered gibberish. The evil spirits seemed to have
claimed her, and he wondered if he should intervene and try
to save her or leave her. Soon the buzzards would begin to
circle.

Her cries grew muted and finally quieted altogether. Having made up his mind, Lone Wolf rose from his hiding place
and went down the slope to the woman. He bent over her,
noting her size and thinness.

She was very ugly, even for a white woman. Her face was

red, with little brown spots all over it, her lips cracked and bleeding. A smudge of dried blood dirtied one cheek and her hands were filthy, the nails black and blood-encrusted.

Opening his water pouch, he knelt beside her and raised her shoulders. She moaned a protest, rolling her head from side to side until he placed the mouth of his water pouch to her lips. Then she jerked and reached greedily for the skin, her lips drawing in the water in a sucking motion. When he tried to draw the pouch away, she uttered a cry and gripped it tightly, spilling some of the precious drops.

"No!" Lone Wolf said sharply, and jerked the skin away. The woman sank back against the rocks, giving in once again to her stupor.

Lone Wolf rose and, searching along the rocky path, gathered enough knobby wood to start a small fire; then, drawing the mule meat from his parfleche, he set it to roasting over the coals. The smell of cooking meat seemed to revive the woman, for she moaned again and raised her head, fixing him with a wild stare.

"Food," Lone Wolf said in English, indicating the cooking meat. She made no answer, and, turning his back, he carefully turned the sizzling slabs. A sound behind him made him turn. The white woman stood over him like an angry spirit, a tomahawk raised, her eyes black and wild, her red hair standing out about her head like bloodied feathers. With a shrill cry, she brought the tomahawk down on Lone Wolf.

Chapter 2

*L*ONE WOLF SAW the glint of blade and rolled to one side, landing back on his feet to face the madwoman. The force of her swing had carried her forward and sideways so she teetered over the flames, her back to him. Lone Wolf leaped forward and wrapped his arms around her, pinning her arms to her side. She screamed, kicking out with her long legs. One leather boot caught him in the shins, making him loosen his grip.

Quickly she spun and raised the tomahawk. Lone Wolf reached for his knife, but it was not at his waist. It lay against a stone, near the fire where he'd turned the meat. He launched himself forward against the white woman, letting the weight of his hard body slam into hers. He heard the yelp of pain and *whoosh* of air as he bore her to the ground.

Still she struggled, with far more strength than he'd anticipated. Grunts of pain and despair emitted from her half-opened mouth and she strained against him, trying to free her hand with the tomahawk. Lone Wolf's strong fingers gripped her bony wrist, pinching into the thin muscles until the tomahawk clattered to the rocky ledge. She lashed out with her feet, landing kicks about his calves and thighs, grinding her heel into his moccasined foot, and when her hand was free, she drew back her arm and swung it, landing a blow against the side of Lone Wolf's face.

Anger surged through him. Never had an enemy counted coup against him, and now a woman had done so. She must be an evil spirit, indeed, to possess so much power. Drawing back his fist, Lone Wolf punched her chin. Her head snapped back and she drew a sharp breath, but still she didn't lessen her attack against him. Lone Wolf aimed a punch low to her stomach, and the tall, thin body went limp in his arms, sliding slowly to the ground.

Lone Wolf leaped away, then squatted to study the woman. Was she feigning unconsciousness to put him off-guard again? She lay grasping her stomach and groaning. Tears streamed from the sides of her eyes and flowed down her face to the rocks below. Finally she turned her head and looked at him, her strange, pale eyes bright with defiance.

"Go ahead, you murdering savage. Kill me the way you did the rest of the people on the wagon train. I'm not afraid to die!"

Her words amazed him, for they were brave words. He had little doubt she meant them, for when he reached forward to retrieve the tomahawk she'd wielded, she did not flinch or draw away but only waited stoically.

Lone Wolf looked at her for a long time, carefully choosing the white words he must use to make her understand.

"Cheyenne did not kill your people," he said quietly. "Sioux."

"*Pah!*" She sat up and spat her disbelief. "What difference does it make which tribe attacked the train? You're all the same!"

Lone Wolf considered her words, mystified that she should think the Cheyenne part of the Sioux Nation. "*Tsitsitis* are not brothers of the Sioux," he said. "*Tsitsitis* are different."

"I thought you said you were Cheyenne," she answered suspiciously.

"Cheyenne is white man name for *Tsitsitis*. We are known as The People."

Colly made no reply, digesting what he had said. It made little sense to her. She knew there were various tribes, for

Jim Farley had told them something of the prairie Indians, but she'd assumed they were somehow all related.

"I Lone Wolf," the Indian went on, then waited expectantly.

"I'm Colly Mead," she snapped, then pulled herself up, for the smell of burning meat had reached her nostrils and she glanced at the fire. Her stomach tightened at the thought of meat. She'd had none in so long.

Lone Wolf saw her look and guessed her hunger. Crossing to the fire, he used his knife to spear the charred strips of meat from the flame. Impaling one piece on his knife blade, he held it out to her.

"Eat," he ordered.

Distrustfully she stared into his dark eyes, wanting to refuse, but the smell made her faint with hunger, and, in the end, she reached greedily for the roasted meat. It burned her hands so she dropped it on the ground, then quickly picked it up and juggled it from one hand to another as she took a first bite. It was tough and gamy-tasting . . . and the most delicious thing she'd ever eaten! She chewed, mindless of the grease that slid down her chin. Before the piece was half-chewed, she swallowed it down and bit off another piece, cramming it into her mouth until her cheeks puffed out on either side.

Lone Wolf's eyes gleamed with humor as he watched her chew. Aware of his scrutiny, Colly grew ashamed of herself and contrived to eat more slowly, taking smaller bites. Lone Wolf squatted nearby, but well out of range of her reach, his manner wary as he chewed his own meat.

"Ummm, this is good," Colly said—by way of gratitude for his sharing. "What is it? Deer, elk?"

"Mule," he replied.

"Mule!" Colly glanced back up the trail. "Oh!" She thought of the patient, weary mule that had died trying to get water. Suddenly her hunger was gone and her stomach cramped. She laid aside her meat and wrapped her arms around her middle, trying not to moan.

Lone Wolf regarded her solemnly. "Eat too fast," he said. "Not chew food!" He made chewing motions with his teeth. They flashed white and even against his dark face as he smiled.

Miffed at his behavior, Colly made no answer, simply staring back at him, nor did she smile. Lone Wolf's grin faded and he continued eating in silence.

"Could I have some more water?" Colly asked.

Lone Wolf hesitated, glancing from her to the water bag hanging nearby. Reluctantly he put down his food but kept hold of his knife as he brought the pouch to her.

"Do not spill," he admonished before handing her the bag.

"No, I won't," Colly said, and quickly drank, lest he change his mind. When she drew the bag away, he took it from her, giving her no chance for a second drink.

"Sleep now," the Indian ordered, and, feeling better, Colly sighed and lay back against the rough stone.

The glow of coals made a peaceful, cozy oasis in the sea of blackness that surrounded them. How long had it been since she'd had a fire? She curled on her side so she could watch the dying embers. They brought back memories of nights on the wagon train, when the chores were done and it wasn't time yet to turn in, so people strolled from one wagon site to another, visiting and speculating on what the new land held for them. Now they all knew: it held the darkness of a grave. Reminded of her circumstances, Colly rolled on her back and sat up.

"What are you going to do with me?" she asked the Indian warrior, who crouched on the other side of the dying fire.

"Lone Wolf take Colly Mead to safety," he said, without hesitation, so she believed him.

"You're taking me to the fort?" she cried incredulously.

"No!" His sharp denial punctured her ballooning hope. "*Tsitsitis* not go to white man's fort. Only bring trouble. Lone Wolf take to village of his people. Safe there."

"To an Indian village?" Colly said. "You're kidnapping me."

"What is kidnapping?" Lone Wolf asked.

"You're taking me against my will," Colly accused.

Lone Wolf shrugged. "If not will to go to the village of *Tsitsitis*, Lone Wolf kidnap."

"Then why don't you just kill me now—or do you want your people to torture me?"

Lone Wolf's face changed, became somber. "We do not torture those white eyes who come to our village."

"How do I know you're not lying?"

Lone Wolf sprang to his feet, his knife in one hand, his legs spread, his face twisted in an ugly scowl. "Lone Wolf, war chief of the Dog Soldiers, does not lie."

Foolish words, Colly thought. She was uttering foolish words that would only get her killed. She must appease this savage and hope he meant what he said, that he would take her to his village. How much better would that be, though? She remembered too well the mutilation of the men and women of the wagon train. Would such savages hesitate to do the same to her? A thought struck her for the first time. The bodies she'd seen were mostly men, with only a few women and no children. Where had the children been? Kidnapped! Taken back to the Indian village . . . for what? Torture? Jim Farley had told of how some of the warring Indian tribes took captives, using them as slaves, adopting those who pleased them.

She looked at the savage man across the fire. His dark eyes glinted dangerously in the light of the fire. He'd not hurt her so far. In fact, he'd saved her life, giving her water and food. He'd made no move to touch her until she'd attacked first. Could he have spoken the truth, that he intended only to help her? Yet why wouldn't he take her to the fort, to her own people?

Going to the white man's fort only brought trouble, he'd said. So he was afraid of the white soldiers and what they would do when they found out about the train. That meant he and his tribe must have attacked the train—and she was the only living person who could tell the soldiers what had happened. He couldn't let her live. He must surely mean to kill her. For some reason he'd chosen not to do so now. Her thoughts whirled until she was hopelessly confused.

She must escape. She must wait until he'd relaxed his guard and escape. She'd heard the whicker of a horse back along the trail. If she could slip away while he slept and make her way to the horse . . . He'd never catch her. What about his men? Was he alone? He couldn't have attacked the train on his own. That meant there had to be other Indians out there in the foothills, waiting!

"Where are your men?" she asked abruptly, looking around.

Lone Wolf saw the calculation on her face. He'd seen such looks before on the white faces when they planned to cheat the Indians. He was sorry he'd saved her. "My men are there," he said, nodding to the east, "and there," he pointed to the west, "and there." He indicated they were surrounded. "The *Tsitsitis* are everywhere. This is their land."

"Why don't they show themselves then?" Colly challenged.

The Indian's dark, enigmatic stare was unwavering. She looked away first.

"They will show themselves when it is time," he answered mildly; then, sliding his knife into the leather sheath at his waist, he lay back without benefit of pad or blanket.

Colly watched him for a while, uncertain of what she should do, and when the fire's embers had cooled and still he'd made no movement, not even to the twitching of a muscle, she got to her feet and took a step toward the trail. Instantly he was towering before her, his dark, bare chest an invincible wall cutting her off from escape, his dark eyes sinister hollows in his stern face. He said nothing, demanding no explanation, but the tension radiating from his taut body made her back away.

"I—I need some privacy," she stuttered.

"What is privacy?" he asked stonily.

"I . . . need to be alone—to relieve myself."

He made no answer, his dark eyes glaring at her while he sifted her strange words, seeking their meaning, and at last he nodded as if he understood.

"No privacy!" he commanded. "Relieve self here." Folding his arms across his chest, he made a great show of turning his back.

"But I can't . . ." Colly said to that implacable back, then shrugged in defeat. "Never mind," she said, stepping back to the fire. She didn't see Lone Wolf's grin.

"Lie down on ground," he ordered, shoving her slightly. Though his actions were not rough, Colly guessed they were not meant to be argued with. She did as he'd ordered and glared up at him. Lone Wolf lay down again, this time close enough for their feet to touch. Immediately Colly drew her booted foot away, but Lone Wolf grabbed hold of her ankle in an iron grip.

"No!" Colly cried out, trying to kick him. He yanked her foot next to his again and lashed the two together with a braided rawhide rope.

"What are you doing?" Colly demanded, her heart beating like a drum in her ears. She didn't like the feeling of his strong, hard fingers gripping her ankle or the feeling of helplessness his presence invoked. She was more courageous facing the prairie by herself than she was facing this savage man.

Panic spilled through her and she lashed out with her other boot, catching him against his shoulder. The contact was solid and sharp, and she knew she'd hurt him. Finding satisfaction in that, she drew back her foot and kicked again, this time aiming for his head. She heard his grunt of pain as the tip of her boot struck his chin; the rope binding them loosened and she tore at it with her fingers.

A blow against the side of her head sent her flying backward; she lay dazed, gripping her jaw with her hands and choking back sobs. The Indian ignored her, silently retying the rope around their two feet.

"Sleep now!" he ordered, and, turning on his side, he seemed to fall asleep immediately.

So much for escaping, Colly thought as she lay nursing her bruised jaw and staring through tear-moistened eyes at the star-studded sky above. What was she to do now? Nothing much to be done. She'd been foolish to try and make her move so soon. He hadn't trusted her. He'd known instantly what she'd planned. Patience! She must use patience—and she must sleep and wake, and eat mule and drink his water, and, when she was stronger and the right moment presented itself, she'd be ready.

So thinking, she lay back and forced her weary mind to empty itself of the fear that gripped her. Wrapping her thin arms around her aching stomach, she stared at the velvety sky and thought of nights back in Tennessee when the heat of day lay over the land, driving a body from his bed to seek a breath of coolness on the front porch.

Many an evening she'd sat watching the moon rise, listening to the buzz of the grasshoppers and dog day cicada, the call of the Blackburnian warbler, and the scurry of salamanders and lizards beneath the porch. Mama could never abide sitting on the porch after dark, but it never bothered Colly. She'd watched the rising moon and felt an aching loneliness that she could never quite define and never knew how to overcome. Life was filled with such lonely yearnings for unnamed things, she figured, and a body just had to accept it. But now, lying on a rocky ledge, her leg tied to the leg of a strange and awesome Indian, she thought she'd never felt such yearning or lonesomeness.

Fatigue finally claimed her and she woke at the gray light of dawn, nudged to awareness by a not ungentle moccasined foot. Lone Wolf towered over her.

"We go," he said, staring down at her. In the light of day she could see that he was far handsomer than she'd supposed the night before, a strapping, tall man with finely chiseled features and lively, intelligent eyes. Self-consciously she ran a rough hand over her straggly, tangled hair and around to her face. Her skin was sunburned and tender, her lips cracked, her nose bulbous and red. Her clothes were filthy and hung on her scarecrow figure. She must look a sight. Suddenly aware of how silly such thoughts were in the face of her predicament, she jammed the shapeless felt hat over her head and stood facing him, her eyes nearly on a level with his.

"Water!" she croaked, thinking she would never again have enough of it.

Lone Wolf handed her the pouch and said nothing as she drank long and deep. When she'd lowered the pouch, he handed her a hunk of cold, charred meat from the night before. Colly's aching stomach turned, but she took the burned mass and forced herself to tear off a chunk and chew it. Her teeth hurt, feeling loose in her mouth from lack of proper diet. She ignored the pain and the nausea as her stomach protested the ingestion of something so foreign as mule meat. Unable to take another bite, she handed the meat back to Lone Wolf, who carefully wrapped it in his parfleche.

When he was ready, he motioned her forward along the path. Steadily they descended for several hundred yards; then they came to a tiny clearing where two horses had been left to graze. They were sleek and sturdy. Lone Wolf motioned her to one and turned to the black stallion, slinging his parfleche over its flanks and placing a leather saddle on its back.

A pad was placed over the back of the second horse, and from this she assumed she was to ride bareback. Without waiting for Lone Wolf's instructions, she sprang onto the horse's back and once seated, with the rawhide reins in her hands, felt a thrill of power, of possibilities. She could gallop away down the trail before Lone Wolf could even mount. With such a horse beneath her and not a plodding mule, she could get away, she was sure of it. But where would she go here in this vast land? While she debated, Lone Wolf leaped into the saddle and with a quick flick of his strong wrists subdued the spirited animal.

When the stallion was brought under control, Lone Wolf

whirled to look for Colly. She noted the look of surprise and satisfaction when he saw she'd made no move to get away. With a grunt he led the way down out of the foothills and headed north. Docilely Colly followed, but her thoughts were feverish. She'd done well not to flee. He was an expert horseman. He would have caught her in a matter of minutes. By staying, she'd won a small measure of his trust. She was pleased with her decision. Now she concentrated on their northward trek. Somehow she'd have to find her way back over this path. She wanted to remember it.

They traveled back the way she'd come, veering away from the site of the burned wagon train, turning north once again, away from the Platte River. They traveled without speaking, Lone Wolf leading the way. She imagined to some onlooker seeing them from afar they might appear as an Indian and his squaw, so docilely did she follow.

Lone Wolf pushed forward without pause, seeming to know instinctively the lay of the land and where each hill and valley led. Late in the afternoon he paused and placed a bone whistle to his lips. The sound was sharp and piercing. He waited, and, receiving no answer, blew again, then, taking up his reins, moved forward across the changing flat plains. The long prairie grasses had given way to a shorter, stunted variety. The rich greenness succumbed to the burned browns and siennas of the raw northern plains.

The sun beat down on their backs, but Lone Wolf seemed not to notice, nor did he pause to drink from the water pouch. Colly licked her dry, cracked lips and tried not to think about the brackish-tasting liquid. She fixed her gaze on the broad, tanned back of the rider ahead and set to wondering what kind of people the Cheyenne were. Stretching her mind back to those happier times on the wagon train when Jim Farley had regaled them with his experiences among the tribes, she tried to remember what he'd said of the Cheyenne.

"Stay away from their women," he'd admonished the young men. "Their men'll cut you down for even thinking about them. The women ain't much better. And if'n you do get one off alone, it don't do you no good noway. They wear the dad blamedest contraption around their legs, what you might call a chastity belt.'' He'd stopped talking when he'd seen Colly was standing nearby listening. "Sorry, ma'am,'' he'd said, and sauntered away while the young men had snickered with glee at his latest revelation. But there had been more long conversations with Brother Davey and Papa. Slowly the words came back to her.

"Cheyenne 'bout the best of the heathens,'' Farley had revealed. "They ain't as bloodthirsty as the Sioux, but when you git 'em riled, you can't tell much difference anyhow. Don't matter who the tomahawk belongs to, if'n it's liftin' your scalp.''

Faint reassurance, Colly thought, shivering and glancing at the figure ahead. Lone Wolf's body was erect in the saddle, his long, glossy blue-black hair curling in the wind as it brushed his shoulders. She found herself fascinated by that hair. She'd never seen a man with long hair before. She would have thought it womanly, but somehow it wasn't. He rode his pony with easy familiarity, his long legs sleek and muscular in their rawhide leggings. What kind of men were the Cheyenne? she wondered idly. Did they have families like the white men, or did they just breed with any female of their species like animals? Her cheeks burned at the direction her thoughts had taken. Still, the earthy necessities of the farm and husbandry carried her thoughts onward. Lone Wolf was a fine specimen. If he'd been a stallion back on the farm, she would have given him leeway to cover their best brood mare.

Lone Wolf paused and swung around, addressing her for the first time since they'd left their campsite. His dark eyes were direct and fierce as they met hers. Colly was glad for the floppy brim of the battered hat.

"My men are there,'' he said, pointing to the distance. Colly followed his line of direction and saw a herd of horses moving through a dry, flat prairie toward a rim of mountains. Even from here, she could hear the shrill cries of men as they galloped about, keeping the horses herded close.

Taking out the bone whistle, Lone Wolf blew into it, and this time Colly recognized the high, piercing call of the eagle. The shrill cry echoed along the hills and was answered. Grinning, Lone Wolf stood high in his stirrups and waved; then, motioning her to follow, he spurred his horse down the hillside, toward the milling herd.

Colly paused, watching him ride away. He'd taken for granted that she would follow. Now was her chance, while he was still galloping downhill. He wouldn't know she was gone until he reached the bottom and, by then, he'd have to wheel his horse and ride back up, a feat that would take far longer than her riding down the other side. Colly put her thoughts to action, slapping at her mount's shanks.

Giving little thought to the safety of the Indian pony, she urged it down the hillside. Rocks and dust rose around them as they gained the flatland below. Applying her booted heels mercilessly, Colly bent low over the horse's neck. The well-trained pony responded, stretching his long legs in a full-out gallop. The prairie wind whipped at Colly's face and she bowed her head against the sleek horseflesh so her hat wouldn't fly away. She took no chance of turning in the saddle to see if she was pursued but willed the horse forward.

A whistle, shrill and urgent, cut across the staccato of galloping hooves, bringing her horse up abruptly.

"Giddap!" Colly cried, kicking its sides and slapping the reins. The horse sidestepped nervously, whickering and rolling its eyes. The whistle came again and the horse turned back, trotting easily.

"No! You can't go back there!" Colly cried, sawing at the reins in an effort to turn the animal. The horse shook his head fiercely, and she nearly lost her grip on the reins. Resigning herself to the inevitable, Colly slumped forward while the Indian pony carried her back to its master.

Lone Wolf waited at the bottom of the hill, his face grim and implacable. When they were near enough, he reached forward and took the reins from her.

"Get off horse," he said sternly.

Colly raised her head and glared at him. "What?" she asked warily.

"Get off horse," Lone Wolf repeated. "Walk."

"You—I can't . . . I'm too weak and tired to walk very fast," she stammered.

"Walk," Lone Wolf reiterated. "If decide to leave, not take Lone Wolf's horse."

"I see!" Colly snapped, sliding down from the horse's back. "You aren't concerned about losing me at all, only your precious horse."

"Horse belong to Lone Wolf," he answered. "White woman belong to self." Trailing the second horse behind him, he started back up the hill.

Furious, Colly stared after him for a long time. She wouldn't follow him, she decided. She'd strike out her own way. Hadn't he as much as said she was free to go? She licked her dry lips and thought of her thirst. Lone Wolf carried his water pouch with him. Reluctantly she started up the hill after him.

Lone Wolf never once looked back to see if she followed. Obviously he didn't care either way, she decided, and contrived to keep up with him. The grade was steep, the sun hot, and she arrived at the top sweating and gasping for breath. Lone Wolf was already halfway down the other side, giving her no chance to rest or catch her breath. Far ahead, the horse herd and his men were nearly out of sight.

Cursing Lone Wolf and the very hills themselves, she stumbled after him. At the bottom of the hill, she saw he was moving across the valley floor without seeming to give any thought to her. Colly took off her felt hat and wiped at the sweat that beaded her brow. Then, clamping it on her head again, she marched forth. Anger carried her a good portion of the way, helping her ignore the heat and dust and uneven ground she crossed. But thirst won out over anger, fear overcame outrage, so that when she finally stumbled into their camp, her defiance was gone. Stumbling to the pouch of water, she eagerly raised it to her lips, but Lone Wolf was there to take it from her.

"Water!" she demanded desperately; then, realizing she had no right to demand anything, she softened her voice. "Please!"

Lone Wolf waved his arm to one side of the grove of stunted trees where they'd camped. Colly's lips tightened, thinking he was ordering her out of camp.

"Plenty water," he said.

Colly looked again and saw the silvery, incandescent stream of water at the edge of some boulders. "Water!" she cried, running toward it. "Fresh water!" She half stumbled, half fell into the cold, clear stream, burying her face in the sparkling liquid. Her mouth opened and she gulped in great swallows, choking and gasping in her hurry. When at last her thirst was surfeited, she raised her wet face and looked back at the circle of curious eyes that studied her. Lone Wolf's men were very much like him, tall, well-built men with brown, muscular bodies, covered only by leggings, or in some cases mere breechcloths. Their hair was long and often braided and decorated with a topknot of feathers.

Colly sat back on her heels and stared at the men. They made comments among themselves and laughed uproariously. Somehow she sensed their words had been about her and were derisive. Had she not seen similar behavior among the young men in Tennessee? They had called her "old maid" and "Mr. Colly Mead" behind her back—just because she'd worked her father's fields and stood as tall as they.

Lord, she must look a sight if even these savages looked at her the same way. All well and good, she reminded herself. She was no longer looking for a husband—and certainly not among these brutes. She wanted only to remain alive and somehow make her way back to Tennessee. Better to be mocked by those you knew and understood than by a strange heathen bunch like this. Raising her chin high, she got to her feet and stood with her hands on her hips, glaring at the onlooking men.

"What're you looking at?" she demanded. "Haven't you seen a white woman before?"

This only occasioned more comments and laughter from her audience, and one brave made so bold as to step forward and take hold of her bedraggled red braid.

"Stop that!" Colly shouted, and slapped at him. Nimbly he danced aside.

Angered by the sneering humor in the Indian's dark eyes, Colly snatched up a dead limb and chased after him. With a wild yelp, the man leaped out the way, but another took his place. Colly swung her club, but he danced aside, his voice shrill and mocking. Another call rose from behind her, and Colly whirled, her club raised, and, like the first two Indians, this brave wheeled away, yelping and doing a kind of jiggling shuffle. They took turns presenting themselves before her, taunting her, challenging her. She swung her club time and again until at last she stood exhausted, her head bowed in defeat, the stick drooping in her hand.

Lone Wolf came upon the scene, and, seeing what had transpired, stepped close to Colly as he turned to berate his men. Without hesitation, Colly raised her club and struck out, hitting his shoulder as hard as she could. Only when he'd rolled away from the blow did she see it was Lone Wolf. She hadn't meant to strike him, yet her anger was such that he seemed a suitable enough target, so she followed after him, her stick raised again.

Lone Wolf rolled to a stop and rose on his knees, his hands upraised to deflect her blows. His long fingers closed around the stick and it was wrenched from her hand. With a cry of rage, Colly launched herself at him, her fist doubled, to land a blow on his ear. Lone Wolf gripped her shoulders and fell backward, carrying her with him, rolling on his back with a force that flipped her into the air. She landed flat on her back, the air knocked from her.

Lone Wolf was on his feet crouching over her, his arms extended to continue the battle if she wished. Colly rolled onto her side and brought her knees up to her chest, cradling her bruised and aching body, wrapping her skinny arms around her skinnier knees and giving way to the misery she felt. She made no sound, for she'd learned at an early age that her father had no pity for weeping. Yet she lay unable to hold back the feelings of fear and stress and fatigue that gripped her battered soul.

How much must she endure before she could die peacefully? she wondered bitterly. Even here, in the wilderness, among heathen savages, contempt was heaped on her head. Had God no mercy for her?

Lone Wolf looked at the pitifully thin, ragged being and wondered if he'd done right to save her. He felt her despair and wished he could give comfort, for she was brave and fearless. Yet each man must choose his own destiny to live and die, and he sensed she did not desire death. Slowly he walked back to the campfire and seated himself. His men were silent as they watched him.

"She is a warrior woman," Doll Man said finally. "She is not afraid."

"Her spirit is strong," Lone Wolf answered.

"What will you do with her?" Little Bear asked cautiously.

"If she will go, I will take her to our village," Lone Wolf answered, and, tired of any more questions for which he had few answers, he rose and took a piece of freshly roasted prairie rabbit to the stream where the white woman lay.

"Here is food," he said, but she made no answer, nor any move to take the food from him. She lay as he'd left her, with her legs drawn up. Her eyes were wide open and unblinking, as if she'd gone into a trance. Perhaps the spirits were visiting her, giving her a vision, Lone Wolf decided, and placed the meat on some leaves close to her head. When she woke from her trance, she would be hungry.

He walked away, wondering if the spirits would help her rise and travel on with them. He shrugged. He'd done all he could for her. Settling himself beside the fire, he fell asleep instantly.

Colly heard him approach and smelled the food he brought, but she seemed gripped in some great void that would not release her. She lay in the darkness and heard the stream tumbling at her feet, and smelled the water, and the moist earth, and dreamed without closing her eyes of the quiet green ponds at home with the water striders and whirligig beetles floating on the surface, and the lady ferns and trout lilies growing on the banks, and in the shaded places of the woods the red fruiting cup of the soldier lichen.

These beloved things lay ahead of her. She had only to reach for them and they would be hers again. She heard the call of the yellowthroat and the raucous cry of the kingfisher, seductive and promising. She could go back home. She could. She had only to touch the lemony ball of sunshine that lay ahead. With a joyous cry she reached for it, felt the prickly nettle of a bush, and awoke from her dream, feeling the hard ground beneath her and seeing the cold prairie sky above her. In despair she cried out, the sound so wild and tumbling in the darkness, Lone Wolf and his warriors sat up and peered through the shadows.

"It is an evil spirit," one cried.

"It is the spirit of the Warrior Woman, struggling to be free," Lone Wolf said, and lay back, unable to sleep for the rest of the night.

When at last the bright rim of orange-red light stained the eastern horizon, casting its warming light over the land, he rose and made his way down to the stream. The strange woman sat on its banks plaiting her hair. She'd already washed herself, for her face was clean and her ragged clothes damp. She'd eaten the food he'd brought her. The bone lay on a rock nearby, picked clean. She raised serene eyes to him when he approached, but she said nothing. He noted something new in her attitude, a resignation, a wisdom of the ways of life.

"I wish to go to your village," she said finally.

Lone Wolf studied her face. Her skin was pale beneath the redness caused by the sun and held many spots, even on her arms. He'd seen other white people spotted in this manner and knew they accepted it. Her face was thin, her nose longer than the Indians, her lips narrow. It was not an unpleasant face! He liked her eyes; though they were pale like the white eyes, they held many things he wished to know. Nodding his head, he grunted.

"Today you will ride," he said, and knelt beside the stream to bathe himself. He was unaware she stood beside him until he felt her touch against his shoulder.

"Thank you, Lone Wolf," she said softly. "I will not run away again."

Before he could answer she'd turned aside and made her way back to the campsite. Lone Wolf watched her go, noting how she limped slightly; then, shrugging aside his curiosity, he turned to his morning bath.

Chapter 3

THEY SET OUT early, still heading north. The browns
and golds of the prairie had given way to rolling hills
of greenery, pine forests, and towering hardwood trees. Beneath their deep shade they moved like cool shadows, caught
now and then in bright spangled dollops of sunlight that broke
through the thick canopies overhead. Lone Wolf's men
herded the horses forward with a minimum of racket, as if
awed by the spirals and green arches of the forest cathedral.
Even Colly shivered, sensing that God did, indeed, live in
such a place as this.

They came to a tumbling river with the sunlight caught in
its swift waters and, turning westward again, followed its
meandering course.

Colly stayed close to Lone Wolf, showing him she could
be trusted. He sensed the change in her and grunted with
satisfaction. Her treatment by his people would depend on
how she behaved toward them. The *Tsitsitis* were leery of the
white eyes. If she tried to run away, taking a horse or other
things that did not belong to her, she would only bring their
wrath down on her head. Lone Wolf noted how she had
ceased fighting her predicament and tried to make amends,
even to helping herd the horses.

Courage without wisdom was foolhardy, Old Bear Man
had told him once in his youth, and Lone Wolf believed this.

He was pleased that the white woman understood this as well. With this new wisdom, she seemed far braver to him now. Surreptitiously he watched her, seeing how her long, lanky form jostled awkwardly with every movement of her mount. She wasn't used to riding horses bareback, he surmised. He noted her thin cheeks and long jawline, her thin body and legs, which were nearly as long as a man's.

She looked ragged and dirty in the worn white man's clothes, yet there was a certain pride in the set of her shoulders. The ugly hat hid her wonderful eyes. Her tattered braid flopped against her sharp shoulder blades with every step of the Indian pony. She had been silent ever since those brief moments by the stream when she'd thanked him. Lone Wolf wondered where she'd come from and who her people had been. Was she the daughter or wife of some great white chief?

Quelling his curiosity, he turned his attention to the trail ahead. Soon they would come to the village. It had been many moons since he last saw his family and friends. Speculations about the white woman were lost in his eager anticipation of his homecoming.

At midafternoon, they topped a rise and led the horses down into a canyon that acted as a corral. After milling restlessly, the horses settled down to munching on the sparse grass. Puzzled that they'd halted so early in the day, Colly dismounted and watched the flurry of activity. A lone scout was dispatched, and from this she wondered if soldiers were somewhere nearby.

However, Lone Wolf and the rest of his men seemed unconcerned. Going down to the river, they plunged into the cold, clear water and swam about, splashing and dunking one another with many good-natured shouts. Surely they wouldn't make such noise if they feared the presence of soldiers.

Averting her eyes from their half-naked bodies, Colly settled herself beneath a tree to see what would happen next. When Lone Wolf and his men had tired of their swim, they climbed out of the river and sat drying themselves in the sunlight. Their voices held an edge of excitement, as if they awaited some looked-for event. Finally, when their taut, muscular bodies were dry, the warriors rose and drew fresh clothes from their parfleches: fringed leggings, finely beaded moccasins, and soft leather shirts decorated with quills and beads, which they belted at their waists with ornately beaded sashes.

With great care the men groomed their hair, rebraiding it into smooth, thick ropes on either side of their heads, and ornamented it with eagle feathers and strips of otter fur. Using bone tweezers, they plucked the hair from their faces, even their eyebrows, and painted the parts in their hair. Last of all, they covered their faces with thick, colored clay in various symbols, the meaning of which Colly could only guess.

As she watched them, Colly grew more alarmed. During the past few days of travel with Lone Wolf and his men, she had told herself that they were people who were not so very different from her own, after all. They still required a fire to warm themselves and food to nourish themselves. Though they appeared far hardier than Brother Davey and his congregation, Colly had noted that Lone Wolf and his men exercised many of the travel habits and precautions of the emigrants.

Unable to endure the high level of stress with which she'd coped the past fortnight, she'd soothed her fears with these thoughts. Now, seeing the hideous painted faces, her small reassurances crumbled and she was left, once again, with doubts and fears about her fate.

Lone Wolf approached, and she cringed backward against the tree, intimidated by his ferocious mask. His dark eyes seemed even more fierce surrounded by the black-and-white paint daubs.

Lone Wolf saw her fear and was perplexed. Why should she be afraid now? he wondered. "Go now!" he said roughly, and was unaware his tone and manner seemed even more menacing.

With her heart thudding in her chest, Colly rose swiftly and remounted. Instinct told her she must obey now or things might go very badly for her. Lone Wolf's men leaped into their saddles and spurred their horses toward the herd they'd captured. With wild, exuberant yells they set their steeds to galloping forward over the next rise. Colly kicked her horse to a brisk gallop to keep up, topping the rise along with the men and horses.

She had only a glimpse of conical-shaped objects on the valley floor below and milling figures. The conical shapes were obviously tepees. With victorious cries the warriors guided the thundering herd down the hill and circled wide so they approached the Indian village from the east. As she followed close behind, Colly peered to either side, taking in as much detail as she could. The tepees were made of some kind of skins stretched over long, slender poles. In front of the tepees sat tripods with decorated circular disks like those carried by Lone Wolf and his braves.

Old women draped in furs sat before cooking fires, where kettles of food simmered. Dogs barked, children screamed gleefully and ran after the returning warriors. Men and women hurried toward the melee, their faces bright with smiles, their guttural voices calling greetings.

As nearly as Colly could tell, the village was circular, with only an opening facing eastward. Lone Wolf and his men drove their herd right into the center of the village and brought it to a halt. Horses whinnied, adding to the confusion, then settled down as they caught the scent of people.

They weren't wild ponies, after all, Colly thought as men and women stepped forward to run experienced hands over the sleek, foam-slathered coats. Comments were called back and forth, and Colly was reminded of Saturday afternoons back in Tennessee when the women gathered in the general store to buy bits of calico and supplies and the men gathered near the corrals to inspect the livestock and call out prices.

A tall man stepped out of a specially decorated lodge set the first in line of the crescent. His bearing was so dignified, Colly had no need to see how the people fell back in deference to know he was someone important. His leather shirt and leggings were bleached nearly white and draped softly over his stooping shoulders. His braids were gray, his weathered brown face creased with wrinkles, but his eyes were keen and piercing. Lone Wolf made his way toward the chief.

"Greetings, White Thunder," he said, raising his right hand in a sign of friendship.

"Greetings, Lone Wolf. You have done well." The old chief nodded toward the milling horses. Although Colly couldn't understand the words they spoke, she could see by the smile on the old man's face and the way his hand clasped Lone Wolf's that he was pleased with the horses the braves had acquired. Silently she waited until the old chief's gaze swung around to her. She heard his guttural tones and knew he was asking about her. Lone Wolf answered at some length. The old man nodded thoughtfully, his brows pulled down in a scowl while he queried his young war chief. At last he smiled and turned to the rest of the villagers, his hands raised for attention. He spoke a few words, and the villagers uttered sounds of appreciation, their faces once again bright with anticipation. Lone Wolf spoke to his men, who led the horses from the village circle. Then he turned toward Colly.

"Come," he said, signaling her forward.

Colly dismounted and followed after him. She was perfectly aware of the curious stares directed toward her by the villagers. Their dark eyes were bright, their faces unsmiling. She felt a nervous tremor pass over her. Was this where she met her final fate? she wondered briefly. Her heart thumped wildly in her chest. Her legs trembled with the desire to run, but she followed Lone Wolf through the silent crowd of dark-skinned people to a plump middle-aged woman with fine dark eyes. Beside the woman stood a younger, slimmer version of herself.

Red Bead Woman watched her son approach, her pride all

too evident in her gaze. Lone Wolf was a son to make any
mother proud. When his father had been killed in battle
against the Pawnee, Lone Wolf had avenged his death, and
so greatly was he respected he'd been made a war chief at a
very young age. When he went out on the war path or a
raiding party, as he'd just done, she worried incessantly about
him. Now he was home, his tall body loping easily toward
her.

"Greetings, *nah koa*," Lone Wolf said, embracing the
older woman.

With a sharp, puzzled look Red Bead Woman answered
in kind. "Welcome, my son. We have missed you these many
moons and are happy you are with us again."

Red Bead Woman returned Lone Wolf's embrace and
turned a questioning eye toward Colly. "You have brought a
captive?"

Colly's head jerked up and she glared at Lone Wolf.

"I found her along the trail, *nah koa*," he replied. "The
Sioux attacked the wagon train that carried her people."

The woman turned a searching gaze on Colly. "How is it
she has escaped?"

"She will tell you her story," Lone Wolf said. "I wish
you to take her into our lodge and care for her. She will be
of much help to you, for she is strong and able."

Red Bead Woman shook her head doubtfully. "She is too
skinny to be strong," she said, "but I will take her into our
lodge if you wish."

Irritated at being discussed so openly, as if she weren't
even there, Colly expelled her breath gustily through her nostrils and tipped her chin high.

"She is full of pride," Lone Wolf said in his own language, "and easily offended, but you must not mind this. If
she is too much trouble for you, tell me and I will deal with
her."

"I think I will have no trouble," Red Bead Woman answered, and, stepping in front of Colly, fixed her with a stern
eye.

"What are you called?" she demanded crisply.

Colly was taken aback but decided it was best to answer. "My name is Colly Mead," she answered. "What are you called?"

Ah, she does have spirit, Red Bead Woman thought, and introduced herself. "This is my daughter, Black Moon," she said, indicating the young woman standing nearby. Black Moon's dark gaze was derisive as it swept over Colly's caked, dirty hair, all the way down the filthy calico bodice with its torn-off tail and her father's battered woolen trousers, to the cracked, mud-covered boots.

Colly knew her appearance was unprepossessing, but there was little she could do about that now. Silently she waited, her gray eyes flashing indignantly as she endured Black Moon's perusal. The fact that Black Moon was truly beautiful made it all the more difficult.

The Indian girl was only as tall as her mother, but her figure was slim and lithe. She wore a soft deerskin dress ornamented with beads, brass buttons, and soft fringes. Her glossy dark hair was parted in the middle and pulled to either side of her beautiful oval face. Bits of strung tortoiseshell and beads decorated the tips of her braids. So perfect did her features appear that Colly held her breath, wishing she could have possessed such beauty. But she did not and, attending to her own situation, she glanced at Lone Wolf and waited.

"You will come to our lodge," Red Bead Woman said. "Come." She led the way among the tepees, and Colly followed behind. Satisfied with his solution concerning the captive woman, Lone Wolf turned away, striding across the circle to join his friends in their exuberant celebration.

Colly was stiffly aware of Black Moon following behind and contrived not to clomp along in her badly fitting boots. They passed several tepees where women were busy over their cooking fires, preparing kettles of food. There was to be a great feast in celebration of the returning warriors and the many horses they'd brought to add to the wealth of the village. Red Bead Woman explained all this with evident pride for her son's accomplishments.

"What about me?" Colly interrupted finally. "What are you going to do with me?"

Red Bead Woman paused, her eyebrows rising slightly over her dark eyes. "You will live with us until the white soldiers come for you. Then you may go," she answered serenely. "But you must work as we all do."

"Yes, of course I will," Colly answered, relieved to know at last what the Cheyenne had in mind for her. "Then I am not a prisoner?"

"Lone Wolf did not say so," Red Bead Woman answered. "He is the one who found you and saved you. He may do with you as he wishes."

"I see." Colly's elation had dimmed. To think that her destiny lay in the hands of a disgruntled warrior who thought nothing of knocking her to the ground was disheartening. Another thought struck her and she gripped Red Bead Woman's arm. "When will the white soldiers come?"

Red Bead Woman shrugged her shoulders. "I do not know."

"Do they come often to your village?"

The Indian woman shook her head. "They have never come here."

"Then how will the white soldiers know I am here at your village?"

Red Bead Woman shrugged again. "I do not know, but they will come to know it one day." She continued to walk.

Colly hurried to catch up with her. "One day?" she wailed in frustration. "Then Lone Wolf and his braves *did* attack the wagon train," she accused.

Red Bead Woman whirled and stared at her with such anger-filled eyes that Colly backed away a few steps.

"My son is wise," Red Bead Woman said. "He would not attack the white men. He knows this will cause war. The Sioux want war with the whites." Her words and attitude were so fierce that Colly knew she spoke the truth.

"I'm sorry. I—I didn't mean to cause offense," she stammered, but Red Bead Woman took no more time to explain things to her. She paused before a large skin tepee, and, with a quick glance indicating Colly should follow, ducked her head and stepped inside the small oval-shaped opening. Colly followed.

Inside, she blinked her eyes, trying to accustom herself to the darkness after the bright sunlight. Finally she was able to make out the interior of the lodge. A rectangular fire pit was built at the center of the lodge, while all around the skin walls, on a slight ledge of dirt and sod, rested sleeping pads of skin, filled with sweet prairie grass. Between each bed were backrests, rough tripods made of sapling and covered with leather. Between the poles of the tripods were stored parfleches of extra clothing, utensils, and food supplies.

Sweet grass had been scattered over the ledge, its fragrance filling the air in a not unpleasant manner. The floor around the fire had been cleared of prairie sod, the hard soil swept clean of all dust and loose dirt. From the lodge poles hung various items: water pouches, arrow quivers, and shields. The effect of the whole was one of orderliness.

Crossing to one of the tripods, Red Bead Woman pulled out a parfleche and searched among its contents. Finally she turned back to Colly, a soft skin garment and a pair of plain moccasins in her hands.

"First, you go to the river and bathe," Red Bead Woman directed, and Colly's cheeks stung with shame that the Indian woman considered her dirty. Well, she was, but it wasn't her fault, nor was this her normal state. Her embarrassment stayed nonetheless. She found little humor in the memory of the whites' scathing epithets of "dirty savages" when they spoke of the Indians. It seemed some of the Indians had little better regard for the white men.

Taking the garment from Red Bead Woman, Colly turned to the door. "Where is the river?" she asked.

"Black Moon will take you," Red Bead Woman answered, and waved her daughter forward. With an expression of distaste, Black Moon led Colly from the lodge.

"Lone Wolf must be your brother," Colly said, seeking some conversation that would lessen the girl's hostility.

"Lone Wolf, *nahnih*," Black Moon answered in the Cheyenne tongue, and, since Colly had already surmised their kinship, she interpreted the Cheyenne word to mean "brother."

"Do you speak English?" Colly persisted, knowing she'd have little chance to communicate if Black Moon did not. Stubbornly Black Moon remained silent.

"Was that old man back there your chief?" Colly tried again. "He looked very wise."

Still Black Moon refused to answer her.

They'd reached the bank of the river by now and the Indian girl turned sharply, moving quickly to a secluded spot where bushes grew out into the shallow waters, creating a natural screen. Other women were already there swimming. When they saw Black Moon, they let out a cry of greeting, then came forward to study the new arrival.

Some of them had not yet dressed after their baths, and Colly caught glimpses of bare copper breasts and sleek buttocks. The women hurried up the bank and donned buckskin dresses. Gaily they chattered among themselves, casting bright glances at Colly's awkward figure.

Cheeks flaming, Colly placed the clothes Red Bead Woman had given her on a nearby rock, then sat down to unlace her boots. That done, she stood up and looked about her. The women waited expectantly. Colly cast a quick glance at the water, considering bathing in her waist and trousers as she had done on the trail, but the prospect of a real bath was too appealing.

Loosening the rope that held her father's trousers on, she let them slide around her ankles and kicked them off. The women gasped and stared openly at her long white legs. One of them rattled off something, and the rest laughed. Black Moon snickered.

Angrily Colly unbuttoned her tattered dress bodice. "I didn't laugh at them," she muttered under her breath. Black Moon looked at her in surprise.

"They are not white and spotted like a fish," she said in perfect English.

Colly stared at her in amazement.

"You *do* speak English," she said accusingly.

"What is English?" Black Moon returned. "I speak the tongue of the white man."

Dumbfounded by such logic, Colly only stared at the Indian girl, then turned to the river. With her bodice shed, she was clad only in her unadorned cotton camisole and drawers. They were gray from lack of proper laundry facilities on the wagon train and the fact she'd worn them day and night since her parents became ill.

The stink of her own body assailed her nostrils, so she readily plunged into the icy waters, and, since she was unable to swim, stood in the shallows, flapping her arms to warm herself. Black Moon removed her doeskin dress and waded out to her.

"White women do not use soap to bathe themselves?" she asked curiously.

"You have soap?" Colly asked in disbelief.

Black Moon held out her hand, revealing the soft, pulpy center of some wild plant. Dubiously Colly looked at it.

"Take it," Black Moon urged. "It will make you clean."

"What is it called?" Colly asked, taking the piece of pulpy stalk. Following Black Moon's directions, she rubbed the mess between her palms until a lather appeared. Delighted, she glanced at Black Moon, then worked the soap into her hair, hastily working her braid loose so her hair flowed around her in the current.

"This is the stalk of the soapweed," Black Moon explained. "We use it for many things." Black Moon paused. "White women do not use such a plant?"

Colly cast the young girl a quick glance. Black Moon's

face was earnest. "We make our soap of lye and lard and ash," she explained.

"These things we use to soften hides!" Black Moon cried, amazed that the white women should put such things on their own skins.

"How is it that you speak Eng—the white man's tongue so well, yet you know so little about us?" Colly asked.

"I know many things about you," Black Moon flared. "A trapper lived with my people when I was a girl. He taught us many things. How to speak the white man's tongue. How to use the white man's guns and cook in the kettles of iron. We know many more things about you than you know about us."

Colly shook the water out of her rinsed hair and looked at Black Moon. "I daresay you're right about that," she said. "Does *nahnih* mean 'brother'?"

Black Moon's smile was superior, but she nodded her head in agreement.

"Tell me some other Cheyenne words," Colly urged, perceiving that the more she learned of these strange people, the better for her.

Black Moon dropped her hostile air and leaned back in the water, floating on her back. She raised one gleaming brown arm to point to trees, bushes, rocks, and water while she told Colly the names for them. Colly listened intently, repeating each one several times to be sure she was saying them properly.

"That is enough for today," Black Moon said finally, tired of her role as teacher. She glanced at Colly and her brows drew together in consternation.

"They do not wash off," she said, pointing to Colly's freckled arm.

"No," Colly answered, trying not to mind the attention her freckles received. Even in Tennessee, the thick smattering of spots had occasioned comment, for most women strove to keep their arms and faces protected from the sun. Still, they'd been fairly earned, working the fields as she had done.

"How did you get them?" Black Moon persisted, unaware she caused offense.

"From the sun," Colly mumbled, lowering her arms beneath the water.

Black Moon peered at her own arms. "The sun does not give such spots to the Cheyenne," she noted. "Must be bad medicine."

Miffed by the Indian girl's assumed superiority, Colly folded her arms as if protecting them from anyone's view. "Magic medicine," she grunted disdainfully, and led the way back to shore, where several women still tarried, talking to one another and waiting for another glimpse of the white woman with the pale, ugly body.

Curiosity overcame good manners, so some of them stared openly at this strange, gawky creature who looked more like a man than a woman. The wet cotton camisole clung to Colly's chest, revealing her small, pointed breasts and skinny rib cage. Even her buttocks were skinny, they saw, and they clucked their tongues with mock sympathy.

Only her hair, loosened around her shoulders and still streaming with water, occasioned cries of envy. They crowded close, touching the orange-red strands, then drawing away as if expecting to be burned. Seizing her arm, they looked at her freckles, too, and rubbed at them as if to remove them. Colly jerked her arm away and glared at them.

"The sun gave them to her," Black Moon whispered, and the women drew back, regarding her with some awe.

Even Black Moon was mesmerized by Colly's vivid hair. Quickly, without benefit of a comb or brush, Colly plaited the heavy, wet strands into a tight single braid down her back, then reached for the leather garment Red Bead Woman had given her.

She could, she realized, pull it on over her wet undergarments, but Black Moon was there, gesturing for her to take off the limp rags. Shaking her head vehemently, Colly refused, but Black Moon advanced on her, clearly resolved to be obeyed.

"We must burn white man clothes," she said, drawing her fine, dark brows into a scowl. "Must burn everything that white man sickness touch."

"Oh, I see," Colly said, straightening. Once again she'd underestimated the Indian's behavior. Turning her back—and casting a quick glance to see that no men were present—Colly slipped out of the pitiful gray rags that constituted the last tie to all that was civilization. Now she truly felt like a heathen.

Without a word, Black Moon took the offending garments and handed Colly a long piece of soft, fine doeskin. Colly looked at the strip of hide, not sure what she was supposed to do with it, until Black Moon showed her how to loop it between her thighs and fasten it front and back over a single rawhide sash tied at her waist. Such a garment was, she realized, somewhat like the breechcloths Lone Wolf's men had worn, no doubt the equivalent of a lady's underdrawers. The hide was not unpleasant against her skin, but she felt strangely naked about the hips.

The long doeskin dress was drawn over her shoulders, and Colly felt the brush of the soft hide against her bare nipples. The sensation was strangely sensuous, making her uncomfortably aware of her body.

Black Moon handed her the moccasins and helped her lace them on correctly. They reached high up on her legs, almost to her knees. Although the dress, obviously intended for Red Bead Woman's shorter frame, was woefully short, Colly found she was modestly covered, yet unencumbered by skirts and petticoats. Following Black Moon up the path to the village, she marveled at the comfort of the Indian clothes.

Red Bead Woman was waiting for them, her plump face thoughtful as she watched their approach. The tall white woman limped, unaccustomed to the soft soles of the moccasins. Soon, though, her feet would toughen. Concern for the white woman's momentary discomfort was not what brought the frown to Red Bead Woman's face.

Why had her son brought this woman to their village? Had not their prophet, Motsiiu, warned them only harm would come from their association with the whites? Why had Lone Wolf ignored such a warning, especially when the white soldiers had already proven themselves hostile to the Cheyenne people? What would this strange white woman's coming mean to their village? Red Bead Woman guessed that Chief White Thunder was even now sitting in his lodge mulling over these same questions.

Black Moon and Colly had reached Red Bead Woman's lodge, so the Indian woman put aside her ponderings and bent to stir the pot of food.

"There is to be a feast," she explained, without looking at the white woman again. The pale eyes gazed at her too directly, making her nervous. "You will stay here at the lodge."

The white woman made no reply, and Red Bead Woman glanced around to find her staring at the savory pot of food. The wide, pale eyes seemed huge in the thin face and held the same silent yearning Red Bead Woman had seen in the eyes of the Cheyenne children when the winters had been long and hunger stalked the people like an angry coyote. Taking up a wooden bowl, Red Bead Woman filled it with the steaming mixture.

"Eat now," she commanded. The white woman hesitated only a moment; then, gripping the bowl with trembling hands, as if fearful of spilling even one drop of the precious contents, she crouched beside the fire, and, before Red Bead Woman could tender a carved bone spoon, dipped dripping chunks of meat and roots out with her fingers and popped them into her mouth. Black Moon's face curled with disgust at such bad manners, but Red Bead Woman averted her face with some understanding. Once she had known hunger like that. She felt a stirring of pity for the white woman, then quickly clamped it down.

At first the white woman gobbled her food, half choking it down, and just as suddenly set the half-filled bowl aside.

Grimacing apologetically at Red Bead Woman, she gripped her stomach while her shoulders shook with spasms of pain. The Indian woman nodded her head in understanding, and, disappearing inside the tepee, fumbled among the pouches hanging from the lodge poles until she'd found what she sought. Returning to the fire, she cast some dried, crumbled leaves into a bone cup of boiling water, then handed it to Colly.

"Drink this tea," Red Bead Woman said. "It will take the pain away."

Hesitantly Colly reached for the cup and sipped the hot liquid. It burned a fiery path to her stomach, and almost immediately the pain eased. Gratefully Colly smiled at the Indian woman and continued to sip the hot tea, uncertain if it was the mysterious leaves Red Bead Woman had used or the fact that her stomach had at last been given enough hot food. Either way, she was beginning to feel better.

"Thank you," she said, holding out the empty cup.

"You have not eaten much food for a long time," Red Bead Woman observed.

"Food got kind of sparse on the wagon train," Colly explained. "Then when Mama and Papa got sick, I was too tired to cook just for myself. I'd run out of food when Lone Wolf found me. I—I guess I would have died if he hadn't come along."

Red Bead Woman grunted. "Many buffalo do not come to the hunting ground of the white man?"

"We don't have buffalo back in Tennessee," Colly said, and Red Bead Woman liked the quiet, soft sound of her voice. "Papa and me, we grew some cows and a couple of hogs. In the fall and winter we'd hunt deer and squirrel. Once in a while we'd have possums, although Mama wasn't much for possum meat. She thought decent folk shouldn't eat them." She stopped talking, aware she'd run on. It had been comforting to share something of her homeland with this kind woman.

But the past days had been long and arduous. Her stomach

was filled for the first time in a long time and the fire warmed her from the creeping evening chill. She was safe for the moment. A sense of well-being settled over her and she yawned, stretching her jaws wide.

"Come," Red Bead Woman said, and, rising, led the way into the lodge. "You will sleep here," she said, indicating a bed pad to one side, well away from the fire pit. Silently Colly sank to the pad and closed her eyes, falling at once into a deep sleep.

Before Red Bead Woman left to join the festivities, she checked on the sleeping woman. Lone Wolf had said she'd tried running away, but Red Bead Woman had no fear of that happening now. She had drugged the tea she gave the white woman. She would sleep long and deep.

Red Bead Woman felt no guilt as she left the lodge to join the celebration, for she'd seen many things in the pale eyes and thin face. The white woman was exhausted, her spirit flagging from her ordeal. She needed food and rest to recover her strength and her will to live. Knowing she'd done all she could for the moment, Red Bead Woman hurried to join her tribesmen in their honor of her son.

Colly's sleep was dreamless, deep and warm and dark, more comforting than anything her sun-seared days had offered. Gratefully she embraced the oblivion offered by her sleep and for a time knew peace. Then her spirit, too strong to accept defeat—even so minute a one as the drugged tea Red Bead Woman had offered—pushed to the edge of awareness, so Colly lay half dreaming, half awake.

She heard the high shrieks of revelry as the Indians celebrated their good fortune over the Arapaho. She heard and misunderstood the wild abandon of the animallike cries. Anyone capable of making such sounds must surely be capable of attacking a wagon train and murdering innocent people. There was no conscience, no honor in such a cry, only a primitive triumph of survival. Her subconscious heard and understood that primal cry. It echoed in her soul, wakening her, so she answered its call with a cry of her own and sat up, peering through the darkness with dilated eyes that saw nothing.

Slowly her vision cleared and she saw through the open flap of the tepee a bright orange fire and dark figures leaping and dancing around it. Pressing her fist against her mouth to still any more screams, she lay back against the grass-scented bed, her body rigid, her eyes terror-filled. Not until morning, when she heard the Indian known as Red Bead Woman creep into her bed, did she relax her vigilance and sleep again.

Chapter 4

*H*AUNTING NIGHTMARES RECEDED in the warm golden light of morning. Colly jerked awake and lay still on her grass-and-skin bed, her huge gray eyes moving from side to side as she took in the interior of the skin lodge. She'd forgotten all that had befallen her—and for a moment thought she was still on the wagon train and the soft skins above were the flapping canvas covering. Slowly memory returned and she drew in her breath and sat up, fearfully searching for the hideous painted figures of her nightmare, but the lodge was empty. The gentle voice of Red Bead Woman could be heard without, answered by the sharper, clearer tones of Black Moon.

Colly rose from her bed and stumbled to the door of the lodge. Facing east as it did, the opening was filled with sunlight. Colly stepped into the buttery light and raised a hand to shield her eyes.

"You are awake," Red Bead Woman greeted her. "Come and eat."

Colly felt no hunger but sat beside the fire as Red Bead Woman had bid her. Now that her eyes had accustomed themselves to the sunlight, she looked about, feeling her spirits rise. She had survived her first night in the Indian camp and she'd been treated with kindness so far. It was foolish for her to expect anything worse. Ashamed of her suspicions

54

in the face of Red Bead Woman's graciousness, she smiled and took the bowl of hot mush the Indian woman proffered. It had a strange nutty flavor, and Colly struggled to eat it without showing her distaste. Finally she set the bowl aside.

"Soon your stomach will grow again and you will eat more," Red Bead Woman said. Her expression was not unkind, but Colly sensed a guarded air about her. Glancing around the village, Colly noted few people were about.

"Where is everyone?" she asked warily.

Red Bead Woman shrugged. "Cheyenne people rise early. Not good to sleep while the sun is up."

"I'm sorry I slept so late. I'll get up earlier tomorrow."

"Ummm," Red Bead Woman grunted, neither condemning nor excusing Colly's lateness.

"I heard things in the night, cries and screams," Colly said hesitantly.

"Our people celebrated the return of our warriors and their horses," Red Bead Woman replied. "They stole many horses from the Arapaho."

"Why do they steal horses?" Colly asked.

The Indian woman shrugged. "The Arapaho steal horses from the Cheyenne. We steal back."

"What about the wagon train?" Colly finally found the courage to ask. "How can you be certain your warriors didn't kill my people?"

Red Bead Woman nodded as if she understood Colly's doubts. Rising, she crossed to the lodge door and returned with two tomahawks in her hand. Thrusting them out, handle first, she invited Colly's inspection.

"Cheyenne tomahawk," she declared, pointing to the one with zigzag lines resembling lightning. "Sioux tomahawk!" she said, indicating the other.

Colly recognized the tomahawk she'd removed from Brother Davey's body. The markings were obviously different. Relief was clear in her eyes when she met Red Bead Woman's gaze.

"Thank you," she said, and, grunting with satisfaction, the Indian woman returned the tomahawks to the lodge.

Returning, she took down a water pouch and emptied the contents onto the ground. "Go to the river and bring back water," she instructed, holding out the pouch.

Startled by her actions, Colly looked from Red Bead Woman to the puddle of water seeping into the ground.

"That is dead water," the Indian woman explained. "We drink only living water."

Colly's eyes filled with comprehension as she took the water pouch. Red Bead Woman halted her going with a touch. "We have many ways that are different from the white man's. Cheyenne ways good for Cheyenne."

Colly smiled then, a wide, joyful thing that lit her pale eyes wondrously and warmed her thin face. "Cheyenne ways may be good for white men, too," she said.

Caught in the wonder of that smile, Red Bead Woman made no response, and Colly turned toward the river. Watching her go, Red Bead Woman thought she could understand what had prompted her son to bring this woman to their village. She was different from many of the white eyes. Red Bead Woman wasn't certain just what that difference was, but she'd caught a glimpse of it in the spirit of that smile. Oddly troubled now, she turned back to the fire. She must talk to Lone Wolf about this strange woman, but he hadn't returned from last night's festivities and she wasn't certain when she would see him again.

Colly hurried to the river, wanting to complete her chore quickly and well to disprove any notion of slothfulness Red Bead Woman might have gained about her. She followed the path Black Moon had taken the day before, intending to climb above the bathing area to dip fresh water, but as she neared the shallow banks where the women had bathed, she heard voices and turned to see who was at the river. Her thin cheeks burned with color as she glimpsed tall, lean bodies with broad, muscular shoulders. Her gaze collided with fierce dark eyes and she darted back along the trail, horrified that Lone

Wolf had caught her peering down at the nude bathing men. She hadn't known, but how was she to tell him that?

She had no need to worry that Lone Wolf thought her indecent. He'd seen the embarrassment in her face before she ducked away, and he knew she hadn't meant to see the men bathing. He was pleased by her modesty. He had been thinking of her as he floated in the river, wondering if his mother was pleased with their—Lone Wolf paused in his thinking, uncertain of what to call her. She wasn't a guest, neither was she a captive, so she couldn't be a slave, and yet he was responsible for her being here.

Sometimes he wished he hadn't rescued her, for her presence was troubling to him and to the others. Yet something had compelled him to follow her, and he'd been unable to leave her to die. Perhaps the Great Spirit had some special plan for this white woman. Perhaps that was why he'd been sent to save her. Lone Wolf thought again of the strange, glowing eyes and hair like the twisting, leaping flames of a hot fire. He must be patient, he thought, for surely the spirits had a reason for bringing her to them and would, in time, reveal those reasons.

Colly climbed high above the bank, skirted the bathing place, and dipped her water from the river before returning to Red Bead Woman's lodge. All the way, she refused to think about the tall Indian she'd seen at the river. He was a heathen, a godless creature, uncivilized, animallike, living here on the prairie in a house made of animal skins. She must think of him in no other way, for to do so would surely be a sin against God—and would damn her soul to eternal hellfire.

She must strive to do all she could to survive and never lose sight of the fact that she would one day be rescued. When that day came, she wanted to walk among her own kind with her head high, knowing she'd done nothing indecent. All the way back to the village, she sought to remember Brother Davey's brim-fire-and-damnation sermons.

As Colly returned the water pouch to Red Bead Woman,

a loud, singsong voice called from the other side of the village. An old man seated on an equally aging horse rode around the circle of tepees. He rode from the opening in the east to the south, then around to the north. All along his path people came out to hear his words. Colly listened intently, and although she couldn't understand his song, she began to hear a rhythm and knew when he repeated something.

"What does he say?" she asked Red Bead Woman, who had also stopped her work and stood listening.

"He tells us what the chiefs have decided for us this day," she answered. "We will camp here for a while longer; then we will go to look for the buffalo."

The old crier had reached the other side of the opening to the village circle, but instead of riding across it, he turned and retraced his steps, still calling out his message. People who'd come out to listen now turned back to their work. Red Bead Woman gathered up her bone needle and her sharp knife. She'd been invited to spend the day helping a friend sew a new lodge. She glanced at Colly.

"Spotted Woman will go with Black Moon and the other women to collect wood," Red Bead Woman continued, but unaware of the Indians' name for her, Colly only stared at her blankly. Red Bead Woman motioned to Black Moon, and the younger girl took hold of Colly's arm, yanking her to her feet.

Colly cast a troubled glance over her shoulder but followed the girl, who fell in with a group of chattering, laughing young women. One of them, a slim, pretty girl called Burning Star, seemed her favorite. Sideway glances were cast Colly's way, but no one spoke to her.

Young boys had risen early and ridden into the hills to drive in the herd of horses. Now Lone Wolf and the other men came forward to select favorite mounts that would be tethered in front of the tepee for their convenience throughout the day. Black Moon and the women went forward to choose horses for themselves.

Lone Wolf saw Colly waiting to one side and cut a mount

from the herd. Slipping a rope halter over its head, he led it to her. Without meeting his gaze Colly took the reins and led the horse to a boulder, where she mounted bareback.

With her long legs astride, her short dress rode up, revealing her knees and a goodly portion of pale thighs. Casting a surreptitious glance at Lone Wolf, she tugged at the leather skirt. Lone Wolf's face was immobile as he gazed at her, his dark eyes raking over her face and dress and finally down to her bared knees. He gave little notice to her exposed flesh, raising his gaze again to meet hers.

"Go into hills with women to gather firewood?" he asked.

"Yes, I'm going with Black Moon," Colly answered, forcing herself to meet his gaze with far more serenity than she felt.

Lone Wolf gazed into her eyes for a long moment that made her lids twitch in an effort not to look away first. Finally he leaned forward and gripped her mount's reins. "Lone Wolf's horse," he said. "Do not take."

"No, I won't," she flared, cheeks flaming with anger. She felt the fool that she'd worried over her exposed knees when all he'd been concerned with was his horseflesh. "In fact, if you prefer, I won't ride your horse at all." She started to dismount, but Lone Wolf crowded his horse close, so she was forced to stay mounted. She settled onto the back of the horse again, but her head was held uncommonly high.

Once again, Lone Wolf reached out, and this time his hand fell against her bare thigh, his long fingers biting cruelly into her pale flesh. "Lone Wolf's woman," he said sternly. "Do not run away."

"I—I am most certainly not your woman," Colly sputtered indignantly, brushing her hand against his as if to rid herself of some pesky mosquito. But Lone Wolf was not to be so easily deterred. His firm grip remained on her bare knee, his dark eyes captured her gaze, quelling her rebellion.

"Lone Wolf does not use the white man's words so well." His dark gaze lifted to her hair. "Spotted Woman rescued by Lone Wolf. Lone Wolf responsible until white soldiers come.''

Colly recognized the name Red Bead Woman had used earlier and guessed it was the name given to her because of her freckles. So bemused was she by this discovery that she did not at first grasp the import of Lone Wolf's words. When she did, she met his stern gaze.

''Do you mean that since you've rescued me, I belong to you?'' she asked.

Lone Wolf nodded with satisfaction. ''Stay at Lone Wolf's lodge. Lone Wolf protect, bring food. Spotted Woman must work, gather wood, not run away. If Spotted Woman run away, Lone Wolf must punish.''

Colly shivered at his warning. She knew by his demeanor that he meant what he said. He'd given her fair warning. Now, satisfied he'd delivered his message, he released her knee, and, wheeling his mount, galloped away without a backward glance.

Colly watched him go, anger coursing through her at his high-handed manner. She must work, indeed. Red Bead Woman had already told her that and, of course, she intended to work for her keep. No one had said Colly Mead was not a hard worker. She would prove to this arrogant savage warrior that he had no need to order her about.

Furthermore, if she decided to leave the village, she would do so. But when she did, she would plan carefully, taking not only a horse, but a water pouch and food so she might survive. She'd learned much about the prairie in her short weeks traveling on its teeming flatness. She would learn more, though. She needed to learn the way to the nearest fort, and when she knew that, no Indian warrior, no matter how menacing, would keep her from going.

Feeling better about her small inner defiance, Colly cantered after Black Moon and the other young women. She was so caught up in her interchange with Lone Wolf that she gave little notice to the snickering comments Black Moon and her friend, Burning Star, directed toward her. They traveled some distance from the river, angling upward into forested mountain slopes. Finally they approached an area filled with dead wood and fallen trees, where they halted. Dismounting, the women began to gather dead branches.

"Spotted Woman help," Black Moon ordered, drawing down her brows impatiently.

Colly slid off her horse and set herself to the task of gathering dead wood. She was amazed at the industry of the women, who dragged large pieces of fallen tree trunks and fastened them so their horses could drag them back. Likewise, others had fashioned travois, onto which they tied bundles of wood. When everyone had a considerable load of wood, they turned their horses back to the village. All the while they talked amiably among themselves. There was much laughter and good-natured antics.

Back in the village, Colly followed Black Moon to the tepee she had occupied the night before. Memory of Lone Wolf's claims made her question the younger girl.

"Is this Red Bead Woman's lodge?" she asked tentatively.

Black Moon's face brightened with a superior smile. "This is the lodge of Lone Wolf," she answered.

"I see," Colly said, and then another thought occurred to her. "Does Lone Wolf live here, too?"

Disbelief crossed Black Moon's face. "This is the lodge of Lone Wolf," she repeated sharply, and turned toward the river. "Come, we will search for duck eggs."

Colly thought about trying to explain but decided against it. She hurried to catch up with the Indian girl. All day the women worked at one task or another, often chatting or laughing so the time passed quickly.

Finally Black Moon turned to Colly. "We will bathe now."

Gratefully Colly followed her to the river. Now that they were alone, she turned back to the subject that troubled her the most.

"Is it true I am Lone Wolf's property?" she asked, and her voice held so much misery that Black Moon's impatience softened.

"Lone Wolf rescued you," she answered gently.

"And I must obey him?"

Black Moon looked away, an old anger twisting her pretty mouth. "I must obey him, too," she said bitterly.

Something in her voice touched Colly; she forgot her own misery and studied the Indian girl. "Why must you? You're his sister," she said.

Black Moon's head lifted proudly, and her eyes were dark with pain as she spoke. "It is the way of the Cheyenne that a woman must accept her brother as a guardian."

"And you object to this?" Colly asked encouragingly.

"I must marry a man I do not want because my brother says so." Black Moon's dark eyes flashed with fire before she lowered her lashes.

"Perhaps if you told Lone Wolf you don't want to marry the man he has chosen . . ."

"He knows," Black Moon said.

They walked in silence the rest of the way to the river. Once there, Black Moon immediately stripped off her clothes, all save the chastity rope twisted around her thighs, and plunged into the river. Still unaccustomed to such openness, Colly followed more slowly, keeping on the loincloth tied at her waist and holding her hands over her small breasts until she was in the water. She stood watching Black Moon swim.

"Why would Lone Wolf make you marry someone you don't love?" she asked when Black Moon paused nearby.

The Indian girl sluiced the water from her face and hair and turned a troubled face to Colly. "He does this to repay a debt of gratitude," she answered slowly. "When my father was killed by the Pawnee, Little Bear protected his bones and took them to a safe place where the enemy could not find them. He did this at great risk to himself. Such a deed must be honored. Lone Wolf has promised I will be Little Bear's wife."

"Perhaps you'll grow to love Little Bear," Colly said, moved by the girl's story.

Black Moon rolled her eyes at the white woman in exasperation. "That is what my mother has said, but I do not think this will be. Little Bear is a cruel man. He grows angry at many things." Not wishing to continue the conversation, she floated away, swimming with long, lazy strokes before coming back to help Colly with more Cheyenne words. The Indian girl's manner had softened considerably. She was almost friendly, until Burning Star hailed her from the shore; then she clamped on the old hostile glare and swam away from Colly.

Red Bead Woman had returned to the lodge by the time they returned. She sat skinning fresh rabbits that Lone Wolf had brought in earlier. Colly glanced around the village, but, catching no glimpse of the tall, broad-shouldered Indian, she relaxed a little. At Red Bead Woman's orders, Colly put more wood on the fire and helped around the lodge. The sun was sinking below the line of trees on a distant ridge. Coolness flooded the camp that had baked all day in the sun. Firelight glowed inside the skin tepees, turning them golden. In the distance youngsters swooped across the ground like quick-darting birds, their shrill voices echoing on the quiet evening air.

Red Bead Woman showed Colly how to impale the rabbits on sharp sticks over the campfire and turned her attention to something else, leaving Colly to tend them. Carefully she turned the meat, making sure it browned evenly without burning. Once again the sounds of the village assailed her, the low throb of small skin drums and the answering boom of a larger drum, the shrill notes of a flute, barking dogs, neighing ponies, and, out on the prairie, the long, lonely howl of a coyote.

She couldn't adjust to the hustle and bustle of the camp. It reminded her of the wagon train and the confining, caterwauling presence of people locked together in too intimate a contact by their mutual fear of the unknown. Colly longed for the quiet of the farm, when the chores were done and her time was finally hers. Solitude was sweet then. She thought of the prairie, vast and lonely beneath the sky, just beyond those mountains and forests. Even the prairie was better than this press of people. Then she heard the distant howl of the coyote and shivered. Suddenly she was grateful to be here with these people, alien as they were. No matter how savage and backward they might seem to her, they were human beings placed here on this earth by the same God who must surely have a purpose for them all.

The meat had scorched during her mooning. She snatched it from the fire and in her hurry bumped against Lone Wolf's shield resting on its tripod. It rolled across the ground and came to rest against the hot stones of the fire pit. Colly hurried to snatch it up, but a charred black burn marred the painted surface. Not knowing what to do about it, she stood holding the round disc as Lone Wolf approached the campfire. When he saw her holding his shield, he came to an abrupt halt, his expression turning dark with anger.

"I—I'm sorry," she stammered. "I knocked against it and it rolled across the ground and fell against the hot stones. I'm afraid it's been scorched." She held the shield out to him.

Without a word, he took the shield and stood staring at her so fiercely, she grew frightened.

"I—I didn't mean to do it," she stammered. "Mama always said I was as clumsy as—as a mule . . ." Her voice dwindled to a halt and she stared back at the Indian man. She was aware Black Moon and Red Bead Woman had come to the fire, though neither of them spoke.

Finally Lone Wolf turned away, disappearing into the dark with his shield. Colly looked at Black Moon and Red Bead Woman.

"He's angry with me," she said inanely.

"It is bad luck to handle someone else's shield," Red Bead Woman said, crossing to the fire.

"It would have burned if I hadn't picked it up," Colly said defensively, and lapsed into silence. The women waited and soon Lone Wolf was back, stepping out of the dark shadows with a shrunken old man following him.

"He has brought Dull Knife," Red Bead Woman said, with evident relief. Colly knew at once he was the medicine man of the village, for he carried several pouches upon his person. His leather shirt was painted with many symbols and he wore necklaces and several amulets of bear teeth and leather.

He fixed Colly with a stern, unblinking stare and asked her to relate what had happened. Hesitantly she told him. Black Moon acted as interpreter. When she had finished, he nodded with satisfaction and spoke in a wavering voice that seemed to gain in strength.

"He says you have not harmed the shield by touching it," Black Moon translated. "You tried to save it from harm."

"That's true!" Colly cried, relieved the old man had understood.

Red Bead Woman began to extinguish the campfire, rolling the hot stones away and spreading dirt over the place where the cooking fire had been. When she was finished, Dull Knife placed the shield back on the ground and covered it with a buffalo robe. Seating himself on the ground, he stared into the distance, and Colly wasn't certain if he'd gone into a trance or was engaged in special prayers. Lone Wolf seated himself by the medicine man and waited.

After some time had passed, Dull Knife rose, and, taking out a bowl made from a box elder knot, he pulverized dried leaves until they were a powder. Building a small fire, he sprinkled the powdery mixture over the flames, then, removing the robe from the shield, he passed the shield through the smoke.

"Why is he doing that?" Colly whispered.

"To purify the shield," Black Moon answered.

Dull Knife handed the shield back to Lone Wolf, who placed it back on its tripod. Colly made a mental note to avoid that area at all costs. His task completed, the old man disappeared into the darkness. Lone Wolf glanced at Colly, his dark eyes unreadable in the shadowy light.

"There is food?" he asked pointedly, and Colly knew he intended that she get it for him.

"I'm afraid I've burned it," she said stiffly, holding out a tortoiseshell filled with blackened meat. Lone Wolf grunted, tore off a fat hind leg, and bit into it with square white teeth. His dark eyes studied her for a moment; then he stalked away.

Colly tried not to be intimidated by his presence, but it was growing more difficult with every encounter. Now, to know that she belonged to Lone Wolf, that he could do with her as he wished, was even more alarming. What if he decided to force himself on her? She'd heard the women on the train whispering of the horrors Indians forced upon their women captives. Her eyes grew large as she strained to peer into the shadows after Lone Wolf. Was he out there somewhere, watching her, lusting for her?

"Lone Wolf!" someone shouted, and was answered from across the circle. Colly spun around, her face burning crimson. Obviously he wasn't out there in the dark watching her, she thought, then grinned at herself. He hadn't touched her on the trail, except to knock her flat when she'd attacked him. There was little to make her believe he wanted her. The thought of any man lusting after her stringy body was ridiculous.

Red Bead Woman and Black Moon returned, and all three women crouched beside the fire nibbling the fresh rabbit in a leisurely fashion. Red Bead Woman's face was serene, her dark eyes dancing with humor as she related the events of her day and the stories that had been told by the women working on the lodge.

Colly sensed a kind of peace had fallen over the village, though the noises of many people engaged in different activities created a hum. Nonetheless, there was a certain ease, as if the day had been all it should have been. Laughter was softened, voices gentled by the sweetness of the evening.

One by one the campfires were tamped down for the night. The village grew quiet as children and the older folks went off to bed. Colly lingered by the dying coals long after Red Bead Woman had yawned and retired to her bed. Black Moon sat on the other side, peering at Colly intensely.

"Spotted Woman tired now," she said coaxingly.

Colly hugged her shoulders against the evening chill and gazed at the brilliant stars twinkling in a black velvet sky. "I slept late this morning," she said, "so I'm not tired yet."

"Spotted Woman grow cold sitting in the dew without a robe?" Black Moon tried again.

"No, I'm fine. Don't worry about me," Colly said, reluctant to surrender this feeling of contentment that had spread over her. It was almost as good as being back home in Tennessee.

Black Moon sat silently contemplating the white woman. Finally she stood, and without a backward glance she stalked away into the darkness. Colly watched her go, wondering what had caused the flare of rage she'd seen on the girl's face. Pushing Black Moon's hostility to the back of her mind, she concentrated once again on the sky, searching for the North Star and Orion's belt. Somehow finding these things made her feel closer to home. She sat on the ground, her arms hugging her knees to her chest for warmth, and gazed at the sky, recalling every detail of the farm—from the grain in the weathered gray wood of the barn to the narcissus growing around the back porch step.

Time lost meaning to her until she felt a presence nearby. She whirled around on her buttocks, her wide eyes darting this way and that, trying to pierce the blackness. She saw Lone Wolf immediately. He was a dark silhouette against the moonlit clearing. He moved forward, towering over her, yet not really menacing after all.

"Spotted Woman sits alone," he said, and his voice was oddly deep and soothing.

"I . . . was enjoying the night," Colly said. "It's very

peaceful, the way it used to get of an evening back in Tennessee.''

"Ten-see?" he repeated.

"Tennessee." Colly repressed a smile, guessing instinctively the warrior wouldn't want to be laughed at. "We had a farm back there."

"If white man had land in Tennessee, why does he come here to take Indian land?" Lone Wolf demanded.

"I don't know," Colly answered, thinking of the blue haze over the hills back home. "I don't know."

Lone Wolf grunted and stalked into the tepee. The peacefulness of the night was gone, but Colly continued to sit by the fire, waiting until she thought Lone Wolf would be asleep. Then, dousing the last of the flames, she rose and entered the lodge.

Involuntarily her gaze darted to the pad where Lone Wolf lay. Although his body was still, she sensed a tension in the long brown limbs and guessed he wasn't sleeping. Creeping to her own pad, Colly lay down and drew a deep breath, willing herself to relax and sleep. But as before, the strangeness of her surroundings and the people sleeping around her proved too much, so she lay rigid and wakeful far into the night. Sometime later she heard someone entering the lodge.

"Black Moon?" she whispered.

"Shhh!" came the reply, and Colly knew it came from Black Moon. Lone Wolf grunted and rolled over in his sleep. Black Moon froze. When he'd settled into a deep sleep again, she scuttled into her bedroll and pulled the robe over her head. All was quiet in the lodge. Colly lay pondering Black Moon's behavior. If she'd been promised in marriage to a man she did not favor, then whom had she gone off with this evening?

Colly woke with a start the next morning, and, seeing the other inhabitants of the lodge were still sleeping, she crept out of her bed. Lone Wolf was still abed, his robes tossed to one side. He wore only a breechcloth, and the early rising sun cast a golden light over the inside of the tepee and its inhabitants. He looked like some bronzed pagan god sprawled across the furs.

Quickly Colly averted her eyes and made her way outside. She would start a cooking fire, she decided, raking the coals from the previous fire. Fiercely she concentrated on what she was doing so her idle mind wouldn't dwell on the sight of Lone Wolf's half-naked body. Patiently she coaxed a flame, added some dried twigs and sticks. Struggling with the dead wood and branches they'd dragged to camp the day before, she sought to break them into more manageable pieces.

Hearing a sound, she whirled, a gasp escaping her lips. Lone Wolf stood before her. He'd donned no other clothes except his moccasins. His bare chest was before her, and for the first time she noted that he had several deep scars. The rest of his skin was a deep, smooth brown. She couldn't seem to find a safe place to rest her eyes. At last she turned back to the resisting branches.

"I was just trying to get some wood for the fire," she said, yanking at a particularly long piece.

"Spotted Woman use axe," he said, pointing to Red Bead Woman's tool propped against a tripod next to the fire.

"Thank you," Colly said, and felt angry that he turned away without offering to help her. "Of course, you could probably cut it better than I."

Lone Wolf paused and looked back at her, his brown eyes amused by her suggestion. "Firewood work for woman, not warrior," he answered arrogantly, and strode away toward the river.

"Seems like all the chores are woman's work," she called after him, but he didn't look back. No doubt he and the rest of his friends would loll about the river all morning, leaving all the heavy chores for the women to do. No wonder people called them lazy, no-account heathens.

So thinking, she picked up the axe and went to work on the branches, cutting them into manageable sizes in no time. Taking an armload back to the fire pit, she added short logs to the greedy flames, then sat back to watch it for a time. But morning was not a time for contemplation and reflections. A restlessness assailed her, so she took up the water pouch, and, taking great care to choose a path that would take her well away from the bathing men, she walked to the river and filled the pouches with living water.

Red Bead Woman and Black Moon were up by the time she returned to camp. In the distance she could see the boys heading to the hills to drive in the herds of horses. Another day had begun.

"This is good," Red Bead Woman said, surveying the things Colly had already done. Colly was surprisingly touched by the kind woman's words. She liked Red Bead Woman and wanted to please her.

As Black Moon sat on a log and groomed herself, Red Bead Woman hurried through the combing and braiding of her long hair and the application of red paint to its part. Colly sat and watched the women. They were as careful in their appearance as a fastidious white woman, taking great care to bathe themselves and ornament their clothes and hair.

Suddenly aware of her own tangled hair, impatiently braided without the use of a comb, Colly seated herself on the ground, turning her legs to the side as the Cheyenne women did, while she unbraided her hair and raked through its tangles with her fingers. She was unaware of the becoming picture she made, for Colly had never once considered herself attractive in any way. But now her hair tumbled around her shoulders, shiny and fiery, as if with a life of its own.

Red Bead Woman raised her head from her cooking and stared, and even Black Moon, who'd seen the red mass loosened before, paused in her grooming to watch the white woman. But it was Lone Wolf, who had come along the trail from the river all fresh and vital from his swim, upon whom the loosened curls had the greatest impact.

He saw the fiery strands spilling about her shoulders, saw the Sun God caught like a halo around the bent head, and his heart was moved as in his first vision. She seemed clothed in skins of gold and her hair was aflame. He felt the air leave his chest and closed his eyes. Still he could see the dancing sun rays. Then the white woman moved, blocking the light of the Sun God, so Lone Wolf could see her face with her great, wondrous eyes turned toward him. They held the mysteries of many worlds, the wisdom of the heavens, the sadness of the deer before the hunter's arrow pierces its heart.

With that same sad, contained air, she caught up the flaming strands in her hands and twisted them into a single braid. Now she was the strange, ugly white woman again.

Lone Wolf's breath returned to his body and he strode to the fire and seated himself with his back to the white woman. Silently he ate the food his mother speared into a wooden bowl for him. When he was finished, he rose, and, taking up his weapons, bid his mother farewell. With great strides, he stalked across the village circle to join his friends. They would spend their day in the hills hunting the deer and elk. He tried not to think about the white woman, or her sad eyes, as he rode away.

Chapter 5

THE DAYS FELL into a rhythm for Colly. The old crier made his rounds each morning, advising the villagers of the day's events. After he'd passed, Red Bead Woman set Colly to some tasks. She gathered wood and tended babies and fetched water. She helped weed the small gardens of beans and corn the Cheyenne had started along the riverbanks.

When the men returned from their hunting trips, she helped unload the horses of their burdens, skinning and cutting up the game while Lone Wolf took his horses down to the river to wash away the blood. She learned to stake green hides on the ground, scrape away the hair, and chip away the blood, fat, and flesh that still clung to the underside. At first she often left gouges, but Red Bead Woman patiently showed her how to hold the scraper made of bone until she was able to leave the underside fairly smooth. She remembered watching Papa work up the skins he'd trapped in the streams back in Tennessee.

She learned quickly and worked hard, pausing only now and then for a few minutes rest. Red Bead Woman watched the tireless thin body and clucked her tongue in approval. The white woman was a strong, good worker and her eyes and hands were steady. Red Bead Woman taught her how to use the flesher, a piece of elk horn bent at a right angle and set with a keen steel-edged blade, to thin the hides.

Colly made no objections to working with the hides, taking pride in the results as she learned to rub, smooth, and soften the skins. But when Red Bead Woman brought the grayish mixture of pulverized brains, liver, powdered soap-weed, and grease to be rubbed into the hide, she balked. Only by shutting her eyes and gritting her teeth could she bear to put her hands into the slimy concoction. Wrinkling her nose at the smell of it, she worked it into the hide as Red Bead Woman showed her. Soon she was up to her elbows in the obnoxious mixture, with daubs of it on her chin and cheek.

Having a sense of being watched, Colly glanced up to find Lone Wolf seated on his horse a short distance away, his dark eyes regarding her intently. A man she'd heard called Doll Man waited patiently. Colly paused, studying the two men, holding her hands in front of her with obvious distaste. Lone Wolf made a comment to Doll Man and the two laughed before galloping away from the village.

Colly gritted her teeth, seething with anger at the two men's callousness and the injustice of women's roles. What if Lone Wolf and Doll Man had to tan these hides? she thought. They wouldn't be so quick to rush out and hunt. But she knew she was being unfair.

She'd begun to see the truth of the roles men and women played in the village. Contrary to her first impressions that the men were pampered and lazy, seldom doing anything, she'd seen how important the hunting forays were in feeding the village. Without the men's efforts the village would starve. She'd also seen how they returned weary and sore from their long hours hunting for game. Sometimes they were even injured.

Furthermore, she'd noticed how the men, even when they appeared to sit idle, were often engaged in the making of weapons or concerned themselves with the protection or governing of the village.

Her understanding of the women's role was changing as well. She saw how the women ruled the camp, how they chose their tasks, doing them at their own leisure, taking pride in their accomplishments and even voicing their opinions to husbands and fathers. If they didn't speak out in councils, their wishes were certainly made known. More and more, Colly realized the extent of the Cheyenne civilization and a tiny bud of admiration began to grow.

One morning when the dead water had been replaced with living, the morning meal had been eaten, and the town crier had made his rounds, the women began to strike the tepees. Red Bead Woman and Black Moon took down the pale skin covering of the lodge and, taking down the slender poles that had held it, they formed a travois, a hide-covered stretcher that would drag behind the horses. They worked quickly and efficiently, as if they'd had great practice.

"What is happening?" Colly asked in dismay, trying to help.

"Chief White Thunder and the council have decided we will move the village farther onto the prairie. Soon the buffalo will come and we must be ready."

"What about the beans and corn? You can't just abandon them," Colly protested, thinking of the hours she'd put in tending the gardens and toting water for the new plants.

"They will be here when we return," Red Bead Woman answered, without pausing at her work.

"We're coming back here?" Colly asked, and didn't even notice that she'd included herself in the tribe's comings and goings.

Red Bead Woman noticed, though, and at last she paused to study the white woman. Colly had filled out in the days she'd been here. Her cheeks would never be plump as Red Bead Woman's were, but they were less hollow. Her thin arms carried more flesh and might even achieve some form of roundness if she continued to eat well. Red Bead Woman nodded with satisfaction. Spotted Woman would never be beautiful with her spotted, pale skin, which reddened after a day in the sun, and her tall, thin body, but she was looking better.

"On the prairie we may find some soldiers," Red Bead Woman said. "You would be pleased to return to your own people?"

Colly made no answer, shocked at the conflicting emotions rushing through her. "Yes, of course it would please me," she said, and turned away to help Black Moon lash their belongings to the travois.

Traveling across the prairie with the tribe of Cheyenne was, in some ways, not unlike traveling on a wagon train, and yet it was different. They left the wooded hills, retracing the trail Lone Wolf and his men had taken weeks before, moving onto the broad, flat face of the prairie single file, their numbers becoming insignificant in such sweeping vastness. Colly felt the old fears seize her, the sense that she was a speck of humanity lost in a world too vast and awesome for man to conquer.

At first, riding beside Red Bead Woman and Black Moon, she was silent, morose, intimidated by her return to the prairie. She held herself in rigidly, her elbows tight to her thin sides, her head bowed. She would not acknowledge or interact with this strangely familiar world of flatness. She was lost again, feeling only the anguish of her parents' death and the massacre of the wagon train. She would close herself away from the pain, pulling the walls of a smaller, more confining, yet eminently less frightening world around her.

But the sound of people, of voices calling in lighthearted gaiety, of horses plodding along, of children laughing and crying came to her, giving her heart. Despite herself, she raised her head and faced the empty, fearsome plain. The Cheyenne seemed to feel no such timidity. They moved through the landscape with the happy anticipation of a homecoming.

Colly was touched by their childlike exuberance. She saw, in their unself-conscious expressions of joy, the child she once had been. Standing barefoot on the slippery, muddy banks of Hangingfly Pond, she'd looked at the sun glinting on the green-scummed water and listened to the cries of the frogs and insects, and, raising her face to a perfect cloudless sky, she'd known that contentment and joy that reached soul deep and changed you a little bit so you never saw the world quite the same again. The Cheyenne people, moving across the landscape of this alien world, felt it. Perhaps that was what gave them courage.

Colly drew in her breath and pulled out of line, watching this band of nomads as they passed. She'd come to know some of them; some faces still held no names. But it seemed she was more akin to them than she had been to the people on Brother Davey's wagon train. This could not be, she thought, and, troubled, pulled back into line.

That night they rested in a temporary camp in the middle of the prairie, surrounded by waist-high grass and covered by a blanket of star-studded sky. Colly sat alone beside the fire and mulled over the confusing thoughts that had come to her on the trek.

Red Bead Woman and Black Moon had gone off to join their friends in a game of chance. Red Bead Woman, Colly had learned, was an inveterate gambler. The bulge of her parfleches gave mute testimony to her prowess with games of dice and cards.

Black Moon had remained secretive and aloof, disappearing for long hours. Colly had noted that such disappearances usually occurred after a handsome young warrior known as Gentle Horse had walked past their tepee.

Colly's thoughts turned to Lone Wolf, as they did with increasing frequency of late. She could hardly help her awareness of him, she told herself crossly, since they must share the same lodge. No matter how she tried to minimize her contact with him, she often raised her head and found him staring at her with dark, fathomless eyes.

Sighing, Colly pushed all thought of the tall warrior from her mind and, unbraiding her hair, attempted to comb out the tangles with her fingers. She wished she'd asked Black

Moon for the loan of her comb before she'd left. The fire warmed her, the hum of the village was comforting, the wide expanse of sky was uplifting, and she found herself humming an old hymn they'd often sung in Brother Davey's church. The feel of her hair between her fingers was silken and oddly stirring. She wasn't sure how long she sat, with her legs turned primly to one side as the Cheyenne women sat, humming her tuneless little song, raking her fingers through her long hair. She wasn't sure how long Lone Wolf had been watching her, but as she became aware of his presence, she jumped and cried out.

Quickly he stepped forward so the light from the fire fell on his features. He held out one hand and in it lay a comb of porcupine quills.

"Lone Wolf give to Spotted Woman," he said, holding out the comb. The firelight accented the curving slopes of his bare arms and shoulders. His eyes were obsidian, reflecting the light as well; his handsome face was impassive, expressionless.

Colly took the comb and looked up at him. "Thank you, Lone Wolf," she said, but he only grunted, as if the giving was of no import, and stalked away.

Colly sat staring after him, wondering what had prompted him to give her the comb. She knew from the way Black Moon cared for hers that it was a valuable possession. Colly examined the comb more thoroughly, seeing the care with which it had been made. Leather had been stretched over a small strip of wood and the quills of the porcupine trimmed and glued to one edge. Colly drew it through her hair, feeling it drag through the tangles. She didn't know what to think of Lone Wolf's gift, but she was pleased with it.

The next morning, they broke camp and moved farther south. To live on the prairie, they must find a river or a tributary for water. White Thunder seemed to have no doubts of where he led his people, nor did they entertain any unease. They pressed forward, filled with good humor and a sense of adventure, until at last they came to a river that Red Bead Woman told her was called the Niobrara.

Here the women set up their lodges. Unlike the temporary camps, where robes had been flung down on the trampled prairie grass, the women began a laborious cleansing of their new lodge sites. Once the huge skin cones were raised and the smoke holes properly adjusted, the women set about cutting away the sagebrush and prairie sod from inside the te-pees, leaving a ledge around the walls for their beds and backrests.

Colly helped Red Bead Woman carefully cut the sod into even chunks so the floor of the lodge would be smooth, scooping the dirt with a spoon and her bare hands onto a skin to be dragged outside.

When all the sod and dirt had been taken away from the lodge, Red Bead Woman sprinkled water over the cleared ground and she and Colly swept away every loose bit of dirt that remained. When they'd finished, the floor of the lodge was as neat and hard-packed as any dirt floor could be. Next they gathered fresh sweet grasses from the prairie and spread them about the ledge before spreading the bed pads and robes and setting the backrests in place. The last thing they did was prepare a fire pit. It was not circular as the white men made it, but rectangular in shape, with the four corners pointing to the East, West, South, and North.

When they'd finished, Red Bead Woman brewed tea from a red leaf wood and they sat resting. The hot liquid tasted not unlike the green tea Colly had once tasted back in Tennessee, and it was strangely rejuvenating.

Once again the camp settled into an easy rhythm. Each morning Colly rose and walked to the river for fresh water. Once again the crier circled the camp, singing out his messages of coming feasts or lost property and other camp news. Thanks to Black Moon, Colly could begin picking out words here and there and could answer the other women with simple responses. She felt elation at this skill, as if she were overcoming some nearly insurmountable barrier.

What did it really matter? she asked herself. One day she would leave the village. If the white soldiers didn't come and find her, she would set out to find them. But the summer was passing quickly, and she sensed an urgency in the Cheyenne as they prepared and stored food for those winter months when food would be scarce.

Scouts were sent out to search for buffalo. Lone Wolf was among them. When they didn't return at the end of each day, the people knew they had not yet found the great woolly bison. In the meantime, the villagers stayed busy. Women hunted along the riverbanks for berries and chokecherries, which they dried for use in the winter. So great was her hatred of the prairie that Colly was surprised at the harvest it yielded.

The Indian women gathered plums and sand cherries, bull berries and currants, all of which they pounded so finely that the seeds and pits were thoroughly broken up. Then they pressed the fruit into flat, thin, rectangular cakes and laid them on a skin in the prairie sun to dry. When they had dried thoroughly, the cakes were packed away in small rawhide sacks and stored in the larger parfleches. Colly came to have great respect for the Cheyenne woman's ability to find food on the inhospitable land.

She was reminded, too, of the women back home who gathered wild berries and cherries and canned them for the winter. Once again she saw how the differences between the two peoples were not so great after all.

Just when she'd decided the women had gathered all the prairie had to offer, they came up with something else. One morning Red Bead Woman brought out bags and special sticks fashioned at one end with a sharp, hardened point and on the other with a cross handle.

"Come. We'll gather *pomme blanche*," she said, giving Colly a stick and a leather pouch. They joined the other women and children who had gathered.

Mounting their horses, the women rode through the prairie with a singular purpose. At last they came to a slight hill with a small valley beyond, and there they dismounted and spread out, searching among the plants until they found a patch of what they wanted.

"This is the way we dig the *pomme blanche*," Red Bead Woman said, gripping the handle of her stick and leaning over it so the weight of her body helped drive it into the hard ground. With an expert flip of her wrist she turned out a clod of dirt, which she broke apart with her hands, revealing a root. With a cry of triumph, she held it up for Colly to see. Other women along the shallow valley were calling out to one another while they held aloft brown roots with soil still clinging to them.

"Spotted Woman try now," Red Bead Woman said, and Colly bent over her stick, shoving it awkwardly so it barely pierced the hard soil. Red Bead Woman had made it seem so easy. Colly straightened, withdrew her stick, and tried again. This time the pointed end sank deep into the earth and she turned out a root. Red Bead Woman snatched it up and held it aloft, indicating Colly had harvested it. There were answering cries of encouragement, so, flushed with success and gratitude at their kindness, Colly set to work, neatly turning out rows of roots. When several were dug out of the ground, she went back and gathered them into her bag.

Red Bead Woman watched her methodical way of working, acknowledged that it was better than the way she had always done it, one at a time, and promptly set about turning out a line of roots before gathering them up. Her respect for the white woman grew.

Colly's back grew stiff and her hands hurt, but she couldn't stop. There was something immensely satisfying in this labor of gathering food, reminding her of the days back on the farm when she'd finished plowing a field and knew her labors would produce food that would feed them throughout the winter. The sun burned on the back of her neck, making it sting with sweat, and more perspiration dripped off her brow and ran down her cheeks in muddy runnels. She didn't really mind. She was used to sweat and hard work and the taste of soil between her teeth. She was happy. Her thin arms moved rapidly, her bony elbows flashing in the sun, loosened tendrils curling around her reddened face.

"We have enough," Red Bead Woman said, touching her elbow.

Colly straightened and looked around her. The leather pouches were all filled and the women were resting. Some of the younger women were tossing their daggers, end over end, in a kind of game to see who could throw it the farthest. There was much laughter among them, and the losers paid up with clumps of root. Soon some of the sacks were not as filled, while others bulged. Through it all, the girls chattered shrilly, like scolding squirrels quarreling over acorns. Soon the older women called to the girls and the roots were loaded onto the horses.

Their progress back to camp was slower, for their horses were laden with bounty. The late slanting sun seemed warmer than ever. Colly longed for a bath in the river. She pushed at the sticky tendrils of hair and wished for the floppy hat that had protected her face from the sun.

When they neared the camp, Black Moon and some of the other young women let out shrill warlike cries. People in the village ran to look and the girls flapped their blankets to draw their attention. With an answering whoop, the men leaped on their ponies and tore out across the prairie toward the root gatherers.

Colly saw that Lone Wolf and his men had returned and were among the riders approaching them. She was touched by their welcome—until she saw that the men were intent upon stealing their hard-earned bounty. Using parfleches for shields they rode toward the women. The girls began to pelt them with sticks and dried buffalo chips they'd gathered. Some even threw their precious roots.

Open-mouthed, Colly watched this tomfoolery, wondering that these people could find cause to play and laugh even after a hard day of work. No man had approached Colly. She sat on her horse, with her bags of roots tied behind. Suddenly Lone Wolf loomed from the side, his big hand outstretched to relieve her of her bag of hard-gained roots. Without thinking, Colly lashed out with her digging stick, slapping his arm with the handle. Lone Wolf's hand was deflected, his horse charged past, and he turned to face her with new respect in his eyes.

"*Pomme blanche* belong to Spotted Woman," she said in her best imitation of Lone Wolf's gruff voice. "Lone Wolf not take!"

Laughter bubbled within her at the astonished look on his face; then she saw the answering humor. Gathering his reins, he let out a wild whoop and galloped back toward the village, his long black hair flying in the wind. The other men followed, and the women continued into the village without any more trouble. Feeling very pleased with herself, Colly dismounted and reached for the heavy bag of roots. Lone Wolf was there beside her, taking it down and leaving it at her feet. His dark eyes glinted with lights as he stared into her eyes.

"We have found the buffalo," he said proudly.

"Oh, Lone Wolf, that's good," she answered, one slim, dirt-crusted hand going automatically to touch his arm. She felt the warm, smooth skin beneath her fingers and drew back, aware she might have given offense by touching him thus, but Lone Wolf's smile was warm, his white teeth flashing in his dark, handsome face. He exuded health and vigor. Energy radiated from his large, well-built body. She felt its tingle and turned away, her cheeks blushing. Lone Wolf saw the maidenly blush and understood its meaning. He drew away, snatching up the reins of the horse and leading it away.

Troubled, he thought of the white woman as he led the horse to the river to drink. He'd been half-afraid of her, believing her a spirit that had taken human form and come to test them. But the night he'd given her the comb, he'd seen the pleasure of a woman in her eyes at the gift and had realized she was not a spirit after all. She was but a woman, yet possessing as she did the mysteries of a woman, he was drawn to think about her.

Tonight he'd seen her blush and knew she had been thinking of him. He wasn't sure he wanted this feeling between them. Once he'd had a wife of his own, but she'd been killed in a raid by the Pawnee. He'd loved Dawn Rising On A Hill and he'd not been inclined to claim another wife.

The white woman was of another world and, although she worked hard and accommodated herself to Red Bead Woman's directions, she was not of their people. She didn't know their ways. One day she would return to the white soldiers. He would no longer think of her. So saying, he put Spotted Woman out of his mind and sauntered back to the village to join his friends. Tonight they would celebrate. Tomorrow they would leave for the buffalo grounds.

Colly felt restless and troubled, the contentment of the day's labor erased by a single touch of a fingertip against an arm, flesh against flesh, as Brother Davey would have said in his hell-and-damnation sermons. Colly was silent during the evening meal, quietly helping Red Bead Woman wash and peel the roots they'd gathered. They were eaten raw and tasted like chestnuts.

"Don't eat too many," Red Bead Woman warned. "Make you very sick." She hugged her stomach with her broad brown hands.

Colly grinned. "Thanks for the warning," she said.

Together the two women cut the roots into strips and put them on drying racks near the fire. They'd no sooner finished than a cry went up that a feast and dance were to take place.

"Spotted Woman come, too," Red Bead Woman said firmly, and, although Colly wished only to bathe and go to bed, she knew she couldn't refuse.

Taking a piece of soapweed, she hurried down to the river to bathe, assuming Black Moon had gone ahead without her. But when she reached the bank, Black Moon was nowhere to be found among the high-spirited young women.

Colly had grown used to stripping off her clothes and

plunging nude into the water, even under the curious eyes of the women. Now they no longer noticed her, nor she them. She waded into the stream until the water was at her shoulders, then kicked her feet out and made a few tentative stabs at the water. She'd been trying to learn to swim and was sure she'd soon get the knack of it. She missed Black Moon's company, surly as it sometimes was. Now she wondered where the girl had disappeared to.

At last she climbed out of the water, her skin and hair glowing from the brisk scrubbing she'd given both. Automatically she reached for the rawhide she used to tie her braided hair, then, on a whim, paused. All around her, pretty young women were readying themselves for the feast and the dance. The light giggles and preening reminded her of the square dances back home—when the young girls groomed themselves, their chatter filled with the handsome young men they'd see at the dance.

She'd never joined them, never been a part of the heady, breathless anticipation in those first innocent, tentative steps toward mating. Now she felt the fluttery tightening in her stomach and didn't recognize its meaning. Impulsively she laid aside the leather thong and, taking out the quill comb Lone Wolf had given her, she set about freeing her long, curling tresses of its tangles.

When it lay about her shoulders and back in gleaming, smooth curls, she rose and donned her dress, suddenly wishing for something new to wear. She paid no attention to the other women as she returned to Lone Wolf's lodge. She was struck by the realization that she had at last acknowledged it as his. Her thoughts were full of the young war chief, her thin cheeks flushed, her eyes glowing with special lights. Only when she stood before the lodge door did she chastise herself.

What if Lone Wolf were within preparing himself for the feast? He would see her face and loosened hair and guess the secrets she was unwilling to accept herself.

Hastily she sat before the fire and rebraided her hair, jerking the rawhide into a tight knot so it wouldn't unravel. She was Colly Mead from Tennessee, she repeated over and over like a litany. One day she would leave this savage land and the people who lived upon it and return to that gentle, rolling country of her birth. So resolved, she rose and stepped through the lodge door to encounter Lone Wolf's mother.

"This is for you, Spotted Woman," Red Bead Woman said, holding out a soft doeskin dress decorated with quills and beads. Colly could see the decorative work had been exquisitely done.

"I couldn't wear this," she said, taking the dress and holding it to the light so she might better see the fine work. "It's far too fine for me."

"It is from the hides you prepared. I have made it longer to cover your legs properly."

"You did all that work for me?" Colly exclaimed, deeply touched by the gift.

"Spotted Woman is a hard worker. She never complains or gives trouble," Red Bead Woman answered, her dark eyes warm and sincere. "Besides, Lone Wolf asked me to make you a dress."

"Lone Wolf?" Colly's head jerked up, her brows pulling together in confusion and beginning anger. "Why should he care what I wear?"

"Spotted Woman feels anger for Lone Wolf?" Red Bead Woman asked in dismay.

Seeing the other woman's distress, Colly shook her head. "No, not—not anger exactly," she stammered. "It's just that he claims I belong to him."

"This displeases you?" Red Bead Woman said hopefully. Perhaps she needn't have worried after all.

"I belong to no one!" Colly asserted, crossing the brushed floor to the ledge where her bed lay. Whirling, she faced Red Bead Woman. "It isn't that you've been unkind to me," she explained awkwardly. "But I want to return to my own people. Why can't he take me to the fort?"

Red Bead Woman had wondered this herself. She knew

the Cheyenne avoided contact with the white soldiers whenever possible, but would not the risk be worthwhile to return the spotted white woman to her people? Colly waited for an answer. Red Bead Woman turned away, hiding the renewed concern for her son and his captive.

"Lone Wolf has never treated you like a slave," she said slowly, as if listing all the reasons why she worried. "He has shown kindness and generosity," she said, waving at the dress. "He has fed you and clothed you and kept you safe. You must trust that he will return you to your own people."

Colly sensed the defeat in the older woman's stance and didn't understand its cause. Believing she'd brought about Red Bead Woman's despondency, she quickly crossed the tepee and placed a strong, thin arm over the other woman's shoulders.

"I've not been unhappy here," she said, realizing her words were true. She'd even known moments of contentment and self-worth. She was sorry she'd destroyed Red Bead Woman's ebullient mood. "I'll be patient," she said softly, "and I'll wear the beautiful dress to the feast tonight." She hesitated, then said in the sketchy Cheyenne she was learning: "I feel honored that you made it for me." Startled, Red Bead Woman looked at her.

Colly smiled, coaxing an answering response from Red Bead Woman, but as she turned aside to change her clothes, she was unaware of the speculative look Red Bead Woman was giving her. The Indian woman had been alarmed to hear the Cheyenne words fall from the white woman's lips. Now with her back stiff, she finished her own grooming.

"I'm ready," Colly said breathlessly, and Red Bead Woman turned to find her standing in the middle of the lodge.

She wore the new dress and waited, her gray eyes shining, her expression anxious. The long dress fit better than Red Bead Woman's shorter, wider versions. She'd cut this dress smaller and longer so the long, flowing skin fell below Spotted Woman's knees. Red Bead Woman saw that Spotted Woman had put on some weight. No longer did she look like

an apparition from the spirit world. The soft doeskin clung
to her small, pointed breasts and slender waist and hips. She
looked like a woman and, although she would never be beautiful as the Cheyenne women were, there was a touching
elegance to her fine eyes and slender form. Would Lone Wolf
see this beauty in the white woman and be drawn to it?

"Do I look all right?" Colly asked when Red Bead Woman
remained silent.

The Indian woman nodded curtly. "Spotted Woman looks
better," she said honestly.

If Colly had hoped for better praise than that, she quickly
hid her disappointment behind a tremulous smile and followed Red Bead Woman out of the lodge. They gathered the
pots of food they'd prepared and carried them to the village
circle, where they were added to the rest of the banquet.

A large campfire had been built in the middle of the clearing, and White Thunder and the important men of the council were seated at one side. Lone Wolf was among the young
men given a place of honor for having found the buffalo.
After that first glance, Colly looked away from the sleek,
handsome warrior.

For most of the evening, Colly stayed beside Red Bead
Woman. She'd caught a glimpse of Black Moon once or
twice, but the Indian girl seemed busy with her own friends.
Colly couldn't blame her, for in a few days, when the buffalo
hunt and all its hard work were behind them, Black Moon
was to be given to Little Bear in marriage. The girl had
grown more sullen with each passing day. Colly wondered
if Lone Wolf was aware of how unhappy his sister was at the
prospect of becoming Little Bear's wife.

As the hours passed and the gaiety of the feast grew more
evident, Colly felt a loneliness seep into her. Although she
nodded at those women she'd come to know at root gathering
and berry picking, she felt isolated. The old shyness that had
often tied her tongue back in Tennessee crept over her until
her smile faded and her expression grew stiff and forbidding.

When the banquet was done and the Indians readied them-

selves for the dance, she wandered away from Red Bead
Woman and the others. No one stopped her as she walked
down to the river. She'd earned that trust from the Cheyenne
by her behavior around the village. She'd never tried to run
away.

Now as she stood by the river, she wondered why that was
so. She hated the prairie and was afraid of facing it alone,
she told herself, but she knew that wasn't the full reason. Although she yearned for the old life back in Tennessee, some
part of her seemed pulled forward—toward some unknown
destiny that would forever link her with these untamed people.

She refused to think about Lone Wolf as she strolled along.
The moonlight lay on the water in great golden patches, like
a crazy quilt Mama had done once. Beyond was the prairie,
dark and brooding. Light laughter disturbed her melancholy,
so she paused, not wanting to intrude upon a couple who
might have slipped away to court. The laughter came again,
low and provocative and familiar, joined now by deeper,
masculine sounds. Colly headed back to the village. She'd
reached the outskirts of the circle when she heard voices on
the trail ahead.

"Black Moon," someone called, and Colly recognized
Little Bear's voice. The laughter behind her showed the couple had not heard. Without thinking, Colly plunged back
down the bank to the river.

"Black Moon!" she called urgently when she was nearly
upon the couple. She heard a gasp, and two dark shadows
pulled apart as she ran into the clearing.

"Spotted Woman!" Black Moon snapped, exasperated by
the interruption.

"Little Bear and Lone Wolf are searching for you!" Colly
interrupted the angry tirade before it could begin. "They're
but a few steps behind me." She whirled and faced the young
warrior standing beside Black Moon. "They must not find
you here, Gentle Horse," she said in her skimpy Cheyenne.

"I will stay and face them," he said stubbornly.

"Now is not the time," Black Moon whispered, her face and voice stricken with despair. "If Lone Wolf is angry and will not listen, he will only forbid us ever to see each other again. And Little Bear—" She shivered. "You must go."

A sound along the trail made them whirl. Little Bear was upon them. Lone Wolf followed close behind. Colly saw the anger in his face and the set of his shoulders and felt the tenseness in the young warrior who stood beside her. Suddenly she knew that if Gentle Horse challenged either of the men now, he would be killed by the stronger, more experienced Little Bear. Without thinking she whirled and pressed herself against Gentle Horse.

"Lone Wolf!" Black Moon said in feigned surprise. "Why have you left the feast? You are an honored guest."

Lone Wolf made no answer, his dark gaze taking in the three of them. His glance froze when it reached Colly standing so close to Gentle Horse. Black Moon made another attempt to speak to her brother, but he brushed her aside.

"I see my brother, Gentle Horse, has also left the feast to sit in the company of women," Little Bear said, glaring at the young brave. "This is not the way of a warrior."

"Even warriors seek the solace of a woman he favors," Gentle Horse replied defiantly.

Little Bear's face seemed to darken in the deep shadows and his suspicious gaze swung from Spotted Woman to Black Moon.

"And which woman do you favor?" Lone Wolf asked, with deceptive quietness. For the first time, Colly realized she had unwittingly made things worse for Gentle Horse. She was considered Lone Wolf's property; therefore to approach her was nearly as bad as to woo Black Moon when she'd been promised to another. She took a quick step forward, her hand held out beseechingly.

"Do not tease Gentle Horse so," she began in halting Cheyenne, and then, because her knowledge of the language wasn't good enough, she was forced to switch to English. "I have grown melancholy of late, missing my people, and I asked Black Moon to walk along the river. Gentle Horse saw we were unaccompanied and followed us to protect us.''

Lone Wolf knew she was lying. She saw his disbelief in the stiffness of his mouth and the half-lowered lids of his dark eyes, but she couldn't back down now.

''Are we not allowed to walk along the river on a night when all the camp celebrates its good fortune?'' she went on.

He had no obvious answer. She could see the bunching of muscles in his shoulders as he opened and closed his fists.

''Little Bear,'' Black Moon said impulsively, stepping forward.

''*Nah Kahim* will return to the campfire with Little Bear,'' Lone Wolf said, using the Cheyenne words to refer to his sister. Black Moon hesitated as if she meant to defy him, then stalked away. Little Bear cast a final warning glare at Gentle Horse and followed.

''Gentle Horse has no reason to stay,'' the war chief continued. ''Lone Wolf will protect his own property.''

The young warrior snorted in anger and turned up the path. Only Colly was left to face Lone Wolf's wrath. He strode forward and gripped her arm. She was stunned at the harshness of his grasp and the force of his anger. His face was wild and savage as he shoved it close to hers. She could feel the heat of his breath against her cheek.

''Lone Wolf rescued Spotted Woman. She belongs to Lone Wolf. If she goes with another man, Lone Wolf will beat her.'' He released her arm as abruptly as he'd seized it. So untamed was the look of him that she remembered when he'd first rescued her and she'd fought him. He'd used force to subdue her then, and she wasn't sure if he would do as he'd threatened. She'd never known the threat of violence from a man before and rage twisted through her, hot and self-righteous.

''If you beat me, I will take your knife and carve your heart from your chest,'' she said, repeating the words she'd overheard one of the other women use. Lone Wolf seemed taken aback by her boldness. Colly's chin jutted forward obstinately.

"I do not belong to Lone Wolf," she snapped. "I belong to myself. You have no right to tell me what I may or may not do." Her tall, slender body was trembling with rage.

Lone Wolf knew he must quell such defiance. Failure to do so would signify a weakness on his part. His arm swung forward, his broad, tanned hand opened so his blow would not hurt her. Yet he halted before he could strike her. She hadn't flinched or looked away. Her great gray eyes glared into his and he caught the scent of her body, familiarly feminine, yet alien. He stood with his great hand scant inches from her face, his dark eyes boring into hers.

Her gaze remained unwavering, yet something in her eyes changed. Lone Wolf dropped his hand and backed away. Colly's breath came in gasps that caused her chest to rise and fall. She blinked and he was gone, soundlessly, through the underbrush.

She stayed for a long time by the river, staring at the bright orange patches on the water and thinking of Tennessee and her mother. She felt adrift, and Tennessee and all the familiar, beloved scenes shifted through her head in an ever-fading pattern. Soon, soon they might be gone forever.

At last the mist from the river chilled her and she climbed the path to the warmth of the village and the campfires and the people.

The campfire had died down now and shadows flickered across the hard-packed ground. The people were gathered in a circle, their faces expectant. A hush had fallen over the crowd. White Thunder and the other councilmen waited stoically, their seamed, bronzed faces impassive. Firelight danced in the expectant dark eyes of the children. The women whispered to one another and giggled. Black Moon stood beside her mother. Little Bear, his face scowling, was seated with the other young warriors. Gentle Horse was there as well, his face somber. Lone Wolf was not to be seen.

Feeling shaken by what had occurred between them at the

river, Colly had no wish to see him again. Turning back to the lodge, she'd taken no more than a step or two when a drumbeat, low and throbbing, began. It was accompanied by a low, singsong chanting. Something in the air pointed to the specialness of this dance. Colly turned back to the lighted circle.

The figure of a man entered the circle, his legs moving rhythmically to the chant, his heels thudding with every drumbeat. His head and upper torso were decorated with a headdress of an eagle, his outspread arms covered with white-tipped eagle feathers representing the mighty wing span of the soaring eagle. The dancing figure tipped first one arm and then the other near the ground before curving them upward to simulate the flight of the bird.

The muscular brown body swept forward in a rolling, graceful figure eight. Colly watched, enthralled by the power and beauty of the dancer. She wasn't sure just when she knew the figure was Lone Wolf. The knowledge just seemed so right that it neither startled nor distressed her. Her pulse drummed in her head and she became a part of the dance. She was unaware that she moved, shifting her weight from one foot to the other, remaining where she was, yet moving in synchronization with the rest of the undulating circle.

The chant rose, more insistent, and instinctively she understood its message. It was a prayer, a plea that the buffalo hunt would be successful, that the hunters' arrows would pierce true and deep, that their horses would be fleet, that they would all be worthy of this gift from the gods. She knew all this without anyone interpreting the dance. She knew and became one with these people, with the tall warrior who spun and swooped and with those who moved in a circle.

And when it was done, she stood dazzled, as if left on an island, while all around her, starlight and magic rained. She turned away then, not wanting to speak to anyone, not wanting to see faces and dark eyes filled with laughter and joyous anticipation, not wanting to touch the magic that was wrought.

Yet she could not rid herself of the image of Lone Wolf, for he had halted the dance in front of her and his dark eyes had gazed deep inside her and found her secrets . . . and she could not deny them. She felt frightened and fearless. She was no longer inside her skin, the familiar skin of the world she'd known. She stood on an edge of something. She had only to reach out. Not yet! Not yet!

She lay on her pallet and tried to think of Tennessee, and the pond, and the fields, and the blue-misted hills, but their image would no longer come to her.

Chapter 6

THE SOUND WAS like thunder. A thousand hooves beat against the prairie floor. Dust billowed behind the dark, humpbacked animals in a great black cloud that encompassed them all. The hunter and the hunted gave no notice. They raced side by side in a contest of life and death, pitting brawn and muscle, endurance and cunning, and in the end the hunter won.

Fearlessly the warriors guided their ponies close to the undulating waves of stampeding buffalo. Commanding their well-trained mounts by the pressure of their knees, they set arrows to bows and released them, driving them deep into the humped furry backs. The sharp points reached into the hearts of the mighty beasts, draining the blood from this vital organ and instantly bringing them to their knees. They dropped to the ground, and the rest of the herd swerved around them as if of a single mind and body.

Colly watched with the other women from a distant ridge, awed by the spectacle before her. Never had she seen such beasts as these, never so many. They were like an ocean, unceasing, without end. Like the prairie, savage and frightening. Yet Lone Wolf and the other warriors had ridden down to meet the thundering herd, armed only with their handmade bows and a few guns, their voices raised in shrill, triumphant cries. Never had she seen anything so recklessly brave. When the race was done and the survivors had fled over the flat prairie, bodies of the dead buffalo littered the landscape for more than a mile.

"Come," Red Bead Woman said, kicking her horse's belly, and the women started down to the fallen bison.

The men were already there, claiming their kills in loud, vibrant voices, swaggering and boasting of their prowess. Some had bent to cut the tongues and livers from their kill, which they ate raw. Colly turned her head away, sickened at the thought of such an act, and remembered the taste of mule blood when she'd fought to survive.

Now the women joined in the festivities, crying congratulatory words to the hunters, measuring the size of their kills. Some women had already drawn their sharp knifes and bent to the task of skinning the great beasts.

Colly followed Red Bead Woman and Black Moon as they made their way to one of the bigger hulking corpses. Lone Wolf had already moved along the kill path to seek out his other targets. He'd done well.

Colly was grateful not to have to meet him face-to-face. She was still too bothered by her thoughts of the evening before. In the light of day she'd told herself she'd gone slightly mad from the moonlight. In the light of day it was easier to believe that.

Red Bead Woman knelt beside the dead buffalo, her sharp knife slicing easily along the exposed belly and around the fetlocks and tail. In no time, the skin was peeled away. Colly tried not to show her squeamishness. On the farm, she'd shouldered any chore without reservation—save that of slaughtering in the fall. Even now, as she stood beside the silent mounds of dead buffalo, she could remember the protesting squeals of the hogs as they were captured and butchered. This was no different, she reminded herself, and knelt beside Red Bead Woman, the better to follow her instructions.

Red Bead Woman cut away the choice pieces first, carefully wrapping the tongues, noses, and liver in a skin before going on to the rest. A receptacle was placed to catch the blood when Red Bead Woman pierced the large jugular vein. Hunks of muscled flesh were cut away from the bones and wrapped in skins to be hauled back to the makeshift camp, where they would be cut into strips and dried. Likewise the thick pad of fat along the back and neck. The lungs were cut away and saved, as well as the stomach and intestines. Even the joint and marrow bones were broken and carried away. When they were finished, there was little left for the buzzards. Red Bead Woman set Colly to work on another carcass and moved along the path to a third.

Colly tried to work in the long, practiced strokes of Red Bead Woman. Black Moon came to help her strip away the hide.

"Spotted Woman did not tell Lone Wolf about Gentle Horse and Black Moon," she said, her expression nonchalant, her brown, nimble hands suddenly clumsy at their work.

"I thought it best not to," Colly answered, gazing at the younger girl's averted face. "Why don't you tell Lone Wolf that you have feelings for Gentle Horse?"

"He knows," Black Moon said in a low voice.

"And yet he makes you marry another man?" Colly asked. "That's not fair, even if Little Bear did bring back your father's bones. You can't be expected to give up your own happiness for such a deed."

"It is the way of the Cheyenne," Black Moon said.

"You could just refuse. Lone Wolf couldn't make you."

Black Moon turned to face Colly then, her eyes dull with hopelessness. "Not to marry Little Bear would bring dishonor to my family, to Lone Wolf, and I could not do that. I am Cheyenne." She paused, her eyes searching Colly's face for some sign the white woman understood what she said. What she saw made her shake her head.

"Spotted Woman has pity for me. There is no need. I am Cheyenne!" She rose and walked away, and Colly knew that in some way she'd offended when she'd only meant to help.

She turned back to the mound of raw flesh she must somehow butcher. Setting her teeth and her knife, she began carving as Red Bead Woman had done. Soon she was covered with blood. Her nostrils were filled with the gore of death. The hot sun beat down on her head. Green bottle flies had come out of nowhere, buzzing around the carcasses, lighting on the women's blood-smudged faces.

When it seemed she could bear no more, she glanced up to find Lone Wolf staring at her. He'd left the other hunters and ridden his horse along the path of the buffalo, searching for the woman with the red hair. He had acquitted himself well on this hunt and he wanted to see the admiration in her eyes. But Spotted Woman crouched before the dead buffalo, her knife flashing in the afternoon sun, her lips pursed in distaste, her silvery eyes darkened with revulsion.

Lone Wolf sat watching her for a long time, thinking of the strange way she behaved. At last he understood. The white women did not butcher meat as the Indian women did. She was unaccustomed to this work, yet she toiled on, trying to overcome her disgust.

At that moment she straightened, one hand going automatically to the ache at the small of her back. Their gazes caught and held, and Lone Wolf heard her catch her breath. She seemed not to breathe at all. A warm prairie wind caught a tendril of red hair and swept it across her cheek; the sun blazed a halo around her head. Her hands and forearms and the front of her doeskin dress were stained with blood. At her feet lay the large chunks of meat she'd dutifully cut away.

Lone Wolf slid off his horse and crossed the trodden grass to her. She waited, her eyes dark as a summer sky during a storm. When he reached her, he took hold of a bloodstained hand and stood studying it, searching for words to reach her. Finally he lifted his head . . . and her steadfast gaze was there to meet his.

"Buffalo are necessary for our people," he said, wishing he were better versed in the white man's tongue.

"I know," she replied.

"The gods give them to us. We must make use of every

part to sustain life.'' He switched to Cheyenne, wishing she could follow.

''I know,'' she repeated, this time in Cheyenne. ''I will learn—and next time will not be so bad.''

Next time! They both stood listening to the words and what they might mean if they wished it so.

''Come, I will help you carry this back to camp,'' he said, and bent to wrap the chunks of meat in the fresh hide.

Together they tied the bones and meat to the travois and even on the back of Colly's horse. She would be expected to walk back, she knew. But when Lone Wolf had settled into his own saddle, he held out a strong brown hand for her, his dark eyes somber as they met hers. Colly took hold of his hand and felt the heat of his palm against her own and the strength of his fingers wrapped around hers. She was pulled onto the back of the horse and sat stiffly, holding herself away from him, her hands resting lightly on each thigh. Lone Wolf took hold of her hands and brought them around his middle, then, taking up his reins and that of the packhorse, he started toward the makeshift camp.

Colly let her body sag against his, feeling the warmth of his skin. Her small breasts tingled as they flattened against the hard contours of his back. She should pull away, but she could not. She leaned her head against his shoulder and drank in the smell and feel of him, wild and untamed. A primitive longing shuddered through her and she gave no thought to anything except to clasp the strange new feelings closer.

Lone Wolf felt the convulsive grip of her strong thin arms around his waist, felt the heat and weight of her against his back. Passion surged through his veins as strongly as the pulse of a war cry. At a walk he led his favorite war pony over the prairie, leaving the others behind them, and when at last he came to a fast-flowing creek, he stopped and lifted Colly from the saddle and led her to the water.

Silently they waded into the cold, clear stream until the water was past their knees, and then he bent to scoop water over her blood-covered arms and hands and finally her dress, his large hands stroking away the stains, brushing over her breasts and thighs until at last she stood clean, heart thudding, cheeks flaming. Neither of them had spoken. No words were needed.

His arms drew her tightly to him, his mouth, firm and strong, touched hers. Her soft lips parted and she tasted him. The ground shook beneath her feet, so she clung to him. Their figures meshed in the hot afternoon sun. The cold, swift water raced around their ankles.

Colly's hand brushed across Lone Wolf's broad back. She wanted to know every part of him. Each touch, each new discovery, cried for more—until she feared she might never be satisfied again without his presence. The kiss ended and she bowed her head against his shoulder, trembling with unfamiliar emotions. That she, old maid Colly Mead, should feel this way was a wonder to her. She gave no thought to anything else, only the moment and the man who held her.

Lone Wolf drew away and stared into her face. His expression was stern and troubled, and she felt her joy drain away as she looked on the bronzed face and torso of the man who had awakened such forbidden desire within her. For a moment Brother Davey's face wavered before her, followed by Mama's and Papa's and all the other members of the wagon train who had died—and whose bones must even now lay bleached and white in the same hot sunlight that warmed Lone Wolf and her.

He saw the rejection in her face, the twist of horror at what she was doing and who he was. He'd seen such a look many times on the faces of the white men, just as he'd seen the same lust on the faces of some of their women. Spotted Woman was like those women, curious about his dark skin and physique, contemptuous of his heritage. Anger raged through him and he stepped away from her.

"At the rising sun, Lone Wolf will give Spotted Woman a horse and meat. Doll Man and Gentle Horse will take her to the white man's fort in the mountains."

Stunned, Colly stared at him, torn between joy at the news and a confusion over the feelings he'd aroused.

"You're—you're sending me away?" she stammered.

"It is what you asked of me," he replied stiffly.

"May I stay until after—after the buffalo feasts—until Black Moon's marriage to Little Bear?"

"There is nothing to see of a Cheyenne marriage," he answered stonily.

She waded forward and placed one slim hand on his arm, much as she had that day by the river when she'd promised not to run again.

"Please allow me to stay a few more days," she said. "Black Moon is my friend. She's unhappy about being given to Little Bear."

He drew away. "Black Moon is honored by this marriage," he snapped.

Colly drew a breath and followed him out of the stream, barely pausing as she slipped on the wet bank.

"You don't understand," she began, thinking she could make Lone Wolf see how unhappy his sister truly was by this marriage. "She doesn't want to marry Little Bear. She loves someone else. She's only doing this because she doesn't want to disappoint you or bring dishonor to her family. I'm sure now that you know the truth, you'll let her marry the man she really loves."

Lone Wolf whirled on her, his eyes blazing. "Black Moon marry Little Bear. Love not needed. It is a white man's word and means nothing."

"It means everything to a woman," Colly said. "Why do you think we endure the hardships and heartaches? Why do we turn our backs on families and friends to follow our husbands into wildernesses? Why do you think we risk a shallow, unmarked grave in the middle of a prairie? Why do you think I asked to—?"

Many of her words he didn't understand, but he understood the passion in her eyes and the sudden coloring of her cheeks before she turned way. He stared at her bent head, his own chest rising and falling with each tight breath, and the magnitude of what was between them touched him.

"Tomorrow, Doll Man take you to Fort Laramie," he said, and when she turned a tearful, appealing face to him, he motioned her into the saddle. She climbed up with no assistance from him, and, when he was seated in front of her, she held herself away from him, her fists clenched on her thighs, her wet rawhide dress chilling her breasts.

They arrived in the makeshift camp without speaking. When they halted before the lodge, Colly slid off the horse. With averted face she went directly to the travois and worked the knots loose.

Red Bead Woman had seen them arrive together and her heart was troubled. The fact that they acted so stiffly toward each other only increased her fear. They didn't act in a natural way, like two people who cared little for each other. Their jaws were stiff, their eyes hooded as if to hide anger and pain.

Colly carried the meat to the campfire and set about carving out thin strips to be hung and dried. Lone Wolf cast one last glance at her bent head and stalked away. Red Bead Woman hurried to show Colly how to clean the small intestines and stuff them with chopped meat and berries. She longed to ask Spotted Woman how she happened to ride to camp with Lone Wolf, but she was fearful of the answer. She concentrated instead on the task at hand.

They cleaned the stomach and hung it up to dry. It would be used as a water pouch. They cut open the lungs and set them to dry. Later, roasted on the coals, they would provide a delicious meal, Red Bead Woman explained to Spotted Woman.

The bones were split for the marrow and a clean stomach lining was filled with the blood they'd collected. Red Bead Woman had let the fire burn down to coals and now she placed the rennet in a bed of hot ashes, tapping it constantly with a stick, rolling it over until the blood boiled and cooked.

Strips of buffalo meat had been anchored over the hot coals and the smell of searing meat rose from the village.

At every campsite the people gorged themselves on the fresh meat. Even the lodges of the old and needy were filled with laughter and goodwill, for the hunters had sent gifts of meat to those less fortunate. Everyone shared in the celebration. The hunters crossed from one campfire to another, telling of their particular exploits and sharing the meat from the cookpots. Lone Wolf did not return to his own campfire that night. Colly hadn't expected he would.

"Why does Lone Wolf force his sister to marry a man she does not love?" she demanded of Red Bead Woman, unable to keep her peace any longer.

"You do not understand the ways of the Cheyenne," Red Bead Woman began. They'd paused in their labors to rest and eat. Now she put aside the bowl of buffalo meat and gazed at the white woman. Was this the reason Spotted Woman and Lone Wolf had quarreled? she wondered.

Colly brushed aside Red Bead Woman's stock answer. "I've heard enough of the Cheyenne ways," she snapped. "And I know Little Bear did a brave and wonderful deed, but is that a reason for Black Moon to be made unhappy?"

Red Bead Woman sighed. She was not immune to her daughter's unhappiness. "Little Bear brought back the bones of my husband, Lone Wolf and Black Moon's father. We owe him a great debt. For a long time he has wanted Black Moon for a wife. Four times the snows have come and still she hesitates. This year she must marry him. If she does not, she will shame Lone Wolf, so he may choose suicide and deliberately seek death in battle."

"Simply because Black Moon wouldn't marry Little Bear?" Colly gasped incredulously.

Red Bead Woman's nod was barely perceptible. Her brown eyes were somber. Colly studied her sad face, wondering what Red Bead Woman would do without a son to provide for her. At last she understood Black Moon's dilemma and she sighed in defeat.

"You are right," she said quietly. "I do not understand the Cheyenne ways. I will say no more."

Although they worked long hours after dark, there was much left undone before fatigue drove Red Bead Woman to bed. The bones to be fashioned into cups and bowls and knifes were piled to one side, the undressed meat stored in their original hides and made safe against marauding animals. Long after the camp had quieted, Colly sat by the fire, thoughtfully combing her hair and thinking of the things Red Bead Woman had said. The thought that Lone Wolf could be forced to take his life in shame if Black Moon refused to marry Little Bear seemed barbaric. Suddenly she was glad Lone Wolf was sending her back to Fort Laramie. She wondered how she would feel to be back in the white world. She could hardly remember what her past life had been, so intensely had her emotions been engaged here in the Cheyenne camp.

A shadow flickered in the dying coals and she whirled to find Lone Wolf standing over her.

"What is it?" she asked, sensing something had changed. His gaze was intense, the slope of his shoulders unyielding, yet his words caused her heart to leap.

"Tomorrow we hunt buffalo again," he said. "Doll Man will hunt as well."

"Does this mean I won't be leaving?" she asked in a whisper.

"Not tomorrow," he answered, and stalked away, but something of his own confusion and tension was left behind. She sensed he was as torn as she.

Thoughtfully she sat holding the comb he'd given her and thinking of their kiss at the stream. She would have given herself to him today, until the memory of all her friends and family rose to haunt her.

How could she surrender to her feelings for a man whose heritage included such barbaric acts? Perhaps the Cheyenne hadn't attacked Brother Davey's wagon train, but they had attacked others. She'd heard too many stories around the wagon train's campfires. Yet to judge Lone Wolf by the senseless acts spoken of by Jim Farley seemed unfair.

She'd lived among the Cheyenne for weeks now. Although there were many things she could not accept, she was beginning to understand their faith and simplicity, even to admire their sense of honor and truth. She thought of Red Bead Woman, who had been a kind teacher, and beautiful Black Moon, who willingly forfeited her own happiness for the sake of her brother's honor.

She thought of Brother Davey and his congregation and realized she'd been comparing them for weeks. Such a comparison was not always flattering to Brother Davey and his followers. Confused beyond belief—and knowing the next day would be as demanding as the one just past—she rose and entered the lodge.

She hadn't realized Lone Wolf had returned to it. Now, by the light of the moon shining through the lodge flap, she saw his long, sinewy legs and felt herself tense. Closing the flap, she crept through the darkness to her own pallet. She lay listening for the deep, slow breathing of masculine slumber, but there was none, only the tense silence of a man as confused as she.

Lone Wolf was gone when she awoke the next morning. Colly helped Red Bead Woman and Black Moon break the temporary camp and trail after the hunters. They heard the thunder of hooves and the shouts of triumph long before they topped the final ridge. Spread out below them were a number of carcasses, just as the day before. But the hunters had fallen silent, casting evasive glances over their shoulders, taking little glory in the sharing of tongues and livers.

"What's wrong?" Colly asked, sensing the disquiet.

"I do not know," Red Bead Woman answered.

The women made their way down to the hunters, talking among themselves. No one made a move to claim the great shaggy carcasses that sprawled in the prairie grass for nearly a mile.

"It is a bad omen," a woman called Magpie said, coming

to join Red Bead Woman's group. "A white buffalo has been killed."

The other women shook their heads in disbelief and rolled their eyes.

"Lone Wolf has ridden back to the main camp to bring White Thunder and Dull Knife." Colly knew that Dull Knife was a very important medicine man in the village and guessed the situation must be grave indeed.

"Why is it a bad omen to kill a white buffalo?" she asked Red Bead Woman. "Their hides would be beautiful."

Magpie heard her question and incredulously repeated it for all the women to hear. They buzzed among themselves, unable to understand how the white woman could be so ignorant of basic knowledge.

"The white buffalo comes from the place far to the north," Magpie said, pointing in that direction. Her eyes were round with awe. "The place where the buffalo comes from the ground. A white buffalo is the chief of all the other buffalo; to kill one would displease the buffalo gods who protect them." Magpie paused and glanced around at the other women, pleased with her narrative.

"We cannot use the white buffalo robe." Red Bead Woman took up the story. "We cannot even dress it until Dull Knife returns. "He alone knows the power to remove the taboo for this. We must wait."

The other women nodded and began to work on the other buffalo that had been felled. Late in the afternoon, Lone Wolf returned, accompanied by White Thunder and Dull Knife. The women laid down their butchering knives and walked to the place where the men surrounded the white buffalo. Before the hide could even be taken from the cow, the medicine man began his ceremony. Lone Wolf stood by to do as he was told, for it was he who'd had the misfortune to fell the animal.

Dull Knife built a small fire from prairie grass, then, from burning sage and other aromatic grasses, he gathered the ashes and strewed them to the four corners of the earth. When he'd finished with his prayers and ceremony, he turned to Lone Wolf, who alone must remove the hide, for he was the man who had felled the great beast. Solemnly he bent to his task and loaded the hide on his own war horse. Colly was surprised at the respect shown to the white buffalo hide until she realized such respect would be shown to any chief.

The people moved away from the carcass of the white buffalo. "No one may eat meat from it," Red Bead Woman explained, "or the buffalo may never return to this place."

The women returned to their jobs of securing the meat of the other buffalo, working quickly now, for they would not remain in their temporary camp. White Thunder would lead them back to the Niobrara River and their summer camp. Everyone worked late into the night preparing the fresh meat so they could haul it back to camp. No one approached the white hide, which had been placed at one end of the camp.

"Cheyenne women may not dress the hide," Black Moon said. "It is forbidden. When we return to the village, Dull Knife will paint it and make a sacrifice of it."

"Will the bad omens be lifted then?" Colly asked, thinking of Lone Wolf.

"Only Dull Knife can tell," Black Moon replied, and returned to her work.

The trek back to the village was not as jubilant as it might have been. Though their parfleches were stuffed with meat, and still more was tied to the travois that trailed behind nearly every horse, the people felt uneasy. What did the appearance of the white buffalo mean? Had they offended the gods by accidentally killing it? Even the women did not chatter as they normally would have done.

The villagers who'd been left behind came out to greet the returning hunters with joyous faces. In spite of the presence of the white buffalo hide, there would be feasting and fresh meat that night. Voices rang with anticipation. Lone Wolf had fallen behind the other travelers, and now, when all were within the circle of lodges, he rode forward to the center of the camp circle and dismounted. He made no move to take the hide from his horse. Instead he crossed to the lodge of Old Wolf and entered. The old warrior had not come out to greet the returning hunters. The villagers waited, and soon Lone Wolf and Old Wolf came out of the tepee and walked to the war horse. Lone Wolf stood aside, and Old Wolf cleared his throat and pointed to the west.

"It was there in the land of the Ute," he began in a sing-song voice. Colly didn't know all the Cheyenne words, but enough to understand what he said. "I saw a Ute warrior coming. I stepped behind a tree and, when he drew near, I sprang upon him, pulled him from his horse, and killed him with my knife."

The people listened to the narrative of how Old Wolf had counted coup pulling an enemy from a horse. Only he was qualified to pull the white hide from Lone Wolf's horse. Old Wolf finished his tale and stepped forward, striking the white hide with his stick. Then, pulling it from the horse, he reverently placed it on the ground.

Dull Knife stepped forward and set a pole into the ground. The people drifted away, the women to set up their lodges once more and put their meat to cooking over their campfires and the men to build a sweat lodge of willow branches. When the sweat lodge was finished, Dull Knife, his thin, wiry body naked and painted with red symbols, painted the hair side of the skin blue before folding it and tying it to the pole. All the while, his frail old voice was raised in prayers.

Now the women and children returned, bringing offerings of beads and fine moccasins and other gifts. Solemnly they passed before him, and each time Dull Knife paused to run his hands over the arms and bodies of each supplicant, chanting a prayer for long life, health, and abundance for each of them.

When all the offerings had been bound inside the hide, it was tied shut and left to hang as an offering to the Sun God. Now Lone Wolf and Dull Knife entered the sweat lodge along with the other men of the village. A fire was built and stones heated. Water was brought from the river to pour over them.

The men stripped away their clothes, purging their bodies in the hot steam and their minds with prayers.

When his prayers were completed and his body purified in the sweat lodge, Lone Wolf left the hut and stood before the white buffalo hide. The sun had not yet risen, but the villagers had gathered, drawn by some sense of drama. The old medicine man approached the young warrior and took out his knife.

Seeing him raise the dagger over Lone Wolf's back, Colly made to cry out, but Red Bead Woman's grip was sharp on her arm, her scowling face urging her to silence. Colly searched the older woman's eyes. Surely she would not remain so calm if Dull Knife meant her son harm. Even the accidental killing of a white buffalo could not be cause enough to kill one of the war chiefs. Colly pressed her hands against her mouth to quell any further cry as Dull Knife cut long strips in Lone Wolf's back just over his shoulder blades.

The warrior made no grimace of pain; his face remained impassive. Thongs of rawhide were run through the slit flesh and tied off. Buffalo skulls were attached to the other end so they rested on the ground.

Once again the medicine man burned a knot of sage and prairie grass, offering the sacred ash to the sky, the ground, and the four directions of the earth. Then he stepped back, and Lone Wolf, dragging his painful burden behind him, began at one end of the village circle and moved around in the direction of the sun. Blood seeped from the torn skin and rolled down his back.

No sound was made by the villagers, no offer of help. Only the eyes of Red Bead Woman and Colly glittered with tears. Colly clenched her teeth so tightly, her jaw ached from the strain. Her broken nails bit into her palms as she strove to be as silent and respectful as the others. To make an outcry on Lone Wolf's part would discredit this thing he did to lift the bad fortune the death of the white buffalo might have brought to his village.

Slowly, painfully, he made his way around the circle, and

when he reached the opening, he dragged the buffalo skulls out onto the prairie to a hilltop. There he took a position on top of one of the buffalo skulls and stood facing the sun as it rose over the prairie.

"What's he doing now?" Colly demanded, gripping Red Bead Woman's arm.

"My son will stand on top of the buffalo skull without eating or drinking. His face will be turned to the sun until it sets tonight."

"Why is he torturing himself like this?"

"To bring good fortune to his village," Red Bead Woman answered.

"This won't do it," Colly flared, angry at the pain and deprivation Lone Wolf must endure.

"You do not understand our ways," Red Bead Woman said. "You are not Cheyenne."

Colly watched her walk away, hearing the warning in those words. For the first time she realized Red Bead Woman was fearful of her, and she didn't understand why. She turned to watch the lone figure standing on the hilltop, his face raised to the sun.

Throughout the day she paused often to gaze at his unwavering figure, trying to guess what might be going through his mind, what drove him to endure the endless hours at the mercy of the sun, his wounds undressed. By the end of the day, she felt as if she herself had been standing on that hilltop, her flesh skewered and raw.

At last, Doll Man and Little Bear climbed the hill and helped him down from the buffalo skulls. Colly saw him stagger, but he remained erect. The thongs were released from his flesh, and slowly the men made their way back to camp. The buffalo skulls were brought and placed in the opening of the village circle. Dull Knife cut away the drawn-out flaps of skin. With ceremony and prayers, he held each piece to the sun and ground and to the four directions, then buried them in the ground.

Colly tried to get close to Lone Wolf to say some encouraging words, but he was surrounded by his friends, who bore him back to the sweat lodge. Before he was carried inside, Colly saw his face and drew back in awe. Here was not the face of a tortured, defeated soul. Lone Wolf's eyes shone with a depth of spirit and pride such as she'd never seen. Slowly she walked back to the lodge and sat before the fire to puzzle over all she'd seen and learned of the Cheyenne.

Dull Knife wrestled long into the night to understand why this event had happened to Lone Wolf. Though the smell of cooking meat and the revelry of the people came to him, he did not quit the lodge. Nor did Lone Wolf. In the morning, when the sun rose on the distant rim of the Mother Earth, the old medicine man rose and left the lodge. At last he knew why the white buffalo had come to them and he knew what must be done to appease the gods. He hurried to White Thunder's lodge—wondering what the old chief would think when he learned the purification involved the white eyes, Spotted Woman. . . .

Chapter 7

WHITE THUNDER SAT unmoving as Dull Knife related his tale. When the old medicine man was finished, he sent for the men of his council and for Lone Wolf, who, it was thought, would one day sit on the council. The flap of White Thunder's lodge was drawn together, signaling no one must enter, and the council pipe was lit and passed to each man. When it had been around the circle once and returned, White Thunder nodded to the old medicine man, who rose and once again told of the message the Great Spirit had sent him.

The men of the council listened with care, for Dull Knife had proven his wisdom and dedication in the well-being of the tribe's spiritual life. They nodded gravely as he offered his interpretation of the white buffalo cow that had come among them.

"This is a warning from the buffalo gods," he said somberly. "The buffalo herds will come no more to our prairies. They will dwindle in number until they are gone forever, and the Cheyenne will be left to wander the plains, weeping and gnashing their teeth, tearing at their eyes with their nails for those who will die without food and shelter."

Lone Wolf listened and shivered with dread, for already the fear was upon the Cheyenne that the coming of the white men would destroy the Mother Earth and carry away her

111

bounties. Gifts of which the Cheyenne partook sparingly, not wishing to offend the Mother Earth with greed. Now as Dull Knife spoke, Lone Wolf wondered what the years ahead held for him and his people. He had fasted throughout the night, purging his body of its impurities, striving for his own vision that would tell him what to do about the white buffalo hide and with the white captive woman. No answer had come and he was left weak and more troubled than ever. Now to hear that the white buffalo had brought only a message of death for his people made his head swim and his sight dim. He gritted his teeth and clenched his fist tightly so he would show no weakness before this august gathering.

"When the white woman came among us, we did not heed the implications of her presence," Dull Knife said. "Lone Wolf has told us of how out of all those white men on the wagon train she alone escaped death. He has told us how he rescued her yet again from death on the trail when she was without food and shelter. Her plight will become that of the Cheyenne if the buffalo fail to come. Who will save us?"

"Perhaps Spotted Woman was sent to show us another way," Tangle Hair spoke up. Dull Knife nodded in satisfaction. The men of the council leaned closer to listen.

"Perhaps there is another way we can assure the buffalo come again," Dull Knife said. "One way we can stop the white men from abusing our land and taking our game. We must link our destinies to theirs, turn a friendly face to them. We must open our minds to the white men and show them our ways. We must take their women as our wives and give our own women to them. The children of such matings will inherit the ways of both nations, the white and the Cheyenne, so our grandchildren will know the way to care for the Mother Earth and be free to seek the buffalo here on her land."

"The children of such alliances are not wanted by the white people," Tall Man said bitterly. "They are scorned in the forts of the white men and sent back to their Indian villages."

"This will change." Dull Knife's gaze turned to the young

war chief. "Lone Wolf found Spotted Woman. He saw that her spirits were strong and he followed her. He has told us how she drank the blood of the mule in order to gain strength and continue her journey. This is the deed of a warrior. Lone Wolf has said she fought like a warrior."

He paused to let his words sink into the minds of his listeners, then continued. "It was Lone Wolf's arrow that found the heart of the white buffalo cow. Now I have seen the vision of him wed to the white buffalo. His children will lead the next generation of Cheyenne."

Lone Wolf's head came up; his black eyes darkened in consternation as he puzzled over the medicine man's message. Dull Knife took up his narration once again.

"Lone Wolf must take Spotted Woman as his wife," the old man said. "This the spirits have revealed to me. This must be done."

Lone Wolf sprang to his feet. "The white woman is to be returned to her people. I have given her my word on this."

A murmur went around the circle of men. All of them knew Lone Wolf could not go back on his word, yet they must fulfill the vision of Dull Knife in order to lift the bad omens caused by the white buffalo's death. The pipe was passed about again as the wise old men tried to find a way out of their dilemma.

White Thunder offered the answer. "No one understands the way of a woman's will," he said. "Just when we think it is as a mountain, she bends like the wild grass upon the plains giving way to the wind. It is the fate of all men to try to understand the ways of women. Perhaps we will find Spotted Woman's will to leave the Cheyenne and return to her own people is not like the mountain, but like the prairie grass bending before the will of the gods—"

"You do not know this woman as I do," Lone Wolf interrupted.

"She is a woman. Perhaps if she were courted . . . if not by Lone Wolf, by some other warrior. It is rumored she walked along the river once with Gentle Horse,'' a chief observed.

"Not Gentle Horse,'' Lone Wolf said loudly, rising to his feet.

"My vision showed Lone Wolf wed to the white buffalo,'' Dull Knife warned.

"Do you wish to try to bend the spirit of Spotted Woman?'' White Thunder asked mildly.

"I will try,'' Lone Wolf said gruffly.

"You will court her, wooing her gently like the young braves swooning over our comeliest maidens?'' White Thunder insisted.

"I will try!'' Lone Wolf answered.

Soon after, the council broke up. The old men left the lodge of their chief and walked among their family and friends, but none of them spoke of what had been said. All had been sworn to secrecy until Lone Wolf had had a chance to woo Spotted Woman.

Colly had no knowledge of what had transpired or how it would affect her. Diligently she worked beside Red Bead Woman drying and storing the meat they had gathered. They boiled the fat from the bones of the fat buffalo cows and made a liquor of sorts. In this, Red Bead Woman boiled the flesh of a yellow calf and *pomme blanche* roots. They boiled the buffalo heads to form a kind of glue and tanned the hides for use for new lodges, and, finally, fashioned the bones into spoons and bowls and finely carved ornaments for the ears and clothes. Each day Colly was more awed by the uses the Cheyenne made of every part of the buffalo. Only the bones and hooves were not used for food. Even the hides were sometimes boiled and eaten.

"I remember one winter when the buffalo had been scarce. Hunger lay over our village so that we took down our lodges and boiled the skins to stay alive,'' Red Bead Woman reminisced. "I was only a girl, yet I remember it always.''

"How awful for you,'' Colly said, her gray eyes dark with sympathy. "What did you do for a home?''

"We shared the lodge of others until the buffalo came again and then we made new lodges."

"What would you have done if the buffalo had not come?" Colly asked. Red Bead Woman paused in her work and stared at Colly.

"Buffalo always come," she said, with absolute certainty.

But after Spotted Woman returned to her work, Red Bead Woman sat wondering why the white woman had posed such a question. Troubled, she went to Dull Knife, who only nodded his head wisely. He saw this as yet another sign that the white woman had been sent to them as a sign and only through her could their way of life be preserved.

Lone Wolf knew nothing of courting. He was no longer a young buck randy as a bull during rutting season. He had loved Dawn Rising On A Hill and still mourned her death. No longer was he inclined to carve flutes and make up pretty tunes to woo the heart of some young maiden.

Yet he remembered the first day of the buffalo hunt, when Spotted Woman had ridden behind him, her strong arms clasped about his waist. He thought of the softness of her body beneath his hands when he'd sluiced water over her dress and the fire her gray gaze had ignited in his loins.

He could have taken her then, along that tumbling stream. He'd been shaken with passion for her, but her reaction had angered him. He'd seen that moment of hesitation and read all the disdain and revulsion the white world had shown toward the red man in that look. How could he overcome that?

Anger filled him. He had no wish to wed her, yet he must fulfill Dull Knife's vision. The vision hadn't said he must care for her, only that he must take her as his wife. He would woo her and mate with her, but he would not give his heart as he had done to Dawn Rising On A Hill. So resolved, he sought the soft wood along the river with which the young men made their flutes and he practiced the notes before going to stand outside his own lodge to play them.

When Red Bead Woman heard the first tentative notes of the flute, she didn't realize they were played by Lone Wolf.

Her bright gaze leaped to her daughter, who sat staring pensively into the flames. At the first sound, Black Moon had looked up, believing, hoping, the notes were Gentle Horse's. Then she sank back. She had forbidden him to seek her out again. In two days' time, she would marry Little Bear. She must accept the inevitable. It would have been nice if the suitor were Little Bear wooing her, but she'd already seen him at the lodge of his friends, drunken and belligerent. Little Bear gathered with a crowd of young bucks who had defied White Thunder's orders and bartered for whiskey from Mexican traders. Black Moon's pretty mouth turned down as she contemplated a life with the brash, undisciplined warrior.

Colly also raised her head at the first note of the flute. There was a sadness to the tune, like a mourning dove pining for her nest. It touched some sore, hollow place in her heart. She folded her hands over the awkward seams she'd drawn in the buckskin and sat listening. She might never have known who the perpetrator of the sad little tune was if Red Bead Woman had not risen from her seat and stood staring across the fire pit.

Colly swiveled on her buttocks and found Lone Wolf standing to one side of the lodge, a wooden flute to his mouth. Surprised that such a keen warrior as he should engage in the making of a fragile song, she openly stared at him. He brought the tune to an end and lowered the flute, his dark gaze boring into her.

Automatically Colly glanced away and turned back to the fire. Her back was stiff and straight, her chin high, her lips trembling and pale. She hadn't seen him since their encounter by the stream. Now her mind skipped over every remembered detail of his appearance. How tall he was, how broad his shoulders beneath the soft doeskin shirt, how rugged and handsome his face, how fine his eyes.

Her fingers trembled and she pricked herself with the bone needle. She cried out softly and placed her finger to her mouth to draw away the blood. She sensed he was still there. She felt the heat and energy of him, though he stood well away. Then there was a scuff of leaves and she knew he'd left. Red Bead Woman and Black Moon gawked after him.

"Why would he play a flute by his own lodge?" Black Moon demanded. Her huge eyes turned to Colly and understanding crept over her. "He woos the captive woman!" she said.

"Be still, Black Moon," Red Bead Woman said.

"It is so!" Black Moon insisted. "Why would he wish to take you for a wife? You are ugly and spotted and—"

"Black Moon!" Red Bead Woman's voice was sharp. Her daughter fell silent. "Go to bed," Red Bead Woman ordered, and, sullenly, Black Moon walked to the tepee, but she did not enter.

All this had transpired in but a minute, and throughout, Colly sat silent, stunned by the fact revealed to her. When Black Moon had left the campfire, Colly raised her gaze to Red Bead Woman and saw her distress. For the first time she realized the Indian mother did not want her son to woo a white woman.

"Black Moon is wrong," Colly said quickly, not wishing to hurt Red Bead Woman. "He didn't even speak to me."

"It is true. He courts as one of the young suitors moon outside a maiden's lodge," Red Bead Woman lamented.

"I do not desire his courting," Colly answered. "Soon I will return to my own people."

"Will you?" Red Bead Woman's eyes reflected the light of the campfire as she stared at Colly. "I have watched you these many weeks as you embrace the ways of our people. I hear our words tumble from your mouth and think to myself, 'She is becoming Cheyenne.' "

"No!" Colly cried, then paused as she thought of what Red Bead Woman had said. It was true she'd grown comfortable among the Cheyenne people. Part of herself was held aloof while she planned her return to the white world, but the other part of her reached out for the laughter and ideas and ways of the people. Part of her had reached for

Lone Wolf without giving thought to the consequences of such an act on Red Bead Woman. She'd worried only about her own reputation, her own needs. Now she stood revealed before Red Bead Woman, and her cry of denial was found a lie.

"I'm sorry if I've displeased you, Red Bead Woman," she said, rising to stand before the woman. "I have known much confusion over these past weeks and months, but I've also known much happiness. I do not wish to hurt you. I will tell Lone Wolf he must not court me. I'll leave at once."

"It is too late," Red Bead Woman said softly. "I have seen this thing grow between you and wondered where it would end. Now we will all know." She raised her face to Colly, her pain showing. "He has always set his feet on a path the rest of us could not follow. Even Dawn Rising On A Hill could not hold him from the paths he chose. Now he has won many coups and gathered much honor for himself. I had hoped he would marry a Cheyenne girl and I would see my grandchildren playing around my lodge."

Colly was shocked by the dislike reflected in Red Bead Woman's attitude. She thought of the careless cruelty of Black Moon's words. The whites had no corner on meanness and bias. Lifting her chin high, she met Red Bead Woman's gaze steadfastly.

"I have not sought out your son's attentions," she said, with quiet dignity, "nor did I desire to come here and live in your lodge. Since your feelings toward me are very clear now, I will remove myself and seek shelter elsewhere until Lone Wolf can take me to Fort Laramie." She turned away and then paused, trying to decide where she might go. She was glad neither woman could see her face, for tears had filled her eyes and rolled silently down her cheeks. A gentle touch on her elbow made her stiffen her back.

"Red Bead Woman has no wish to offend Spotted Woman," the Indian woman said contritely. Colly's heart flooded with forgiveness, which she had no time to utter, for Red Bead Woman continued.

"I will ask my friend, Magpie, to let you stay at her lodge." Red Bead Woman walked away toward Magpie's tepee. Colly twisted her head and shoulders to stare after the broad departing back. She'd forgotten the tears that still stained her cheeks. Black Moon saw them and hurried forth.

"You are not that ugly," she said placatingly. "You are just different from the Cheyenne." She paused, and when Colly made no answer, she went on awkwardly. "I've gotten used to your spots."

"They aren't spots. They're freckles," Colly said. "They aren't an affliction. They're caused by the sun. Many people have them."

"Not the Cheyenne!"

Colly laughed then at the sheer absurdity of human nature. Black Moon smiled tentatively. Then, hearing the pain even in the laughter—and seeing the tears she had caused—she stepped forward and threw her arms around Colly's shoulders.

"I don't want you to leave our lodge," she wailed. "You have been a friend. You did not tell anyone about Gentle Horse. I have repaid you with insults."

"It doesn't matter, Black Moon," Colly said bleakly, patting her on the back. "You only told the truth. I am ugly and spotted. Even the white people think so."

Red Bead Woman returned, all out of breath. "Magpie has said you may stay with her."

"I will go there then," Colly said, stepping away from the two women. Leaving them was as hard as leaving Tennessee had been. A shadow loomed out of the darkness and Lone Wolf stepped into the light.

"Where are you going?" he demanded.

"I'm going to Magpie's lodge until you can take me to the fort."

Anger crossed his face. "Spotted Woman wishes to return to her people?" he asked, as if surprised and disappointed.

Colly hesitated, staring at the three people who'd grown so important to her, not just for her existence, but for so much more. Perhaps that was why the revelations of this evening had been so painful. She respected Red Bead Woman and tried to emulate her in her work and demeanor, drawing strength and independence with each new skill she learned. She was touched by Black Moon, who, shallow and self-centered though she might seem, had nonetheless set aside her own desires for those of her family.

She dared not think about Lone Wolf and the conflicting feelings he'd awakened. She was unaware her eyes had turned to him, that they silently pleaded with him. Lone Wolf saw that mute beseeching and felt his heart swell. Yet Red Bead Woman stood beside him, hostile and angry.

"Go to Magpie's lodge," he said to Spotted Woman. "It is best for now."

Colly heard his words and turned away, hiding the hurt they evoked. Quickly she walked across the square to the tepee of Magpie, whose husband, Tall Man, sat on the council.

"Welcome to our lodge." The Indian woman greeted her warmly, and some of the tightness eased around Colly's heart. Magpie showed her to her pallet, and, after a few words of gratitude, Colly sank onto the furs and turned her back to the rest of the tepee, feigning slumber.

Instead of sleeping she thought back over all that had occurred. She felt pain at Red Bead Woman's rejection, drew comfort from Black Moon's conciliatory words and hugs, and, finally, remembering those first tentative notes of Lone Wolf's flute, she felt a flutter of joy.

He was courting her, Red Bead Woman had said. Courting her for all the village to see, which meant that he planned to ask her to be his wife! What would it be like to be the wife of a man like Lone Wolf? What satisfaction and wonder would there be in his touch? What joy to carry his child, a child so beautiful that even Red Bead Woman could not help but love it—even if it was not pure Cheyenne.

For a while she dreamed that all this could come about, and her dream gave her a beauty so radiant, Black Moon would have exclaimed upon it had she seen it. But Colly had learned dreams were not reality and she must face the truth. Such a union with Lone Wolf could never happen, even if they both should want it, for they would be faced not only with the prejudice of the white world but that of Red Bead Woman as well.

Lone Wolf watched Colly walk away and knew by the set of her shoulders that she was unhappy. He looked at Red Bead Woman's set chin and saw her anger. Only Black Moon seemed neutral to the controversy that had arisen.

"This must be, *nah koa*," he said.

"She is white," Red Bead Woman answered. "She will bring trouble."

"Dull Knife does not say so."

"You have spoken with him about this?" Red Bead Woman asked. His intentions were far greater than she'd realized.

"I have been before the council," Lone Wolf answered. "They do not oppose this union."

Red Bead Woman bowed her head in defeat. "I wish you and Spotted Woman happiness."

"Will you help her? She has no family to represent her."

Red Bead Woman nodded. "She will be as my own daughter," she replied, and went into the lodge, where she might sit alone and contemplate her son's decision. She had no animosity toward Spotted Woman. Indeed, she held the white woman in some esteem, for she never failed at her tasks and was a tireless worker. The white woman was straightforward and without guile.

The only real objection Red Bead Woman had against her was that she was not Cheyenne; she feared the woman's presence among them might bring trouble. Now she must put aside her fears and welcome Spotted Woman as a member of the family.

Perhaps it was as well. In two days' time, Black Moon would go to the lodge of Little Bear to become his wife. Red Bead Woman would be without a daughter. Many times she had wished Lone Wolf would take a wife. At last he had. A thought came to her and she smiled, feeling lighter of heart.

Perhaps after he had taken Spotted Woman as his first wife, he would take a Cheyenne girl for a second wife. Their lodge would be filled with children then. Red Bead Woman fell asleep trying to choose a suitable Cheyenne girl to become her son's second wife.

It seemed strange to waken in someone else's lodge, to rise and see someone else's face other than Red Bead Woman's and Black Moon's. Without being told, Colly spilled out the dead water and went to the river for living water. She brought wood for the fire and helped prepare the food, then set herself to working on a hide Magpie had not yet finished. So diligently did she work that Magpie was moved to tell her friends of the white woman's virtues. Red Bead Woman heard her friend bragging about her houseguest and drew her eyebrows together in displeasure.

"Do not grow too used to her help around your campfire," she snapped. "Soon, Lone Wolf will claim her as his wife and she will return to his lodge."

"You have trained her very well," Magpie said, wishing to appease her friend's ire.

"She is intelligent and learns quickly," Red Bead Woman answered, not wanting to take credit upon herself—and wishing also to add to the image of the woman who would become her daughter-in-law.

"She will be a credit in the lodge of your son," Magpie answered, then tactfully changed the subject. "Tell us about Black Moon's marriage."

On the day of Black Moon's wedding to Little Bear, the village rose and began to prepare extra food, for a wedding was reason enough for a feast. The town crier circled, calling out news of the coming nuptials. Gifts were collected and made ready. The bride had not been seen.

Wearing her best attire, she waited nervously in her tepee

until the time had come to go to the lodge of her new husband. The villagers gathered to watch her ride forward and be presented. Colly looked at Black Moon's impassive face and wondered what trepidation the young girl must feel to marry a man she did not love. As she was received at Little Bear's lodge by his family, Black Moon gave no evidence of her true feelings. She was carried into the lodge and the flap lowered, and the villagers turned away, whimsical smiles curving their lips as they remembered or anticipated their own wedding days.

Colly turned back to Magpie's lodge and paused midstep. Lone Wolf stood before her. She hadn't seen him for two days and her gaze drank in the sight of him—the broad shoulders, the strong, bronzed features, the dark wings of her eyebrows, the blue-black hair hanging straight to his shoulders, its edges ruffled by a breeze. She couldn't see beyond him. He filled her vision. Even when she lowered her gaze, she could still see the long, muscular legs encased in soft doeskin, the long, thin feet laced in moccasins.

One brown hand shot out, crossing her lowered gaze. Lone Wolf opened his fist to reveal two fragments of a rounded rock. The jagged edges had been placed together tightly.

"I found this by the river when I bathed this morning," he said in Cheyenne, and she struggled to follow his words. "It reminded me of Spotted Woman."

Colly reached for the stone and the two halves fell apart in her hands. The center of the stone was exposed, crystalline and fragile, reflecting light and colors of mauve and pink, the hidden beauty within the common rock revealed at last. She stood staring at the two pieces and felt tears prick her eyelids, so moved was she by his words and gift.

Her face was so radiant when she raised it to him, he drew a deep breath and stepped away from her, afraid he might pull her to him here in front of the whole village. His heart sang at the feelings revealed in her eyes. He gave no thought to his resolve not to care for this white woman. Her glance turned his heart. He walked away from her then because he knew to stay would bring speculation among the villagers, but he carried the radiance of her smile and the brilliance of her glance in his mind; they came to him time and again throughout the day, bringing that same surge of wonder.

Colly carried the beautiful stone to Magpie's lodge and sat on her pallet staring at the sparkling depths. She gave no thought to the white soldier's fort or of returning. She thought of Lone Wolf and what would be between them now if he brought her to his lodge as his wife. So overwhelming were her thoughts that she placed the two halves of the rock together and carefully stored it in her bed pouch. Rising, she went about her business, but she gave no thought to the small tasks her hands performed. Her mind was too full of the handsome, tall warrior who looked at her with glowing dark eyes that reflected her own heart's desire.

When the feast began, she craned her neck looking for any sight of Lone Wolf. He was seated with the other men, partaking of the delicacies the women had prepared. After consuming the dishes of roasted tongue and liver sprinkled with gall, dried roasted buffalo lungs, thick, fresh buffalo steaks, cooked *pomme blanche* roots, and pounded fruitcakes, Little Bear's family passed out pieces of red cocklebur to the children. Delightedly they sucked on the wild licorice stick and watched their parents prepare to dance.

An air of gaiety pervaded the camp circle. The chants and drumbeats began, and even Colly was pulled into the circle of dancers by Magpie. Seated with the other warriors, Lone Wolf watched across the fire as she concentrated on the steps, flinging back her head now and then to laugh. She was fire and light, her gray eyes sparkling, her red hair flaming in the firelight, her strong, slender body moving rhythmically, tirelessly, with the drumbeat. He watched her dance, and when the dancers paused to rest, he rose, and, taking his blanket, went to her before the whole village.

She saw him approaching and waited expectantly. His gaze never wavered from hers. She heard the murmurs of those around her but gave them no notice. Her eyes and thoughts were only of this tall, lean warrior coming to her.

When he reached her, Lone Wolf opened his blanket and drew her within its confines. The drums began again and they moved as one with the beat, their breaths mingling, their hearts racing. They touched beneath the blanket, their hands exploring cheeks and chins, his long arms wrapping around her waist, his hand possessive on the curve of her hip, her slender, calloused hands spreading wide over his broad chest, feeling the muscle and sinew of the man.

Her nostrils flared, drinking in the exciting scents of freshly bathed flesh, leather, prairie winds, and all the other masculine smells that were his. She was like a wild prairie flower, willowy, resilient, sturdy, fragile, and pleasing to his nose and eye. He placed his tongue against her nose and tried to taste the golden spots there. Her skin was salty and sweet, a contrast that delighted him.

They talked very little, sometimes murmuring words only lovers understand, falling silent in between. Their feet moved to the rhythm of the music; their hearts moved to a rhythm that was theirs alone. The villagers saw and smiled. Red Bead Woman brushed away the last vestige of her disappointment and beamed.

Black Moon watched her brother and Spotted Woman move around the dance circle and cast a desperate glance around, searching for Gentle Horse. Unerringly she found him. He stood apart, his countenance dark, his eyes bleak. Their gazes met across the heads of the people and her expression softened.

Little Bear saw the change on his bride's face and glared at Gentle Horse. His hand tightened possessively on Black Moon's arm, causing her to wince. She looked into her husband's face and saw the cruelty there. At first he did not loosen his painful grip and Black Moon feared she might faint from the agony of it. Then he released her, his lips curving in a cruel smile.

"Gentle Horse seems unhappy tonight," he said gently. Fear spiraled through Black Moon.

"I do not know," she answered. "I have not spoken to him."

"That is good," Little Bear said approvingly. "Gentle Horse is not a strong warrior as I am." He puffed his chest and preened a bit. "I often worry that he may someday be killed in battle."

Black Moon's eyes filled with tears. "Gentle Horse has been a good friend, nothing more," she replied.

"That is good," Little Bear repeated, and turned away from her then.

Black Moon dared not look at Gentle Horse again. He'd seen the pain cross her face, and now she sat with her eyes downcast, not as a chaste new bride might sit, but as one subdued and frightened. His anger at Little Bear grew and he stalked away.

He couldn't stay here watching while Little Bear claimed Black Moon as a wife. Mounting his pony, Gentle Horse rode out onto the prairie. Above the drumbeat and shifting feet of the dancers, no one heard him leave. Seated beside her new husband, Black Moon sensed he was gone. Her expression remained serene, giving no hint of the anguish she felt inside.

When the dance was finished, Lone Wolf walked Colly to the lodge she shared with Tall Man and Magpie. His face was somber as he removed his blanket from her shoulders.

"Does Spotted Woman still wish to return to her people?" he asked.

Colly drew a deep breath, knowing she'd been asked to finally choose. "I have no family with the white men," she said, hedging. "Red Bead Woman, Black Moon, and Magpie are my family."

"You do not speak of Lone Wolf," he said quietly.

"I do not know how to speak of my feelings for Lone Wolf," she answered. "I will do as Lone Wolf wishes."

"Will you come to my lodge as my wife?" he asked, his hands gripping her shoulders, his dark eyes boring into hers.

Joy swept through Colly. "Yes," she whispered. "Yes."

"What of your white people? Have you no desire to see them again?"

"I belong to the Cheyenne now," she answered.

Lone Wolf studied her radiant face. "You belong to Lone Wolf now," he said, and walked away from her while he still could. When he was a few paces away, he turned and shouted back to her. "In seven days there will be a full moon. It is a good time for a wedding feast." He was gone then, disappearing into the dark shadows.

Colly lay awake for most of the night, forcing her memories back to her childhood and the farm, back to the teachings of her father and mother, the sermons of Brother Davey, the beliefs and traditions of that small farm community. She did this because she knew she must understand finally all that she was giving up before embracing the Cheyenne ways. She must never look back on this moment with regret.

She remembered everything she could and examined the culture of this wild people, asking herself if she was willing to give up all she'd known to live the life of a nomad in a strange, alien land. She thought of Lone Wolf and knew she could. Yet what if he died? Theirs was a dangerous existence. How would she go on? She thought of Red Bead Woman, widowed and content with her son and daughter nearby. She couldn't go on so bravely without Lone Wolf.

At dawn she rose and walked along the river. In the distance stood the tall silhouette of a man, and she knew it was Lone Wolf. She thought of Red Bead Woman and her expectations for a Cheyenne wife, and she knew Lone Wolf weighed the tenure of his life thus far against the unmarked days ahead. Both of them were taking steps away from their own people and forging a new place for themselves. That they contemplated such a step so carefully showed the depth of the commitment they were prepared to make.

The sun topped the horizon, sending its warmth and light

over the dark prairie, and in that instant, Colly put aside all
doubts about her decision. She was part of something outside
herself and the narrow world she'd known. She was no longer
from the white world. It had already forgotten her—and she
was willing to let it go.

She was part of the sky and prairie and the people sleeping
in the tents behind her. She was part of the tall, invincible
man standing on a distant knoll, embracing his dreams and
goals, accepting his sense of all that was right with life. She
was part of all this and more, and yet she remained herself,
Spotted Woman, soon to be the wife of Lone Wolf. She
spread her arms wide, embracing the sunlight and Mother
Earth. Her voice raised in a joyous cry, ringing along the
riverbank.

Standing on a small hill, Lone Wolf wrestled with his
thoughts. Dull Knife had said this step must be taken to fulfill
the vision, and so he willingly made this choice to marry
Spotted Woman, but his heart told him this was so much
more. He was touched by her in the very depths of his soul.
He couldn't imagine racing across the prairie on his war pony,
hunting the elk, or sitting before his campfire without Spotted Woman there with him.

As the sun flowed over the rim of the earth, he felt his
heart lighten. He'd sought no vision, yet he had one of the
tall, thin white woman with her fiery hair neatly braided, her
gray eyes luminous, carrying their child in her belly. He
heard her cry from across the river and remembered another
time when her cry had come to him, compelling him to follow. Now he understood why he'd lingered here through the
night, seeking answers and reassurances. He'd known the
moment he heard that first cry that he was no longer a whole
man. From that moment he had needed her, had sought her
out. Only with Spotted Woman would he be complete again.
He heard the joy in her cry and his fear diminished. They
had chosen their destinies—and they were forever the same.

Chapter 8

*M*AJ. JOHN BUFORD halted his detachment of mounted riflemen and pressed his feet hard against the stirrups, thereby easing the weary ache of his buttocks. They were a three-day ride from Fort Laramie, and the major felt no anticipation in reaching the sprawling log encampment that once had been a trading post. In fact he had no enthusiasm at all for his appointment to this godforsaken land.

He'd made powerful enemies in Washington, no doubt about that. His seduction of a prominent senator's underage daughter had brought him to this demise. He'd hoped the affair would further his career, but he hadn't reckoned on the force of Washington's clacking tongues or the fury of a doting father. The whimpering cow had actually thought he would marry her in spite of her father's objections. John David Buford was not so foolish as all that. Wordlessly he'd taken his punishment, an assignment to a distant outpost where he'd have no contact with innocent young women and little chance for advancement.

He'd been assigned to Col. David E. Twiggs of the Second U.S. Dragoons, who was commander of the Western Division of the Army. Having heard the rumors connected with young Buford's transfer, Colonel Twiggs had immediately assigned him to Comdr. Winslow Sanderson's detachment of mounted riflemen, who were given the command of establishing a military post at the fork of the Laramie and North Platte rivers. They'd ended up purchasing the trading post itself for that purpose and the detachment was bivouacked within its sturdy walls. Since then the assignment had been pure tedium, trying to stay clean without the rudiments of civilization, trying to amuse oneself with the uneducated rabble Sanderson commanded, and trying to figure some way to be transferred back East.

The only things to relieve that numbing boredom were the wagon trains that poured through the fort on their way to Oregon and California. Many an unsuspecting father noted his daughter's sparkling eyes and pink cheeks without realizing she'd been closeted with the handsome Major Buford.

When there were no wagon trains, Buford availed himself of the Indian women who accompanied their husbands to the fort to trade. They could be had for a pint or two of whiskey. With their senses dulled by the raw liquor, the drunken warriors seldom noticed how cruelly their wives were used by Buford.

Still, Buford was restless, his finely etched features twisting with petulance as he surveyed the rolling foothills they must yet cross before reaching Fort Laramie.

"Sir, the scout's coming back," Lieutenant McKinney said beside him. Buford glanced at the young officer. He'd come closer to liking Fitzgerald McKinney than he had anyone at the fort. Untried and given to hero worship of the first order, McKinney had been easily dazzled by Buford's West Point polish and embellished tales of Washington politics.

"Looks like he's traveling fast," Major Buford observed, taking out his army-issued binoculars and training them on the hills behind the approaching scout.

"Doesn't look like anyone's out there," Lieutenant McKinney offered, looking through the binoculars.

"No doubt he saw something that spooked him." Major Buford sighed with exaggerated impatience. "These Indians turn coward once you tame them. I don't know why the army uses them."

"They know the terrain better than we do, sir," McKinney said needlessly. "I reckon if he's coming back, it's got to be something. Stone Calf's pretty reliable."

Major Buford cast his protégé a telling glance, and the young man quickly ducked his head, sorry he'd even appeared to contradict his superior.

The Indian scout, a half-breed Cheyenne, kneed his horse up the incline and reined in amid a shower of dust. "Something ahead," he said, pointing back in the direction he'd come.

"Surely you can be more specific than that," Buford snapped.

"Wagon train," Stone Calf grunted.

"Hellfire! The fools should have been over the mountains by now. They'll never clear the passes before the snows fall."

"All dead," Stone Calf said.

"Dead?" Buford studied the scout and his lieutenant. He would have liked to avoid the unpleasant task he knew awaited them, but Stone Calf and McKinney waited for his orders with expectant faces. Behind him the detachment of rifle soldiers muttered among themselves. They were supposed to guard the travelers on the trail. They took this news badly.

"Show us where you found them," Buford ordered Stone Calf, and the half-breed turned back down the trail. The major waved his detachment forward and followed the scout, all the while cursing a certain senator back in Washington.

The buzzards had long since completed their job. What they hadn't plucked away the wind and hot sun had baked into dust, so the bones of the emigrants lay stark and white in the sunlight. The half-burned wagons lay silver gray and mute.

"Jesus," a young private muttered, and leaned from his horse to retch. He was still new to the army and the harsh realities of the West.

"Lieutenant McKinney," Major Buford barked.

"Yes, sir!" McKinney drew himself upright in the saddle,

but his mouth was white-rimmed and pinched-looking and his freckles stood out in his pale face.

"Form a burial detail. Keep an eye out for anything that might tell who they are."

"Yes, sir!" The young lieutenant turned back along the line to relay the major's instructions.

"Wonder how long the poor devils have been out here?" Sergeant Crook said, glancing at the late August sky.

"It doesn't really matter, does it?" Buford snapped. "They're dead. Go help Lieutenant McKinney and his detail."

"Yes, sir," the sergeant answered, saluting because he knew the major was a stickler for protocol. Cold-blooded bastard, he thought as he joined the other men in their gruesome task.

Stone Calf rode back to the major, his expression unreadable, his gaze never quite meeting Major Buford's.

The lieutenant handed over a weathered and stained book. "Sir, we found something here. Looks like a Bible."

Buford opened the cracked leather covering. " 'Brother Samuel Davey,' " he said, reading the faded writing. In exasperation he slapped the Bible closed. "Some damned fool seeking glory and riches in God's name." Lieutenant McKinney looked shocked at his callous statement. Buford ignored him and sat looking at the burned wagons. "Looks like Indians caught up with them."

"Yes, sir," McKinney answered. "Most of 'em were scalped."

"Anything to tell us which tribe?" McKinney shook his head, but Buford wasn't looking at the lieutenant. His narrowed gaze was fastened on the stoic face of the scout. "What do you say, Stone Calf?"

The scout made no reply.

"Think maybe some of your fellow countrymen attacked this train?"

"Sir, we've had no trouble with the Cheyenne," McKinney said, for he liked the half-breed. "More than likely it was the Sioux. We've been hearing rumors they were acting up."

"That so, Stone Calf?" Buford demanded. "Or did you find something out there?"

Stone Calf's dark eyes flashed with anger. He blinked and the anger was gone. He held out one hand and opened his fist. A sash worked with quills and beads lay on his open palm. Major Buford snatched it up, holding it aloft to study.

"You know whose this is, don't you?" he demanded, fixing Stone Calf with a hard gaze.

The Indian remained silent, as if reluctant to accuse anyone, then raised a finger to point at the sash. "Work of Cheyenne women," he said.

Major Buford's handsome features stretched into a triumphant leer. "I thought as much."

"Are we going after them?" McKinney asked.

Buford's gaze went to the foothills; three days' worth between him and whatever comfort the rough fort offered. But a thought had come to him, a plan to win his release from this hellhole. His report of their finding the burned wagon train and the burial of the dead would garner him some praise, but how much greater that glory would be if he could take back the news that he'd found and punished the murdering Indians who'd done it. He glanced at the lieutenant and then at his scout.

"Yes, Lieutenant, we're going after them."

"The prairie's mighty big, sir. We might not find them out there."

Buford nodded at the silent scout. "He knows where to find them." Stone Calf's eyes flashed hostility, but he made no protest.

"Reassemble the men, Lieutenant," the major ordered. "Stone Calf, lead the way—and see you send us on no wild-goose chase."

Within minutes the detachment was on its way, turning away from the foothills and heading back into the prairie on a northwesterly course.

* * *

Colly had never known such contentment, such utter sense of rightness about her life. In the days that followed, she prepared as best she could for her coming wedding to Lone Wolf. Now she realized the importance of having moved to the lodge of Tall Man and Magpie. Magpie's eyes glittered with anticipation as she schooled Colly in the ways of a Cheyenne marriage. Colly listened attentively. Having made her choice, she wanted to embrace all the ways of the Cheyenne.

Her happiness was troubled only by the aloofness Red Bead Woman showed her when she went to her lodge the day after Black Moon's wedding. Seeing the plump, kindly woman seated beside the fire, diligently working on a skin, Colly paused. This was Lone Wolf's mother, soon to be her mother-in-law, and she wished to mend the rift that had driven her from their lodge.

"Good morning, Red Bead Woman," she said, seating herself beside her old mentor.

The Indian's plump face was calm and unreadable as she glanced at the white woman.

"I see you're preparing a new costume for someone. May I help?"

Red Bead Woman fixed her with a stern gaze. "I have no need of your help," she answered; then, seeing that her denial had caused hurt, she continued: "This costume is for a special Cheyenne ceremony. Only Red Bead Woman may work on it."

Colly's face cleared, her features lighting with one of those smiles that transformed her to beauty. She understood that Red Bead Woman was held in high regard among her sisters of the Quill Society, a prestigious needlework group. The women were allowed to work on ceremonial robes only after they'd proven their worthiness, not only with quill, bead, and needle, but in an exemplary character as well.

Colly felt affection well for this good woman. She knew that in the eyes of white society Red Bead Woman would seem primitive and heathen, but now that Colly had come to know her, she realized Lone Wolf's mother was a woman of high moral principles. She followed the tenets of the Cheyenne laws faithfully. If she had been one of Brother Davey's congregation, she would have been admired. Instead the white world, which had little understanding of the Cheyenne ways, would only belittle her. Colly felt saddened at such a thought. Timidly she reached out a hand to touch Red Bead Woman's shoulder. The Indian whirled to face her.

"I'm sorry. I didn't mean to startle you. I only wanted to say that I'm sorry for the misunderstanding between us." She swallowed her pride and rushed on. "I miss you and would like to come back to your lodge."

"That cannot be," Red Bead Woman said. "One day you will return here as my son's bride. Then you will be in charge of the lodge. I must do as you tell me, but until that day, you may not return."

Stunned, Colly stared at Red Bead Woman, unwilling to believe she could be so petty. "I will never presume to boss you around," she said. "I'm sorry you think I would try."

"What is 'boss around'?" Red Bead Woman asked, but Colly had already jumped to her feet and was stalking away toward Magpie's tepee.

She made no mention to Lone Wolf about her bout with his mother. But when he came to call that evening after dark, bringing his blanket to insure them some privacy as they sat and talked in full view of Magpie, who had suddenly become their chaperon, he sensed something was troubling her. His heart froze and he wondered if she was having second thoughts. Yet her slim body rested against his side with complete trust and acceptance.

"Tell me of your childhood," he said in Cheyenne, wanting to learn as much as he could about her so he might better understand her moods.

"There's not a lot to tell," she answered. "I was born and grew up on a farm in Tennessee."

"Tell me about this farm."

So she told him of the blue mists on the hills and the rich, black soil where they could grow nearly everything, of the creek running through the woods, rushing and chuckling over red sandstone and pebbles, of the pond and the geese that flew over in the fall on their trek from the north, of squirrels that flew and puffballs that exploded when touched, sending a shower of brown spores into the air, of the birds—the thrasher, the warbler, and the bluebirds—and of the green, green ferns growing along the creek banks.

He listened to her recital and heard her love of the land and the things that grew on it. He heard a touch of longing she thought she'd put behind her and, in the days that followed, he often came upon her at the riverbank and lured her away from her tasks with a gift of a beautiful pony or a roughly carved bird. Taking her hand, he would lead her to the green ferns growing along the riverbanks, pointing out the prairie chickens, the insects beneath the grass, and the common warblers that made their homes in the long-stemmed privacy of the prairie grass. He'd always felt her fear of the prairie and understood now that fear existed because she didn't know the land that was to be her home. Slowly he taught her about the prairie, delighting in her wonder. Though her dislike of the great plains never receded, she was a little less afraid of it.

Summer had passed. *Wahkahuneishi*, the time of the Plum Moon, was nearly upon them. It had been a plentiful season for the tribe. The buffalo gods had been generous. No retribution had been visited against the tribe for the killing of the white buffalo chief. Parfleches bulged with extra food. There were many thick robes.

New lodges had been made. They stood pale and pristine in the late summer sunlight, their smoke holes unstained. Chief White Thunder's lodge stood out, with its vivid circle representing the sun. The old lodge skins had been taken down and made into clothes, especially robes for the old people, since the smoke from the many campfires had further softened the skins.

The time of the Cool Moon was upon them, the time when the dry dust blew in one's face and the leaves began to turn. The Cheyenne prepared for the coming time of the *Mahk he konini*, the Big Freezing Moon.

On the first night of the new Plum Moon, Lone Wolf drove thirty of his best horses through the village and up to Tall Man's lodge. Colly, well aware of the meaning of such an event, stood blushing and tongue-tied while the two men went through the formalities of Lone Wolf asking for her hand in marriage. Tall Man and Magpie had agreed to act as her family since she had none. When the arrangements had been concluded to everyone's satisfaction, Lone Wolf mounted his sleek black pony and gazed down at Colly. His eyes were bold, his glance smoldering. Colly felt her breath catch and her nipples tingle beneath the soft buckskin dress. With a whoop of joy, Lone Wolf galloped away. The villagers, who'd been watching unabashedly, turned away grinning. Tall Man turned to Colly and his wife.

"Ten horses for you," he said, nodding to Colly. "Ten for Magpie, and ten for me."

"I shouldn't take any of the horses," Colly protested. "They were meant for you."

"You cannot go to Lone Wolf like a pauper," Magpie answered. "That would shame us, your parents."

Colly grinned at the garrulous woman and hugged her quickly. Though she would never hold Magpie in the esteem she did Red Bead Woman, she found she liked the generous-hearted woman.

"Now, come. We must gather gifts to send to Lone Wolf and his family," Magpie said elatedly. Having no daughter of her own, she was enjoying being a part of the marriage plans.

The gifts were duly sent to Lone Wolf's lodge, and Colly was stunned at the number and quality. Since Lone Wolf had offered generous gifts for his bride-to-be, thereby raising her standing considerably in the eyes of the villagers, Tall Man and Magpie, acting as her foster parents, must give gifts of equal value. They were determined not to be considered wanting in their response. Twenty horses, five colts, three glossy, thick buffalo robes, one gleaming copper kettle, five pairs of moccasins, and ten new arrows were offered as the bride's acceptance gifts. The village buzzed with excitement.

Her cheeks flushed, Colly waited for Lone Wolf to return that night to court her, but he remained away. Tall Man and his friend, Tangle Hair, returned from their trip to Lone Wolf's lodge.

"Tomorrow you will ride to Lone Wolf's lodge to become his wife," Tall Man said.

"So soon?" Colly asked tremulously.

"She will be ready," Magpie answered.

Tall Man grunted and left the lodge. He'd seen the excitement in his wife's eyes and knew there would be little time to relax in his own lodge this night. Resigned, he followed Tangle Hair across the circle ground to his lodge. The two old friends settled before the fire and lit a pipe.

Colly glanced at Magpie but said nothing. Now that the moment of her marriage to Lone Wolf was nearly upon her, she felt jittery. Though her heart and mind were undaunted over her choice, she was, nonetheless, shaken by the thought that soon she would be with Lone Wolf in an intimate embrace.

What if he no longer found her desirable? What if in her ignorance she behaved badly, becoming too wanton or not passionate enough? More than ever she wished Lone Wolf had come to see her this night—or that she had someone to talk to frankly about all her fears. She was an old maid who'd never been told anything about the act of love. She knew how the farm animals went about it, but surely it was different for humans. Magpie chattered brightly until finally Colly's preoccupation silenced even that prattling tongue. Colly crept into her bed and lay rigidly awake until the morning sun stained the eastern horizon.

The day of her wedding, Colly rose headachy and nervous, a state she'd not been subjected to in her entire life. Not wanting to listen to Magpie's well-meaning chatter, she left the tepee and walked down to the river. She felt restless, her firm resolve crumbling at the edges. She wanted to see Lone Wolf, to look into his dark eyes and see his slow, warming smile. Yet she felt too timid to go to his lodge and ask him to accompany her.

So she went to the river alone and stood staring into the muddy, tumbling water. It seemed as thick and muddled as her head. She turned away; then, catching a glimpse of something on the other bank, she paused. How plainly she recognized the silhouette on the other side.

He stood straight and tall, his hands outstretched to the eastern sky in mute supplication. Streaks of red and orange stained the horizon as the sun pushed its way past the last hard line of darkness and offered its light and warmth to the Mother Earth. Standing in the early morning dusk, Colly hugged herself against the chill and felt her heart lift. She had little doubt that the distant figure was Lone Wolf. Seeing the reality of his tall, strong body relieved her anxiety somewhat. He must have felt the same concern as she and come here to pray. She was heartened by this evidence of his faith. Such a man would not treat her cruelly.

Colly returned to Magpie's lodge with a lighter heart—until she remembered that her fears had not been of Lone Wolf's treatment of her, but of her own behavior in the marriage bed. Would he be patient with her? Would she disappoint him? All her bridal jitters came back; she could scarcely stand still as Magpie helped her dress in her finest clothes.

Colly had spent the past weeks making a dress for herself from the skin of a young deer. She'd tanned the hide herself and was proud of its smooth softness. She'd taken special pains with the cutting and sewing of the garment and was pleased with the results. Despite her best efforts, her skill in tanning was not carried over into her quill- and beadwork. Now and then an awkward stitch showed. Wisely she'd kept the design simple, perhaps too simple, for Magpie clucked her tongue and hurried to offer necklaces of beads and bone to ornament her costume. Gratefully Colly accepted. She wanted to appear beautiful to Lone Wolf. For that reason she left her hair loose and flowing down her back.

When it was time, she mounted the sleek white pony Lone Wolf had given her. The villagers were gathered near Lone Wolf's lodge, waiting with eager, expectant smiles. When they saw Colly's hair, they sighed with admiration.

Colly's heart was thudding with excitement by the time she reached Lone Wolf's lodge. The flap opened and she expected to see him stroll forth, but Red Bead Woman and Black Moon appeared. Colly's heart contracted painfully. Was Red Bead Woman going to denounce this marriage publicly?

One glance at the Indian woman's face dispelled her fears. Red Bead Woman and Black Moon were smiling broadly as they stepped forward to greet her. Colly dismounted, and the pony was led away. Red Bead Woman took her hand and led her to a blanket spread before the lodge opening. She pressed Colly down, so she sat in the middle of the blanket. Then the two women took hold of either side, lifted Colly, and carried her inside so, according to Cheyenne custom, she didn't step or walk across the threshold.

Carrying their blanketed burden to the back of the lodge, they proceeded to remove her clothing. Red Bead Woman brought out a dress made of the softest bleached elk skin ornamented with exquisite bead, quill, and elkstooth designs. Colly recognized the garment Red Bead Woman had been working on that day by the fire. Her gaze flew to Red Bead Woman's smiling face.

"I couldn't allow you to help me make your wedding dress," she said softly.

"I thought you were still angry with me," Colly whispered.

"You are my daughter," Red Bead Woman replied. "I welcome you to our lodge."

Tears stinging her lids, Colly threw her arms around the woman, who had been her friend all along. Then Black Moon insisted on hugs. Smiling sheepishly, they moved apart and busied themselves with the rest of the dressing ceremony.

Red Bead Woman slipped the beautiful dress over Colly's shoulders and nodded in satisfaction. Once again they seated Colly on the beautiful robe and set about combing and braiding her hair. They painted her face and the part in her hair and hung bone and copper ornaments about her neck and ears until she was afraid to move, for fear of clanking. When all was ready, they stepped to the door of the lodge and threw back the flap.

Lone Wolf entered, his dark eyes shining, his gaze catching Colly's. He was splendidly dressed in new soft doeskins ornamented with quills and beads along the yoke and down the sleeves. Even his leggings and moccasins were decorated with dyed quills. Colly recognized Red Bead Woman's fine hand.

Lone Wolf smiled at her and crossed the lodge to sit beside her on the robe. His demeanor was almost shy toward her, something she found eminently endearing from so powerful a man. Yet his attitude did little to dispel the lump of excitement that sat in her stomach. He'd never looked so handsome. She'd never been more aware of his masculinity.

Now the feast was to begin, and the villagers hurried to partake of the food Red Bead Woman had prepared. Black Moon moved among the villagers, seeing they were made welcome. Red Bead Woman brought dishes of food to Lone Wolf and Colly, cutting the food into bite-sized pieces. Colly felt no hunger and nibbled at the food halfheartedly. Lone Wolf, too, seemed preoccupied.

At last they were allowed to rise and leave the lodge. They walked to the camp circle and took a place of honor next to Chief White Thunder. Colly smiled tremulously at those who called good wishes. Gifts were dispersed to all the guests.

Darkness fell and the campfire was built higher, so it gave off much illumination. By its light the villagers began to

dance, the young unwed women flirting with the single warriors while their mothers reprimanded them from the side-
lines. A second wedding in their summer camp had set a
mood of gaiety and all had heard the story of Dull Knife's
prophecy. They were especially grateful to Lone Wolf and
Spotted Woman for fulfilling the vision so the buffalo would
come again.

Finally came the time when Lone Wolf stood and held out
his hand to Colly, pulling her to her feet. Amid cries of good
wishes, they took the path from the village center down to
the river. Lone Wolf guided her along the bank to a secluded
clearing, where a small tepee had been set up. Colly paused
and looked at him.

"This will be our honeymoon lodge for a few nights," he
said softly.

His large, rough hand was gentle on her arm. The moonlight cast a pale shadow on the river water. Colly shivered.

"You aren't cold, are you?" he asked. "Do you want to
go into the lodge?"

"No, I'm not chilled," Colly denied hurriedly, and did
her best to suppress another shiver. "Let's look at the moonlight on the river."

"I will make a fire," Lone Wolf said. When he had a
small fire burning warmly, he went into the tepee and came
out with a warm, soft robe. "Come," he said, spreading it
on the ground near him.

Hesitantly she crossed the dark ground to the warmth he
offered. Lone Wolf pulled the robe around them both, so
they were encased as they had been in his courting blanket.

"Tell me some more things about your farm in Tennessee
and the tribe you lived with," he said, placing an arm around
her shoulders and drawing her against him.

Nervously she began to talk, but as the heat of his body
warmed hers and the familiar strength of his arms soothed
her, she began to relax and she told him funny tales of her
childhood and ways of her people. Now and then she paused

to yawn. Finally her head dipped and rested against his shoulder.

Now Lone Wolf began to talk, telling her of his childhood, of being placed on the back of a pony as soon as he could walk, of his grandfather, who had taught him his duties as a man, of his first buffalo hunt, and of how his father had given away a horse when he went on his first war party.

Colly listened to his words, picturing a slim, fearless boy learning to become an honorable man to make his father and grandfather proud of him. She longed to hear everything about his life, but she hadn't slept the night before and the warm fire was making her sleepy.

When Lone Wolf felt her breathing, deep and slow against his neck, and saw how she struggled to stay awake, he lay back in the robe, cradling her against his side. One large hand stroked her hair and back in a soothing, mesmerizing motion.

"Sleep, my wife," he crooned in her ear, and despite herself, Colly sank into blissful slumber, cherished and comforted by Lone Wolf's presence as she had never been before. Dimly, in the distance of the prairie, she heard the cry of a coyote, but she was no longer troubled by it. Lone Wolf was beside her. She was his wife. She smiled in her sleep, and Lone Wolf, who lay holding her, wished she might open her eyes so he could look into them.

He had a need and a desire for his new wife, but he'd sensed her nervousness. Cheyenne men had been taught to be patient with their new brides and often lay many nights just talking, until they no longer felt anxiety about consummating their marriage.

Lone Wolf had known Colly was a maiden—he'd seen it in her blushing cheeks and shy glances—and he was prepared to wait until she was ready. Cradling his wife close, he closed his mind to the tumbling thoughts of the pale, long-limbed body beside him and concentrated fiercely on his last encounter with the Arapaho. Tonight he wished their camp were nearby so he might ride down on them and dispel some of this restless energy in a battle. Then he glanced at Spotted Woman and felt her warm body slumped against his, and he was glad nothing would disturb their time together. Soon, he promised himself. Soon.

Chapter 9

WHEN COLLY AWOKE, her new husband was gone. She lay on the bank of the river trying to orient herself, thinking she was still unwed and had fallen asleep beside Red Bead Woman's cooking fire; then memory flooded back and she sat up. The little honeymoon lodge sat behind her, empty and unused. Drawing her knees up to her chin, Colly sat brooding, remembering how patient Lone Wolf had been with her and how miserably she'd failed as a wife by falling asleep on him. Wherever he'd gone, he must be regretting his marriage to her.

Suddenly he was there on the path leading from the bathing area of the river. Colly turned, expecting to see a stern, accusing face, but his eyes sparkled with good cheer. His tall body exuded energy. His hair had been neatly parted and plaited into two braids with bits of otter fur and bone ornaments added. Colly saw that he'd taken great care with his appearance. He smiled when he saw she was awake, and Colly felt all her fears drain away. She returned his smile.

Lone Wolf seated himself beside her and proceeded to remake the fire, which had burned out during the night. Colly watched him for a moment, taking in his sleek form encased in its soft doeskin and the strong, bronzed features. She thought how handsome he was. He leaned forward to blow

145

gently on the blackened embers. Immediately they glowed to life.

"I'll do that," she cried, mortified at her failure to have rebuilt the fire and prepared his morning meal like a proper wife. Quickly she reached for a pile of small twigs at the same time Lone Wolf's hand closed over them. She felt the surrounding warmth and strength of his palm over her own slim hand and felt the tingle all the way up her arm. His gaze boldly met hers.

Shyly she withdrew her hand and placed the twigs over the coals. Silently she watched the tiny flames begin to grow and was consumed with awareness of the man beside her. She felt his shoulder brush against hers as he rose, and glanced up questioningly.

Lone Wolf walked to the little lodge and soon was back with a pot of food that had been stored there. He put it to warming over the cheery little fire, and Colly sat with pinkened cheeks, berating herself for not having gotten the food herself. When the food was heated, she reached for a bone spoon and wooden bowls, but Lone Wolf gently pushed her away and dished up the stew himself. His smile was wide and generous as he handed her a bowl. Thinking this might be part of the Cheyenne rituals, Colly relaxed, and, taking the dish, sat back. She'd been too excited to eat anything the day before, and she was hungry. After Lone Wolf had begun to eat, she used a sharp stick to spear out pieces of meat and root and vegetables.

"I saw a turtle down at the river this morning," he said in Cheyenne. It was the first time either of them had spoken this morning.

"What kind was it?" she asked, eager for some excuse to begin a conversation between them.

"It was a water turtle," Lone Wolf answered. "A very bad turtle, for they go to war against the Indians."

"Go to war?" Colly repeated.

Lone Wolf smiled indulgently. "Have you not heard the

story of the turtle chief who went to war? I will tell you if you promise not to laugh.''

Colly shook her head, but her eyes were already sparkling with humor, for she'd learned the Cheyenne loved to tell stories and they often had humorous endings. She set her empty bowl aside and watched her husband's face while he began to relate the tale of the sly, determined turtle who waged war against the Indians.

''There was a great camp of water turtles, and, not far away, some people were living—many lodges,'' Lone Wolf began. He was careful to tell the story exactly as it had been told to him, for to do otherwise showed disrespect to the Cheyenne. If he did not relate the story as it should be told, the person who had given it to him could take it back.

''The head turtle spoke to all these people and said: 'Now let us go out on the warpath. I have found many Indians camping near this place. Let us go on the warpath against them and kill their chief.' ''

Colly knew how jealously the Cheyenne guarded their storytelling and knew this was one of Lone Wolf's gifts to her. She sat quietly watching her husband's face while he related the story of how the turtles traveled all night until they reached the Indians' camp.

''The turtle went into the chief's lodge, took hold of the chief's throat, and choked him—and he died—and the turtle bit off his hair.'' Lone Wolf paused dramatically. ''When daylight came, the turtle leader crawled under the bed and stayed there all day.

''In the morning the chief of the Indians was found dead and the old crier went through the camp and called out, directing people to find out if there were any enemies about who might have done this thing.

''After the young men had gone, the chief's wife took down the lodge, for they were going to put the chief's body in another place. While they were moving the lodge, they found a turtle in the ground under the bed.'' He paused again, grinning this time. Colly repressed a giggle at the sly turtle.

"They chose another chief," Lone Wolf continued, "and called upon him to say what should be done. The chief said: 'Let us see what we can do to kill him. He is the one who killed our chief.' "

"Some of the Indians said: 'Let us put him in the fire'; but one said: 'No, we cannot burn him, his shell is too hard. Let us cut his head off.' Another said, 'No, let us hang him,' and a fourth said, 'No, let us drown him.' To all of them this seemed the best, and they decided that the turtle should be drowned."

Lone Wolf stopped speaking and glanced at Colly to see if she was beginning to see the preposterous humor of all this. Her gray eyes were sparkling, so he continued. "Then, the next afternoon, they took him down to the water and a great crowd of people went with them to see him drown. The man who was going to drown him was painted up and he carried the turtle out to the center of the pond. The turtle acted as if he was very frightened." Lone Wolf's face twisted into a grimace of fear. He spoke rapidly now, denoting something was about to happen. "As the man was going to let the turtle down into the water, the turtle turned his head and bit the man, and the man was frightened and sank into the water with the turtle." He paused, rolling his eyes. "Then everyone on the shore was afraid and no one dared to go down into the water to help the man who had sunk."

His expressive telling of the story was mesmerizing. Colly remained still as he finished relating how the turtle bit off the man's hair and returned to his own camp, where everyone had supposed he had been killed. Once there he tied the Indian's scalp to a stick and danced over it. All the other turtles, who had done nothing, went about the camp dancing and singing for joy, and the brave turtle continued to be chief of the turtles.

By the time Lone Wolf had finished his tale and leaned back in smug assurance he'd told it well, Colly was holding a hand across her mouth to keep from laughing, not only at the bold turtle but at her oh-so-arrogant husband. He glanced around to see if she was properly impressed by him, and when he encountered her sparkling eyes, they laughed together. Lone Wolf was pleased he'd made his wife laugh.

"Come, we will ride," he said, taking her hand and pulling her up.

They mounted the horses that had been left tied nearby and galloped out onto the prairie. The autumn chill had fallen away from the morning. The sun shone warm and bright on their backs. It seemed to Colly that such days as this must never end, they were so perfect. They rode far out into the prairie until the tall grass came nearly to their knees, even though they were astride their horses. Colly paused and looked backward in the direction they'd come. The parted grass was already filling in, all evidence of their passing fading. An easy breeze had sprung up, moving the heads of the prairie grass in sweeping waves of color. They rode on, delighting in each other, pleased at their time together.

In the evening they returned to the small lodge beside the river, where together they built a fire and prepared their food. Colly was unaware of how beautiful she'd become with her blushed cheeks and brilliant eyes. After they'd eaten, she sat by the fire and unbraided her hair. As she reached for her prized quill comb, Lone Wolf took it from her.

"I would like to comb your hair," he said, and waited for her nod of assent. Carefully he pulled the comb through her rich, gleaming hair, smoothing it with his hands, marveling at the fiery color.

Colly sat very still under his hands, her head thrown back, her eyes closed against the sheer pleasure of having her husband tend to her hair. When he'd finished and her hair lay around her shoulders in a shiny curtain, he put aside the comb and pulled her into his arms. His kiss was gentle and restrained, asking nothing more than this tender exchange of love. When it had ended, he held her, cradling her against his side while they stared at the campfire. Sometimes they spoke of something they'd seen that day on the prairie or of some thought they'd had. Sometimes they were silent, listening to the flowing river and the night sounds of the animals that dwelled along its banks. Colly sighed, deeply contented.

When the fire had burned down, Lone Wolf rose and led her to the skin lodge. Colly followed willingly, her heart thudding in her chest. This interlude between them had been filled with such tenderness and love, she was ready to give herself to this man. But Lone Wolf pushed her down on the thick pad of furs and lay down beside her, still fully clothed. Taking her into his arms, he kissed her tenderly, and, sighing, pushed her head down on his shoulder.

Colly relaxed against him, taking in the smell and feel of him, all of which were becoming endearingly familiar. She waited, uncertain of what came next, but Lone Wolf only began to talk to her, telling her of Cheyenne customs and of great battles he'd fought, and how he'd counted coup on his enemies. His words were not full of bravado. He told her simply, as a husband might relate details of his job. She sensed he spoke of these things so she might better understand him.

Listening, she marveled that she'd ever considered the Cheyenne men as lazy. Theirs was a duty of feeding and protecting the women and children who depended upon them. Colly felt reassured by his recital, for she could see he was as great a warrior as he was a hunter. She realized he wanted her to understand he would never fail her. She was touched by his attitude.

The night crept by too swiftly, and still Lone Wolf talked on. Colly grew tired, and, rolling onto her side, she wrapped her arm around his waist and dozed off. She never knew when Lone Wolf stopped talking, but when she woke in the morning, she was still entwined in his arms and his strong features were softened by sleep.

She lay beside him for a long time, wondering why he hadn't claimed his rights as her husband. Did she not please him after all? She lay very still so as not to disturb him, but he seemed to sense the stiffness that had crept into her body. As soon as he stirred, she rose swiftly and made her way down to the river. She didn't want him to see how troubled she was.

Lone Wolf felt her leave his side and groaned and rolled over. His dreams had been of Spotted Woman. He had tried his best to use restraint, as all Cheyenne husbands must do with their new brides. He had done so with Dawn Rising On A Hill. She had worn her chastity rope for more nights than he had fingers before she'd finally been coaxed to take it off. He meant to show Spotted Woman the same respect, but each night beside her was more difficult than he'd expected. He found himself wondering about her.

He remembered that day at the stream when he'd washed the blood from her dress. His stroking hands had felt her breasts, small yet firm, and the flat planes of her stomach, and the slight mounding between her thighs. Now he wondered about the long length of her thighs and the color of her hair at their juncture. Would it be flame-colored like the hair on her head? Would she be spotted beneath her clothes? He hoped so. He liked the small golden spots she called freckles.

Sighing he rose and headed toward the river to bathe. He had no desire to meet other men today, so he turned aside to find a different spot. Following a seldom-used path he came out upriver and paused, for his wife stood in the shallow water. Her clothes lay on the bank and she stood gleaming and wet, her pale skin catching the rays of early sun. Her hair seemed to have caught fire, and her slim figure was gilded with sunlight. He saw the milky whiteness of her stomach and thighs, the soft contours of her breasts, the darker aureole of her nipples, the nest of red-gold curls at her mound.

He must have made a sound, for she whirled and stared up at him. Her lips formed a circle but no sound came. Her long, slender hands went to cover her breasts, the act of modesty only making her seem more sensuous. Slowly Lone Wolf walked down the bank, his dark gaze holding hers.

When he reached the water, he waded in without bothering to remove his moccasins.

She met him halfway, her slender arms reaching for him, her face raised for his kiss. There was no tenderness in the kiss they exchanged, only a hunger they'd both tried to ignore for the past two nights. Her soft lips parted beneath his and he tasted the sweetness of his wife, like the summer berries they'd gathered in the marshes.

His strong arm slid around her waist and knees and he carried her up the riverbank to a grassy knoll. They were alone in a secret bower, hidden from view by the wall of green branches. Only the river opened before them, serene and discreet in all its knowledge. Placing Colly on the soft, green bed, Lone Wolf stood gazing down at her in wonder. She blushed beneath his intense gaze, but she didn't shrink away. Reverently he touched her, marveling at the softness of women in all their hidden places. He stroked her, learning the feel of her body. Colly trembled beneath his touch, and when he drew away, she opened her eyes and gazed at him in mute appeal.

Hastily he stripped away the doeskin shirt and leggings. She'd seen him before in only his loincloth, but she'd been too discreet to gaze upon him openly. Now she did, seeing the flexing, sinewy muscles of his thighs, the hard-ribbed flatness of his stomach, the flaring curve of muscled chest and shoulders. He was magnificent. Her gaze moved to his face, to the high cheekbones and chiseled jaw, the strong nose and dark, intelligent eyes. She saw the love there in his gaze, and the flare of passion, and her body and soul answered in a like manner. She held her arms out to him and he removed the breechcloth. Now he stood before her naked and proud. She gazed at his rigid manhood and felt her body readying itself for him.

Lone Wolf lay down beside her. She felt the brush of his throbbing staff against her thigh and her legs parted automatically. All things of the world outside fell away from her. She gave no thought to her childhood teachings. She was a woman couched with the man she loved beneath God's clear sky and it felt right and good.

She expected pain. She'd heard the women talk around their quilting frames, telling of the shame they'd endured in the marriage bed. She'd heard them lament over the lustfulness of husbands, who were otherwise thoughtful and undemanding. She'd heard and believed them when they'd said mating was a duty a woman must bear. But there was no sacrifice of honor here between Lone Wolf and her.

Slowly—and with surprising knowledge—he courted her fire and passion, never taking the next step until he knew she was with him, and when he raised his hard, long body over hers, she felt no fear, no shudder of dread. When he pierced her maidenhead, she cried out for only a moment before wrapping her long limbs around him and moving with him. She'd never guessed it could be like this between men and women, this great reaching together toward a pinnacle never scaled before, and when they stood atop that high place, she felt the shudder of consummation and willingly followed Lone Wolf into a new world of their own.

"Cheyenne!" Stone Calf said. Major Buford raised his head and sniffed the wind as if he might find what he sought in this manner. But the gleaming bones of the buffalo gave up no secrets.

"How long ago were they here?" Buford asked.

Stone Calf shrugged. "Two moons."

"Damn!" Buford swore.

"We don't know they're the same tribe that attacked the wagon train," McKinney pointed out, and fell silent under Buford's intense gaze.

"They're the ones out here. Which way did they go, Stone Calf?"

The Indian scout studied the land. "Too long. No signs."

"Well, which way do you think they went?" Buford snapped.

Stone Calf remained silent, his dark eyes staring into the

distance. Finally he pointed to the west. "River of Niobrara. Maybe go there."

Buford studied the guide with narrowed eyes, then nodded to McKinney. "Let's go," he called. Without waiting to see that his men followed, he galloped away in the direction Stone Calf had pointed.

During the days they'd been tracking the Cheyenne, he'd grown more determined to find and punish them. If he could return to his commanding officer claiming such a success, he would probably be sent back East. He'd ignored the grumblings of his men, pressing onward, although their supplies were running low.

In the afternoon they topped a slight ridge and saw in the distance a group of horsemen, six in all. A deer was slung over the back of a packhorse.

"Indians," the major said, studying them through his binoculars. "Who are they, Stone Calf?"

The scout narrowed his eyes and peered through the white officer's glasses. "Cheyenne," he answered reluctantly.

"They look peaceable enough," Lieutenant McKinney said.

"Look, sir. They've got some game," Sergeant Crook pointed out. "I sure could stand to have me some fresh meat."

The major grinned. "Let's go down and get some, Sergeant," he replied softly.

Lieutenant McKinney cast him a startled glance but made no comment. Deep in his soul, he felt what they were about to do was wrong, possibly even against government policy, but he also knew it would do him little good to protest. The major was in charge.

At the sergeant's signal the men swept down the rise and galloped toward the unsuspecting horsemen.

Doll Man was the first to see the approaching riders. "Soldiers," he called, pointing them out to the other men. Silently they watched the soldiers bear down on them. Little Bear brought up his rifle and checked his ammunition.

"Do not fire," Tall Man said. "They may be friendly."

"Pah!" Little Bear spat out. "Look at the way they rush toward us. They mean us no good."

"If you fire, we won't know if they meant to be peaceful or not," Tall Man pointed out, and since he was an elder and a member of the council, Little Bear knew his word must be obeyed. Silently they waited.

The soldiers quickly surrounded them. "What're you Injuns doin' out here?" Sergeant Crook demanded, coming to a halt before them. Major Buford was trailing behind them. He brought his horse to a stop some distance back, well out of the range of fire, should there be any.

The warriors remained silent, although they'd understood the words the white eyes had spoken.

"Ask 'em what they're doin' out here," the sergeant instructed the half-breed scout.

Stone Calf spoke to the warriors in Cheyenne, and they answered.

"We've been hunting and we're taking meat to our village."

"Ask them where their village is," Major Buford demanded when he heard Stone Calf interpret their words.

His manner was so intense that the warriors conferred among themselves. When Stone Calf relayed the major's commands, they pointed in a direction different from that in which the village lay.

Major Buford studied their closed faces. "I don't believe them," he said. "Tell them that!"

Stone Calf hesitated, knowing the seriousness of calling a Cheyenne a liar. Reluctantly he conveyed the insult. Immediately Little Bear drew himself up. His hands gripping his rifle warningly.

"Tell them they may go, but they must leave the packhorse with the deer," Major Buford continued.

"We won't give it up," Little Bear spat out.

"It is best we do so now," Doll Man said. "We are outnumbered."

Major Buford sensed that the outcome of this encounter hinged on what he did next. ''Draw your arms,'' he ordered his men, and they did so, their expressions menacing.

Doll Man and the other warriors conferred among themselves, and, with a nod of agreement, relinquished the pack-horse bearing their deer.

''Tell them they may go,'' the major ordered Stone Calf, and the scout did as he was ordered, his gaze lowered so the warriors could not see the shame in his eyes.

Tall Man spoke sharply to Little Bear, who sat staring murderously at the major. The warriors dug their heels into the sides of their ponies and with wild whoops galloped away.

''Guess them Cheyenne ain't the fighters we heard they was,'' Sergeant Crook commented. He spat tobacco through his teeth to show his contempt.

''Fire!'' the major ordered, and his men took aim at the departing backs.

An old warrior fell beneath the onslaught of bullets; another sagged in his saddle. Little Bear galloped ahead, then swung around and charged toward the line of soldiers, his arrows flying with swift, deadly accuracy. Some of the other warriors did the same. The line of soldiers was thrown into confusion as some fell from their horses, wounded and dying. Doll Man used their confusion to recover the body of the warrior who'd fallen.

''Take cover and fire at will!'' Major Buford cried, sliding off his own horse and drawing his pistol. Carefully he took aim and fired. Another warrior fell. They drew back and gathered out of range to confer.

''Let's attack them again!'' Little Bear cried wildly.

''There are too many. Tall Man is already dead. We will all be killed,'' Doll Man answered. ''We must warn the village.'' The others nodded their heads in agreement and they withdrew.

''I think we needn't fear those murdering devils anymore,'' Major Buford said, turning to assess the damage.

"Sir, we have wounded men here," Lieutenant McKinney reported.

"How many?"

"Four, sir. One of them won't live to make the fort."

"Any dead?" Buford demanded impatiently.

"Three men, sir."

Buford cursed.

"Are we returning to the fort, sir?"

Buford was stunned at the number of men who'd fallen in the brief skirmish. Defeat sat in his mouth like bitter gall. He couldn't continue the search with dead and wounded men. He'd have to return to the fort. Livid, he stared across the prairie to the distant horizon, where the Indians had been lost from sight.

"We'll go back to Fort Laramie," he said, "but we're coming back. We're going to find those murdering devils."

Slowly the men gathered their dead and wounded and the Indians' deer, which had cost them such a grave price, then turned west toward Fort Laramie.

Colly woke and lay snuggled against her husband's side. She'd never known such happiness. They'd not left their tepee since yesterday morning, when Lone Wolf had come to her at the river. The hours had passed quickly, filled with passion and laughter and discovery. Only when she'd whimpered a tiny protest had Lone Wolf recognized her distress and held himself in check. Now he lay with his arms and long, muscular legs sprawled across her, claiming her even in sleep. She would never grow used to the wild surge of joy his presence brought her. She heard the ghostly hoot of an owl and shivered, snuggling closer to her husband's powerful body. Soon she fell asleep again.

"Lone Wolf!" The call was loud and insistent, penetrating her dreams. She felt Lone Wolf draw away from her and heard him answer softly. The tepee was still dark, but she could see the gray light of dawn when he opened the flap and stepped outside. She lay still and listened to the voices. She couldn't hear the words, but the tone was one of urgency. The flap was thrown back and Lone Wolf entered. He crossed to her at once.

"What is it?" she asked, sitting up on her elbows.

"Tall Man has been killed. Stands In The Timber and Red Arrow were wounded."

"Oh, no," Colly cried, thinking of Magpie. She'd doted on her kindly husband.

"White Thunder has ordered us to break camp immediately and move back to the Cheyenne River camp."

"I'll go at once and help Red Bead Woman," Colly said, rising. Quickly she donned her clothes and gathered the robes. As she stepped out of the small tepee, she turned and looked around the campsite. She had known much happiness here, brief though it was. Now she set about dismantling the small lodge. Using the lodge poles, she made a travois as Red Bead Woman had shown her and loaded the lodge skins and robes on it. In very little time they returned to the village.

All was chaos. Women and children worked furiously to gather their belongings and take down the lodges. Colly hurried to help Red Bead Woman, and once their things were packed on horses and travois, the women turned to help Black Moon and Magpie. The grieving widow had rent her clothes and cut deep scratches in her face and arms. Her eyes were dull and she spoke to no one.

Colly dismantled her lodge and packed her travois. By sunup the camp was gone. Only a circle of fire pits showed where the lodges had rested.

The journey north was somber. There was little talk and no laughter. Even the children were silent. They traveled quickly, pausing only when dusk forced them to it and rising early to be on the move again with the first light.

Colly saw little of Lone Wolf during the day. He rode with the other warriors on the flanks and at the rear of the column. Scouts ranged in a wide, protective circle, keeping watch against white soldiers who had no compunction about stealing food that belonged to the Indians and then shooting them in the back. Colly was quiet during the journey, horrified that her own countrymen had acted so cowardly. At night she stayed close to her own campfire, suddenly conscious of dark, hostile eyes that watched her.

The third day out they began to relax their vigil. Tomorrow they would reach the river and join the other tribes for a few weeks before moving into the hills, where they would set up their winter camp. The danger seemed behind them. Although they mourned the death of Tall Man, a respected warrior and member of the council, they understood that life must go on.

Doll Man was honored for having brought back his body. Stands In The Timber and Red Arrow were healing. Already White Thunder and his councilmembers were discussing the war chief who would be chosen to take Tall Man's place.

That evening they called a council. Everyone was invited. The villagers hurried to White Thunder's lodge and, entering his door, turned immediately to the right to find places to sit. Great care was taken not to step between anyone already seated and the fire, for to do so was considered bad manners. The old chief was seated on his bed at the back of the lodge. His councilmembers were seated on either side. It did not escape the attention of anyone there that Lone Wolf had been given a place of honor at the chief's left side.

Colly stood just inside the door, well back from the center fire pit. When all were within the chief's lodge, the flap was closed. No one might enter or leave during the pipe-smoking ceremony. Everyone watched reverently as the ceremonial pipe was brought out and filled with red willow bark and tobacco. The lodge was silent, for no sudden noise must be made during this time; even the women who were preparing dishes of food for the councilmen were careful they did not knock the dishes together.

Sprinkling powdered buffalo chips over the tobacco bowl, White Thunder lit it; then, pointing the pipe stem first to the sky, the ground, and the four directions, he intoned the words:

"Spirit Above, Smoke. Earth, Smoke. Four Cardinal Points, Smoke." He drew on the pipe four times. Then, holding it straight up, for the stem must touch nothing, he passed it to his left.

Lone Wolf took four puffs from the pipe and passed it along. Some of the old men who sat on the council passed the bowl along without smoking, for it was their habit not to smoke if women were in the lodge.

When the pipe had been passed around the semicircle and back again, White Thunder carefully emptied the ashes into a little pile near the fire. With studied movements, he put the medicine pipe away, then turned back to face his people. All who were present were aware of the significance of this pipe-smoking ceremony. White Thunder had clearly shown that Lone Wolf had been chosen to sit on the council. Colly felt her heart swell with pride as she looked at her husband.

"Now we will hear the storyteller," White Thunder said, and the villagers murmured among themselves, for they loved to hear the tales of Old Man Talking.

The old storyteller had sat among the men of the council and smoked the pipe with them, but now he was brought into the middle of the lodge. Slowly he passed his hands over his legs, arms, and head, promising to tell the stories as they were related to him. He paused, peering at the cracks in the flap.

"He must be sure night has fallen," Black Moon whispered. Colly hadn't known she was nearby. Now she leaned closer to hear her sister-in-law's words with a sense of belonging to a family. "He must tell his stories only at night. If he tells them in the daytime, he will become hunchbacked."

Colly smiled at the whimsy, and Black Moon placed an arm around her waist. The two women stood thus as Old Man Talking began his tales.

"I will tell you of an adventure of that trickster, *Nana bosho*," he said. The children smiled with delight, but no one made a sound. To talk during the narrative or stir about was very bad manners.

Old Man Talking told them of the wily coyote, *Nana bosho*, and of how two Indian girls got the better of him by putting burrs in his hair, and of how the greedy fellow nearly drowned trying to gather plums from a pond when they were but a reflection of the plum tree growing beside the pond. Colly laughed with the others. White Thunder had been wise to call this council and allow Old Man Talking to entertain them. Faces that had been tense and fearful for the past few days were once again cheerful, and their laughter came easily.

At last Old Man Talking raised his hands, and they knew he was about to tell them a different kind of story. He spoke solemnly, telling them of a man who understood the speech of the wolves and thus was able to save his people.

Colly knew Old Man Talking had chosen this story to honor Lone Wolf. She was touched by the graceful ways of these people. At last the stories were ended and the flap thrown back. Colly waited outside for Lone Wolf to join her. When he came from the council, she threw her arms around him.

"I'm so proud of you," she cried.

Gravely he removed her arms from his waist and stepped back, his demeanor serious. Intimidated by this new air of dignity, she fell into step behind him and followed him toward their lodge. Once they'd gained the privacy of their tepee, he whirled and swept her into his arms, pressing quick, hungry kisses on her laughing mouth. They made love urgently, quickly, then lay beside each other resting. Colly ran her hand over his bare chest, her sensitive fingertips brushing against each curve and slope of muscle and each roughly puckered scar from his sacrifices.

"Is the danger over?" she asked sleepily.

Lone Wolf paused a long time before he answered. "The danger from the soldiers will always be with us," he said quietly, "but for now we are safe. Soon we will be in our

winter camp and the snows will come. The soldiers won't
find us then.''

"Why do they hunt you down like this? The Cheyenne
have done nothing.''

"They do not believe that.''

"It saddens me that our people can't understand each other
better.''

Lone Wolf thought of Dull Knife's words the day he revealed his vision. He reached for Colly, cuddling her close,
his cheek resting against hers. "Perhaps our two nations will
be friends and will live as one. Perhaps we are the beginning.
Our children will carry the blood of the white man and of
the Cheyenne.''

"Our children.'' Colly sighed, distracted from her original complaint. "I never thought I would have children, and
I may even now carry your seed within me.''

Lone Wolf hugged her close, but his face was grim, for he
was remembering a prophecy Old Man Talking had revealed
once about a time when the buffalo disappeared from the
land, and the skin of the Cheyenne had turned pale, and they
grew hair on their faces as the white eyes wore. "You will
be controlled by them,'' the old man had said. "The white
people will be all over the land, and at last you will disappear.''

Lone Wolf lay beside Spotted Woman, his wife, and wondered what manner of son they would make between them.

Chapter 10

"*T*HE MURDEROUS DEVILS attacked us without provocation. We were forced to defend ourselves. We took down seven of their men before we drove them off."

"That hardly sounds like the Cheyenne." Commander Sanderson sighed, studying Major Buford. The major stood at attention, his demeanor stern and correct, *too* correct for Sanderson's liking. He'd heard whispers of the brutality Buford showed the Indians who came to the fort, so now he sat weighing the truth of his words.

"Sergeant Crook and Lieutenant McKinney were there, sir," Major Buford said smartly. His gaze never wavered.

Sanderson stood up and paced the log-bound perimeter of his office. Once it had been part of a storage room for the post general store, but partitions had been built providing living quarters and offices.

"You say they attacked you?"

"Yes, sir!"

"How many were there?"

"Approximately thirty, sir."

Sergeant Crook's eyes widened at the exaggeration, but he said nothing.

"These may be renegades, not connected with any particular tribe."

"Yes, sir," Major Buford agreed. "But if we don't do

something to stop them before springtime, when new wagon trains roll through here, we'll have more massacres on our hands.''

"That's true, Major." Sanderson paused, pulling at his lower lip. He was a tall, spare man assigned to command this fort; his experience at other posts had taught him to go slowly and not jump to hasty conclusions. Still, the evidence was irrefutable. A wagon train burned out, its members slaughtered, and now this attack on one of his detachments.

"You've done well, Major Buford." Sanderson turned to face his junior officer. "You say you think the village was near the site where you were attacked?"

"Yes, sir," Buford answered. "The Indians were traveling in a northeasterly direction, but when we questioned them as to where their village was, they pointed dead west. They already had a good-sized buck on their packhorse. I figure they were traveling to their village with it, not away from it."

"Quite right, Major. I want you to take a detachment, extra supplies, and ammunition, and see what you find. If you do come upon their village, don't attack. Just see if you can get any information on the renegades that have been causing the trouble."

"What if they prove hostile, sir?"

"Defend yourselves, Major."

"Yes, sir." Buford saluted smartly and swung around. McKinney and Crook followed him to the door.

"Lieutenant McKinney, I'd like to speak to you," Sanderson called, and the young officer paused. Sergeant Crook sent him a warning glance before closing the door.

"Yes, sir?" McKinney returned to the front of Sanderson's desk. His Adam's apple bobbed nervously as he swallowed.

"You've been uncommonly quiet throughout this report." The commander fixed him with a stern glare.

"I had nothing more to add, sir," he answered.

"Tell me, Lieutenant, do you enjoy serving under Major Buford?"

McKinney smiled briefly. "Yes, sir."

"He's a competent officer?"

"Yes, sir."

"Was Major Buford's account of what happened in your encounter with the Cheyenne correct?"

McKinney hesitated, his loyalties torn. Sweat broke out on his brow and upper lip. "Yes, sir!" he said finally.

Sanderson hadn't missed the hesitation or the nervousness. Something was not as the major had reported it, but he was loath to dig deeper with a petty officer. Obviously Major Buford occasioned loyalty in his men and that counted for a great deal out here, where discipline could become lax. He had no wish to undermine that loyalty. He could only trust that Major Buford was an honorable man in the end.

"That will be all, son," Sanderson said finally, and with evident relief, Lieutenant McKinney quit the room.

"What did he talk to you about?" Major Buford demanded when the lieutenant exited the building.

"N-nothing, sir," McKinney answered, for he was certain that was all the conversation had been about. He was unaware he seemed evasive to Buford and that a twinge of distrust had crept into Buford's opinion of him.

"Get your gear ready; we're leaving as soon as the supply wagon is loaded," Buford ordered, and strolled away.

"Yes, sir," McKinney called, but as he readied his bedroll and other gear, he wasn't as eager to go on this outing with Major Buford as he once would have been.

Ice was forming a light skin along the riverbanks and in the ponds. People were forced to break away the cold crystals before plunging into the water for their daily bath. Colly marveled at their fortitude. Only by steeling herself for that first shock of cold could she force herself into the icy river. Once she'd bathed and donned her clothes, she felt invigorated, but if the truth were known, she would have much preferred to snuggle down in her warm robes and sleep an extra hour. Lone Wolf's teasing challenge always drove her from their bed and down to the river. Soon it would be the time of the Freezing Moon and they would depart this camp and go deeper into the hills to spend the winter.

Colly enjoyed this time of peace. She never thought of her white name. Upon their arrival back at their river camp, she'd hurried to check on the garden she'd helped tend when she was first brought to the Cheyenne camp. All the women busied themselves with harvesting the corn, beans, and squash from the garden, grinding the corn into meal, drying the beans, and storing them in small leather pouches. This was a time of visiting with members of other camps. The women gathered often to indulge in their favorite games of chance.

The boys from the different camps formed teams for ball games played with a leather ball and wide rackets made of net. The men busied themselves with council meetings to decide the meaning of the skirmish between the white soldiers and the Cheyenne warriors. They decided to wait and see what further moves the white soldiers would make. Soon they would be high in their winter camps, unreachable because of the mountain snows.

Colly and Black Moon had become closer since that night with the storyteller. She had sensed then that her sister-in-law was unhappy, and at times when they'd bathed together, she'd seen dark bruises on her arms and shoulders, as if she'd been forcefully struck. When she attempted to speak to Black Moon about the bruises, the girl had simply turned away. Colly didn't bring up the subject again, but she took extra care to seek Black Moon out.

She thought of speaking to Red Bead Woman about her daughter's plight, but the Indian woman was preoccupied with helping Magpie, who still grieved for Tall Man. Here, too, Colly felt the burden of caring. Tall Man and Magpie had been generous to her before her marriage. Sometimes, when she knew Red Bead Woman was busy elsewhere, she would take her sewing and go to Magpie's lodge. Sometimes no words were said, but Magpie seemed to draw comfort from her presence.

Colly's attempt to quill and embroider as finely as Red Bead Woman had greatly improved. She took considerable pains with the moccasins she was working on, for she meant them as a gift to Lone Wolf. She always smiled when she thought of the handsome warrior who was her husband. She saw that he was a man of considerable wisdom, often choosing the most peaceful way of handling any problem that arose. In the few short months since his election to the council, he'd won the respect of all for his wisdom and restraint—all except Little Bear, who'd grown envious of Lone Wolf's high stature.

At the same time, it seemed that Little Bear was becoming more reckless. Often he talked among the young warriors, inciting them to anger against the white soldiers. White Thunder called him before the council for a reprimand, but that hadn't stopped the young hothead. Furthermore, he'd begun to take a bullying attitude toward the other villagers, striding through their midst arrogantly, kicking dirt in their cooking pots, shoving aside the young boys who tried so hard to emulate the older warriors.

Black Moon's expression grew more troubled as the weeks passed. Everyone knew Little Bear had become more abusive to her. Their voices were often heard in arguments that ended with the sound of blows.

"Do you not know of your sister's plight?" Colly asked Lone Wolf one evening when Black Moon had come to her, sobbing and bruised.

"It is not the way of the Cheyenne to interfere with a man and his wife," Lone Wolf answered shortly, "and you must not encourage Black Moon to be disobedient. Little Bear has not the patience that I possess with a sassy wife." His playful grin turned her thoughts from Black Moon's plight. But Lone Wolf was all too aware of Little Bear's abuse and had in fact given the fiery warrior a veiled warning. It seemed to have done little good. He knew his old friend had grown jealous that he, Lone Wolf, had been chosen to sit on the council instead of Little Bear. His behavior had ended Little Bear's chance of having a similar honor.

One day the peace of the village was rent by the sound of screams and shouts. Most of the men were out hunting. The women were gathered in small groups, sewing and gossiping. At the sounds of violence they looked around in fear. Black Moon ran from her lodge; her elk-skin dress hung in tatters, and her legs and arms were bleeding from gashes. Screaming, she ran through the village, dodging among the tepees with Little Bear close behind shouting hoarse obscenities. Black Moon tripped and fell, and Little Bear was upon her, his fists pounding her face and body. Black Moon broke free and ran toward Lone Wolf's lodge, where Colly was waiting, a stick of wood in her hands.

"Quickly, go inside. You'll be safe there," Colly cried, and Black Moon took shelter inside the tepee, sobbing and huddling down on a pile of robes. Red Bead Woman hurried to her daughter's aid.

"Black Moon," Little Bear bellowed, coming to the lodge.

"Leave her alone," Colly said. "You've hurt her enough."

Little Bear's lip curled contemptuously as he tried to shove past Colly. She raised the stick of wood and brought it down on his shoulders. Little Bear ducked and jumped aside. Colly gave him little chance to retaliate. Following after him, she swung the stick again and again, each time landing a well-aimed blow. Little Bear howled with rage and indignation. The watching women laughed to see the arrogant warrior brought to heel by a woman. In trying to duck the relentless blows Colly rained on his head and back, Little Bear tripped and went sprawling across a campfire, the contents of the pot barely missing him. Yelping with pain from the glowing coals, he leaped up and made a hasty retreat, the laughter of the women ringing in his ears.

Colly watched him run toward the river, and she tossed aside the stick of firewood. Hurrying inside, she knelt beside Black Moon. Red Bead Woman had bound up the deep cuts on her legs and arms, but nothing could be done about the puffy bruises on her face. One eye was already swollen shut and a deep cut distorted her pretty mouth.

"Thank you," Black Moon whispered to Colly.

"He'll never do that to you again," Colly said.

Red Bead Woman said nothing, but her eyes spoke of her gratitude. Black Moon's sobs quieted and at last she fell asleep.

Thoughtfully Colly rose and went outside. Since Black Moon's marriage, Gentle Horse had joined one of the other bands. Colly knew they were camped farther along the river. Taking one of the horses always kept hobbled near the lodge, she rode along the riverbank until she came to the camp of the Omisis band. An old man came to greet her.

"I am looking for the lodge of Gentle Horse," she called. The old man pointed out the way.

When she stood before Gentle Horse's tepee, she hesitated, not certain of what she meant to ask of him. He'd heard her approach and now he came to greet her.

"Welcome, Spotted Woman," he said. "I have heard of your marriage to Lone Wolf."

"It is not for Lone Wolf I have come," Colly began, and, taking a deep breath, related all that had happened to Black Moon since his departure from the band.

"I will kill Little Bear," Gentle Horse said. His expression was so ferocious, Colly wondered how he'd ever earned his name.

"Killing Little Bear isn't the solution," she said.

With an effort the warrior brought his anger under control. His dark eyes studied Colly. "Thank you for bringing me this news of Black Moon," he said quietly. "Go back to your lodge now and do not worry. Little Bear will never harm her again."

"You can't kill him," Colly insisted, but knew her pleas fell on deaf ears. Gentle Horse strode away from her, and, catching up the reins of his horse, mounted and spurred it to a fast gallop.

"Gentle Horse," Colly called, leaping astride her horse and going after the warrior, but Gentle Horse was soon lost to sight. Dismayed at what damage she may have caused by her good intentions, Colly turned her pony homeward.

Should she tell Lone Wolf? she wondered. But Lone Wolf and the men did not return to the camp that night. The women knew they must not have found game and so had camped out in the hills. Finally, unable to bear the suspense, Colly told Red Bead Woman what she had done.

"You can't stop what is to be." Red Bead Woman replied with such serenity that Colly wondered if she wanted Gentle Horse to kill Little Bear.

She sat by the campfire long after Red Bead Woman had gone to her bed, pondering over events until she fell asleep by the fire. A noise caused her to jerk awake. She sat up and looked around. Shadows shifted at the back of the lodge.

"Little Bear!" Colly cried, grabbing up a stick of firewood and preparing to protect Black Moon.

"Spotted Woman, it is I, Gentle Horse," a voice called softly.

"Gentle Horse?" Colly repeated warily. "Step forward and show yourself."

The dark shadows moved and Gentle Horse stepped into the dwindling firelight. There was a movement at his side and Black Moon showed herself.

"Black Moon, what are you doing out here?" Colly whispered.

The young girl shivered in the evening air and pulled a robe tighter about herself. "I'm running away with Gentle Horse," she said, and her bruised face lit with happiness as she gazed at the tall warrior.

"Where will you go?" Colly asked, going to take Black Moon's hands.

"My tribe is moving to its winter camp tomorrow. We'll travel ahead of them until we are well away, then join the others," Gentle Horse explained. His arm lay about Black Moon's small shoulders protectively.

"Go with care, my friends," Colly said, hugging Black Moon.

"You've been a good friend, my sister-in-law," Black Moon said. "Perhaps I will see you again one day."

"In the spring," Colly answered, gripping her hands tightly.

They exchanged a final hug, and Colly stepped back. Gentle Horse and Black Moon disappeared into the shadows. Colly stood for a long time, listening for any sign of discovery, but the camp was silent. Had she done right in letting Gentle Horse and Black Moon leave? She missed Lone Wolf and wished he were here. Slowly she doused the campfire and entered the lodge. Red Bead Woman sat beside the fire pit, feeding knots of grass to a small fire.

"They are gone?" she asked.

"Yes," Colly answered.

"No one tried to stop them?"

"No one."

"This is good," Red Bead Woman said, and rolled herself into her bed robes. Colly knew they would never speak of this night again, but she feared now for Lone Wolf's response when he learned what had happened.

"Will Black Moon's running away bring dishonor to Lone Wolf now?" she asked.

Red Bead Woman sighed. "Black Moon did as her brother commanded. Little Bear beat her many times. The dishonor is on Little Bear."

When Lone Wolf and the other men returned the following afternoon, Little Bear met them outside the village and lodged loud and long complaints concerning the conduct of Lone Wolf's wife and sister. He demanded Black Moon return to her own lodge and insisted on following Lone Wolf to his tepee. Colly was seated outside the lodge when the men rode up. Lone Wolf looked down at his wife and noticed the nervous shift of her eyes did not match the serene expression she wore.

"Little Bear has said you beat him with a stick of firewood," he said, pulling his brows into a fierce scowl to hide his laughter.

"Yes, my husband, I did," Colly answered. Lone Wolf was amused by her attempt at meekness.

"He has complained that you caused him to injure himself in our campfire."

"That is true, my husband."

"He says that you encouraged his wife to stay away from his tepee and her wifely duties."

"Is it a wife's duty to endure her husband's beatings?" Colly flared, then composed herself.

"We will speak of this when we are alone," Lone Wolf said, with mock sternness. "Now Little Bear has come to claim his wife."

"She's not here." Colly couldn't contain a triumphant glance at the disgruntled warrior who had so abused his wife. Little Bear's face puffed up with rage.

"That is a lie. She's inside," he cried.

Lone Wolf drew himself up and faced his brother-in-law. "You dishonor me when you call my wife a liar," he said.

Little Bear's anger dwindled somewhat when he realized he'd given offense to Lone Wolf. Although he was envious of his friend, he also feared him. "I wish only to have my wife back," he answered sullenly.

"She is not here," Colly repeated firmly. "You may step inside and see for yourself if you wish."

Little Bear slid off his pony and stalked to the lodge. At first all was silent; then a bellow of rage could be heard and the crashing of belongings. Quickly Lone Wolf dismounted and entered the lodge. Almost immediately Little Bear was propelled outward. He stumbled backward across the ground and fell ignominiously on his backside. Lone Wolf was right behind him.

"Your manners are very bad, Little Bear. You do not honor a man's lodge."

"I honor your lodge as your sister has honored mine," Little Bear sneered. Rolling to his feet, he drew his knife, brandishing it menacingly. Lone Wolf crouched, his hands held up in a defensive position, his eyes cold and hard as he watched Little Bear.

"Little Bear!" Chief White Thunder stalked forward. "Put away your knife. You have no enemies here. Your wife has run away with another man. You should take it with better grace than this."

"Gentle Horse," Little Bear snarled. "I will find him and kill them both."

"Why don't you leave them alone? Haven't you brought her enough misery?" Colly cried.

Little Bear fixed her with a cold eye. "I will remember that you have helped them," he said. "You are also my enemy."

"Then I am also your enemy," Lone Wolf replied.

A flicker of fear passed over Little Bear's eyes and he backed away. Casting a last baleful glance over his shoulder, he mounted his horse and galloped away.

"Have care, Lone Wolf and Spotted Woman," White Thunder warned. "Little Bear has become a bad Indian."

"Thank you for your help," Colly said before Lone Wolf's tight grip on her arm propelled her into their lodge.

Bedding and cooking pots were strewn everywhere from Little Bear's rampage. Colly knelt and began tidying the lodge. She knew Lone Wolf was angry with her, but she wasn't sure why. He stood glaring down at her, his face in shadows, his eyes impatient.

"I'm glad you've returned," she said by way of making a peace gesture.

"It is good I returned when I did," he answered shortly. "Otherwise my wife might have needed to battle Little Bear alone."

"I did it once. I'm sure I could have bested him again," she replied.

Lone Wolf knelt beside her then, taking the cooking pots and robes from her hands and grasping her shoulders. "Do not dismiss Little Bear too easily," he warned. "He is filled with rage and he never forgives a slight. You have ridiculed him before the village of women and helped his wife run away.''

''But that is not the Cheyenne way,'' Colly pointed out. ''Cheyenne men treat their wives as equals. Why could Little Bear not do the same with Black Moon? He deserved to have her run away. And you . . . You should have helped her. You are her brother.''

The accusation hung between them, and Lone Wolf wondered if she'd ever understand the subtleties of their culture. He'd been bound by unspoken customs of their people not to interfere. Secretly he was glad Spotted Woman had fought off Little Bear and was happy Black Moon had escaped her abusive husband, but he feared now what retribution Little Bear might mete out to the firebrand, Spotted Woman.

Nothing more was heard from Little Bear for several days, and Colly guessed he was trying to track down Black Moon. She worried obsessively until Little Bear returned empty-handed. Colly was made all too aware of his arrival and his anger. One afternoon, as she sat tanning the hide from a doe Lone Wolf had brought in, she looked up to see Little Bear seated on his horse staring at her. His gaze was so hate-filled, she blanched and dropped her scraping tool.

When Lone Wolf returned to the lodge that evening, he told how Little Bear had tried to track Gentle Horse and Black Moon, but the Omisis band had traveled to their winter camp and the trail had been obliterated by their passage. Colly felt relief flood through her.

''Thank God. He can't harm them now.''

''Be careful, Spotted Woman,'' Lone Wolf said that night when they lay snuggled in their bed robes. ''His anger burns brighter now than before and he has no other target but you.''

''I'll be careful,'' Colly whispered, remembering the way Little Bear had glared at her earlier.

A few mornings later, when the air was crisp with cold and an icy vapor hung over the river, the crier made his rounds, informing all to strike their tepees. They would begin their final journey back to their winter camp.

"Where is the winter camp?" Colly asked as she and Red Bead Woman began disassembling the lodge.

"It is high in the foothills," Red Bead Woman answered, "where the trees grow tall and the air is pure. There is plenty of wood and much game—deer and antelope and elk. Life is good there." She stopped talking abruptly and gazed off to the north. Colly crossed to her at once and put a hand on her arm.

"Life will be good for Black Moon, too," she said softly. "Gentle Horse will care for her and protect her. He loves her very much. She is happy with him."

Mutely Red Bead Woman nodded. In silence they continued breaking camp.

The journey to the winter camp took two days. Little Bear often made his presence known to Colly and always when Lone Wolf was scouting ahead on the trail. Colly tried not to be intimidated by him, but she was growing uneasy.

They traveled high into the hills, where rocky bluffs rose majestically and tall pine trees soared to regal heights. The piercing cry of the eagle and the sighing rush of the wind through the pines were like a hymn to Colly. She'd never seen such beauty. Her hatred of the prairie was left behind her in a newfound love of the hills rising in black silhouettes in the blue-misted distance and the shaded, scented, sun-heated valleys through which they traveled. It seemed they'd reached the loveliest valley of all, deep within those hills, when they halted and word traveled along the caravan that here would be the place of their winter camp.

Immediately the women began to set up their lodges. This time thin hide liners were added, hanging about halfway up from the poles and falling to the ground with a generous enough allowance to tuck under the bed pads. They used rocks to weight down the outside of the lodge. Any air that penetrated the skins would flow upward, thus providing a draft for the fire without pouring cold air onto the inhabitants. When they were finished, the lodge was surprisingly snug against the coming winter winds. Colly was impressed by the simple ingenuity of the Cheyenne.

The rectangular fire pit was dug in the center of the lodge and the smoke flaps adjusted against prevailing winds.

"Come," Lone Wolf said, catching her hand. "Your work is finished for a while. I have something to show you."

"I should stay and help Red Bead Woman," Colly protested halfheartedly. Lone Wolf smiled at her.

"Stay, if that is what you wish to do." His eyes danced with mischievous lights, and Colly laughed and called to her mother-in-law.

"I am going with Lone Wolf for a while. Why don't you rest until I return?"

"Go, go," Red Bead Woman said, waving at them. "I will warm myself beside the fire."

"Will you be all right?"

"I am well," Red Bead Woman answered, but Colly noted the spirit had gone out of her. She'd been despondent ever since Black Moon ran away with Gentle Horse. Although Lone Wolf waited outside the tepee with their horses, she couldn't walk away without making some attempt to cheer Red Bead Woman.

"Nah koa," she said, kneeling beside her. Red Bead Woman's head came up at the intimate address. "May I call you mother?" Colly asked quickly.

Red Bead Woman nodded sadly. "I have no other daughter now that Black Moon has gone."

"Could I not be your daughter as well?" Colly asked. "I won't try to take Black Moon's place, for I know she'll return someday. But my mother was killed on the Oregon Trail and I have no one, either."

Red Bead Woman's eyes held hesitation as she met Colly's gaze. "You do not hold anger for me because I cast you out of our lodge before your marriage to Lone Wolf?" she asked piteously.

Colly threw her arms around Red Bead Woman. Two

chubby brown arms returned the embrace. "Is that what you thought?" Colly drew back to peer into her face. "I thought you disapproved of me as your daughter-in-law because I'm white."

Red Bead Woman sat silent for a long moment, then raised her head. A tiny smile quivered at the corners of her mouth. "You are not all white," she said impudently. "You have lovely spots."

Colly laughed with her.

"Your heart is good and kind and brave," Red Bead Woman went on. "You work very hard. I am lucky to have so good a daughter."

"Thank you, *nah koa*," Colly said. "I shall call you mother from now on."

The sound of Lone Wolf's war horse, Taro, stamping impatiently, reminded them that Lone Wolf waited—and probably with as much impatience as his horse.

"I will return soon," Colly said, rising and waving good-bye.

Watching his wife's luminous face, Lone Wolf wondered what had given her such a happy glow and decided he'd done right to invite her to go for a ride.

He led her high into the hills, stopping now and then to point out a bright golden thicket of paper birch and mountain maple. He cut away from the path and entered the dark serenity of a white pine forest. Their passage was muffled by the spongy needles padding the forest floor, barren of grass here, which could not grow in the deep shade. They rode past a beaver stream, where the aspens along the banks had been cut by the animals' sharp incisors to build their dams and houses. Their passing caused a frenzy of tail slapping as the furry creatures sounded an alarm; then all was silent as they rode on. Farther along a young bull moose fed on water plants, raising his head to stare at them curiously before continuing his feeding.

Colly was aware of the roar of water long before they reached the fall. They guided their horses up a last rocky slope and sat staring at the plunging white water as it poured over a ledge and fell to a hollowed-out basin below before racing away over stones and rapids.

But Lone Wolf did not pause until he'd led her along a high ledge above the waterfall. There, hidden by bushes and gold-leaved mountain maples, was a small cave leading back into the mountains.

"It's so dark," Colly said when they'd dismounted and stood peering inside.

"There's nothing to harm you," Lone Wolf reassured her, and, taking her hand, pulled her inside to explore. They peered around the rocky walls carved out by some ancient stream that had long since dried up, for the floor of the cave was covered with silt and sand. Finally they returned to the ledge and stood gazing out over the narrow valley and stream.

"It's beautiful," Colly said breathlessly. Her eyes shone when she turned to Lone Wolf. "Thank you for bringing me here."

"You are happy here in the mountains?"

"Who would not be happy in such a beautiful place?" she replied.

"You do not like the prairie?"

"No." Colly took a deep breath. "The prairie holds only death."

"It also brings life to the Cheyenne, for it is on the prairie that the great buffalo come. You must learn not to fear it."

Colly was touched by his perception. She held out a hand and took his. "I will never be afraid if you are at my side," she answered.

His kiss was deep and slow, and she knew he had brought her to this place so they might be alone. He led her to the edge of the waterfall and spread a robe on the grassy bank. Seating himself, he pulled her down beside him. His kiss was passionate, his stroking hands gentle yet demanding. Colly gave herself to his touch, shivering as he awakened those special feelings only he could bring to life. They made love slowly, wonderingly, sometimes barely moving, yet feeling each throb, each shudder of the other's body more keenly than ever before. Her heartbeat thundered in her ears, shutting out the roar of the waterfall, and when Lone Wolf plunged against her and stiffened, she was beside him in their ultimate triumph. Only after a very long time was she able to hear the waterfall again.

Hi ko mini, the time of the Freezing Moon, had arrived. The mountain maples and aspen lost their golden leaves and reached barren arms beseechingly to the winter sky. Snow fell on the distant peaks and dusted the skin lodges, but all within were snug and warm. Geese and trumpeting swans winged southward in a steady stream. And then the first real snow fell on the valley.

Lone Wolf roused Colly from her warm robes and forced her to go out into the crystalline air. The snow lay all feathery and fragile along the tree branches. All around the camp, people had come out of their lodges to marvel at the pristine beauty. Their voices rang out gaily and the children raced through snowdrifts, scattering the mounds hither and yon until their mothers called them back to their lodges.

Colly gathered a handful and threw it in Lone Wolf's face. His shout and warning growl sent her scurrying. His long arms caught her without any trouble and he bore her to the ground, where he rubbed her face in the cold, wet accumulation.

"This is *qali* snow," he said, gathering a handful and holding it out to her. Colly could see the fragile hoarfrost crystals. "It's very heavy and will make the trees bend and break." Colly didn't believe him, but when the days passed and the delicate flakes added their wet burden to the young saplings, she found that Lone Wolf had told her the truth.

The men stayed in camp more now, sitting around their campfires, smoking and gossiping. Some worked on their weapons. The arrow maker was kept busy smoothing and straightening shoots of red willow or rosebush within his grooved sandstone slabs. Seated beside the fire in the evening, Lone Wolf answered Colly's questions about his weapons.

"The deep grooves on either side of the arrow shaft permit the blood to escape so the animal will weaken."

"What are the zigzag lines?"

"They represent lightning. The arrows are stronger and will kill the animal."

"Why are there feathers on one end?"

"To influence the flight of the arrow."

"Why do you use turkey feathers when you use eagle feathers for everything else?"

"Turkey feathers are not damaged by wetting with blood. Eagle feathers are."

"Will you teach me to shoot?"

"If you wish."

"Where are you going?"

"To the lodge of White Thunder. He does not ask so many questions."

Colly knew the men sat listening to the old ones discuss past events of war and great journeys to distant places and tribes. Growing boys would creep inside the lodges and sit along the wall behind the old men so they might listen and learn.

She had never known such happiness. Her estrangement with Red Bead Woman had ended. Black Moon was safe and happy with Gentle Horse—Colly was certain of that—and she was wonderfully in love with her husband. Even the sneering presence of Little Bear ceased to irritate her. She grew complacent. She grew careless.

Chapter 11

"SPOTTED WOMAN, ARE you going to gather wood today?" a voice called from outside the lodge. Colly poked her head out the flap to find Burning Star, a young woman who had been Black Moon's friend. Since the day she'd defended her sister-in-law against Little Bear, Colly was often sought out by the other young women. She was grateful for their friendships, for she missed Black Moon.

"Red Bead Woman and I will join you," she called, and withdrew back into the tepee to pull on warm leggings and lace up grass-lined moccasins. Last she drew on a new robe Red Bead Woman had made for her. It was thick and warm and decorated with quills and paint. Red Bead Woman was similarly engaged, taking extra care to don warm clothing. Since the first snows, the winter winds had grown cold and cutting and the campfires burned greedily, requiring more wood.

"We must stop at Magpie's lodge," Red Bead Woman called as they paused outside the lodge to collect their horses. The passes had not yet filled with snow, so the horses could still be used. The two women made their way around the village circle until they reached Magpie's lodge.

"Come out, Magpie," Red Bead Woman called. "We must go gather wood before the blizzards come."

Magpie poked her head outside the door and stared at

them. Her once lively eyes were dull, and her skin hung on her tall frame. She still grieved from the death of her husband and had become morose.

"I have enough wood," she said. "I will stay here today."

Colly nodded at the pitifully inadequate pile of wood outside the tepee. She dismounted and brought the reins of her packhorse to Magpie. "Will you come help us then? We have need of wood. You may ride our packhorse."

Magpie searched Colly's beseeching face and finally nodded. "If you need me," she replied hesitantly. Throwing a robe about her shoulders, she climbed astride the placid packhorse. Her eyes seemed a little brighter as she watched Colly mount and settle the thick, richly decorated robe around her shoulders.

"You have become a woman of means, daughter," she said. "Your robe is very fine."

"It is a gift from Red Bead Woman," Colly replied. "It is of great value to me." She ceased speaking as she noticed Little Bear ride by. As always, his dark eyes were filled with hatred. Colly wheeled her pony sharply and led the way to the village entrance, where the other women were gathered.

"The men have been gone overly long at their hunt," Magpie commented as they rode along.

"All save Little Bear," Colly said bitterly. "He and his friends do nothing to help feed the village, only sit by their campfires drinking the bad whiskey they get from passing traders."

"They claim they are left behind to protect the village," Burning Star said.

"*Pah!* They are too drunk to protect anyone," Red Bead Woman said briskly. "They are parasites."

Colly had remained silent after her first lament. She was gratified to hear that others found Little Bear as objectionable as she did. They rode far along the mountain tracks, leaving the main trail to search amid the dense thickets and ranks of majestic red pines. The wind had risen on the high ledges, screaming over the rocky tors, swirling the thin snow in small eddies at their feet. But here beneath the towering trees, the wind was held at bay. All was silent, and in the smooth patches of snow lay tracings of a snowshoe hare's passing and the deeper, longer, striding hoofprints of a moose. Farther on they caught the milling tracks of a wolf pack.

"This is far enough," Red Bead Woman called, casting a quick glance at the sky. Ominous black clouds had blown over the distant peaks to the west. "A blizzard is coming. We must be quick."

The women scrambled from their horses and began gathering the dead wood that lay beneath the trees. Some climbed into the lower branches to tug down dead limbs caught there. Colly worked beside Magpie and Red Bead Woman, tying the heavy limbs to a travois. The heavy clouds were directly overhead now. Large fluffy flakes drifted down, swiftly coating their shoulders and their mounts' flanks. Wearied by her labors, Magpie sagged against her horse. Gripping the stirrups to remain upright, she shivered with a sudden chill.

"Magpie, you are ill," Red Bead Woman cried, coming to help her old friend.

"It is nothing," the shaking woman answered, but her lips were blue with cold, her eyes bright and feverish.

"Take this," Colly said, shrugging off the heavy, brightly patterned robe Red Bead Woman had given her.

"You will be c-cold," Magpie protested, but Colly fastened the robe high around her, forming a hood over her bent head.

"But what of you?" Magpie gasped.

Colly drew out the blanket that Lone Wolf had once used in his courting of her. "I will use this," she said, drawing the thin, striped woolen blanket around her shoulders and head, forming a hood much as she had formed for Magpie, with only her eyes showing. "It's warm enough!" She gave the ill woman an encouraging grin.

The other women had already mounted and formed a line down the mountain path. Colly and Red Bead Woman got Magpie on her horse. Then, mounting themselves, they fell in at the rear of the line. The heavy snowfall was already filling in the path they'd made earlier. The wet flakes fell thick and silent and ominous. A *qali* snow, Colly thought, remembering what Lone Wolf had told her. The weight of it could bend and break a sapling in no time. Trails could become impassable, passes filled and lost. The women moved ahead steadily, knowing to tarry was deadly. Colly cast a glance over her shoulder at Red Bead Woman, who tugged on Magpie's horse. They had fallen behind and could barely be seen through the thickly falling snow.

"Red Bead Woman," Colly called, and pulled her horse to a stop to wait for them.

There was a scurry of hooves against the packed snow and the high-pitched cry of a spooked horse.

"Magpie!" Red Bead Woman cried. Turning her horse on the narrow trail, Colly rode back to them.

"What is it?" she called. Her voice seemed muffled and weak in the dense silence of the snowy hills.

"Magpie's horse spooked and ran back up the trail," Red Bead Woman called. "I'll have to go after her."

Colly heard the fatigue in her voice. "It's too narrow to turn your horse here. I'll go after Magpie. Try to catch up to the other women and tell them to wait for us."

Red Bead Woman nodded and prodded her horse down the trail. She intended to tell the women to wait and to return to help find Magpie.

Colly rode back up the trail, urging her recalcitrant horse forward.

"Magpie!" she called, but there was no answer. The deep prints of her horse were quickly filling. Colly kicked her moccasined heels against her horse's belly. He balked, made nervous by the heavy snowdrifts. Up ahead a horse screamed in pain; then the trail was silent.

"Magpie!" Colly screamed, and was answered by the silent falling snow. She pushed her horse forward up the trail, searching along the edge of the path for any sign of a horse having slid off the narrow ledge, then tumbling down the wooded slopes.

"Magpie!" she called again and again.

She found the horse at the edge of the trail, floundering helplessly in a bloodstained snowdrift, his eyes rolled in fear and pain. Colly paid it no attention, for her quick eye had picked out a familiar brightly painted robe.

"Magpie, are you all right?" she called, sliding off her own horse and plowing a path down the slope to the still mound. "Magpie, speak to me. Tell me you're all right."

Colly rolled the mound over and drew back, gasping with horror. Magpie's head was bashed in on one side, blood and hair matting the ugly wound. A bloody rock lay nearby.

"Magpie," she whispered, and the woman's eyelashes fluttered briefly against her sickly white face. Colly raised Magpie's head, cradling her shoulders against her chest. The lips worked soundlessly.

"Don't try to talk. Red Bead Woman and the others will be here soon. We'll take you back to the village and you'll be warm . . . and the medicine man will tend your wound." She knew she was babbling. She patted Magpie's cheeks as one would to soothe a sick child, and all the while she heard the death gurgle.

"M-Ma . . ." Magpie mumbled.

"What did you say? I didn't hear you," Colly said, holding her ear closer to the woman's lips.

"B-Bear-r-r . . ." Magpie whispered, her life leaving her in one long, sighing breath.

"Magpie?" Colly whispered, unable to believe the once vibrant woman was forever silenced. But Magpie's features had gone rigid and her black eyes gazed at the pale sky, unblinking against the snowflakes that fell into them.

Gently Colly brushed the snow from the old woman's face and closed the sightless eyes. She couldn't bear to leave her here in the snow, so she sat rocking her, thinking of all the things that had gone into making Magpie the woman she was.

Magpie's body grew stiff, and Colly was aware the rigidity was not caused by death alone. Magpie's body was already freezing. The cold, wet snow had surrounded them, half burying their legs, so Colly had to struggle to pull herself free of its clutches. Standing, she was more aware of the cold, aware that she, too, could freeze if she didn't do something.

The thin courting blanket wasn't heavy enough. She looked around for shelter, but there was none—and no sign of Red Bead Woman or any of the other women on the path above. Perhaps they had decided not to wait for her. To do so would put their lives in jeopardy as well. She accepted this thought without rancor. She understood it was the way adopted if one was to survive here in this harsh, unforgiving land. Still, she couldn't allow herself to die without trying to live.

Much as she hated to disturb her old friend in death, she knew she must recover the robe. It was thick and warm and would go a long way in protecting her. With some difficulty, she worked it free from Magpie's stiff form. With the thick buffalo pelt around her shoulders, she struggled back up the embankment to the trail. Her horse waited against a rocky ledge, his head hanging, his reins looping on the ground. The snow had accumulated to a level near his knees. The poor horse was nearly helpless.

Magpie's horse had fallen silent, its lifeblood seeping into the snow. Magpie had gasped out a warning about a bear before dying. A bear must have torn the bloody gash in the horse's throat. Magpie had been thrown clear, escaping the tearing claws only to suffer a fatal blow to her head from the rock below.

Colly peered around, trying to penetrate the thick curtain of snow. There was no sight or sound of a bear waiting to attack her. Yet the silence was eerie, making her uneasy. The real danger was from the blizzard, she thought, scoffing at her fancifulness.

Wading through the snow, she caught her mount's reins, and, leading him against the rocky overhang, guided him to his knees. When the horse was lying down, she crawled between it and the ledge, burrowing down in the snow. Using the robe she'd taken from Magpie, she spread it over herself, forming a roof of sorts against the falling snow. The wet snow beneath chilled her to the bone, but she soon became immune to it, concentrating on the warmth of the pony and the protection of the robe overhead.

She would survive, she thought fiercely. She would survive and return to Lone Wolf's lodge, and lie in their bed feeling the warmth and strength of his body next to hers, feeling the passion and wonder of their love. She would survive!

She thought of Red Bead Woman. Had she gone ahead with the women or was she even now out there on the trail searching for her? Colly hoped not. It would do no good for both of them to die. She thought of Lone Wolf, of the grief he would endure if both his mother and his wife died. "I hope you are safe, Red Bead Woman," she whispered, then set to worrying about her husband.

The hunters had not returned before the women had set out to find wood. How could she know that even now he wasn't frozen and lifeless somewhere? Her thoughts became more torturous than any discomfort she endured from the cold. The hours passed slowly. She half dozed in her cold bed and lost track of time and place, living in her daydreams of happier times, short as they were, with her husband.

She remembered every moment between Lone Wolf and her, from the first moment they met until he kissed her goodbye for his last hunting trip. She chuckled, remembering how fierce he'd seemed, how frightened she'd been, how she'd fought him and finally come to trust him. She thought of his face the night he gave her the comb, of his hands smoothing over her breasts and thighs as he washed away the blood at the buffalo hunt, and of his long, sinewy body looming over hers in the privacy of their honeymoon lodge as he taught her the joy of becoming a woman loved.

Her robe was heavy with the weight of snow. Her icy grave

was dark. She lay as still as death, her mind floating away from the pain of her body. Dusk fell over the land, but she neither knew nor cared. In her feverish dreams, she heard her name called from a great distance and she struggled to answer, yet something kept her earthbound. The warmth of the horse bore against her back, ensnaring her, anchoring her to the Mother Earth so she couldn't float free to the Father Sky.

Lone Wolf was like a madman. Time and again he drove Taro up the steep path, urging the uncomplaining horse forward. With great heart the beast struggled to obey his master's command, but finally even stamina and heart were overcome by the deep, drifting snow.

Red Bead Woman waited in the village below, dragged there by the other women, who wouldn't leave her to wait on the trail alone. So she'd returned, resisting and weeping, only to find Lone Wolf had returned from his hunting trip. She'd told him that Spotted Woman and Magpie were lost in the mountains in the blizzard.

His face had been terrible, bleak and stark, his fists clenching and unclenching. He'd gone out before the blizzard abated, disappearing in the white, swirling mists like some ghostly wraith. He'd gone looking for a woman such as he'd never known before. His mind told him she was dead, but his heart denied it to his last breath, his last ounce of strength.

He blazed a path through the heavy snow, pushing forward until his pulse pounded in his ears and his chest hurt with the effort of drawing a breath of the icy, vaporous air. Up the mountain path he pushed, calling her name. The others followed, wanting to help yet knowing it was useless. This was not the first time the great snows had snatched a life. Now there were two, perhaps three, if the war chief did not stop his madness and give up.

White Thunder sent one of the younger councilmen up the mountain trail with a message that he must give up and return to the village, but Lone Wolf ignored his chief's admonition.

Spotted Woman was up there somewhere in the mountains, perhaps even now struggling to live, believing he would come for her. He couldn't seek the warmth of the lodge fire knowing she was cold and lost. So he struggled on, and the warriors and hunters who were his friends formed a human chain from the village high up the mountain path, with their rawhide ropes linking them together against the blinding snow. Somewhere up ahead a man struggled against the forces of the Mother Earth to save one woman. Yet each of them knew this was no ordinary woman, just as Lone Wolf was no ordinary warrior. Dull Knife's vision had revealed this white woman was part of their destinies. Remembering this, they, too, made the effort to save her.

"How do you know this was a Cheyenne camp?" Major Buford demanded of his Indian guide. His pale blue eyes were derisive, his bearing haughty as always.

Stone Calf did not like this white officer. He saw the contempt in the major's face for the red men. He'd heard the stories about the way he treated Indian women and he recognized the lies against his Cheyenne brethren. He'd tried to tell someone at the fort the truth of who provoked the attack with the Cheyenne warriors, but no one would listen.

"Boy, are you calling your superior officer a liar?" one young officer had declared, and Stone Calf had backed away, knowing to pursue this would only bring retribution down on his own head. So now he'd led the white soldiers to this place by the river, and with each mile he'd felt the weight of his betrayal of his father's people.

Stone Calf had been conceived by a warring Cheyenne renegade and a captive white woman who had survived the rigors of her captivity only long enough to give birth to a son. The moment she'd seen his broad-featured face and the coal black hair and dark eyes, she'd turned away from him as if he'd been the spawn of the devil himself. In the days that followed she'd willed herself to die and so she did, her body left somewhere on the prairie. Her son had been left with a band of Cheyenne who'd adopted him.

But Stone Calf had known he didn't belong with them, and when his father had come for him, he'd willingly left the village and followed his father's renegade band. In his youth he'd stood outside post gates, begging for whiskey for his father. When he grew hungry, he'd done odd jobs for the white men. He'd earned his place among them as a guide, but he'd never felt any particular kinship for them. They couldn't accept the half of him that was Indian, and he couldn't forgive the half of himself that was white, so he was caught between two worlds, trying to find a place where he fit. He did not fit in with this white officer with the curling lip and contemptuous gaze.

"Well, great Indian tracker. How do you know this was a Cheyenne campsite?"

Stone Calf waited before answering, gauging that moment when his silence conveyed just the right amount of insolence without bringing wrath down on his head. When he felt Major Buford's anger was on the point of boiling over, he raised a hand and pointed to the circle of fire pits.

"See the opening to the east? This is the way of the Cheyenne." He got off his horse and walked to one of the fire pits. "See the four corners of the fire bowl? This is also the way of the Cheyenne."

He sprang back into his saddle and sat stoically waiting for the major's next command. There was a glimmer of triumph in his eyes, but then it was gone. His face was impassive.

Major Buford studied Stone Calf. He hated the smug Indian guide. He was well aware Stone Calf felt the same for him. One day, Buford had promised himself, he was going to get the half-breed off by himself and then they would see who was the superior one—this savage half-breed with the unreadable eyes or a graduate of West Point!

"Where do you think they've gone now?" he asked, turning his attention back to the elusive Cheyenne.

Stone Calf shrugged and remained silent.

"Would you tell me if you knew?" Buford snapped.

"Stone Calf has brought you here," the guide pointed out.

"But only after the Cheyenne left the site," Buford said. "How long were they here?"

"Sir, we found evidence of a garden back along the riverbank there," said Lieutenant McKinney. "Looks like they return to this spot often. We could set up an ambush for them in the spring when they come back here."

"I don't want to wait until spring," Buford snapped. He glanced at Stone Calf, whose gaze was pinned on the distant mountains. "They're up there somewhere, aren't they?" he demanded. The guide remained silent.

"We're going up there after them," Buford said.

"When, sir?" Lieutenant McKinney asked.

"Now!"

"There's a blizzard coming, sir." McKinney nodded to the sky. "We'd better take shelter somewhere. Here along the riverbank would be best."

"That storm's miles away, Lieutenant. We'll start out at once and camp at the foot of those hills there."

"I don't think we'll make it, sir. These storms travel faster than—"

"You have your orders, Lieutenant."

"Yes, sir." The young officer saluted smartly and guided his horse down along the straggly line of men.

Their faces looked cold and weary. He hated telling them they must go on. Much of McKinney's hero worship of his commanding officer had melted away. His sympathy lay with the enlisted men who must follow Major Buford's inept command.

"Fall in, men," he called. "We'll camp at the foot of those hills yonder."

The battalion set out halfheartedly. The wind rose, moaning along the flatland and whipping snow in the faces of their horses. The tired animals neighed and pranced nervously. When they were halfway to the foothills, the snow began to fall, and within minutes they'd lost sight of the distant line of mountains that had been their guide. They struggled on, the horses threshing through the fresh-fallen snow, falling to their knees time and again until they simply lay down and refused to move.

"Sir, the men and horses can't take this," Lieutenant McKinney shouted to the major.

"Tell them to keep going," came the major's reply. His jaw was set, his gaze feverishly determined.

"Sir, without good visibility we may be traveling in circles. It's best if we draw up the supply wagons and take shelter as best we can."

Major Buford seemed to take stock then and finally nodded. "Good thinking, Lieutenant. Order the men to halt and break out their tents."

"Yes, sir." The lieutenant saluted smartly and wheeled his horse to tell his men. The snow was so deep, his well-trained mount could barely plough through the drifting snow.

"Take shelter," he called. "Break out your tents and take shelter as best you can."

The men scurried to do as he ordered, bringing the two wagons forward and lining them side by side with a good distance between them for men to set up their tents. The wind fought their efforts, so some men simply rolled themselves in the canvas awnings and burrowed into the snow. The cook had arranged a place for Major Buford, who took no time to lighten his horse of its saddle. He dived under the supply wagon and pulled a canvas over himself, leaving only an opening around his face for him to peer out at the white wall of snow. God, how he hated this country. As soon as he'd punished the Cheyenne devils who'd attacked them, he would request a transfer back East. It all depended on his finding and punishing the Cheyenne. Soon, he thought. Soon. They were up there in the mountains and he meant to find them. Soon!

The wind had ceased its maddening scream of fury. The world beyond was silent, save for the distant call of an eagle.

The Indian pony whickered and stirred, kicking with his legs; then, feeling the thick and clinging blanket of snow that entrapped him, he lashed out blindly, floundering to his feet.

Colly felt the cold rush of air against her back, then pushed against the robe that covered her like a shroud. The snow was heavy and unyielding, and she, too, panicked, fearful of being buried alive. Her arms flailed against the restraining snow, pushing it aside, burrowing a path to the sunlight until, like the pony, she was free and stood shaking the snow from herself.

All around, the landscape had changed, sculpted and molded by the snow and wind. Only a slight mound showed where Magpie's horse lay, but the slope was smooth where the dead woman rested.

Colly turned away, contemplating the trail that she must travel to reach the village. There was no trace of their previous journey. She must find her way alone. The memory of her ordeal on the prairie returned to her, vivid and unnerving. She'd trusted the mountains, taken comfort in the towering peaks and scaly walls. Now she knew that death awaited the unwary traveler anywhere in this untamed land.

The prairie had not defeated her; the mountains would not, either. Lone Wolf would come to her as he did before. Taking strength from that thought, she dug out the buffalo robe, and, shaking it free of the snow and ice, fastened it around herself. Then, taking her snowshoes from her saddle, she fastened them on. At first she tried to bring the Indian pony with her, encouraging him to flounder down the trail, but the pony balked and finally lay down, unwilling to risk the danger of the deep snow. Worn out from her struggles with him, Colly took off the saddle and reins and left them alongside the trail. Without them the horse might survive and make his way back to the village in his own time.

Alone, she made her way down the trail, searching for any familiar landmark. Several times she backtracked, taking a different turn and praying all the while. Her legs grew numb from the weight of the snowshoes, but still she plowed on, fearful of spending another night in the mountains alone. Late in the afternoon, when the sun was but a pale shadow in the cloud-laden sky and the coldness crept around the rocky abutments and pine forests with the promise of more snow, she heard a sound that gave her renewed strength—a name floating on the cold air like a distant prayer.

"Lone Wolf?" she whispered. Despite the pain to her snow-blinded eyes, she tried to peer along the trail. "Lone Wolf!" she screamed. "I'm here!" Snow tore loose from a high overhead shelf and tumbled down the slope, pelting her in its passing. She threw herself down on the trail and buried her head until it had passed.

"Spotted Woman!" The cry came again, and she raised her head, her expression joyous. She dared not scream again and loosen more snow overhead. She struggled to her feet and fled down the path, half running, half sliding, laughing and crying.

"Spotted Woman!" Lone Wolf called.

She couldn't see him, but she felt his strong hands gripping her, pulling her against him. She felt the solid impact of his body and clamped her arms around his waist. He was real. He was life, and he'd found her again. She would never let him go.

Other warriors came to join them, but it was Lone Wolf who held her, who whispered gentle words in her ears, who gave her heart again. With her cold face pressed against his warm neck, she told him of Magpie and the bear. Some of the warriors set out at once to follow her trail before the snows fell and obliterated it. If that happened, Magpie would not be found until spring and wild animals would have scattered her remains. Lone Wolf guided Colly to a travois they'd brought, and, despite her protests, made her lie down on it. With Doll Man at one end and Lone Wolf at the other, they bore her down the trail to the village.

"*Aiee*, you've found her!" Red Bead Woman cried, running to meet them. Her eyes were red-rimmed, her face pale with dread as she looked at the figure on the stretcher. When she saw that Colly was alive, she threw up her hands, then embraced her daughter-in-law.

"Magpie is dead," Colly whispered. "I couldn't get to her in time to save her."

"What you have done was very brave, my daughter," Red Bead Woman answered. "You have brought much honor to our lodge."

Colly lay back against the travois while Red Bead Woman walked beside her, gripping her hand and crying out to all they met that her daughter-in-law was safe, and telling of her brave deed. By the time they reached Lone Wolf's lodge, even more stature had been added to the name of Spotted Woman.

Lone Wolf hovered around her as Red Bead Woman brought her hot tea made from the red leaf wood and a bowl of acorn mush mixed with a little bit of buffalo fat. Colly ate and drank and rested by the warm fire while feeling returned to her legs and feet and the pain in her snow-blinded eyes diminished. She slept and woke to eat and drink a little more, then slept again. When she woke a second time, the lodge was dark except for the flickering light from the fire pit; nestled snugly against her was Lone Wolf's long, sinewy body. Colly sighed with contentment and wrapped her arms and legs around his strong body. Her breathing grew deep and slow, so Lone Wolf knew she slept once more.

He lay beside her, unable to sleep, although his body was numb with fatigue. He'd nearly lost her out there in the mountains and his heart still beat with terror at the thought. He'd grieved when he lost Dawn Rising On A Hill, but he'd never felt like this, as if his own life had ceased as well. He was shaken by the depth of his feelings for this white woman. No matter what Dull Knife's vision had been, Lone Wolf thanked the gods for giving her to him. At last he slept, his head pressed against her small breasts, his mighty arms encircling her slender waist, his long, muscular legs imprisoned by her long, slender legs. They lay tangled as one, their breaths mingling, their hearts beating in unison.

Sometime in the night, Doll Man and the other warriors returned from the mountains. They brought with them Magpie's frozen body and news more troubling than her death itself. When Lone Wolf rose and sought out his friends, he was told what they'd found. His face grew grim and he sat for a long time thinking of all he'd heard. His heart was heavy with fear when he rose and walked back to his lodge.

His wife still slept. He stood over her pallet for a long time, staring at her sleeping face, and then he went away. He carried in his heart the memory of Red Bead Woman's words, that Spotted Woman had given Magpie her robe. Yet when they'd found his wife, she'd once again worn the robe. And what of the awful truth Doll Man had found on the trail? Magpie had been murdered—and no one had been there except his wife!

Chapter 12

COLLY WOKE TO bright sunlight streaming through the
smoke flaps. The tepee was warm and cozy from the
blazing fire. Red Bead Woman sat tending a bubbling pot of
elk meat and dried roots. The smell was tantalizing, and
Colly's stomach rumbled with the reminder that she'd eaten
little since her ordeal.

"That smells delicious," she said, sitting up and smiling
at Red Bead Woman. The Indian woman raised a bleak face
and stared at her.

"I will bring you food," she said solemnly, and, filling a
tortoiseshell bowl with a generous portion, she brought it to
Colly. Lone Wolf entered the lodge then and paused when
he saw she was sitting up.

"You are better?" he asked, crouching beside the fire.
His dark eyes were hooded as they met hers.

"Much better," Colly said warmly. "It is good to be back
here with you both. When I was caught in the blizzard, I
thought I would never see either of you again."

"I thought the same," Red Bead Woman replied, without
meeting Colly's gaze. "It is lucky you found Magpie and
were able to reclaim your robe."

"Without it I would have frozen to death," Colly answered, using a sharpened stick to pick at the bits of meat
and roots in the tortoiseshell bowl. But the memory of Mag-

pie lying in the snow took away her appetite and she set the bowl to one side.

"You do not like the food?" Red Bead Woman asked, her dark eyes studying Colly's face.

"I cannot eat, remembering how Magpie died there on the trail all alone. What terror she must have felt when that bear confronted her."

"Tell me about it," Lone Wolf said softly.

"When I got there, she was already hurt. Her horse was on the ground, bleeding from a large gash in its throat. Magpie had been thrown down an embankment. She lay so still, I thought she was dead. I could see that she'd hit her head against a rock. She lived only a few minutes, long enough to say two things to me. I couldn't hear the first words, but then she said the word 'bear' very clearly. That's how I knew a bear had killed her horse."

Colly pressed her hands over her face. "She must have been so frightened there all by herself. If only I'd gone along the trail faster, I might have scared the bear away. I could have done something to save her. She was so kind and good to me when I was a stranger here, always so cheerful and jolly until her husband was killed. It doesn't seem fair."

"How did you get your robe back?" Lone Wolf interrupted her lament of self-blame.

"I sat for a long time, just holding her. But then I saw the snow was growing worse and that I would never make it back to the village before dark. I knew I had to find shelter. I had only the courting blanket and it wasn't thick enough. I took the robe from Magpie's body and took shelter under a ledge with my horse. He's still up there somewhere, along with Magpie."

"Magpie was brought back to the village," Red Bead Woman said. "She was buried properly."

"Her spirit is at rest then," Colly said, taking some comfort in thinking the sad widow of Tall Man rested near her people.

"Magpie's spirit will roam the trails until her murderer is brought to justice," Red Bead Woman said stiffly.

"Murderer!" Colly gasped, her eyes going wide as she gazed from Lone Wolf to Red Bead Woman. The firelight played on their faces, revealing something she'd rather not have seen.

"You suspected me," Colly whispered, shaking her head.

"We know you did not kill Magpie," Lone Wolf said quickly. "You went back to save her."

"But you doubted me. For a moment you thought me capable of such a deed."

"Some thought you might have fought with Magpie to have your robe back," Lone Wolf said.

"Why would I?"

"So you wouldn't perish from the cold. You are a survivor, Spotted Woman."

"But not like that. Not at someone else's expense. Magpie was my friend. Why would you think she was murdered? Didn't you see her horse, how its throat was slashed?"

"We saw many things, Spotted Woman," Lone Wolf said softly. "A knife slashed the throat of the horse, not a bear's claws, and Magpie was not thrown against a rock. She was hit with it. The one who did this left his bloodied prints on the rock."

"No!" Colly sat rocking herself, choking back sobs of grief over Magpie's hapless fate. At last she raised her tear-streaked face. "Why didn't they kill me, too?" she asked. "I must have arrived soon after they struck her."

"Perhaps whoever it was didn't know you were alone," Red Bead Woman said.

"Why did Magpie tell me a bear had attacked her?"

"We do not know the answer to these things, but perhaps the council will. You must go before them as soon as you are well enough."

Colly jerked her head up. "Do I go before them accused of murder?"

"You must simply tell them as you have told us."

"Will my husband sit in judgment of me as well?" Colly asked bitterly. She flung aside the covers and stood up. She was still weak and her knees trembled dangerously, but she pulled her shoulders up sharply.

"Call the council. I am ready to speak to them," she said quietly.

Lone Wolf leaped to his feet and stood before her. "I do not believe you capable of such a deed," he said. For a moment she thought he meant to take her into his arms, but then he turned and left the lodge.

Colly bit back tears of despair and readied herself for the council meeting. When Doll Man summoned her, she was composed and held herself with great dignity. The villagers buzzed as she walked past, each of them speculating on whether she had murdered Magpie.

When she stood before White Thunder's lodge, she turned quickly and met the avid stares of people she'd once believed were her friends. Red Bead Woman's face was filled with sympathy; Burning Star and some of the other young women smiled encouragingly. They, at least, did not believe her guilty. Only a few looked away, uncertain of her innocence. Her chin tilted high, Colly turned and entered the lodge, automatically stepping to the right, as was the proper thing to do when entering someone's lodge.

"Come, my daughter," White Thunder said in his wavering voice, which still commanded authority. Colly stepped to the center of the lodge as he'd indicated. With her moccasined feet placed primly side by side she waited.

"Tell us, my daughter, of what happened in the mountain blizzard," White Thunder began, and Colly repeated her story, much as she'd told Lone Wolf and Red Bead Woman. Now and then one of the men on the council interrupted her to ask a question. Lone Wolf remained silent throughout, but she felt a warmth radiating from him. When all was done, Colly stood waiting. The men looked at one another.

"There was no evidence of our enemies, the Ute, killing our kinswoman?" one councilman asked.

"None!" White Thunder answered.

Dull Knife cleared his throat and spoke. All the council members listened to him carefully.

"Perhaps there are angry spirits at work here against the White Buffalo Woman," the old medicine man said. "Ever since my vision, which has brought her into our midst as Lone Wolf's wife, I have felt a wicked energy directed against her." Lone Wolf raised his head and looked at the old man. Colly stood listening to his words, wondering what Lone Wolf's taking her as a wife had to do with the medicine man's vision.

"The woman known as Spotted Woman wore a special robe made for her by her mother-in-law, Red Bead Woman. The robe is distinctive, so none could fail to recognize it as belonging to Spotted Woman. In the mountains she gave the robe to Magpie, who has no enemies, and Magpie was killed." He ceased speaking, letting the elders draw their own conclusions. Colly felt herself blanch. Dull Knife was saying she was the intended victim! But who? Little Bear!

"Perhaps Magpie wasn't saying a bear attacked her, but Little Bear—" Colly fell silent, aware she'd spoken out in council meeting when she shouldn't have. No one seemed to notice, for their thoughts were on the stark accusations made here.

White Thunder nodded to someone and a man stepped forward to take Colly's elbow and lead her from the lodge. Dazed, she stood in the sunlight, taking in all that had been revealed. Slowly she raised her head, her gaze sliding along the silent faces until she reached one. Her gaze was accusing, filled with anger. She was unaware she'd taken a step forward toward Little Bear until she saw the alarm in his eyes. He stumbled backward, then, regaining his balance, slipped away through the tepees. Through it all, his fierce gaze had never wavered from Colly.

She saw him go and longed to cry out for Lone Wolf, but the memory that Lone Wolf, too, had thought her capable of murder stilled her cry. She raced across the circle to the place where Little Bear's tepee sat. He was already astride his pony. Without pausing to think, Colly ran straight at him, her hands upraised to pull him from his saddle. Her hands settled beneath his rawhide shirt, grasping his arm. Her nails dug, tearing deep runnels through flesh and muscle.

Little Bear shook her off, and, whirling, directed his war pony straight at her. The pony's deep chest hit her a glancing blow, knocking her to the ground. Little Bear brought his horse around, forcing it to ride over her. Colly threw up her arm to protect her face and heard the thud of a hoof on the ground next to her.

"Little Bear!" Lone Wolf's rage-filled cry echoed across the valley like a mighty roll of thunder.

Little Bear whirled and saw the fury in the war chief's face. Fear filled his belly and he kicked at his horse, galloping away over the packed snow until he left the village and its trails behind. His horse plowed through snowdrifts, gasping with the effort. Little Bear peered over his shoulder and saw that Lone Wolf had mounted and was riding after him. Ignoring his horse's distress, Little Bear pushed him forward. They gained a trail into the mountains where the wind had blown the path clear, and he raced forward. Still Lone Wolf followed him.

High on the mountain trail, Taro's superior stamina carried Lone Wolf close enough to reach out and pull Little Bear from his saddle. Head over heels they rolled down a snow-covered embankment, coming to rest on a wide ledge.

Lone Wolf recovered first, leaping to his feet and aiming a blow at Little Bear's head. Little Bear fell backward; his cheek scraped against a jutting stone, tearing through muscles. Blood poured down his face. Drawing a weapon, he backed away, making no attempt to fight back. His eyes shifted from side to side, looking for a way to escape. When he saw an opening, he lashed out with his knife, barely missing Lone Wolf's chest. The two men grappled and rolled on the ground. The knife was knocked from Little Bear's hand and he reached for a rock, raising it high before bringing it down on Lone Wolf's head. The war chief lay still. Little Bear raised the rock again, preparing to kill Lone Wolf as he had killed Magpie.

An arrow ricocheted off the rock. Startled, Little Bear dropped the heavy rock and stared at the ledge above. Doll Man was poised with yet another arrow fitted to his bow. Leaping to one side, Little Bear scrambled down one side of the ledge, half falling, half crawling, until he gained the cover of a thicket.

Doll Man made no more effort to shoot the renegade. He and the other warriors climbed down to the ledge and lifted Lone Wolf's inert figure back up the slope to the trail. There they tied him to his horse and made their way back to the village.

The villagers were abuzz with the latest events. Little Bear's flight had only proven his guilt and cleared Colly's name. Lone Wolf was resting in his lodge, healing from the blow to his head.

The second morning after Little Bear fled, the villagers rose to find that his ponies and weapons had been taken during the night.

The warriors spread out, searching for any sign of the murderer, but Little Bear wasn't found. Three nights later, some of Little Bear's cronies left the village, and it was thought by older, wiser heads that the young hotheads had gone to join Little Bear. There was some worry that the band might bring trouble down on the heads of the Cheyenne by their lawless acts against the hated whites. The only consolation was that the winter snows would slow them down before they caused too much mischief.

In their lodge Lone Wolf and Spotted Woman seldom spoke. When he'd been brought to the tepee with a head injury, Colly had made herself another pallet so as not to disturb him. Now that he was better, she made no attempt to rejoin him. Lone Wolf knew she was hurt that he'd thought her capable of murdering Magpie, but he hadn't guessed how deep her pain went.

She'd remembered the puzzling words of the old medicine man about a vision, and after mulling them over for many hours, she'd turned to Red Bead Woman. Unaware that Spotted Woman hadn't known of the vision and might be offended by any part of it, Red Bead Woman had discussed it freely, telling of how Lone Wolf had courted and wed her as the vision directed. Colly felt betrayed. She'd thought he'd chosen her out of love, not because of some superstitious ramblings of an old medicine man. Silently she nursed her hurt until it grew beyond healing.

Red Bead Woman saw the estrangement between her son and his wife. "You must speak to her," she urged Lone Wolf. "This hurt will not go away by itself."

So Lone Wolf waited until he and Colly were alone in the tepee.

"It is time we talk," he said, lying on his pallet and regarding her with steady eyes. Colly had knelt to add wood to the fire. Now she rose and faced her husband.

"Yes, it is time," she said, and seated herself near him, her feet turned primly to the right side as all Cheyenne women sat.

"I was wrong to doubt you. Deep in my heart I knew you could not have murdered Magpie for the robe. But there is within each of us a darker side that might be capable of this deed, if it meant saving our own life."

"I can understand your moment of doubt," Colly answered calmly.

Lone Wolf studied her closed face, surprised at her words, perplexed at her aloofness. "Then why do you still feel anger toward me?"

Colly raised her gaze to meet his. "I thought you took me as your wife because you loved me. If you do not understand love as we white people mean, then I thought you found me pleasing. Instead I find you married me to fulfill a vision Dull Knife had. You married me to save your people from some evil fortune brought about by the killing of the white buffalo."

"That is so," Lone Wolf said. "I would not have married you if Dull Knife and the Council had not bidden me to do so. I would have sent you back to your people, because our worlds are too different. Even now we cannot be sure that we will remain together. What will happen when the white soldiers come to our village? Will you return with them?"

Colly stared at him, feeling the pain of his words go deep. "If you had loved me as I love you, you would have no need to feel these things. You would know I have made my choice. I won't change my mind."

"Are you certain?" His question was more a statement of disbelief.

Colly turned her face away from him, not wanting him to see the additional hurt his words caused. She'd thought they were special in their regard for each other. It pained her that he hadn't felt the same. She'd given up all hope of returning to her own people, knowing once she'd chosen the Cheyenne as her people, the white world would no longer accept her. She'd done so gladly, embracing his people, his culture, as her own. That he was unable to understand the magnitude of her selflessness hurt beyond words.

Taking her bedding, she retired to the women's lodge, for the time of her menses would soon be upon her. She was grateful for this excuse to leave Lone Wolf's lodge. Perhaps in the days to come she could sort out her feelings. When Lone Wolf discovered she had left his lodge, he grew angry, believing she'd left to defy him. Only Red Bead Woman's sage advice stayed him from approaching the women's hut and demanding her return.

He was frustrated. His words had not brought peace between them. The gulf seemed wider than before and he wondered what he might have said to bridge it. That they came from different worlds was a contributing factor, he had little doubt. Alone on his pallet, he remembered how openly she'd come to him on their honeymoon, how joyous her face when they'd laughed together. He wanted his wife back at his side.

He missed their closeness, but he didn't know how to overcome the barriers that had been erected between them.

In the women's hut, Colly waited for her cycle and was dismayed when no blood showed. Still she rested there, troubled by what this might mean and by the coldness between her husband and herself. After the customary four days, she returned to Lone Wolf's lodge, but she told no one her secret.

They'd lost two men to the blizzard. They'd been found sitting at their posts, guarding the horses, frozen in an upright position, their hands gripping their guns, their unblinking eyes gazing into the distance, their skin white, like ice on a pond. They had to build a fire and thaw them out to straighten their limbs and tie them in their canvas bedrolls. There was no place to bury them in the frozen flatland, so they tied them to their horses.

The supply wagons were caught in snowdrifts and no amount of labor could free them. Major Buford ordered the supplies loaded on packhorses.

"Sir, the men want to know if we're heading back to the fort," Sergeant Crook said. "They're in pretty bad shape, sir. Some of them have come near losing their toes and fingers."

"But they haven't!" Major Buford snapped. "We're going on, Sergeant. We're close to that Cheyenne Indian village. I feel it in my bones. We're going on."

Watching the major's face, his petty officers sometimes wondered if he'd lost his mind, been driven crazy by the prairie and the blizzard. It happened to some men out here. Grumbling among themselves, they pushed off, heading for the mountain slopes.

Lone Wolf grew restless long before his wound had healed. His estrangement with his wife further added to his mental stress. Although she had returned to his lodge, she was more aloof than ever. As soon as he was able, he walked about the village, stopping in the lodges of his friends to smoke a pipe and talk of things only men would know.

The old men told tales of the days of the Iron Shirt, a coat of mail traded through many hands—from the Mexicans to the Arapaho, and finally to the Cheyenne. But a great warrior, Alights On The Cloud, had worn the shirt into battle and been killed. The shirt had been captured by the Pawnee and destroyed. The old men still grieved for this sacred shirt and its magical powers.

Still the Cheyenne possessed an Ancient Scalp Shirt, which could be worn only by a warrior who had counted one or more coup. Lone Wolf knew they were considering giving him the Scalp Shirt to wear in battle. It was a great honor, giving him the same rank as a chief, but one heavy with responsibilities.

Since his marriage to Spotted Woman, he had thought of refusing the honor of the Scalp Shirt. His life would be in constant danger on the battlefield, for he must be the first to advance and the last to retreat and he must pick up his dismounted comrades. In addition, he must not get angry if his horses were stolen or his wife carried off—and he must not seek revenge. Remembering the way he had fought Little Bear, Lone Wolf was not certain he could follow those rules, especially where Spotted Woman was concerned.

Feeling better for having spent time with his comrades, Lone Wolf returned to his lodge, determined to try again with Spotted Woman. He was, after all, a war chief who had proven himself time and again for bravery and cunning. He would not allow his wife to treat him as a guest in his own lodge. He would demand that she show him preference and bend her will to his.

Having buoyed up his courage with such thoughts, he stepped inside his tepee and glared at the woman seated at the fire, calmly sewing a garment of elk skin. Her red braid lay smooth and glossy down her back. She didn't glance up when he entered, but her shoulders stiffened. The slight angered him more. Once she would have flung herself at him, offering him laughter and kisses.

Red Bead Woman saw the scowl on Lone Wolf's face and rose, knowing she must not interfere with the two young people yet praying her son would show some tenderness toward Spotted Woman. Taking her warm robe, she passed through the flap and walked to the lodge of Tangle Hair and his wife, Sun Flower. She missed Magpie.

"Spotted Woman!" Lone Wolf's voice was stern. Colly looked over her shoulder at him.

"You wished something?"

Lone Wolf stalked to the fire, letting his towering height intimidate her. Her gaze remained serene as she looked up at him. Her gray eyes were flat, without emotion.

"I wish the comfort of my wife," he said, without preamble. At first she looked puzzled by his words; then understanding flooded her features.

"I have no comfort to give you," she replied, but her breath came in a short, sighing gasp.

"Then I will take it," Lone Wolf said, clasping her arm and hauling her to her feet. Shock rippled across Colly's face.

"Surely you do not mean to take me against my will?" she gasped. "This is not the way of the Cheyenne."

"To deny the needs of your husband is not the way of a Cheyenne wife," Lone Wolf said flatly. He'd hoped once he made his demands she would capitulate, and, once they'd held each other and made love, the anger would be gone, but her jaw jutted mutinously and her eyes snapped with contempt.

"Is force the way of Lone Wolf then?" she demanded. "Does he have no more honor than Little Bear, abusing his wife at his pleasure?"

"I have no wish to abuse, only to hold her, but her tongue cuts deeply."

"More deeply than the arrow that felled the white buffalo?"

"Your memory is overly long, Spotted Woman. I will not be deterred by your grudge. You are my wife."

She drew herself up, her gray eyes nearly level with his. "Take what I cannot give you then," she whispered.

Their words were like blows between them, wounding and destroying faith and trust.

"I will take what is mine to take," Lone Wolf roared, and roughly yanked her against him. His large hands closed in her hair, disarranging the braid. Impatiently he pulled away the beaded thong that held it. His hands tore at the glossy rope until her hair lay around her shoulders like the fiery plumage of some mystic bird.

Her gaze never wavered from his face, her eyes deep wells of misery and pain. Lone Wolf buried his face in the glorious silken strands, breathing in the fragrance of her hair and body. His own body responded with a familiar passion. His blood soared through his veins, his burgeoning manhood pressed against his breechcloth.

Once he'd touched her, he was lost. His hands slid over her skin, pushing aside the soft skins to reveal the softer flesh beneath. Slowly he undressed her and gazed at her pale, slim body by the light of the fire. His kisses grew deeper, more demanding. So lost in his own needs was he that he didn't notice there was no answering response.

Colly held herself rigid and unyielding. Her gray eyes were bright with unshed tears, her pale face bleak with sorrow. Had they come to this, then? she wondered. Had the love and trust they'd given each other meant nothing, that he could thrust it all aside in the heat of his own lust? She felt his strong arms lift her impatiently and carry her to their pallet. She wanted to cry out her bitter disappointment. She wanted to gnash her teeth and rend her clothes and tear at her hair in grief for all that had once been theirs and seemed forever lost.

None too gently, Lone Wolf placed her on the soft fur pallet and stood to strip away his leggings and shirt. His breechcloth fell away last, revealing his readiness. Even as her heart sorrowed over what was to happen between them, her body remembered the touch of him and opened itself. She lay with her muscles throbbing with the need to wrap themselves around him, but she forced herself to limp passivity.

Lone Wolf loomed above her, his fierce gaze taking in her averted face, the single tear that had escaped and lay on her pale, thin cheek. He saw her pain and felt his own desire dwindle. He could not take her like this. Unwilling to admit defeat, he took hold of her hand and placed her flattened palm against his chest. She made no move to caress him as she once would have done. He moved her hand about, letting her feel his sleek, muscled torso, and then he carried it lower, wrapping her fingers around his engorged member. Still she remained passive. But the whimper she gave told him of her torment. Slowly he removed her hand and rolled away from her.

"Will it always be like this between us?" he asked wearily.

"I do not know," she answered. "I only know how my heart feels now."

"And I know how my heart feels," Lone Wolf answered. "It longs for the loving wife I once had." He paused for a long moment, then sighed. "Do you wish to return to your own people?"

Colly felt her heart contract. Did he no longer want her then? "I have not thought of it," she answered truthfully. "Does my husband wish me to go?"

Lone Wolf rolled over to look at her, one large hand coming out to cradle her chin and bring her gaze to meet his. There was great sadness in his face, and resignation.

"Spotted Woman may do as she wishes," he said, and rose. In silence he donned his clothes and left the tepee.

He strode to the lodge of White Thunder and sat talking to his chief for a long time. Word had come that an old enemy, the Ute, had crossed over the snow-filled mountain passes and attacked the Omisis camp. Believing themselves safe in their winter camp, the Omisis had been caught unawares and many had died. Their warriors were filled with anger and the need for revenge, and they'd sent word asking the men of the White Wolf band to join them.

That night all the villagers were summoned to White Thunder's lodge. The old chief was somber as he faced his people and spoke of the attack on the Omisis band. He also praised his brave war chief, Lone Wolf, who would now wear the Ancient Scalp Shirt. With dull eyes, Colly watched her husband being honored. But when she turned to congratulate Red Bead Woman, she was startled to see the fear and worry mirrored in her eyes.

"Are you not happy for your son's great honor?" she asked as they walked back to their lodge.

"This honor will place him in great danger," Red Bead Woman said, and revealed the grave responsibilities connected with the Scalp Shirt.

Colly felt her chest tighten. She'd had no idea. She must speak to Lone Wolf at once, tell him she still loved him despite their misunderstanding. But Lone Wolf had gone with the other warriors to the sweat lodge and she knew they prepared to join the Omisis warriors.

Tomorrow! she thought. I'll tell him tomorrow and somehow we'll work our way through this unhappy maze together.

But with the first light of dawn, the warriors were gone, riding on their fastest ponies down the mountain slopes—toward the land of their enemies, the Ute.

Chapter 13

"**S**OLDIERS! RUN! HIDE! Soldiers are coming!"
Pandemonium struck the village with the outcry. Most of the men had joined the war party against the Ute, so only old warriors had been left behind to guard the women and children. Mothers gathered their children and ran from one place to another seeking help. Some took shelter inside their tepees, huddling near their fire pits, their arms fiercely wrapped around their children, as if that were enough. Others ran into the woods and hid beneath snowbanks and in thickets.

"Spotted Woman, come quickly," Red Bead Woman called, waving her toward their lodge. Caught up in the momentum of panic, Colly sped across the village circle.

She was too late. The soldiers were upon them, riding straight into the camp circle, letting their horses and numbers intimidate the women, children, and old people who scrambled out of the way. The actual appearance of the soldiers seemed to have taken all animation from the people. They stood rooted to the ground, like slender, helpless saplings in the spring.

Colly paused in her flight, knowing instinctively that to run was to draw attention to herself. Her robe had slipped around her shoulders, revealing her bright hair, so she tugged it high, making a hood, and turned sideways so that she might observe without being noticed. Other women stood thus, their robes hiding their faces, their little ones tucked safely beneath the fringes. Their eyes were wide and distrustful as they waited for the white soldiers to come to a halt.

Colly studied the men on horseback. It had been many months since she'd seen a white face. Some of them were little more than boys with fuzz upon their cheeks; some were hard-bitten, experienced soldiers with little sympathy or kindness showing in their hooded eyes. All of them looked cold and weary.

An Indian dressed in cast-off cavalry pants and a ragged buffalo robe sat on his pony a little to one side of the mounted men. His pale skin hinted at his white blood. His dark eyes gazed straight ahead, not acknowledging either the white soldiers or the villagers. He seemed untouched by his surroundings.

Colly studied the white faces and felt no stirring to return to her old way of life. Even with the rift between Lone Wolf and herself, she was content among the Cheyenne.

The man who rode at the head of the detachment gazed around the village, contempt evident in his eyes. The muscles of his cheeks flexed as if he was gathering spittle to cast out as a sign of his disregard for the Indians.

"Where's your head man?" he called. His voice was loud in the clear, cold air, his Eastern accent clipped and brusque. No one in the village made a reply. The insolent gaze went round the cowed circle of people.

"Stone Calf, ask them where their leader is—" His words were cut off by the sudden appearance of White Thunder.

Colly felt a thrill of pride as she saw the old chief approach. He'd taken time to don his headdress of eagle feathers. It splayed out behind him with every step and fanned the top of his head in a majestic array. He'd also chosen his new robe, with the tales of his many coups painted upon it. His bearing was regal, his weathered face noble and serene as he faced the impatient white officer.

"I am White Thunder," he said in a stately manner. Then,

using the white man's words, he said, "I am leader of the White Wolf band. Welcome to our village."

"I'm Major John Buford of the United States Army," the officer answered grandly. "I'm looking for the band of Indians that camped south of here last summer and attacked a wagon train." In the face of White Thunder's gracious speech, the major's words and attitude seemed harsh and unfriendly. At his tone, Colly could feel the tension grow in the people around her. They remained silent and watchful.

"We have camped many times upon the prairies," White Thunder said, waving to indicate the southern course they took. "We go where the buffalo lead us. But we have never attacked the wagons of the white people."

"Are you sure about that?" Major Buford snapped disbelievingly. The people muttered among themselves. The white officer was calling White Thunder a liar. Never had the chief been so insulted.

White Thunder's face revealed nothing of the affront shown him. "We have not harmed the white men. We fight only if we are attacked."

"Is that so?" Major Buford let his gaze roam around the village. At last his cold blue eyes settled on Colly.

She felt her heart beat faster with some unknown dread. She was certain her face was hidden in the shadows of the robe, but her hand, pale and slim, was exposed as she gripped the edge of the robe. She dared not withdraw it, lest the robe fall from her shoulders. So she stood, not drawing a breath, until the icy gaze moved on to something else. Even then she dared not rest easy. She began to edge backward toward the lodge, where Red Bead Woman stood hidden from sight.

"Where are all your men, Chief?" Buford was asking. "All I see here are old men and women."

"Our men are hunting," White Thunder answered, with equanimity. "They should return soon."

"What are they hunting, eh?" Buford shouted accusingly. "Are they out there looking for some innocent white soldiers to kill?"

White Thunder remained silent for a long time, his shoulders rigid, his dark eyes flat with anger. "Our men hunt for food for the village," he answered finally, his tone as even as always. "If white people are astir in the mountains at this time of year, we have no need to kill them. They will die from exposure and starvation."

Buford's face turned ugly at the chief's words. "That's what you want, isn't it?" he challenged. "You'd like to see all the white people crossing your precious land dead."

"I would like to see the white people return to their own land," White Thunder said quietly. "The white men do not honor the Mother Earth. They take from her and give nothing back."

"Perhaps we will give back something," Buford said. "Perhaps we'll enrich her soil with the blood of the red men."

The women drew back, clutching their children beneath their robes. Colly's heart was pounding so hard, she could scarcely swallow. She longed to step forward and berate the foul major for his savage words, but fear of discovery kept her silent.

A fresh-faced young officer pushed forward and restored a calmer tone to the talk. "Sir, we have no proof these people had anything to do with the wagon train. We can't provoke them into a fight."

The major's head swiveled stiffly, like a puppet whose joints had rusted. "Lieutenant McKinney believes you, Chief," he said quietly. He turned back to White Thunder. His eyes were calmer, the gleam of madness replaced by speculation. His gaze angled to Colly, where she stood clutching her robe high around her. She prayed her red hair didn't show. Instinctively she drew away, inching back toward the tepees.

"Since you say your people had nothing to do with the attack on any of the wagon trains, I'll take your word as truth." He smiled, a flexing of cheek muscles empty of real emotions. He pulled hard on his mount's reins, and it reared its head in pain and danced backward a few steps. Colly felt pity for any animal that fell under the hands of the cruel officer.

"When your men return from hunting, tell them to take extra precautions. I understand these hills are full of all manner of deadly game."

White Thunder made no reply, and with a final flip of a salute—which was more mocking insult than a sign of respect—the major and his men withdrew. The villagers remained where they were until the soldiers had disappeared over a hill; then slowly, as if released from a spell, they looked around, eyes wide with fright.

"It is all right," White Thunder told his people. "Go about your business."

Slowly the women moved to their lodges. Colly knew they would not feel safe again until the men had returned, and even then the threat of the soldiers would haunt them, for never before had the white eyes penetrated the winter prairie to reach their camp. The people felt restless, betrayed, wary.

Colly saw White Thunder converse with Tangle Hair and Old Wolf. The two old men nodded in agreement at something, then went off to mount their horses and ride out over the ridge of hills. Colly knew they were going to follow the soldiers for a time to see if they'd truly left the mountains. She applauded White Thunder's precautions.

Evening in camp was subdued, the mothers keeping their children close by, the elders sending inquiring glances at the distant hills as if watching for the return of Tangle Hair and Old Wolf. Finally at dusk, when the two men returned and made their report to White Thunder, all waited to hear the results. The village crier mounted his horse and made his rounds of the tepees, calling out what Tangle Hair and Old Wolf had observed.

"The soldiers have left the mountains and returned to the prairie. They ride back to their fort." Heartbeats slowed and grins of relief lit the faces of the women, until the old man continued. "Women of the camp, gather your children about you for the night and put moccasins on their feet—so if our village is attacked, our children will not flee into the freezing snow with bare feet." The old man passed on, repeating his message, leaving consternation and unease in his wake.

"What does this mean, *nah koa*?" Colly asked Red Bead Woman.

The old Indian woman shook her head sorrowfully. "In the old days in the Cheyenne camps, we were constantly in fear of attack from *hohe*. Our mothers were admonished to put our moccasins on us when we slept at night. Many times we were awakened to the shrill war cries of our enemies, and we fled into the dark woods." She sighed. "It has been many years since our people have lived with such threats. Now the Ute attack us and the soldiers come to threaten us. It is a bad time." She sat rocking herself.

"It will pass, *nah koa*," Colly whispered, hugging her mother-in-law. But she felt tense with worry as she prepared for bed. She remembered the look in the major's eyes when his gaze rested on her. He'd known she was white, yet he'd not inquired about her or why she was here. The fact that he hadn't done so seemed a bad omen. His duty would be to rescue white prisoners . . . and he had no way of knowing if she was kept against her will or not, if he did not ask.

Perhaps he hadn't discerned she was a white woman, she thought hopefully. Perhaps she was worrying unduly. Tangle Hair and Old Wolf had said the soldiers had left the mountains. They were experienced warriors. What they said must be true. Still, when Red Bead Woman's activities caused Colly to sit up in bed and observe her mother-in-law packing her parfleches with extra food and robes, Colly rose and wordlessly helped her. When the bags were bulging with supplies, Colly leaned back and looked at Red Bead Woman's face questioningly.

"We will take these into the woods and hide them," Red Bead Woman whispered. "Tomorrow morning we can always bring them back."

Wordlessly Colly picked up two of the packs and made her way out of the lodge.

"Come," Red Bead Woman said, and set off at an angle from the camp, keeping well away from the well-traveled paths that led higher into the mountains. At last they came to a place where a scrubby mountain maple spread bony arms to the night sky.

"We will leave it here in the tree so no animals will find it and carry it away." Red Bead Woman tossed a rawhide rope over one of the branches and hoisted the bundles of food high out of the reach of animals. When they were secured, she looked at Colly, then turned back to the village. They did not talk about their nightly sojourn. They huddled on their pallets, pulling their robes tightly about them, thinking of the soldiers winding their way down the mountainside and out across the prairie, wondering where their own men were now. Colly lay thinking of Lone Wolf. He'd gone away without giving her a chance to talk to him, to tell him how much she needed him. They'd parted in anger, and now she wondered what dangers he faced. Was he warm and well fed? Was he wounded and suffering? She couldn't bear the image that came to mind. Shutting her eyes tightly, she listened to the fluting call of a night owl.

The piercing cry of an owl broke the silence. It would be daylight in an hour and the village below lay wrapped in sleepy, careless silence. Wispy streams of gray mist rose from the smoke flaps of the tepees. The dogs were silent, huddled in a pile for warmth near one end of the village. Horses stamped their feet in the packed snow and stood patiently in the predawn chill. The men readied their weapons and tightened their grips on their bridles. The village sentries had been silently dispatched with the skillful sweep of a knife. There was no one to sound a warning. The morning seemed to hold its breath, as if it knew that soon the peace would be shattered by the sound and fury of battle.

At a signal from their leader, the men kneed their mounts

and thundered down a ridge, their voices raised in shrill savage cries.

Lone Wolf led them into battle as was his duty as possessor of the Ancient Scalp Shirt. Fearlessly he rode into the center of the Ute village, his lance held high, the war cry strong in his throat. Ute warriors, still groggy from sleep, stumbled from their tepees, their feet bare in the snow, their hands gripping their weapons in hasty defense. They'd been caught unawares; the momentum of Lone Wolf's charge was too great for them to overcome. They tried to fight while their women and children fled from their beds into the thick blackness of the trees and ravines, but Lone Wolf's Dog Soldiers were everywhere, their murderous tomahawks raised in shiny, unrelenting death strokes. The tomahawk blades did not seek the fleeing women and children. Lone Wolf had admonished his men to concentrate on the Ute warriors. They were the ones who'd brought death and grief to the Cheyenne people.

The Cheyenne fought nobly, counting many coups against their enemies. Lone Wolf was like an avenging spirit astride Taro, racing through the village, his spear and tomahawk flashing with deadly intent in the first pale light of sunrise.

The Ute warriors were rallying, gathering their shields and fitting arrows to bows. Some had made it to their ponies, and now the battle raged more evenly. Some of the Cheyenne warriors fell, but Lone Wolf did not hesitate. His bow sang with the strength of his rage. When his quiver was empty, he rode through the village, plucking a lance from the dead body of an enemy. Turning, he spurred forth again and his mighty arm tossed the simple iron-tipped weapon with such force, it ran through the body of still another enemy and emerged on the other side.

At last the battle turned. The Ute fled after their women into the woods. The Cheyenne men followed them, pushing their horses through shallow snowdrifts, routing out the hiding men.

Lone Wolf reined in his horse and gazed at the Indian who

had ridden onto the path ahead. His horse was large and nearly all white, save for dark fetlocks. The warrior was formidable, and Lone Wolf had little doubt he was one of the Ute's prized warriors, if not their war chief himself. The man sat waiting, and Lone Wolf knew a challenge had been issued.

The warriors on either side fell silent as the two chiefs rode toward each other. Lone Wolf held only a tomahawk. The rest of his weapons were gone. Still he showed no unease. His shield was carried in his left hand, its painted surface held toward the enemy warrior, his dark gaze unwavering.

Taro moved forward as implacably as the sun across the sky. When the men were no farther apart than a hundred feet, they spurred their horses and dashed forward, their muscular arms raised in battle. Their tomahawks clashed like some ancient Excaliburs of a different time and place, but the rage in their hearts was the same as all men know in defending their honor. Their horses whirled and danced as the men vied for a better advantage. The Ute warrior's longer lance pierced the skin of Lone Wolf's shoulder. His eyes did not even flicker at the pain as blood streamed down his arm. His tomahawk flew through the air, its blade glittering, its aim true as it struck the Ute's lance, breaking its shaft. The ragged ends fell apart in the Ute's hand, scratching a long cut along one lean cheek.

The Ute tossed aside the useless weapon and drew out his tomahawk. Lone Wolf was weaponless except for his bow— for which he had no arrows. He slipped it off his shoulder and held it before him. The Ute charged, his tomahawk raised high. Lone Wolf whipped his bow around his head and sent it whirling. The flying bow struck the Ute's arm, knocking the tomahawk from his grasp.

As the momentum of his forward rush carried him past Lone Wolf, the Ute warrior leaped at the war chief, sweeping them both from the saddle and to the ground. They rolled over and over before breaking apart. Each sprang to his feet weaponless, but no less deadly foes. With a shout, the Ute sprang at Lone Wolf. The war chief steadied himself on widespread legs, knees slightly bent, and took the full weight of the enemy warrior, rolling backward, so the thrust of the lunge carried him over Lone Wolf's head. The warrior landed flat on his back, the wind momentarily knocked from his lungs.

Lone Wolf leaped to his feet and threw himself forward. The two men grappled and moved apart, each regarding the other with renewed respect, each finding the other a worthy opponent. There would be no dishonor to die at the hands of such a warrior as these two, yet neither intended to lose. They sprang toward each other, their great hands grasping for key positions that would crush the life from the other.

The Ute's hands closed about Lone Wolf's throat. He felt his air cut off and his chest heaved with the need to breathe. He knew this would be his last struggle if he didn't loosen the Ute's hold on him. His muscular legs lashed backward, striking the Ute in the midsection. Lone Wolf heard the snap of ribs. The Ute stumbled backward, his hands going to his chest, and Lone Wolf leaped at him, carrying him backward, his knee driving into the broken ribs, forcing them inward through soft tissue, into lungs and heart, so the death rattle was cut off and blood spilled from the warrior's mouth and nose.

Lone Wolf sat astride his opponent long after he was sure of his death, gathering strength to rise. Doll Man galloped forward.

"We have defeated our enemies," he cried. "The Ute have fled. They're scattered in the woods. Shall we burn their tepees?"

Lone Wolf raised his head and glanced around. The smell of death filled his nostrils. Snow was already falling over the devastation of the village. His men were busy gathering scalps from the dead, their triumphant yips filling the air. He felt a shiver of premonition and wished himself back in their village. Slowly he shook his head.

"We have done enough," he said wearily. "We will return home." He rose then and leaped into his saddle, taking the reins and sounding the cry to his men. They heard, and, though puzzled that he had allowed the village to remain unburned, they regained their mounts. Brandishing the fresh scalps of their slain enemies on the tips of their lances, they galloped after Lone Wolf.

"What was that?" Colly whispered to Red Bead Woman. The fire had died down to coals and the lodge was chilled.

"Why do you wake me? It is but an owl," Red Bead Woman grumbled, tugging her robes tighter beneath her chin.

"But it has sounded many times in these past minutes," Colly insisted. Red Bead Woman opened her eyes and listened as the hollow sound came again. Her eyes grew wide and she pushed aside the covers.

"Flee," she cried. "The soldiers—" Her warning was cut off by the rush of hoofbeats and the scream of horses in the village center. Shots sounded and the hoarse curses of men filled the night.

Colly leaped to her feet. "Come. We are being attacked." She threw her robe around her shoulders and reached for one for Red Bead Woman. They stuck their heads through the flaps of their tepee.

Soldiers were everywhere, their pistols blazing, their horses crashing into the sides of lodges. As the skins fell around the sleeping inhabitants, the riders shot them in their beds.

"Flee into the woods," Red Bead Woman cried, turning away from the village center, but Colly could not turn away from the cruelty of her countrymen. A small child stood crying beside his fallen mother; a soldier rode forward, the iron-shod shoes of his mount striking the child so he lay still beside his mother.

"No!" Colly cried, and, heedless of her own safety, rushed forward to drag at the booted foot of the soldier, who'd wheeled his mount and was prepared to ride over the defenseless bodies yet again. He struck out with his saber, nearly hitting her, but she leaped away and tumbled in the snow, her robe flying free. She saw the silver arch of the saber as it landed in a nearby snowbank. She sprang up and faced him yet again. He took out his gun and aimed it at her. The gleam of the rising sun gilded her head and figure and shone in his eyes, so for a heartbeat he lost sight of her. When he moved to one side, he saw her plainly and cursed.

"Jesus! A white woman," he cried. "Major Buford! Lieutenant McKinney!"

Colly saw the direction of his cry. The arrogant major was engaged in hacking at a woman who held up her hands in an appeal to save her children. Without thinking, Colly picked up the saber, which had fallen from the soldier's hand, and dashed forward. Even as she did so, she saw the woman fall. Her name was Morning Sun, Colly recalled. Morning Sun! She must remember the name and the woman, who had been a hard worker and proud mother. Morning Sun fell to the ground, her blood staining the white snow beneath her children's feet. The major raised his hackamore again, but Colly was there, raising her weapon, stopping the downward sweep of steel with steel. Startled, the major yanked the reins of his horse and turned toward her, his eyes going wide when he saw the red hair and pale face. Colly's tall, lanky body was fit and well muscled from her months among the Cheyenne. Her arm shuddered beneath the impact of the major's sword, but her clumsy parry held, deflecting his blade a second time.

"Run!" she cried to Morning Sun's children, and they scrambled away from the fighting. Now the soldier who'd first identified her rushed forward to help his superior officer, and Colly knew she had no chance to hold off both of them. All around her, women and old men hobbled, trying to rescue the children, fleeing into the woods beyond. The village was nearly empty, save for the soldiers and those who had died. Flinging her saber at the major, she turned and ran. She could hear the clatter of hooves behind her as a soldier pursued her.

"After them!" Major Buford roared at his men. "Find them and kill them—all except for the white woman."

Blood pumped through her veins, her knees jerked high, and her feet slammed into the packed snow, pushing her forward. She ran with all her might, glad for once she was tall and skinny, but pitted against the strength and stamina of a horse, she had little chance.

She made for the thicket and ran into it, ignoring the pain of barbed branches that dug at her as she passed. The horse couldn't penetrate here. Cursing, the soldier dismounted and pushed his way forward. He could see the woman ahead, her red braid flopping against her thin shoulders. If she were an Indian woman, he'd take out his revolver and shoot her, but the major had said he wanted her alive, so he stumbled after her, cursing and heavy-footed.

"Come back. We ain't goin' to hurt ye. We mean to rescue ye from these devils, take ye back to your own kind," he called, but the tall woman kept running, weaving through the trees and bushes, and the soldier knew why.

"She's gone Indian," he mumbled to himself.

He was gaining on her. She could hear his heavy breathing and his muttered curses. He sounded like an enraged bear. Her sides ached and blood poured from the gashes on her arms. She wasn't sure where she was. There was no other sound of people in these thickets. She leaped across a fallen log and crawled into the hollowed-out depression. The soldier lumbered forward, taking no care to muffle his passing. Colly shrank back against the log as he stepped across and stumbled up the trail. For a moment she was safe, but then he was back, moving more swiftly than she'd thought him capable. His face lit with cruel purpose when he caught a glimpse of her.

"Thought ye could outsmart me!" he cried, crouching before her hiding place. "Thinkin' like an Injun, ain't ye? Won't do ye no good. Come on outta there."

Shivering with cold, Colly crawled out of her hiding place and stood before him.

"Well, look at that hair. Ye shore ain't no Injun."

"Please, leave me," Colly pleaded. "Go back to your friends and forget you ever found me."

"It ain't goin' to work that way, li'l gal," the soldier said, his gray eyes glittering with mean intent. "What'd ye do? Lay with one of them red devils and decide ye like 'em better 'n white men? Like as not, ye ain't had the right kind of white man." He lunged for her, his big hand closing over her right shoulder. The fine stitching of her doeskin dress gave way, scattering beads and quills over the white snow. Her shoulder was exposed to the biting cold.

Colly twisted away from him, running through the snow. Frozen branches slapped against her face. A hand caught her braid and yanked her backward.

"No need to act skittish around me," the burly soldier said. "It ain't like ye're a decent woman. We know what happens to the likes of ye when these savages git their hands on ye. Ye ain't much good for white living no more."

"Please, let me go. I don't want to go back with you."

"Now, ye listen to me. Ye don' want to go back, I ain't takin' ye—but ye have to make it worth my while. Ye understand? I been out here in the cold and snow trackin' ye for a long time. I need a little comfortin', if ye know what I mean."

Colly understood all too well. The man drew her against his stinking body, pressing his foul-smelling mouth on hers. Colly held her breath, twisting away from his grasp.

"Here now. Ye better cooperate, missy," he cried, slapping her across the face.

Colly's head reeled from the blow and her cheek went numb, but she still fought against him. He hit her again, doubling up a fist and striking her as he would a man. She fell into the snow and lay still. He was on top of her at once, ripping at the soft leather, jerking her dress above her knees. Colly felt the cold against her bare thighs and cried out a protest, but it went unheard.

Her flailing hand fell against his revolver and, without

pausing to think, she had it out. She couldn't warn him. He would wrest the weapon from her and take her anyway. She pressed the pistol barrel against his shoulder and fired. Blood splattered against her cheek. The man pulled back, his face registering shock, then anger, as he grabbled for the gun.

Dimly Colly remembered something Lone Wolf had said once—Never aim to wound an animal bigger than you, aim to kill. She placed the barrel against his neck and pulled the trigger again. The shot echoed through the woods.

For a long time she lay with the man's heavy body pressing her into the snow, his warm blood flowing onto her chest. He was dead, and she'd taken his life. Never had she thought she'd ever kill a man; now she lay with his last gasp of life echoing in her ears. She stared at the pale winter sky and wondered why God had turned his face away from all of them this day.

Finally the sound of distant voices awakened her need to survive, and she crawled from beneath the dead soldier. She still clasped his gun in her hand. She saw the box of ammunition attached to his belt, the knife still in its sheath, and her hands reached for these things, tearing them free before she fled into the woods. She moved numbly, automatically putting one foot before the other. She didn't feel the cold against her bare shoulder. She was unaware she still bore the blood of the man she'd killed. She thought only of surviving.

She wasn't sure how far she'd gone. A lone eagle's cry sounded high above her. The wind moaned through the trees. Melted snow fell from branches, plunging downward with a muffled *plop*. At last she paused, dazed and lost. The sun had passed overhead and was near to setting in the west. Colly felt the night cold seeping around her and sank into the snow.

She had no way to help herself. She sat staring at the dead soldier's gun and thought briefly of using it on herself. Then reason returned and she dropped it in the snow while sobs shook her body. The horror and shock of the past few hours claimed her. She felt only shame for her own race. Where did she belong now? she wondered. The village was destroyed, its people scattered in the cold, deadly mountains, and the ones who'd brought this devastation were her own people. She could never return to them.

She was alone again, and death loomed from every majestic peak, every regal pine, from the flat, gray sky that promised more snow to the cold wind whistling over the jagged ledges. She was alone, and this time she had no will to fight against death. She slid down into the snow, accepting the cold as part of death. She thought back to her childhood in Tennessee and the days and nights in the Cheyenne village, and for a while she was almost happy.

The snow warmed her, making her sleepy, making her forget the horrors. Colly laid her head back and stared at the sky. She wasn't going to die after all. She was going to rest for just a little while and then she would rise and go back, back to Tennessee, where Lone Wolf waited for her.

Chapter 14

R ED BEAD WOMAN found her lying still and unresisting in the snow, her pale eyes turned to the sky, a smile upon her lips. Red Bead Woman found her and cried out with horror to think she'd come too late. Then she saw the small flicker of pulse in the long, pale neck and she reached out with an open hand to deliver several stinging slaps.

"Spotted Woman! Come back to us," she shouted. Her fingers explored beneath the bloody dress, seeking evidence of a wound. When she found none, she sighed with relief. Colly blinked and looked around, but her gaze was bemused, as if she already existed in some other world and viewed this one with a fond remembrance.

Red Bead Woman got her to her feet and wrapped a warm robe about her shoulders. Then, leading her as one would lead a docile child, she started back through the woods to the place where the other survivors waited. They skirted the dead soldier, and for the first time Colly let out a whimper.

"Shhh, he won't hurt you," Red Bead Woman murmured as to a child. She'd already guessed what had taken place here. Many of their women had been raped before meeting their death. A few, like Spotted Woman, had managed to escape. Red Bead Woman led her daughter-in-law to the ledge under the riverbank, where the others waited. Night was falling, and they were cold and hungry and frightened. Seeing other survivors, Colly roused from her state of shock and ran forward, embracing each woman, weeping and begging for forgiveness. Red Bead Woman pulled her aside.

"This is not your doing," she said. "We do not blame you. We saw how you fought the soldiers and tried to save the children."

"You forgive me for this?" she asked piteously, and when Red Bead Woman nodded, she put her head on the Indian woman's shoulder and wept. At last the great shuddering sobs halted and she raised her head.

"Are the soldiers still in our village?" she asked.

Mutely Red Bead Woman nodded. Colly looked around her at the weeping women and children. "We must do something to help them," she said.

"We will retrieve our bundles. There is food and warm robes. I need you to help me."

"I will!" Colly said unhesitatingly, and the two women made their way from the riverbank.

The night before, when they'd brought the bundles into the woods and hidden them, it had seemed they'd carried them far from the village. Now the sound of the soldiers in the village and the cries of the women they'd captured seemed much too close. Cautiously they moved through the underbrush, aware a sentry might find them at any moment. Colly raised her head to peer at the warm lodges and the soldiers who loitered there, partaking of the food in the cooking pots and the warmth of the Indian fires. How she despised them all.

Quickly they retrieved the bundles from the tree and made their way back to the riverbank. They passed out the meager supply of food and handed around the extra robes. They needed twice as many, but at least their foresight had alleviated some of the suffering. With their bellies full again, the children nestled against one another beneath the robes and soon fell asleep, their small faces pinched with the fear from the horrors they'd survived. Colly, Red Bead Woman, and the others huddled together, talking in quiet voices, recounting the names of their fallen comrades.

"We must find a place to hide until the soldiers give up looking for us," Burning Star said from between clenched teeth. Her robe was thin and she tried not to give in to the cold. Colly rose and went to sit beside her, wrapping her robe around them both. Burning Star smiled in gratitude.

"The men will be back soon, perhaps tomorrow," she said quietly, but even she did not believe that would happen.

Through the night they dozed, unable to sleep soundly because of the cold and their own uneasiness. Colly lay dreaming of Lone Wolf, of the day they first came to the mountains, when he led her high into the hills and made love to her on the ledge overlooking the waterfall. They had laughed together then, and the sunlight had been golden in the burnished leaves of the mountain maple. Near dawn Colly raised her head and sniffed the air.

"Something's burning," she said. Red Bead Woman and the other women roused and looked at one another.

"The village!" they exclaimed, and scrambled up the bank.

Carefully they made their way through the brush, crawling on their bellies until they were close enough to see. In the sweet, flat valley that had once been their home, the ring of tepees burned, the black smoke rising in the still air. The soldiers were already mounted and ready to withdraw, save for those few who carried torches from one lodge to the next.

"No!" a woman cried, and tried to scramble forward as her lodge caught fire. Hands pulled her back, pushing her flat, smothering her cry, while dark eyes stared at the destruction below.

"Our robes, our food," another woman whimpered. "How will I feed my children or keep them warm?"

When all the tepees were blazing, Major Buford signaled his men. They remounted, and, with a final glance around, they wheeled and left the burning village.

Silently the women waited until they were out of sight,

then rose and moved down the slope to the village. Swiftly they moved among the burning tepees, searching for anything that might have escaped the destruction of the soldiers and the greedy flames of the fire.

One snatched up a pot, another a half-burned robe. She beat it against the snowy ground until the flames were out and held it aloft triumphantly. Some risked the flaming pyre of their lodges to snatch out parfleches with half-burned food and clothing. Others hastened to gather scattered tools, bowls, and spoons. Many of them had been crushed beneath the hooves of the soldiers' mounts. When they'd gathered all they could, they melted back into the woods and thickets, meeting once again on the riverbank.

"What good are these things without our lodges? We will freeze without a place to sleep. Look! It has snowed already during the night and the sky is heavy with the threat of more snow. We will die out here."

"No, we won't," Colly said. "I know a place where we can go. No one can find us there. We will be safe until our braves return."

"Where is this place?" the women cried disbelievingly.

"It's up there"—Colly pointed—"higher in the mountains, near the waterfall."

"I know the place," Red Bead Woman cried. "I'd forgotten it."

"Gather up your things. We'll go there today and then we'll search for food. We will survive, and when our men return, they will find us alive."

Colly's voice rang out in the cold air, instilling hope and a will to survive in those who might have given up and waited stoically for death. The women gathered their pitiful ragtag belongings and wearily followed after Colly. She had no idea how long it would take them to make the distance on foot, or even if she could find the way, for the paths were changed by the snow and ice. But she must try or they all would perish.

Red Bead Woman read her indecision and smiled gently.

"You will find this place for us," she said, with a strong, sure voice that gave Colly courage.

In a straggling line, they set out climbing in the thin, cold air until weariness made them pause to rest. With the children, travel was slow, so Colly despaired of finding the cave before nightfall. Then she found the copse of aspen and mountain maple. They'd been bright gold in their fall leaves; now they stood thin and barren. Farther on she found the stream where beaver dams dotted the frozen, flat creek bed and the place where the moose had fed on water plants. A little farther along and she remembered that here she'd first heard the faint roar of a waterfall. Now all was silent.

"We're nearly there," she called to the weary women and children.

They clambered along the stream bank and came at last to the place where the waterfall poured over the high ledge to the basin below. But now the rushing water was held captive by the icy grip of winter, the plumes of frozen water creating a curtain of white fantasy.

"Up there." Colly pointed to the ledge above the waterfall and began to climb. The women hesitated only a moment and followed after her. When they reached the ledge, Colly turned about, looking for the entrance to the cave. There was none.

"It was here. I know it was," she cried. "There were bushes here that half hid the entrance." Some of the women looked at her with skepticism, but Red Bead Woman motioned to some of them and began to dig. Colly lent a hand, ignoring the cold. Finally they broke through; a small black opening appeared.

"There. There it is," she cried, and the women renewed their efforts, digging with their bare hands.

The cave was as she'd remembered it. Cautiously the women entered, searching for signs of wild animals, and when they were certain they were safe, they stood and stared at one another in relief.

"A fire!" Red Bead Woman said. "Gather firewood. Tonight we'll be warm."

The women scattered and searched among the fallen timber for branches, which they dragged back to the cave. Without the coals of previous campfires to draw from, they searched the creek bed for rocks and flint to start a fire. Before long the cave was warm and comfortable, with a small blazing fire. The children huddled close, cheered by the flames. One of the women rationed the meager supply of food they had left. When all had eaten something, they settled down to rest, feeling considerably more hopeful than they had felt the night before. Tomorrow they would have to search for food.

It snowed during the night. The entrance to the cave was nearly covered again. Any evidence of their trail was obliterated. Taking this as a good sign, the women spread out, searching along the stream beds for evidence of deer or small game animals that might have come to drink. Traps were set. Some of the women fashioned hooks and used large rocks to break holes in the ice and fish for trout. Others sought among the trees for bark and roots that were edible. They carried their meager findings back to the cave and set a pot of food to bubbling. Still, with all their efforts, they went to bed that night with rumbling stomachs.

On the second day one of their snares produced a rabbit, which was skinned and put into the pot, bones and all, for they needed every ounce of nutrition they could find. They longed for some of the tender roots they'd gathered on the prairie or ground acorns to thicken their stew. Still, they made the best of it, joking lightheartedly as they waited for the rabbit to cook, portioning it equally among themselves when it was done, dismayed there was so little to share after all.

The third day the traps were empty and the fish weren't biting. The women gave their children pieces of bark to chew on and exchanged worried glances. The fourth day they boiled one of the buffalo robes. The results were unpalatable and meager. The children drank the resulting brew only because their mothers insisted, and they sat quietly by the fire, their faces pinched with hunger. The younger ones whimpered and clawed at their mothers' chests for half-remembered sources of nourishment. Even those mothers who were nursing found their milk was drying up. Their babies grew fretful and feverish.

"We must do something," Colly whispered. "I can't bear to watch the children suffering like this."

"The men will come soon," Red Bead Woman replied softly.

"But when?" Colly railed. "And why was it so necessary for them to go off on a war party against the Ute now? Didn't they know we needed them?"

"We thought we were safe," Red Bead Woman explained patiently. "Our enemies have never found us in our winter camp."

"What if they have not found the Ute in their winter camp?" Colly continued. "Then all this suffering will have been in vain. They should have stayed in camp. Is revenge more important than life?"

"They did not go to seek revenge alone," Red Bead Woman said. "If they do not repay the Ute for their attack on the Omisis band, the Ute will think our warriors are weak. There will be more attacks in the spring and more Cheyenne will die."

"Is it better for the Cheyenne to die like this?" Colly said bitterly, and rose and left the warmth of the cave. Her anger burned deep as she watched the suffering children. Her own misery drove her to take chances, so, without telling anyone where she was going, she trudged down the mountain, back to the destroyed village.

The fresh snowfall had covered the ugly mounds that once had been Cheyenne lodges. Within those tepees lay the remains of those women unable to escape the soldiers' attention. Who knew what unspeakable horrors they'd endured throughout the long night before their death? Wolves had been at the pitiful remains of those who had fallen outside the lodges. Bones lay scattered about.

Colly clutched her stomach and turned away, unable to witness the horror. Twice in her lifetime she'd seen the misery of man's cruelty to his own kind, for were they not all the same beneath their skin color? Were they not all filled with the need to love and be loved and to raise the human spirit to a nobler plane? Why then did men debase themselves by engaging in barbarism? She longed for Lone Wolf to be there, to share her groping search for answers, to reassure her that his gods and hers were not a lie.

Finally, too sick to continue, she turned back to the mountain cave and the miserable huddle of people who waited for her. They were all she had now of life and humanity, of hope and beliefs. She hurried back to them as one hounded by the saints of hell.

There was no food the fifth day. They gnawed roots and bark and melted snow over their fire for water—and prayed for the return of their men. Colly no longer prayed. She wasn't sure there was anyone to hear their pitiful supplications. She seemed to be dying inside, inch by painful inch. She sat alone against the damp wall of the cave and welcomed the cold cutting edge against her back. Somehow it made her feel she still had a firm grasp on the bitter realities.

When the first call sounded, no one made a move. They sat staring at the fire as if they hadn't heard. The call came again, a high, sweet cry of a bird, and the women shook off the lethargy that had claimed them and looked at one another.

"Our warriors are back," Red Bead Woman whispered, and rose from her seat by the fire. She ran to the door and looked outside. "Our men are back," she called, and with cries of joy the women and children rose and ran to the cave entrance. The men were already climbing the steep path. The women rushed forward.

When the cave was empty, Colly rose as if in a trance and walked out onto the ledge with almost a detached curiosity.

Had Lone Wolf returned then? Or was his body lying wounded and frozen on some distant land of the Ute? She seemed untouched by the weeping and embraces of those around her. Then he came up the hill, his dark gaze searching the face of every woman he passed, his expression anxious until he saw her by the cave entrance.

He said nothing as he came to her, his tall, lean body moving quickly until he stood before her. The dam burst within her then. All the frozen emotions gave way, all the pain, all the fear she'd hidden away rose and she crumbled against him, weeping against his chest. His strong arms held her, his solid body comforted her.

"When we saw the village, we thought you were all dead. We had no idea of where you could be. Then I saw footsteps leading into the mountains and I knew you'd brought them to the cave."

"Without its shelter, we would have died here," she said. "So many have died already, killed by the soldiers. We couldn't find White Thunder or Tangle Hair. Old Wolf is dead. Morning Sun and her children. So many! The soldiers didn't care who they killed."

"White Thunder and Tangle Hair gathered some of the villagers and escaped south onto the plains. They made their way to the camp of the Omisis and sent a message to us."

"There are more people alive?" Colly wept. "I thought we were all who'd survived. I couldn't understand how God could have been so unkind as to let so many die."

"We've brought food for you all. Venison. We'll leave as soon as you're strong enough. The Omisis band welcomes us." Wearily Colly nodded her head. The warriors brought warm robes and caches of meat.

Now that the wonder of finding loved ones had passed, the women hurried to cook the meat and hand it out to their children. Wrapped in warm robes, the young ones sat on the warriors' laps, laughing and playing. How quickly they were able to put the horror behind them. The warriors related their stories of the raid on the Ute village. Proudly they showed off their fresh scalps, telling of how they'd counted coup on their old enemies. The children listened with eyes gleaming, imagining themselves there, riding with the warriors as they attacked the village. Stonily Colly listened and turned away, sickened at the sight of the scalps, mute reminders that what Lone Wolf and his men had done was not so different from what the soldiers had done to them.

Lone Wolf seemed to understand the parallel, for he crouched beside her. "We did not burn their village, or rape their women, or kill their children," he said.

Colly turned her head and met his gaze. He could see she'd been weeping. "No, but you killed their men and took their scalps as trophies. How can you justify such savage deeds?"

"Because we are people in a savage land. We do what we must to survive, just as you did when you killed the white soldier," Lone Wolf replied.

"Red Bead Woman told you?"

"She has told me of all the cruelties you've endured and of your bravery and courage. If not for you, they would have all died."

"I killed a man," Colly said dully. "I took a life!"

"The life of an enemy who meant to dishonor you."

"Yes, I upheld my honor." Laughter at the fire drew her attention again. "But I did not take his scalp. At least I have not become so barbaric as that."

Lone Wolf gripped her arm when she would have risen. "If you had taken his scalp and draped it high from a lance, then all who saw it would have known that you had slain your enemy. They would respect you and know you are not weak. They would hesitate before thinking of doing harm to you. There is a reason for all things in this land, and each thing helps us live as men." His fist thudded against his chest. His voice had risen, and other warriors turned to look at him. When they saw that Colly and Lone Wolf were engaged in a private conversation, they turned away and resumed their own talks.

Colly twisted her arm from Lone Wolf's grasp. "You have

the Cheyenne ways to guide you," she said quietly. "Many of these ways are good. But the white men have laws, too, and I cannot put these behind me, even when they go against the Cheyenne ways."

"Did the white soldiers follow their own laws when they burned our village and killed our women and children?"

Colly's gaze dropped in shame. "Will you seek white scalps for your lances now?" she asked bitterly.

"I do not know. We will go to the camp of the Omisis— and in the spring we will meet in council and determine what we must do about the white soldiers."

Colly kept to herself in this new camp, aware that if she felt troubled by the differences in their two worlds, the Cheyenne also questioned her place among them.

Lone Wolf had chosen not to share the lodge of Black Moon and Gentle Horse. Soon the whole camp whispered that he did not approve of his sister's marriage with the warrior. Black Moon was subdued, hurt, and defiant. Colly wondered if Lone Wolf had chosen not to come to the lodge because of his anger at Black Moon—or because he wished to avoid his wife.

The time of the Light Snow Moon, also known as *Shiivine*, was upon them. March, Colly mused, counting on her fingers. Nearly a year since she'd left Tennessee a lifetime ago. She began to walk alone through the woods, delighting in the first faint runnels of melting snow, but soon the trails were treacherous with mud and melting ice. The men could not go into the hills to hunt without great exertion on their parts. The horses could not keep their footing in the slush. Even the snowshoes were useless against the melting ice. Colly remembered how this time of year had been in Tennessee. The winds had begun to blow warm with the promise of spring, and on the sunny slopes of the balds, the first fingers of bracken fern had begun to uncurl; soon the air would be sweet with the calls of the chickadees as they gathered the wool from beneath the cinnamon fern to build their nests. Each time she thought of home, she waited for the pangs of longing, the restless cravings for things once known and loved, but there were none. Now her pain came from the estrangement between Lone Wolf and herself. He filled her mind and heart.

One day, driven from the lodge by her maddening thoughts, Colly stumbled upon a moose mired in mud nearly to his belly. She could tell he'd been trapped there a long time, for his head drooped with fatigue and his eyes rolled frantically. She hurried back to the village and sought out Lone Wolf. He sat with the other men, repairing weapons. He rose immediately when she approached.

"Greetings, Spotted Woman," he said. "Did you have need of me?" His dark, liquid eyes studied her face warmly.

"I'm sorry to take you from your friends," she answered hesitantly. He shrugged. "I've found a moose caught in the mud and wondered if you might help free him?"

Lone Wolf glanced at the other men, laughter dancing in his eyes. Some of the men grinned and quickly turned away.

"We will be glad to free the moose from the mud," he said, taking up his bow and arrows. "Take us to him."

Colly led the men up the path she'd traveled, all the while thinking of Lone Wolf's tall, muscular body so near her own. Was he as aware of her as she was of him?

They reached the clearing, where the moose still struggled in his muddy prison.

"Shoot him while his legs are bound by the mud," one warrior said, fitting an arrow to his bow.

"Let him free himself; then we will kill him," another argued. "Otherwise, we will have to wade into the mud to rescue the meat."

"You can't kill him," Colly cried. "He's trapped by the mud. It's unfair."

But no one heard her. In no time they'd thrown a rope around the antlers of the moose and guided him to the edge of the quagmire. His spindly legs had no sooner touched solid ground than he was felled by an arrow through his neck.

"No!" Colly cried out; all the warriors turned and looked at her in consternation. She turned and ran down the trail. Lone Wolf left the other men butchering the meat while he ran after Colly.

"Why do you weep for the moose?" he asked when he found her huddled on a fallen log. "It was his destiny to feed the hungry village."

"It seems so cruel that we go on killing people and animals . . . and for what? To sustain our own lives. What makes our lives more precious than theirs?"

Lone Wolf stood staring down at his wife and remembered the time he'd spent in the hills fasting and praying and the vision that had come to him. He remembered Spotted Woman's lonely cry that day on the prairie when she came upon the wagon train. Now he knelt before her, his eyes dark and troubled.

"I do not know why it should be so, that the moose and buffalo must give up their lives to give us life, but it is so. If it were meant for the buffalo to be supreme, he would kill us and feed upon our bodies. So would the moose. This is the order of life on the Mother Earth."

"It's very easy for you, isn't it?" Colly said accusingly.

"We must accept these mysteries, for we cannot know everything," he answered patiently. "Why did the moose appear in the mud today when our food is low and our bellies empty? Why did you walk along that path and find the moose? Why did you come to me? Come, Spotted Woman, put aside your doubts. Accept this gift from the gods and let us feast tonight."

Numbly Colly shook her head, and Lone Wolf went away and left her, disappointed that she did not understand about the moose.

She was disappointed that Lone Wolf hadn't seen the similarity between their plight and that of the moose. If God had placed the moose there in the mud for the Cheyenne, just as he had once produced manna for the Jews fleeing from Egypt, then had he also meant for the soldiers to attack the village?

Had he placed them there in the path of the soldiers so that they might be found and killed? Her head hurt from the effort to understand, and, as she sat and pondered, the smell of roasting meat assailed her nostrils, driving her back to the camp—where she took a piece of the moose meat Red Bead Woman offered and ate it with shameful relish.

Chapter 15

THE TWO BANDS stayed in the mountains until the month of the Fat Moon was upon them. The streams and rivers were high within their banks as rivulets of melting snow poured into them. The ice on the still ponds grew black, then broke apart in fragile chunks of honeycombed crystal that gave out a high tinkling sound when they hit against the rocky shoreline.

The music of spring, Colly thought, standing on a bank. She walked among the woods seeking the first signs of spring: the tightly furled fiddleheads and the tiny buddings of wild-flowers. One day she came upon red fruiting cups of some British soldier lichen and knelt beside them, thinking of all the Tennessee springs when she'd found this same fungus.

The skies were filled with ducks and geese winging northward. She saw great herons, their huge, ugly bodies graceful in flight, and grebes and loons. One day she came upon a whooping crane and started backward, at first intimidated by its height. The bird was nearly as tall as she, standing on its spindly legs. Its glossy plumage was pure white, except for its black face and wing tips. Colly felt joy soaring through her heart and turned about, looking for someone with whom to share this wondrous moment, but she was alone. Saddened, she went away . . . leaving the gangly bird with its fierce yellow eyes glaring unyieldingly upon its world.

Was she like that awkward whooping crane, unable to adapt to a new world? Was she demanding too much? She thought of Lone Wolf and felt lonely. She was more alone now than before she'd known him, for he'd taught her love and shared laughter. She longed for him to come to her now.

Then one day, when the waxy leaves of the marsh marigolds had burst into bloom, and the slender willow saplings had sent forth tender green leaves, and the woods were musty with damp, black soil and decaying logs, Lone Wolf came upon her so suddenly, she knew he'd been following her.

The sun slanted through the newly leafed trees, the breeze was warm on their faces, bringing a waft of pine, and, above all, the turgid, overpowering smell of earth, awakened and fertile again.

They said nothing, their hungry gazes drinking in the sight of each other. Lone Wolf took her hand and led her away from the woods, past stands of white cedar that filled the air with their pungent scent, past patches of tiny, starlike white flowers, to a high ridge where the sun warmed the soil and tangles of berry bushes made a dense private wall of greenery. There they sat upon the soft pad of pine needles and gazed into each other's eyes.

"Lone Wolf misses his wife," he said in English, and she stilled his lips with her hand, knowing he'd chosen her language in an attempt to please her.

"Spotted Woman has missed Lone Wolf," she said in Cheyenne. "I do not understand my anger and sorrow, but it has been like a great buffalo skull that I must drag behind me until I learn the answers to questions I have."

"Have you found the answers?" he asked, with great patience.

Colly nodded. "I fear there are no answers. It is as you say. We must accept some mysteries, for we cannot know everything."

She saw the dawning hope in his eyes. "This will please Red Bead Woman," he said softly.

"Red Bead Woman?" Colly was puzzled at his words.

Lone Wolf nodded. "She has set about finding me a second wife."

"A second wife?" Colly's voice rose sharply. "Do you mean that if I do not return to you as your wife, she will find you another wife?"

Lone Wolf shook his head, sorry he'd brought up the subject. "Even if you return to my bed mat, she is determined I take a second wife."

Colly gaped at him. She'd known some of the men had two wives, but she'd chosen not to dwell on such a habit, certain that Lone Wolf would never take another as long as she was with him. Now she felt jealousy and pain lace through her.

"Is that what you wish to do?" she asked stiffly.

"I have given it no thought," he replied, shrugging. It was the way of his people and not to be worried over. Colly felt her anger building. She thought of striking his smug, handsome face, but his next words robbed her of her rage.

"I have no wish for another wife," he said huskily.

Colly felt her anger melt away. Lone Wolf's arms closed around her, snaring her tightly; his mouth claimed hers hungrily. His lips were firm and smooth, the tip of his tongue hot and pulsing. She opened to him like a flower too long deprived of sunshine and rain.

Her thin arms wrapped around his trim waist, her hands, soft from their winter of inactivity, slid across his back. Then, impatient with the doeskin of his shirt, she pushed beneath his sash and felt the familiar warm sweetness of flesh. Her questing hands found the roughness of scars from his buffalo torture and the sleekness of muscles. Her nostrils drew in the woodsy scent of him, her mouth tasted the piny essence that was his. This was Lone Wolf, her beloved husband, and she'd missed him. What did all her questing matter? She was lost without him. Life had little meaning. If she must choose, then her choice must always be Lone Wolf.

There was a shuffle of dried grasses, the snap of a twig. Colly looked around to see Burning Star had intruded on their seclusion. Her dark eyes were bold as they met Lone Wolf's gaze, her pretty mouth curved in a smile.

"Red Bead Woman has sent me to find you," she said sweetly, casting a challenging glance at Colly. "She has need of you."

"Tell my mother I will come soon," Lone Wolf said, his arm still clasped about Colly's waist.

"She must see you at once," Burning Star declared.

"You'd better go," Colly said, shifting away from him. She'd caught the possessive excitement in Burning Star's glance. Was this the woman who would become Lone Wolf's second wife? Colly remembered they once had shared a robe. They would never share her husband, she vowed.

Lone Wolf sighed and smiled at Colly. "Will Spotted Woman wait here for my return?"

She wanted to, but hurt pride was already making it difficult for her to keep a friendly face. She forced a smile and shook her head.

"I have much work to do today," she answered. "I will be at the lodge of Gentle Horse and Black Moon, if you wish to see me."

He hid his disappointment with a smile, taking her words as a promise that all was well between them again. Colly watched as he followed Burning Star down the path toward the village. The young woman smiled up at him often, now and then brushing against him along the trail. Colly felt sick with despair. She turned back up the trail, finding no comfort now in the early blooming Juneberry bushes, or the delicate flowering wildflowers, or the clear, sweet tones of the song thrush. She had never known such pain.

Late in the day she climbed down the path and returned to the lodge. Her eyes were downcast, her expression filled with sadness as she knelt beside the outdoor campfire Red Bead Woman had built. The Indian woman hummed as she worked. She was reunited with her daughter, and, although she had lost many friends in the sad winter, her son and his wife were also safe. Now she had decided upon a woman worthy to be a second wife. She was very happy.

At first Red Bead Woman did not see that Colly was troubled. Finally her quiet, withdrawn air drew Red Bead Woman's attention. "Are you ill?"

"I am well," Colly answered.

Red Bead Woman watched her work around the campfire; then, torn by the unhappiness she saw in Colly's eyes, she tried again.

"You are unhappy. Why?"

Colly hesitated, but the pain of Red Bead Woman's betrayal was too great. She raised her head and met her mother-in-law's gaze. Red Bead Woman was surprised to see she was weeping.

"I had thought I pleased you as a daughter," Colly began in a low voice. "Although I am not Cheyenne and do not always understand the ways of the people, I have tried to live as a good Cheyenne."

"You are very brave," Red Bead Woman replied. "You saved the women and children when the white soldiers attacked us by leading us to the cave. You fought the soldiers."

"Is that why you resent me?" Colly asked. "Because my skin is white and my people attacked yours?"

Red Bead Woman stared at her speechlessly. "I do not resent you," she said softly.

"Then why do you desire another wife for your son?" Colly's voice broke on a near sob.

Red Bead Woman stared at the tight face of Spotted Woman for a long time. She knew first wives sometimes grew jealous of second wives, especially if they were younger and prettier, but most of the time the Cheyenne wives lived in harmony.

"I thought you would like Burning Star as a sister. She is cheerful and a good worker. She will bring another pair of hands to our lodge and will add laughter. She is strong and will bear healthy children." She stopped speaking, for the pain that fluttered across Spotted Woman's face was too raw to contemplate. The silence stretched between them.

"Is it not the way of the white men to take two wives?" Red Bead Woman asked finally.

Colly shook her head. "They consider one enough."

Again Red Bead Woman was silent. She saw now she had been wrong. Since Spotted Woman had not shared her son's mat for many weeks, she'd assumed Spotted Woman would welcome a second wife to take over such duties. Now she saw that she was wrong and that her meddling had caused more misunderstanding.

"One wife is enough!" she said finally, wishing to take away the pain she'd caused Spotted Woman. Colly only sighed, and when Lone Wolf's long shadow crossed the glowing circle from the campfire, she rose and entered the lodge without speaking to him.

Troubled, he seated himself at the fire and ate from the dish his mother handed him. He had swallowed his pride to come here to the lodge shared by his sister and Gentle Horse. Feeling unjustly injured by such behavior, Lone Wolf stalked away, spreading his bedroll in the lodge of another warrior, but it was late in the night before he finally slept.

What Red Bead Woman had started she could not so easily halt. Burning Star had always had a secret attraction for the tall, handsome war chief. Now she pursued him in the subtle ways of the Indian maidens, giggling when he was near and going out of her way to walk past his lodge. She came often to visit Red Bead Woman, sitting beside the older woman ostensibly to learn some favored stitch, but in reality to win Red Bead Woman to her suit.

Colly had once regarded Burning Star as her friend; now she felt anger for the girl. Black Moon sensed the stiffness between the two women and tried to speak to Colly.

"I can never be friends with her," Colly declared impatiently. "She wishes Lone Wolf for a husband."

"That should not make you angry," Black Moon said. "You will still be his first wife."

"I wish to be his only wife or no wife at all," Colly declared hotly. When she saw Black Moon didn't understand her attitude, she grasped her sister-in-law's arm. "How would you like Burning Star as a second wife to Gentle Horse?" she demanded.

"Burning Star is my friend. I would like her to be related to me in such a way," Black Moon replied, surprised at Spotted Woman's intenseness.

Colly made a scoffing noise in her throat at Black Moon's words. "Would you feel so generous when Gentle Horse took Burning Star into his bed?" she asked, and stalked away.

Black Moon walked to the field, where the men were gathered practicing their skills with lance and bows. Proudly she watched as Gentle Horse wrestled with another young warrior. Though he was gentle in their lodge, touching her hair and smiling often, she was pleased to see he did not live up to his name on the practice field. Watching his strong arms wrap around his opponent and his long legs lash out, she thought of their nights in the robes when his hard body plunged against hers. Would she mind if Gentle Horse did these things to another woman? Suddenly she knew she would—and she began to understand Spotted Woman's anguish.

Thoughtfully she walked back to the lodge they all shared, wondering how she might tell Burning Star she would not be welcomed into their lodge as a second wife. She knew Burning Star. Once she'd made up her mind to something, she never stopped until she had what she wanted. Black Moon had always admired this quality in her friend, but now she disliked her a little for it.

The villagers were recovering from their ordeal. Children whose mothers had been killed by the white men's bullets were taken into other families. New lodges were made. Warriors whose wives had died were looking for new wives among the Omisis band. Each would go to live with his new wife's people, thus depleting the White Wolf band even further. But the thing that most threatened the band's survival was the defection of the young warriors who, angered by White Thunder's passive acceptance of the white soldiers' attack, had slipped away from the camp to join Little Bear's renegade band.

"These bad Indians will bring trouble to our people," White Thunder said when he'd called a council.

The people listened to him and nodded their heads in agreement. Yet the warriors knew they would be called upon to retaliate in some way for the deaths of their people by the white soldiers. Furthermore they knew White Thunder was waiting for the great Sacred Arrow Renewal Ceremony to be held soon.

Now that spring had come fully to the land, people were able to move about freely. Once again the women went into the hills in search of firewood, early berries, and roots. They also hunted the small game animals, setting traps for rabbits and squirrels and turtles, and gathered duck eggs along the riverbanks.

Colly recognized this peace that had settled over the combined village and knew she should feel contentment herself. The hardship of winter was behind them, the memory of the soldiers' attack nearly forgotten in the burgeoning renewal of life. She and Red Bead Woman were in their own lodge again, but Lone Wolf had not rejoined them. Each time she caught a glimpse of Lone Wolf and Burning Star together, she felt like weeping. To make matters worse, she'd missed yet another month of menses and was torn between joy and fear that she might be with child. She fiercely guarded the secret. She could never tell Lone Wolf with this anger between them, for she knew if he took another wife, she would return to the white world. This was one Cheyenne way she could never accept.

The spring and all its fresh new promise flowered quickly into the full-blown glory of early summer. One day a messenger rode into the camp bringing his ceremonial pipe and gifts for the chiefs. He had been traveling far and wide seeking out every Cheyenne camp, meeting and informing them of the place where the Sacred Arrow Renewal Ceremony would be held. Immediately the people began to prepare for the journey to this site. There was much excitement, for the Sacred Arrow Ceremony was a time of spiritual renewal for all the Cheyenne and they looked forward to visiting with their sister bands.

Colly rode her horse in the line of people, feeling, as she always felt, a kinship with these simple yet complex people. But something was different this time, for she accepted the fact that she would never truly be a Cheyenne. She thought about her baby and her responsibility to it. Was it best to let him grow up here with his father's people, unschooled in the white man's ways, or take him back to the white world, where he would never quite belong? Her somber gaze sought out Lone Wolf's figure among the outriders, and, seeing that Burning Star had ridden her pony close to Lone Wolf's and was leaning from her saddle to tell him something, she hissed with annoyance.

Black Moon edged her pony close. "He would not look at Burning Star with so much kindness if you would return to his pallet as his wife."

"I will not buy his attention with my body," Colly retorted. "I am his wife. I deserve more respect than that."

"But you have turned him away. How can you blame him if he seeks out another?" Black Moon persisted.

Hearing her sister-in-law's words, Colly felt her heart squeeze painfully.

"Does he court Burning Star then?" she asked in a low, dull voice.

Black Moon shook her head. "Not yet. But if this anger between you continues, he will surely do so. He may even throw you away at the next dance."

Colly's lips twisted into a bitter smile. How much better the Cheyenne's expression for what was truly a divorce. If she didn't return to Lone Wolf's bed, she was in danger of being thrown away like some useless object.

"Please, try to resolve your disagreement with my brother," Black Moon urged. "I do not wish to see you thrown away."

"If that is what he wishes to do, then so be it," Colly answered stiffly and kicked at her horse, spurting ahead of Black Moon.

Later, when they paused to camp for the night, Lone Wolf sought out his wife and was puzzled to find her stiff-necked and hostile. Angry with her sharp retorts to him, he stalked away, and, when Burning Star came to sit beside him at a campfire, he did not move away. Seeing the two of them huddled together, Colly's heart nearly broke. Pleading fatigue, she went to her bed pallet and hid her face so no one could see her cry.

Red Bead Woman had seen Colly's distress. Furthermore she'd guessed Colly's condition but had said nothing. It wasn't her place to tell such news, but she longed for the moment when her son and his wife would reconcile so she could tell all her friends she would soon be a grandmother twice over.

As for Burning Star, Red Bead Woman was sorry she'd ever started this web of problems, but she could do nothing to halt it. She no longer encouraged Burning Star to sit beside her and sew, nor did she share such skills with her, seeking out Colly instead. Her daughter-in-law had become a proficient seamstress, devising such decorative patterns and beadwork that Red Bead Woman had thought of sponsoring her as a new member for the Quill Society. This was a position of such honor that she'd been waiting until just the right moment to bring it to Colly's attention.

Then, when it seemed things had become as bad between Lone Wolf and Spotted Woman as they could, Lone Wolf talked to Gentle Horse and discovered that Colly had summoned the warrior to his sister's aid and encouraged them to run away together.

"Why are you angry about this now?" Colly demanded when Lone Wolf confronted her. "Would you have her married to a murderer?"

"Little Bear was not a murderer when Black Moon was married to him. If she had stayed with him, he wouldn't have felt anger toward you and tried to murder you. Indirectly you brought about the murder of Magpie."

"How dare you blame me!" Colly cried. "I loved her. She was my friend, too. I gave her my robe because she was ill. It was an ugly trick of fate."

"Everything we do has consequences," Lone Wolf said. "Because you interfered between a man and his wife, you set in motion a chain of events that led to this tragedy—and it still has not ended, for Little Bear is out there drawing away our young warriors. Our band is weakened. If our enemies attack us now, many more lives will be lost. Why could you not accept the ways of our people?"

She stared at him dry-eyed, while her slim body shook with indignation. "If that is so, then you must ultimately share in the blame as well," she said. "You brought me to your village and you took me as your wife. If you had left me to die on the trail, none of this would have happened."

"You speak with clever, empty words that show ignorance and disrespect for our laws," Lone Wolf said sternly. His dark eyes were flat with anger. Whirling, he left her, striding away from the lodge toward the tepee of Dull Knife.

Colly watched him go and thought her heart must truly break. Everything between them seemed to have dissolved into ashes. Entering the lodge, she sat on her pallet, her shoulders rigid. Her eyes were dry and she wasn't sure if it was because she had at last become a true Cheyenne or because her pain was too great to express with tears.

Dull Knife came to find Lone Wolf as he walked beside the river one day. The old medicine chief did not take long to state his concerns.

"There are rumors you intend to throw away Spotted Woman," he said bluntly.

Lone Wolf turned to face the medicine man with a troubled face. "This is not a rumor I have started," he replied. "I have no wish to throw away Spotted Woman, but she is no longer pleased with me as her husband. I believe she would be happier if she divorced me and returned to her people."

"That may be," Dull Knife said slowly. "I have pondered the meaning of all that has occurred this winter. Spotted Woman has saved many of our women and children by taking them to hide in the cave and I have wondered if this is what my vision meant. But I do not believe it is so. She is still needed among our people for some special reason. I ask that you do not set her aside until that reason has been shown to us."

"I will do as you say," Lone Wolf answered. Dull Knife sensed that he was troubled and wished to speak further.

"What is it you wish to ask, my son?"

Lone Wolf told the old man of his accusations to Spotted Woman concerning her help of Black Moon and Gentle Horse and of the clever words she turned against him.

The old man listened, nodding his head. "She is right. If you must blame her, then you must blame yourself, too. We do as we think is best and we cannot see the future and its consequences. You have acted as an honorable man in all things, Lone Wolf. So, too, has Spotted Woman. She is equally without blemish in this. It is true that Little Bear might not have become a murderer if he had been given the incentive, but he was, and his spirit was not strong enough to resist. He is banished from our tribe, but there is hope. Someday he may return to us."

Lone Wolf bowed to the medicine man's words. He knew the way of the Cheyenne was to accept even the worst of the worst back into their folds if that person had truly proven himself worthy. He thought of the hatred on Little Bear's face for Spotted Woman, and he prayed the renegade warrior would never return to their band.

Thoughtfully he returned to the village and took up his

duties as war chief. The people were preparing to travel to the site of the Renewal Ceremony, and Lone Wolf knew he and his warriors would be called upon for many responsibilities in this journey. He put his thoughts of Spotted Woman from his mind.

Four times they paused in their journey to the site of the Sacred Arrow Renewal Ceremony and each time they prayed. The members of the council solemnly smoked the Sacred Pipe to the four directions and to the Great Medicine Spirits above. Colly seldom saw Lone Wolf, for he spent his nights sharing sentry duty or in the medicine man's lodge preparing for the great ceremony.

Their journey was near its end when the column halted and word was sent along the line of men and women that the appointed place was less than an hour's ride away. They would pause here for the rest of the day and prepare for their arrival. Now the people donned their finest clothes, painting their faces and adorning themselves with fine bone ornaments. Even their horses were groomed and painted. Excitement lay over the camp like a summer breeze rippling through the prairie grass, restless and capricious.

Early the next morning the two bands made their way to the camp circle, taking care to approach from the east. All the bands that had reached the appointed place earlier turned out to cheer and applaud the new arrivals as they paraded around the camp circle, greeting old friends and showing off. All hardships and sorrows of the past winter were forgotten. The Omisis and White Wolf bands moved to their appointed places in the circle and began setting up their lodges. Packhorses were unloaded, cooking fires started, invitations to meals sent back and forth. Each day the people busied themselves in a flurry of visiting, eating, gambling, and gossiping.

Then the last band pulled into place in the arc. More than eight hundred tepees stood in place and in the center of the great arc sat the Sacred Arrow Lodge. When all the chiefs had arrived, they hurried to the sacred lodge, the flaps were drawn together, and the ceremonial drumming began.

"We will go into our lodge," Red Bead Woman said, and Black Moon and Colly followed her inside.

As Colly drew the flaps together, she observed that all the cooking fires had burned down and the women and children had closed themselves inside their tepees. Only those warriors who had been designated patrolled the perimeter of the camp. Even the dogs were subdued and silent, slinking about the camp like culprits caught in some misdeed. Finally they settled themselves beside the dying campfires, their heads resting on their paws.

Colly fastened the flaps of their lodge and turned back to Red Bead Woman.

"Now what happens?" she whispered.

Wordlessly Red Bead Woman motioned her closer to the small central fire. "The Sacred Arrow Lodge has been prepared. Now the medicine men will cut away the sod and prepare the inside of the lodge. Then they will erect a sacred altar. For four days there will be special ceremonies that will renew the arrows so they prosper. If the arrows prosper, so will the Cheyenne people."

"What kind of ceremonies will they perform?" Colly asked faintly. She had seen Lone Wolf enter the Sacred Arrow Lodge and feared he might be called upon again to perform some torture upon himself.

"There is much that is secret in this ceremony and known only to the medicine men and the chiefs. There will surely be prayers, and men who are honorable in war will be sent to the lodge of the Sacred Arrow Keeper. They must be worthy men. Lone Wolf will be one of them, for he has become a wearer of the Ancient Scalp Shirt.

"When these men reach the lodge of the Sacred Arrow Keeper, they will be given a fox-skin bundle in which will be the four Sacred Arrows," Red Bead Woman continued in a hushed, reverent voice. "They will take the bundle back to the Sacred Arrow Lodge, where the medicine men will place it on their altar.''

She paused and lowered her voice. ''I do not know all the secrets of this ceremony, but the bundle is opened, the arrows examined. If the feathers are not in perfect condition, a warrior will be given the honor of repairing them. He must be healthy, clean, kind, generous, wise, and brave. He must never be guilty of a dishonorable act. That is why they have chosen Lone Wolf.''

Red Bead Woman's face displayed her pride, despite her attempts to hide it. Colly thought of her husband. He was all those things Red Bead Woman had mentioned and so much more. He tried to lead an honorable life in all ways. Even the day he'd tried to claim his husbandly rights against her will, he'd been unable to, drawing away with shame for even thinking he might do so. Her heart felt like breaking for this honorable man she loved so much. How had they lost each other?

''On the third day,'' Red Bead Woman said, ''the renewal takes place. A tally stick is prepared for every living Cheyenne family.'' She hesitated. ''Little Bear's family may not have a stick, for he has become a murderer. Each stick is smoked in incense to bless each family and give it well-being. On the third day, the medicine men also renew their medicine. Then, at last, on the fourth day, the arrows will be put out for all the men to see. We women must stay within our lodges.''

''Why?'' Colly demanded. ''Are we not worthy enough to see them?''

Red Bead Woman shrugged. ''It is the Cheyenne way.''

Colly opened her mouth to utter a retort; then, seeing Red Bead Woman's face, she swallowed the words. Some things must be accepted, she'd come to realize.

''I hear the arrows are very hard to see anyway,'' Red Bead Woman said by way of placating her. ''They give off a great blinding light.''

"What happens to the arrows after they've been viewed by the men?" Colly asked stiffly.

"They are returned to the lodge of the Sacred Arrow Keeper, who will care for them until the next Renewal Ceremony. After the four days have ended, we may throw back our flaps and leave our tepees, and soon after, the hunts begin." Her face was joyous, so Colly had not the heart to question further into a ceremony that so severely excluded women.

In the four days that followed, she listened to Red Bead Woman and Black Moon and did as they did, observing the rituals required to renew their existence. On the morning of the fifth day, they threw back their lodge flaps and stepped out into the sun-filled morning.

The first figure Colly saw was that of Lone Wolf. He'd emerged from the sweat lodge, where Red Bead Woman had said the chiefs and medicine men must go to be purified so that they could walk among the women and children without danger. He stood tall and proud, his powerful body held with renewed confidence, his expression serene. She remembered the way he'd looked after the buffalo skull torture and wondered at this mystical renewing. Was it not like the white man's own renewal when he stood before the cross and accepted God's gift of renewed life?

Somehow she felt reassured by what she saw in him and, as she stood watching him, he turned to meet her gaze. She saw the softening in his eyes and, slowly, he made his way toward her. His hand reached out to grasp her, but before their fingers touched, a wind blew from the prairie, carrying with it the smell of hail and dust, the smell of danger and death. People paused and looked around, their faces turned to the sky, their eyes filled with fear; then the wind passed on, rippling across the prairie grass like a giant hand passing across the flatland.

The people looked at one another uneasily and cast glances at the white woman in their midst. Now that the Renewal Ceremony was behind them, they could look around and note the occupants of the individual bands. Many of them felt uneasy to see a white face living among them.

A man came to Lone Wolf's side, and in a moment he was gone from her, as quickly as the wind had passed, leaving her standing with her hand still outstretched to him. A shiver ran through her and she turned back to her lodge. Some premonition haunted her. Beyond the circle of tepees lay the great prairie, and she sensed its cold, unrelenting pull on her. She felt frightened not for herself, but for the loss of all she held most dear in life.

Chapter 16

*L*ONE WOLF DID not seek her out again in the days that
followed. The large encampment celebrated its renewal of life, its sense of oneness as a whole society. They
were not just separate bands of people living and warring
upon the land; they were one nation, proud and independent,
masters of the Great Plains and its environs. They were *Tsitsitis*, the people. Their women were chaste, their warriors
courageous, their chiefs wise in all things. They were the
Cheyenne Nation. Even the fear of the white soldiers attacking was not to be acknowledged now.

The council had decreed that the Cheyenne would not
retaliate against the white eyes for the soldiers' attack. A
committee of chiefs would travel to Fort Laramie to lodge a
complaint with the white chief.

The Cheyenne moved out onto the prairie as one body,
seeking the great buffalo, which was the core of their existence.

Colly did not participate in this buffalo hunt as she had
participated the summer before. She remained in the background as much as possible, sensing the resentment the new
bands felt toward her white skin and all too aware that such
open hostility had affected her acceptance by the Omisis and
the White Wolf bands. Red Bead Woman often sought her
out, reassuring her in silent gestures of affection that all would

be well, but Colly wondered how long she would be welcomed among them.

The communal hunt was successful. The buffalo had been found upon the prairie again, and the hunters' arrows had been swift and true. The hunters returned to camp with an abundance of meat, and the feasting began.

"Are you coming to the dance tonight?" Burning Star asked Colly, with uncharacteristic friendliness.

Colly raised her gaze from the buffalo robe she was tanning and smiled briefly. "I don't believe so," she said. "Are you?"

Burning Star smiled eagerly. "Tonight is the Omaha Dance. It is a very special dance."

"Why is it so important?" Colly asked, only half-interested.

Burning Star's smile was triumphant. She giggled a little, but her eyes flashed with malicious brightness. "It is the dance where a man may drum away an unwanted wife. Have you not heard? Lone Wolf is to be leader of the dance."

Colly could think of nothing to say. Pain rippled through her. Burning Star didn't wait for an answer, merely tittering with mischief as she sauntered away. She was certain that her white-skinned rival would soon be disposed of, and she, Burning Star, would take her place as a first wife to Lone Wolf. Such a prospect was exciting to the young maiden; she'd long desired the handsome warrior.

Colly tried to ignore the coming event, but as darkness fell around the camp, she couldn't keep herself away from the dance. Pulling a thin summer robe high about her, she made her way to the camp circle, keeping well back in the shadows. A quick glance around told her that Lone Wolf was not present, although Gentle Horse stood in the shadows.

Colly knew Lone Wolf had not spoken to the warrior since they'd joined the Omisis band back in the winter. If Lone Wolf objected to the union between Black Moon and Gentle Horse, Colly knew Black Moon would not dishonor her brother by disobeying him, even though she carried Gentle

Horse's baby. By the grimness of Gentle Horse's face, Colly knew he was all too aware of this.

A drumbeat began, low and heavy in portent, and Colly forgot all about the tragic circumstances of Black Moon and Gentle Horse in the face of her own unhappiness. Several men moved out into the circle around the fire pit and began to dance. Some stepped forward to strike the drum and cry, "I throw her away." Colly knew their wives were being publicly shamed and her heart broke at the thought that Lone Wolf meant to do this to her.

Suddenly he stepped forward into the firelight. Colly's heart lurched within her chest. The men danced around him. Gentle Horse stood alert, his gaze fixed on Lone Wolf. Lone Wolf moved about the circle with lazy grace, his strong, bare legs moving rhythmically, his body gleaming in the firelight. His long hair was hanging loose and flowing down his shoulders, adorned with a single eagle feather. His chiseled features were somber, as befitted the ceremonial dance. The dance was drawing to a close. Every man participating had struck the drum and cried out his intentions of divorcing his wife. Now Lone Wolf moved close, and, taking the stick, tapped the drum.

"I throw away my sister, Black Moon," he cried in a loud, ringing voice, and threw the stick. It sailed through the air and struck Gentle Horse on the shoulder. The warrior caught the stick and stood staring at Lone Wolf, a smile slowly lit his face. The people around cried out their approval.

"What has happened?" Colly asked a woman standing next to her.

"Lone Wolf has thrown away his sister. The stick has struck Gentle Horse and he will become Black Moon's husband. It is a great honor Lone Wolf has shown his sister."

Joy rose like a great wind inside Colly, and she shoved her way through the milling people until she reached Gentle Horse. Black Moon was already there at his side, her face beaming with happiness.

"Black Moon, I'm so happy for you," Colly cried, embracing the young woman. She drew back and glanced around.

Lone Wolf stood behind her, his dark gaze warm and compelling on her face. Her hand went out to him, and this time he grasped it, pulling her toward him so that their bodies nearly touched. The near contact was more tantalizing than anything Colly had ever felt. Lone Wolf read the desire in her eyes, and, taking her hand, led her from the circle of light. When they were in the dark shadows, he pulled her close, his mouth settling on hers in a long, slow kiss that took her breath away and left her clinging to him for support.

Around the campfire Burning Star saw them leave, and her heart twisted with hatred for the white woman. She stalked away, down to the river, until she found the secret place where Lone Wolf had built a small willow lodge and often came to be alone. She'd discovered it quite by accident and had never invaded his private sanctum before, but now she sat thinking of the warrior she'd admired so long. He had never uttered a word of encouragement to her and had often talked to her of Spotted Woman. Burning Star had felt certain she could woo him away from the ugly spotted white woman, but tonight she had seen the power the white woman held over him.

She shall not have him, Burning Star thought rebelliously, and threw herself on Lone Wolf's pallet.

Lone Wolf stepped back and gazed at Colly. "I have ignored you these many nights," he said in a husky voice, "but not by choice. I have fulfilled my duties as a war chief and as a Cheyenne warrior. I have helped in the Sacred Arrow Renewal Ceremony and the renewal of our people. I had hoped this time might see a renewal of our feelings for each other."

"My love for you never needed renewing," Colly whispered. "I have never ceased to love you. Our worlds are so different, we must at times stumble in our understanding of each other."

Lone Wolf took her hand and placed it against his chest. "My heart cannot beat without you," he declared. "Come with me now." His whispered words were like a fire in her veins. Blindly she followed her husband as he led her away from the firelight and down to the river. They followed the bank until he came to a small tepee made of willow sticks.

"I made this for us," he said. "I had hopes we would come here and be as newly married again."

Her heart soared at his gesture. She rained kisses on his cheeks and mouth and turned to his lodge, which was a symbol of his continuing love for her. Though he was unable to say the words as white people did, he'd shown her in ways that were far more poignant. Colly had no need of anything else. Her body was hungry for his; her heart sang a song of joy and anticipation. She bent low and stepped inside the lodge, sinking to her knees, for there was no room to stand.

"Lone Wolf?" A soft voice came out of the darkness of the lodge. "Have you thrown away your wife as you promised?"

Colly's heart froze with dread. She recognized Burning Star's voice.

Lone Wolf had not yet entered. He did so now, his hand reaching for Colly. Numbly she pushed him away, whirling to crawl out of the wigwam.

"Spotted Woman!" he cried, following her. Colly fled down the river path toward the circle of lodges.

"Spotted Woman!" Lone Wolf's strong hand closed around her arm, jerking her to a halt. He forced her to face him. By the light of the prairie moon, she gazed at his face, searching for any sign of shame at his duplicity.

"Why do you run from me?" he asked, puzzled by her behavior. "Were your words a lie to me?"

"You dare to question me, when you take me to the lodge you share with another?"

"I do not understand your words," Lone Wolf said, thinking in her excitement she had not chosen the right Cheyenne words.

"You forgot to tell Burning Star you'd changed your mind about throwing away your wife. She waits for you back there in your lodge." She jerked free of him and stormed up the path.

"I have never thought to throw you away as my wife," he called after her, but she was too angry to heed his words.

Fighting the tears she hated so much, the tears that were a part of the white world, she made her way to the lodge she'd shared with Red Bead Woman and Black Moon—and once upon a time with Lone Wolf. She would divorce Lone Wolf, she thought angrily. Black Moon had said all a woman must do to divorce her husband was move back with her family. Colly stopped walking, her breath catching in her throat. She had no family. She'd made Red Bead Woman and Black Moon and Lone Wolf her family. Slowly she continued her steps to the lodge and spent a sleepless night upon her lonely pallet.

Lone Wolf walked back to his willow lodge. The words of Spotted Woman made no sense to him. Stooping, he crawled inside and lay on his pallet. He thought of how this moment might have been with Spotted Woman beside him. Instead he lay alone, his pallet cold, his rest fitful while he pondered over the ways of women. He'd seen the desire in Spotted Woman's eyes. Her face had been soft and filled with emotion for him. Her kiss had been as hungry as his, her body yielding in his arms. Why had she changed?

Lone Wolf thought of the times other men had spoken of their wives and their capricious moods. Such times often occurred when women were with child. He sat up in bed, his eyes gleaming. Was Spotted Woman carrying his child? Doubts replaced elation. Would she not have told him so? Besides, he'd held her slim figure against his and there had been no roundness to indicate that a child was growing there. Confused, he closed his eyes and tried to sleep. Tomorrow he would try again with his wife.

The bands were splitting apart, moving out onto the prairie on their own to seek the buffalo and gather roots. The time for visiting was done until the next great Renewal Ceremony, and that might not occur again for several years. Campfires burned late into the night as friends made use of their last days together.

Then the tepees were struck, the travois were loaded, good-byes were said, and the great enclave broke apart. The bands moved out onto the prairie to seek buffalo, dig roots, and collect berries for the coming winter. Although they would travel and live apart, their hearts were united in a common bond.

Colly rode behind Red Bead Woman and Black Moon and wondered where she belonged in all this. The Cheyenne had a very clear idea of their identity. Colly felt lost between two worlds. How would her son feel? she wondered, letting her slim hand curl around her stomach.

Red Bead Woman saw the gesture and wondered when Spotted Woman would speak to Lone Wolf about their child. It would do much to bring them back together. She wondered why they were unable to right their feelings when it was so clear they cared about each other. Red Bead Woman had heard Burning Star's words that Lone Wolf was leading the Omaha Dance, and she, too, had gone, fearful of seeing her son cast away his white wife. When she'd seen them leave the dance together, she'd felt certain the war between them had ended. Still, Lone Wolf did not rejoin them in the lodge. Now that they were on the trail again, perhaps he would.

Red Bead Woman sighed. She wanted grandchildren to hold, and she was fearful the headstrong pride of her son and his wife would take that privilege from her. At least Black Moon and Gentle Horse would produce a child soon, she thought, and fell to musing on the happier reunion of her daughter and her new husband. At last Black Moon seemed to have the happiness she deserved.

The Indian warrior watched the people move across the prairie, their travois laden with their skin lodges and other belongings. He knew they were moving to their summer camp on the prairie, where they would hunt the buffalo and gather *pomme blanche*. How docilely they followed White Thunder.

"They do not go to find the white soldiers who attacked the village," said Crazy Head, a young warrior who had left the White Wolf band to join Little Bear.

"*Pah*, they are no longer Cheyenne," Little Bear scoffed. "White Thunder grows old—and his warriors have become women."

"There are some who still fight as warriors," said Rising Fire, another of Little Bear's renegade band. "Lone Wolf is a great warrior. He now wears the Ancient Scalp Shirt into battle."

Little Bear's face grew ugly as he fingered a scar on his cheek. "I will one day take the Ancient Scalp Shirt from Lone Wolf's dead body," he said.

The braves looked at him, troubled. They were ambitious young men who longed for the chance to go against their enemies and earn their coups. They had no wish to fight their own band. They'd joined Little Bear thinking he would seek out the white eyes and kill them. They felt shame that White Thunder had done nothing to retaliate for the attack on their village. They had not agreed with their chief's request for patience until the Great Council could meet. Now that meeting had occurred, and White Thunder was moving his people to their summer camp. Where was the war party that would avenge the Cheyenne people who had died?

"Do we ride against the white eyes again?" they asked their leader. They had waited patiently throughout the winter months, and, with the spring and the return of the wagon trains, they had ridden down on the white men, killing their teams and burning their wagons. They had kidnapped some of their women, and having none of their own had made use of them before killing them. Now, for some reason, when the trail was thick with wagon trains that could be attacked, Little Bear had brought them here. They saw how the hatred burned in his eyes, but now he did not gaze upon the white faces—he looked at his own people, and they wondered where such hatred would lead them all.

"Do we return to the white man's trail and attack his trains?" Crazy Head demanded.

"Not now," Little Bear said, narrowing his eyes. "We will follow the White Wolf band for a while. I have a wish to see my wife."

"But she has divorced you, Little Bear, and Lone Wolf threw her away at the Omaha Dance. His stick hit Gentle Horse, who has claimed her for his wife."

"I did not throw Black Moon away," Little Bear said arrogantly.

The braves exchanged uneasy glances. "There will be a fight if you try to steal her away," Crazy Head said. "Gentle Horse and Lone Wolf will try to stop you."

"Gentle Horse, *pah*. He is no warrior. As for Lone Wolf, I welcome a fight with him. I have many grievances to settle." Seeing the hesitation on the faces of his men, he roared: "Has he not taken a white eyes as his wife? He is not a true Cheyenne. He has already taken one step into the white man's world. Is it not better to kill him now than to wait until he brings the white man to every Cheyenne lodge?"

Reluctantly his men nodded in agreement. Then, as Little Bear raised his hand and bellowed in defiance, they joined in his cry. "Death to Lone Wolf and his white eyes wife, who has brought the white soldiers to our villages."

When the flat plains echoed with their defiant cry, Little Bear lowered his arm and glared at his men triumphantly. "Death to Lone Wolf," he repeated quietly, and led the way through the green prairie grass toward the trail of the White Wolf band.

"I tell you, sir, we can find these devils," Major Buford said to his superior officer. "We nearly wiped them all out last winter. There can't be more than a handful of them. They've come down to the prairie to hunt buffalo. I know their habits. Stone Calf led me right to their camp last year. They've got to be the ones attacking these trains.''

''All right, Major Buford.'' Commander Sanderson sighed. ''I'd hoped we could avoid out-and-out war with the Cheyenne, but we can't let these attacks on the wagon trains go unpunished. Take as many men as you need and see what you find.''

''Yes, sir,'' Buford said. ''I'd like Lieutenant McKinney, sir, and Sergeant Crook.''

''Lieutenant McKinney has requested he not be detailed to you again,'' Sanderson said. ''Have you two had a falling-out?''

''Yes, sir,'' Buford answered, with a display of reluctance. ''Lieutenant McKinney was insubordinate on that winter detail. I had to dress him down in front of the men. I'm afraid he's holding something of a grudge. But he's a good man and I'd like him along.''

''All right, Major. See if you can't work things out. McKinney is a fine young man. I believe he has a good future in the army.''

''Yes, sir. I believe you're right.'' Buford saluted and left the office.

Once he was out of Sanderson's sight, his pleasant smile vanished and his eyes held a hard edge of rage. How dare McKinney make such a request, thereby raising a question about Buford's command? Buford thought of the young officer and the way he had avoided him ever since that attack on the Cheyenne village. He'd been warned to keep his mouth shut about what had really happened and go along with Buford's report. Maybe he hadn't. Maybe that was why Buford was still in this hellhole, why his request for a transfer this spring had been denied.

Anger, dangerous and retaliatory, raged through Buford. He'd make the snot-nosed young cavalryman pay for his double cross. His auspicious army career just might come to a crashing halt. Buford flicked his riding crop against his legs as he stalked along the parade ground. Yellow Dog, an aging

Cheyenne warrior, sat against the wall of the supply house. His eyes were lackluster, his face dulled from the alcohol he imbibed. Major Buford paused before the aging wreck of a warrior, his hand coming from his pocket to reveal the gleam of coins. Yellow Dog licked his lips expectantly.

"Send Running Deer to my quarters," he said, clicking the coins invitingly.

Yellow Dog wiped his mouth and shook his head. "Not Running Deer," he said. "Send Calf Woman."

"I don't want your wife," Buford said. "She's old and she smells. Send your daughter, Running Deer."

"Not Running Deer," Yellow Dog mumbled, his rheumy eyes squeezing moisture onto his leathery cheeks.

Buford shrugged and shoved the coins back into his pocket. "I had a need for a woman tonight," he said regretfully. "Guess I'll go get myself a drink of whiskey instead." He turned to leave, but Yellow Dog's filthy, thin hand grasped his pant leg.

"Send Running Deer to lodge," he said in a defeated voice.

Buford's lips curled derisively. "That's good, Chief Yellow Dog," he sneered. "That's real good." He dropped the coins into the dust near the old Indian. Yellow Dog scrambled to retrieve them, then rose and spoke to his wife and daughter.

Running Deer was a pretty girl of thirteen who'd only recently achieved her first passage into womanhood, but she had not known the pride and responsibility of such an honor. Her first menstrual period had passed unnoticed by her father and mother. She had bound herself and gone to the water trough to draw water and bathe herself.

Not for her the announcement by a proud father of her journey into womanhood, nor the giving away of a fine horse to commemorate this event. No old grandmother taught her to unbraid her hair and bathe herself. No one painted her body red or burned sweet grass and junipers for her in the menstrual lodge. No one showed her how to purify herself or advised her not to ride a horse during her cycle.

Such advice would not have mattered to Running Deer, for her father no longer owned a horse. If he had, he would have traded it for whiskey. So she had no idea of what her role as a woman meant, or even of her own worth. She had been taught none of the pride of her Cheyenne ancestors. She was a new child of the western movement; she was unaware of her past or her future.

Stone Calf knew, though. He, too, had endured this shame, and he saw what was happening to Running Dear. That one of the soldiers sought her out was inevitable. He'd known this and tried to harden his heart to it. Stone Calf saw Major Buford bargaining with Yellow Dog—and he saw Running Deer begin her long walk across the parade ground to Buford's quarters. He knew she would not be the same girl when she returned.

Angry with Yellow Dog and with the memory of his own father, who had hated the white eyes and had in the end been defeated by their firewater, he took his horse and rode out into the hills, seeking his own kind of renewal in the clean sky and broad, rolling hills. Even here the stain of the white man's hand could be seen in the deep-rutted trails that cut across the land. He rode until darkness lay over the hills, and at last he returned to the fort. As he stabled his horse and removed the saddle, he heard a whimper. He paused, listening for the sound again. It came from the corner of the stable. Stone Calf took a step forward and peered into the shadows.

Running Deer huddled on a pile of hay, her hair undone and twined around her body, her doeskin dress in rags. Dark smudges marred the round curve of one bare shoulder. One small-boned hand was pressed to her mouth as she pressed back another sob.

Stone Calf turned away, shutting out the tiny sound of misery. He relieved his horse of its bridle and gave it hay to eat, then brought it fresh water. When all was well with his horse, he left the stables and crossed to the cookhouse, where he might get something to eat. His ride had made him hungry. He sat on the rough bench and waited while the cook sloshed hot coffee into his tin cup and slapped some beans and burned beef onto a tin plate.

Stone Calf ignored the cook's surly demeanor. He'd never seen him behave any differently to anyone else. He ate slowly, closing his mind to everything except the white man's food. He was half-finished when Sergeant Crook entered.

"You'd better git yo'rself some sleep tonight, chief," the sergeant said amiably. "We're ridin' out early in the mornin'. Goin' to git ourselves some of them Injun devils what've been killin' white folks." The sergeant grinned. "I'm goin' to take some scalps, chief. What d'you say?"

Stone Calf made no reply, and, laughing, the sergeant left the cookhouse. The half-breed scout sat staring at the congealing beans and meat while a rage grew inside him. When it seemed to consume him, he rose from the bench and carefully walked from the cookshack.

"Hey, you didn't eat all your food," the cook shouted after him. "You ain't gettin' any more if you git hungry." When Stone Calf did not turn back, the cook picked up the plate and threw the contents into a bucket. "Heathens don't 'ppreciate when they got it good. Pro'bly ain't used to havin' his food cooked."

Stone Calf walked back to the stable. The whimpering had grown quieter now, but Running Deer still lay where he'd seen her. Angry now with himself, with the girl, and most of all with every white soldier that manned the fort, Stone Calf reached for the girl and turned her over, none too gently. She cried out and raised beseeching, terror-filled eyes to him. When she saw it was Stone Calf, who had occasionally been kind to her, giving her candy or bread, she tried to smile, but her pain was too great.

Stone Calf saw the bruises Buford had left on her young body and cursed the officer. But when he pulled aside the scraps of her dress and saw the blood on her thighs, he drew back. She needed help, greater than he could ever give her, but he knew better than to ask the white women who had taken shelter within the fort. The girl's mother was useless. She and her husband were in a drunken stupor by this time. Stone Calf clamped his back teeth together until his jaw muscles bunched, and he carried the girl to his room off the back of the stable. There he lit a lamp and picked up a bucket.

"Don't go," she cried when he crossed to the door.

"I'll be back," he said, and went out to the horse trough.

With a torn-up army shirt and the cold water, he bathed the blood from her thighs and smeared a horse salve on her cuts and bruises. When he was finished, he handed her another cast-off army shirt and a pair of doeskin leggings. It was the best he could do. Running Deer's eyes were bright with gratitude. Shyly she reached out a hand to touch his arm.

"Stone Calf my friend," she said shyly. He grunted in reply. She tried again. "Stone Calf help Running Deer. Running Deer repay Stone Calf." She took his hand and placed it on her small, unformed breasts, her expression encouraging. When he did not respond, she moved his hand to the juncture of her thighs.

Stone Calf felt the heat of her mound and his blood ran swiftly. He had not had a woman for many moons. Running Deer waited, her flickering gaze displaying a mixture of fear and a desire to please.

"No!" Stone Calf shouted, flinging his hand away and getting to his feet.

Running Deer's expression crumbled. Her small chin trembled. "Running Deer does not please Stone Calf," she said. "Running Deer has nothing else to give."

Stone Calf knelt beside her. "You don't have to repay me for helping you," he explained patiently. "The white man treated you badly. It was wrong. Why didn't you run away?"

"Where?" the girl asked. Stone Calf studied her resigned expression for a long time.

"You will come here," he said gruffly. "I, Stone Calf, take you for my wife."

Her expression filled with joy. Then she thought of her father. *"Ne hyo . . ."* she began.

"I will tell your father and I will pay a good price for you," Stone Calf said. Running Deer lay back against the bedding, her gaze running over Stone Calf and then his room with a proprietary air.

"Stone Calf come to bed?" she asked prettily, and the half-breed sat down on the bed beside the young girl. He did not ask himself what he had done. He looked at Running Deer's pretty face and thought of all the Cheyenne women who had died last winter when he led the soldiers to their village.

They came in the night, not bold and angry as real warriors come, but like the scurrilous coyote that creeps on silent feet so no one knows of his coming until they catch the stench of him. They came in the night and crept to the lodge of Gentle Horse, where he rested with his wife. Beneath the edge of the summer lodge one figure came, and, by the shifting light of the fire pit, sought out the target of his hatred.

Black Moon opened her eyes and saw the shadows against the skins. She screamed and rolled to one side. Gentle Horse reached for his weapon and rose in a single smooth move, but he was too late. Little Bear was upon his back, his arm tugging back Gentle Horse's head, his knife slashing once, twice, and he stood back while the warrior's blood spurted onto his chest.

Black Moon saw Gentle Horse's wound and screamed over and over again, the sound carrying outside the lodge and alerting those who slept nearby. Lone Wolf rolled from his pallet, glancing first at his sleeping wife and mother; then, hearing the screams coming from without, he grabbed his weapon and shield and ran outside. His first thought was that the soldiers had come again, but the village was silent. Only shifting shadows warned of interlopers in the village.

Lone Wolf turned to the lodge of his sister and her husband. Even as he approached the tepee, a scream came from within. Lone Wolf rushed forward and threw back the flap. In the flickering firelight he took in the bloody scene of death. Black Moon, wounded and bleeding from several cuts to her arms and face, tried to crawl across the tepee to her fallen husband, while Little Bear towered above her, his bloody knife at the ready.

"Little Bear!" Lone Wolf cried, and the renegade warrior whirled.

"Lone Wolf," he snarled. "I have come to avenge myself upon you all. I have brought death to my faithless wife and her lover. Now I will kill you and the white eyes you've taken as a wife."

"You will bring no more death to this village," Lone Wolf cried, and sprang forward.

His knife flashed, biting deep into Little Bear's arm. Little Bear swung his knife but was knocked aside by Lone Wolf's shield. The two men circled. Black Moon had reached her husband's side, and, seeing the death wound, began to lament loudly, tearing at her hair and eyes.

Lone Wolf lunged at Little Bear, his knife flashing again, leaving another deep cut that gushed with blood. Little Bear stumbled backward with the onslaught of Lone Wolf's attack. The lodge opening was at his back and he darted out of it, looking this way and that. His braves were scattered about, some running from the White Wolf warriors who had taken up their weapons and were repelling the attack. Lone Wolf stepped out of the tepee, stalking Little Bear with deadly purpose. The warrior backed away, looking for a way of escape.

Drawn from sleep by the commotion, Red Bead Woman and Colly rushed toward Black Moon's tepee. Entering, Colly gasped when she saw the blood-splattered bedding and lodge poles. Red Bead Woman's voice rose in a shrill lament when she saw her daughter. They tried to tear Black Moon from Gentle Horse to tend her wounds, but she fought them, rocking back and forth, her cry like that of a wounded animal. Seeing she could do nothing to help Black Moon at the moment and that Red Bead Woman was nearby, Colly raced out of the tepee to see her husband lunge for Little Bear.

The two men fell to the ground. Lone Wolf's shield flew away to one side, but both men still gripped their knives as they regained their feet. Warily they circled. Colly's gaze was pinned on Lone Wolf. She was unaware that Little Bear's gaze had fixed on her—or that he'd angled too near her—until she felt his arm close around her in a death grip. She fought him, trying to break his hold. His arms were slick with the blood of Black Moon and Gentle Horse.

"Let her go, Little Bear," Lone Wolf cried. "Does the mighty renegade chief hide behind the body of a woman?"

"I have no need of a white woman's body to save my life," Little Bear sneered. "My knife seeks revenge for the wrongs she's done me." He raised his knife high and brought it slashing toward Colly's face. She threw herself to one side, away from the arcing blade. Lone Wolf sprang forward, his arm high, catching the blade with his own flesh.

Lone Wolf's blood splattered onto Colly's cheek and she screamed, her fear for Lone Wolf greater than any regard for herself. Lone Wolf's hands closed around Little Bear's neck and the renegade's hold on her was broken. Colly sprang away from the fighting men and whirled, ready to give aid if Lone Wolf needed it, but his hold on Little Bear was deadly. He tightened his grip, and Colly saw Little Bear's eyes bulge frantically as he kicked out, trying to loosen the strangling hold.

With one last bit of strength, Little Bear lashed out with his knife. It slashed through the skin across Lone Wolf's ribs, momentarily loosening his hold. Little Bear sprang to his feet and began to run. Lone Wolf was up, and, regardless of the flow of blood from his arm and side, gave chase.

Some of the young braves who had followed Little Bear waited with horses. Little Bear sprang onto one and—without waiting to see if his men followed—galloped away. The renegade braves who had been captured turned their eyes away from the sight of their leader's cowardly flight. They had turned their backs on the Cheyenne way, believing Little Bear's words of glory and honor, but there had been no glory in this attack tonight. Shamed, they hung their heads and waited to see what punishment White Thunder and their fathers would mete out to them.

"Are you all right?" Colly cried, running to Lone Wolf. Seeing his cuts, she wrapped a thin piece of doeskin around his arm and pressed another to his bleeding side. Placing his good arm around her shoulder, she wound her arm around his waist.

"Lean on me," she directed, and Lone Wolf did as she'd ordered—not so much because he needed her help, but because her touch on his skin was soft and tender and he needed to feel her near him. For a moment, when Little Bear's knife had arced through the air, he'd feared she'd met the same fate as Gentle Horse. He'd had no time to think, only react. His arm tightened around her shoulder, and she placed her bloody face against his chest.

"You're not hurt, are you?" he asked anxiously.

She merely nodded, not wanting to move her head from where it rested. She could hear his heartbeat, quick and erratic. It matched her own. Once again they'd come so close to losing each other. She would not let pride drive them apart again, even if there were a thousand Burning Stars.

Together they made their way back to their lodge. Colly washed his wounds herself and packed them with special herbs from Red Bead Woman's bag. When she was finished, she lay down beside Lone Wolf, curling against his side. She did not try to call the medicine man, for she knew he was engaged in another lodge where another woman had not been as lucky.

Chapter 17

STONE CALF LED them deep into the prairie. He gave no thought to the hard knot inside his chest. It was as if he'd bound up his emotions and lodged them there so that he could act and think as a ghost spirit. Only when he thought of Running Deer did the hard knot begin to dissolve, so he tried not to think about her. He had sought out Yellow Dog the morning he left the fort and had informed the old man that he was taking Running Deer as his wife. For a bride-price he gave the old man a moth-eaten buffalo robe and his packhorse. It was all he'd had to give, but it had seemed to satisfy the old man. Running Deer was Stone Calf's wife.

Now the half-breed scout pushed through the tall prairie grass, smelling the earth and grass and even the sky but drawing no comfort from it. He had a dilemma, and he wasn't sure how to handle it. If he led the soldiers to the Cheyenne's summer camp, he would bring more bloodshed to innocent people. If he deserted Major Buford, he would be hunted down and hanged. He could go to the Cheyenne people and perhaps they would take him, even knowing he had guided the soldiers to their camp, but he could not face them. Besides, there was Running Deer. He thought of her bright eyes and round cheeks and the blood on her smooth thighs. What would become of her if he did not return?

He led them in circles on the wide prairie, hoping they'd

soon become tired of the chase. Lieutenant McKinney was already suspicious of what he was doing. He'd seen it in his eyes, but the young officer had said nothing. Stone Calf was certain he wouldn't say anything. He'd heard the lieutenant arguing with the major after the winter attack on the village. He'd been against it. Stone Calf knew the major had lied about the villagers, claiming hostile warriors had attacked them first. Now he was going to finish them off. Stone Calf thought of the kind Cheyenne family who had taken him in when he was a child. White Thunder had been a young warrior then; he'd been brave and wise. Now he was a chief of the White Wolf band.

Stone Calf led them in circles on the great prairie. He could not betray the Cheyenne again.

"What do you think, Lieutenant?" Major Buford said, staring at his younger officer. They were gathered around a map of the territory.

The lieutenant shrugged. "It's a big prairie. Trying to find a Cheyenne camp out here is like trying to find a needle in a haystack."

"He found it last year," Sergeant Crook said. "I think he's leadin' us on a wild-goose chase. He don't want to find them Injuns."

"My thought exactly," Buford said, refolding the map. "Sergeant, go get that half-breed and bring him here."

"Yes, sir," Crook said, with a slow grin.

Stone Calf was brought to the firelight. Major Buford reared back against his saddle and stared up at the half-breed for an unnerving length of time. Stone Calf's face remained impassive.

Angry that the scout failed to be intimidated by a superior officer, Major Buford pulled out his revolver and leveled it at Stone Calf's chest. "Do you think tomorrow you might find those Cheyenne we're looking for?"

Stone Calf kept his gaze level on the major's face, letting enough time lapse to show he was unafraid. He looked at the cold face and thought of Running Deer, left broken and bleeding back at the fort. He thought of all the subtle cruelties this careless young man had visited on the Indians at the fort and in the Cheyenne village, and rage boiled inside him, like the hot muds he once found in a high mountain place. None of his feelings showed on his face. His black eyes remained flat, unreadable, so that in spite of the gun he held, Major Buford was the one who felt intimidated. Quickly he glanced at his other two officers and, reassured, waved his gun at the scout.

"You have three days to find us some Cheyenne Indians," he said, "or else we're going to think you're in cahoots with them. You know what they do to traitors, chief? They string them up on a rope by the neck."

Stone Calf's eyes glittered, whether with amusement or hatred, Buford wasn't sure. "In three days I will find Cheyenne Indians," the half-breed said, and stalked away from the campfire.

"I wasn't finished with you," Buford shouted in frustration, then glanced around the camp at his men. They were watching with wide, searching eyes. Buford's face turned ugly. That savage had made him look weak and inept in front of his men. Something else to even the score for. Buford put away his gun and turned toward his tent.

"Tell the men to turn in," he ordered over his shoulder.

Lieutenant McKinney rose to do as he'd been ordered, but his thoughts were elsewhere. What if Stone Calf made good his claim to find Cheyenne in three days' time? What if there was another massacre as there had been back in the winter? He couldn't hide it from his commander a second time. He wouldn't, not even to protect a fellow officer. A man had to live with his conscience.

Stone Calf had no more doubts, no more hesitations. His plan was very clear. He rose early the next morning, before the light had even sliced the eastern horizon dividing the sky and earth into two entities. He rode away into the thick prairie grass, leaving no trace behind him.

"Do you think he's comin' back, sir?" Sergeant Crook asked when they'd discovered Stone Calf's absence.

"He'd damn well better," Buford growled, "or we'll be hunting a traitor."

Stone Calf gave no thought to whether or not he was a traitor. Those were white man words for white man laws. They didn't really touch him. He'd learned a different law those few years he'd spent in a Cheyenne camp, the laws of a man in his own environment. He needed no one else to tell him what was right and wrong, for the answers ran through him like a river.

He circled, in case anyone tried to follow, but eventually he traveled to the place he'd known about for several days, the place where the Cheyenne camp lay along the prairie river. He'd stumbled upon it one day, and, crouching in the grass, he'd watched the people as they crossed from the river to their lodges, the warriors coming and going, their voices light and carefree on the summer air. He'd felt a peace steal over him as he watched them and he wondered if he and Running Deer would be welcomed if they came here to live.

Now he made his way to the camp of the people, knowing that they would never welcome him. Still, he must do this thing. He must repay them for the wrong he'd committed against them.

He approached the village from the east, riding slowly, his hands in plain view so they would know he came as a friend and not an enemy. Some warriors noted the army mark on his horse and, taking up their lances and bows, followed him to the village circle. White Thunder was sent for and came out to see their visitor, who waited somberly on his white soldier's horse.

"Welcome, Stone Calf," the old chief said. "You have returned to our camp."

"I have been here before," Stone Calf said. "I brought the soldiers to your winter camp."

"This I had guessed," said White Thunder. "Have you brought soldiers with you this time?"

Stone Calf made no answer, but the old chief shook his head. "I thought you had not. I saw your shame at the winter camp."

"The soldiers are searching for you again," the scout said, refusing to acknowledge the old man's understanding words. "I cannot lead them astray much longer."

"You have repaid us by this act," White Thunder said gravely. "But we do not understand why the white soldiers attack us so."

Stone Calf's hard gaze moved around the circle of villagers until it reached one woman. "You have a white woman in your midst," he said. "She is believed to come from a wagon train that was attacked before the winter snows. They believe the *Tsitsitis* attacked the train."

"We did not," White Thunder said. "Lone Wolf found her on the trail and rescued her."

"You must return the white woman to the fort or the soldiers will always search for you."

"No!" Colly cried from her place at the back of the gathering. Lone Wolf, who had stood beside White Thunder, tightened his grip upon his lance.

"The white eyes woman known as Spotted Woman is the wife of Lone Wolf," White Thunder said flatly. "She does not wish to return."

Stone Calf studied the tall warrior. His chest and side and one arm were bound as if he'd suffered serious wounds. He shifted his gaze back to White Thunder. "The wagon trains are still being attacked."

"But not by the warriors of the White Wolf band," said the chief, without hesitation, so Stone Calf believed him. "There are men who have broken away from us. They were here two nights ago and attacked our village, killing one of our warriors and wounding another." He nodded toward Lone Wolf.

"I have come across their camp," the scout related.

"These renegades are filled with hate for the white men.

They wish to punish the soldiers for their slaughter of our women and children.''

Stone Calf nodded. ''There is a white soldier who hates the Cheyenne. He wishes to kill us all.''

''Even you?'' Lone Wolf challenged. ''Then why do you ride with him?''

Stone Calf ignored the criticism. He reined his horse sharply. ''I have brought you a warning, White Thunder, in return for the years of my youth.''

When he would have sprinted away, the old chief stepped forward and gripped his pony's reins. ''When you have finished with the white men and need a family, come to the White Wolf band,'' he said, staring into the half-breed's eyes. Then he released the pony and stepped back.

Thoughtfully Stone Calf rode away, White Thunder's words ringing in his ears. He thought again of Running Deer and pictured himself among the Cheyenne people, hunting the great buffalo upon the plains. Perhaps he could return to the world of the Cheyenne. Then he sighed and shook his head.

Once he, too, had had a vision. Filled with the white man's whiskey, he'd heard their boasts and he'd understood that the world of the Indian must come to an end. The tracks of the white man's wagons were already cutting apart the Mother Earth and her blood was the blood of the Indians who fell before the white man's bullets. He could do nothing to change what must come. He could change only this one day, this one battle, between the arrogant major and the Cheyenne.

Stone Calf angled his horse away from the path he'd taken before. He had two days before he must return to the detachment, two days in which to search for the camp of the renegades.

A council was called. The flaps on White Thunder's tent were closed so that no one might enter. The sacred pipe was smoked, and, when it had been passed about and its ashes emptied—and the bowl carefully cleaned and put away—the men of the council began to speak.

"The white woman must go," they said. "She has brought death to our village."

"What of Dull Knife's vision?" Lone Wolf asked.

"We have followed the directions of his vision and our village was attacked, our women and children slaughtered. Our young men have run off to join a renegade band. All this since the white woman has come among us."

"She is not to blame for all this," Lone Wolf argued. "The spirits have directed us. Why would they have told us wrong?"

"Perhaps your sacrifice of the buffalo heads was not enough to appease the buffalo gods for your killing of their chief."

"I will submit myself to any sacrifice," Lone Wolf cried, but all knew he was too weak from his wounds to withstand such a sacrifice now.

"It is too late. The damage is done," other men complained. "The soldiers will hunt us, always finding us when we least expect it, killing us and our children until there are no more Cheyenne upon the earth."

Dull Knife rose and held out his hands. The smoke of the sacred fire curled about his hands and rose to encircle his head. He breathed deeply and opened his eyes. With unhurried measure he looked at each member of the council. "Have you forgotten the vision of the white buffalo?" he asked quietly. "Have you forgotten the sacrifice of Lone Wolf? Do you cast aside his efforts so easily?" His voice had risen to a powerful timbre. Then he spoke quietly again, using the contrast to make his point.

"We have prepared for this time. Now we do not run about blindly like frightened women, blaming one another."

"But the white woman has brought the soldiers upon us."

"It was not the white woman who brought the soldiers to our village. They came because they sought the ones who attacked their wagon train. They believe the Cheyenne did this thing, but Spotted Woman knows the truth and she will tell the soldiers.''

"No!" Lone Wolf cried, leaping to his feet. "She is but a woman. If she tries to go to the white fort, they will kill her."

"Why would they kill one of their own kind?" White Thunder asked.

Dull Knife raised his hands, and in them he held a tomahawk with Sioux markings. "Spotted Woman came to me today after the Indian scout warned us. She told me she took this tomahawk from the body of the wagon train's leader. With this she can prove to the white soldiers that the Cheyenne are innocent of this crime."

"I forbid her to go," Lone Wolf cried.

"This may bring peace between the Cheyenne and the white soldiers."

"This may bring death to Spotted Woman," Lone Wolf cried.

The men of the council were silent. At last White Thunder spoke. "Once she was called Warrior Woman because she was fearless and fought like a warrior. You cannot change her destiny or yours. The gods have sent the Warrior Woman, like the white buffalo, and we must do as is required of us."

Lone Wolf knew White Thunder's words had been meant to shame him, for he was putting his own desires ahead of the good of the band, but his love for Spotted Woman was so great, he couldn't allow her to leave him.

"I will leave the decision to Spotted Woman," he said finally, knowing he could say nothing else.

"So be it," said White Thunder, and the council meeting ended. Lone Wolf made his way back to his lodge in search of Spotted Woman.

She sat beside his mother, tanning a buffalo hide. Her strong, nimble fingers rubbed the mixture of brains and ashes into the skin and her face showed none of the repugnance it had once held. Lone Wolf stood watching her, enjoying the sight of her strong face and flaming hair. She had always pleased him and he had no wish to lose her. They had just resolved the anger between them and his wounds from Little Bear's knives were not yet healed. Was he to have no time to know his wife again? This night he would ignore the throbbing wound in his side and take her to his bed.

He thought of his brother-in-law, Gentle Horse, who lay now in his grave while his widow wept on her lonely pallet. Black Moon had no will to live, not even for her unborn baby. She grieved for Gentle Horse and the brief happiness they had known. Was his marriage to Spotted Woman doomed as well?

Lone Wolf strode to his wife and knelt beside her. Startled, she glanced up at him, a slow smile lighting her face.

"I have need to speak with you," he said, holding out his hand to her.

"You have been to the council meeting?" she said.

Lone Wolf nodded and waited while she wiped her hands and got to her feet. Hand in hand they walked to the river, neither of them speaking. The sun was warm on their heads, the cry of insects loud in the hot grass. No clouds marred the blue canopy of sky, but Lone Wolf took no pleasure in this.

"I do not wish you to return to your people."

"I will not stay with them," Colly answered, turning to face him. His dark gaze warmed her heart, for it spoke of his love for her and his fear at their parting. "Once I have delivered the tomahawk to the fort and told them the truth, I will return."

"They will not believe you. The messenger, Stone Calf, has said this man hates us. He wishes to kill as many Cheyenne as he can."

"But if I deliver the tomahawk, he will have no more excuses for his attacks against us. There are laws that will keep him from it."

"I do not believe this," Lone Wolf answered, growing angry that he could not change things.

"Why would I lie to you?" Colly asked, linking her fingers with his.

Lone Wolf flung her hand away. "You do not wish to remain here as my wife. You want to return to your white world."

"That's not true," she said. She looked at him, seeing the powerful shoulders, the strongly molded features, the dark eyes and long, glossy hair. A necklace of bone and shell hung about his neck and rawhide thongs were tied around his bulging biceps. Everything about him spoke of a man of the wilderness, a man who dominated by his personal strength and magnetism, a man so powerful, he was used to having his way. Now he stood before her, thwarted and frustrated, the very essence of an Indian male, and she wanted to laugh, for he was also like a petulant boy determined to have his way. Yet to laugh would wound his pride.

"If you go to the soldiers' fort, I do not want you back." His eyes were black with rage.

"Lone Wolf, you don't mean that."

"I have spoken," he said in a low, quiet voice that carried more weight than a shout might have. He whirled and stalked away.

Colly watched his stiff departing back and was speechless. And she was angry. Didn't he see what she was trying to do? She must return to the fort for the safety of them all.

Lone Wolf would get over his anger, she was sure of it; but another thought occurred to her. If she waited until he was well enough to ride, he might try to accompany her. He had lost much blood and would be weak for many days, perhaps weeks. She must go alone, and she must go at once.

She cast a quick glance at the lodge where Red Bead Woman still worked on the hide. Inside, Black Moon lay grieving for the death of her husband and Lone Wolf lay angry and impatient over his wounds. She loved each of them and shared their pain and anger and grief, just as she shared their joy. She must also share the danger that would make the tribe safe once more. She had not told Lone Wolf of her certainty she carried his child. She wanted her son to grow up in a world that offered more than death and flight from the white soldiers. She must do what she could to insure safety for their people. When she returned, she would melt Lone Wolf's anger with her revelation about their baby—and at last they would begin to live happily again.

So certain was she of this dream and her part in making it happen that she went immediately to Dull Knife's lodge and told him of her thoughts concerning Lone Wolf.

"It is true; he resists the wisdom of this journey," the old medicine man said. "He is too weak to travel with you. I will speak to White Thunder and make arrangements for someone to take you to the fort."

"They must wait for me to guide me back to the village afterward," she insisted, and Dull Knife nodded in affirmation.

Within a short while they were ready to leave. Colly mounted one of the fine ponies Lone Wolf had given her, and they set out. Doll Man and another young warrior, Bear Rope, accompanied her. They left the village immediately. Lone Wolf was nowhere in sight. Colly knew Dull Knife would tell him of her departure and assure him of her return.

Sergeant Crook crawled down the slight ravine and made his way back to the men and horses hidden in the tall grass.

"Are they Cheyenne?" Major Buford asked impatiently.

"Yeah, they're Cheyenne, all right," Crook said.

Major Buford glanced at Stone Calf. "Are you sure?"

Stone Calf nodded. Then Crook said, "I could tell by the symbols on some of their lodges." He grunted. "They look pretty shabby, though."

"They haven't recovered yet from the beating we gave them last winter," Buford crowed.

"I didn't see many women," Crook said. "Them warriors look like a pretty mean lot. Some of 'em seemed drunk, though."

"Where would they get whiskey out here?" Lieutenant McKinney asked.

"That drummer that was killed last week," Crook answered.

"Order the men to check their ammunition and mount up," Buford ordered.

"Ain't we goin' to wait until dark and try to surprise 'em?" Crook asked, surprised at the major's impatience.

"We'll surprise them now," Buford said. "Mount up."

They rode over the slight swell in the prairie floor, the thunder of their hooves giving away their presence. Little Bear and his men ran out of their tepees, snatching up the rifles they'd collected from the wagon trains they'd attacked. They sprang on their ponies and were ready for the attack before Buford's men reached them. The battle was short-lived, with the sides firing point-blank at each other while horses screamed and reared. The soldiers' superior firing power and accuracy soon overcame the renegades' first clumsy attempts with the firearms. At last Little Bear and his surviving warriors fled across the prairie, pursued by Buford's men.

"We routed 'em, sir," Lieutenant McKinney said. He was feeling far better about this battle than he had felt about their winter one. There had been no women and children present in this camp, and from the rifles among the Indian braves, it was evident they had indeed been attacking the wagon trains.

"A good day's work, Lieutenant," Buford said, smiling winningly at his officer.

"Yes, sir," McKinney said, but turned away quickly, still uneasy with Buford's way of fighting.

Buford's eyes narrowed as he watched McKinney walk away. He hadn't forgotten his earlier resolution concerning the lieutenant. If he needed a scapegoat for anything, Lieutenant McKinney was it.

"Let's head back to the fort," he said, with obvious relish.

"What about the dead Injuns, sir?" Sergeant Crook asked.

''Leave them for the buzzards,'' Buford answered. ''Mount up.''

Colly and her escort traveled swiftly, moving across the prairie far more quickly than the whole tribe was able to travel. They paused at night only long enough to snatch a few hours' sleep and chew some of the pemmican from their packs. At first light they were up and moving again. Colly was surprised at how fit her body had become. Despite her condition, she was able to keep up with the men.

On the third day they caught sight of a line of men on a distant ridge and fell back while Bear Rope went ahead to scout.

''It is the soldiers,'' he said. ''They are returning to the fort.''

''Should we ride down and meet them?'' Colly asked.

Doll Man shook his head. ''I do not know. I do not trust these soldiers.''

''If these are the men who attacked our village and have hunted us, then they must be told that we are innocent of the crimes they claim against us. Do not go down, Doll Man. I'll go alone. They won't hurt me when they see I'm white. Follow at a safe distance and wait for me. I'll ride out from the fort after I've met with the commander.''

Doll Man nodded in agreement. With a final salute Colly reined her pony around and started toward the line of soldiers.

Lone Wolf gasped and sagged against his pony's neck. One hand pressed against his bound side. The knife wound had opened. The bandage was soaked with blood. He rested against the sweaty flesh, breathing in the horse smell of Taro. The scent reminded him of those times he'd galloped into battle on the back of this valiant horse. He gained strength and sat up straight again.

He'd thought he would have caught up with Doll Man and Spotted Woman by now. He hadn't reckoned on his weakened state. Now he pushed himself to stay in the saddle for one hour longer, one day longer, until he reached Spotted Woman. He wasn't sure why he must reach her before she arrived at the white man's fort; he only knew he must. The sun beat against him, trying to defeat him, but he pressed onward.

At last he came to a high place where he could see the depression below. The tall prairie grass had given way to sagebrush and the stunted weeds of the rocky foothills. The fort lay less than a day's ride ahead. But now he made out the line of soldiers silhouetted against the ocher background, their dark uniforms like shadows against the land.

His eyes caught the motion of another rider, and, as he looked, he saw the flaming hair of Spotted Woman. She was riding toward the soldiers. Soon she would be lost to him forever. He would never be able to speak to her again, or touch her hand, or see the light and shadows moving in her eyes. He called to her, his voice hoarse and cracking from thirst. He dug his heels into Taro's sides and the tired horse spurted forward, its great heart given to its master's commands.

Colly was near the soldiers now. She waved and called to them.

"Looks like an Indian woman, sir," Sergeant Crook said.

"Indian woman, hell. That's a white woman. Look at her hair." Everyone was so astounded by the sight of a white woman approaching that they gave little notice to Lieutenant McKinney's uncharacteristic expletive.

"Reckon what she wants?" Crook said, spitting tobacco juice and settling back in his saddle.

"Maybe she's escaped and needs help," Lieutenant McKinney offered.

"Nah, she's in a hurry, but she ain't in that big a hurry, an' I don't see nobody followin' her."

"Look there, sir," one of the men called out.

"By golly, looks like that Injun's tryin' to head her off."

"Stop him," Major Buford ordered, taking out his gun. "Lieutenant McKinney, go after the woman."

"Yes, sir." The young lieutenant whipped his horse forward. A blaze of rifle fire had already gone up, the sound echoing in the hills around.

Startled, Colly reined in her horse and stared at the line of soldiers, her first thought for her own safety. But they couldn't be shooting at her, she realized, and looked around, thinking Doll Man and Bear Rope had been spotted. They'd been right not to trust the soldiers. What she saw caused her heart to leap into her throat. She recognized the sleek black stallion immediately, and she had little doubt about the tall figure in the saddle. A hail of bullets rang out again. The figure swayed in the saddle.

"Lone Wolf!" she screamed, and reined her horse toward him, but a young man in a soldier's uniform was beside her, his hand reaching for her bridle.

"It's all right, ma'am," he reassured her. "They ain't shootin' at you."

Another volley of shots rang out, and Colly screamed, her eyes wide with terror as she twisted in her saddle in an attempt to see Lone Wolf. She saw his big body jerk; the glossy dark hair she'd once disdained flew out around his head like the feathers of a dying eagle. His arms were flung upward and he fell from his horse as if jerked by some invisible string. He hit the ground and his body rolled over and over, then lay still, like one of the stuffed leather dolls the Cheyenne women made for their little girls to play with. Taro came to a halt and stood still, his reins dragging on the ground, his head lowered.

"Lone Wolf! Let me go!" Colly tore at the reins, beating against the young lieutenant's face and hands until he was driven away from her. The horse, spooked by the flurry of activity around him, spun and squealed. Colly fought to get him under control, losing precious minutes when she might reach Lone Wolf. She wheeled the horse and kicked its belly. It spurted away from the lieutenant, but now other men had come to help him. They pressed their horses against the side of hers, cutting off her passage.

"Let me go. I have to go to him," she sobbed, but they captured her reins and turned her horse back toward the line of soldiers. "You don't understand. That was my husband. He meant no harm to you. He only wanted to talk to me. You must let me go to him. He may be alive. I can help him."

She was unaware she'd spoken in Cheyenne until she saw the puzzled faces before her.

"My husband," she said in English, trying to calm herself. "You've shot my husband."

"That was an Indian," one of the men said. He was a short, burly man with a rough face and hard, uncaring eyes. His uniform bore the stripes of an officer, but his lips were stained with the drool of tobacco juice.

"Crook, go see if he's alive," a man ordered, riding forward.

"Yes, sir," the sergeant answered, and galloped out to the place where Lone Wolf lay.

Her breath held, Colly waited while the burly man dismounted and roughly turned Lone Wolf over. She cried out at the soldier's careless handling of the inert body.

"He's as dead as I've seen 'em," the sergeant called back. "Want me to shoot him in the head just to be sure?"

"No!" Colly cried out.

"Save your bullet," the officer called, and turned his cool gaze on Colly. "Ma'am, I take it you lived with the Indians for a spell. Could you tell me how you came to be there with them?"

At first, she couldn't speak; her heart was numb with grief. The world around her seemed not to exist. All was darkness.

"Ma'am!" the officer demanded impatiently. Colly raised her head and forced her gaze to focus on him.

"Who are you?" she whispered.

"I'm Major John D. Buford, head of the Sixth Cavalry

Mounted Rifleman, stationed out of Fort Laramie. Now tell me who you are.''

''I am . . . Spotted Woman, wife of Lone Wolf, war chief of the White Wolf band of the Cheyenne Nation,'' she answered, and her voice grew stronger. Lone Wolf was dead and so was she, but her reason for being here had not vanished. She must tell her story to protect the Cheyenne people.

''Once, I was Colly Mead. I came here by way of a wagon train. Brother Davey Samuel was our leader.'' Briefly she told her story, sitting there in the middle of the foothills, the wind from the prairie blowing against her cheeks. She told her story and relived for a moment the joy and happiness she'd known with the Cheyenne, and when she'd finished, she pulled the Sioux tomahawk from her bedroll and handed it to the major.

''So you see, you have hunted the Cheyenne people for no reason. They are innocent.'' She turned her horse and was surprised to see her way still blocked. Her questioning gaze went back to the major.

''Please, let me pass now, Major,'' she said tiredly. ''I must collect my husband's body and return it to his people.''

''I'm afraid I can't let you do that, ma'am,'' the major said. ''You'll have to come to the fort with me. Once my commanding officer has talked to you, we'll send you back East, where you came from.''

''I have no desire to return East,'' Colly said, panic pitching her voice high. ''My home is here with the *Tsitsitis*. I want to collect my dead husband's body and see it's properly buried.''

''You're coming with us,'' the major snapped. ''Lieutenant, lead the men out.''

''At least let me take my husband's body. I can't leave him here on the prairie like an animal. The coyotes will dishonor his body.''

''Leave him,'' the major snapped. ''We have no time for dirty Indians.'' His blue eyes were filled with contempt for her. She knew what he was thinking, that she herself was dirty because she'd lain with an Indian.

She wanted to rail at him, to tell him his attitude was wrong and hateful, but she saw how whole he was in his belief of superiority and she knew it was useless. Still, she fought against the hands that reached for her bridle, kicking at the young private until the major ordered her feet tied beneath the belly of her pony.

Still she screamed at them, alternately pleading and cursing until she knew she must appear a madwoman. She couldn't go away and leave him alone on the prairie. She thought of his beloved body, so strong and powerful above hers, his hands gentle and warm on her skin, his eyes laughing into hers. She screamed against her sorrow and grief until she was exhausted and lay at last against the neck of her mount, her long, tangled braid drooping over her shoulder, her long legs captured like some graceful crane the young boys had caught in the river marshes. And thus they bore her to the fort, like some broken-winged bird who would never fly again.

Chapter 18

PEOPLE TURNED TO stare when they rode into the fort. Soldiers and emigrants who'd paused in their long journey formed a line to watch the return of the soldiers. They clucked their tongues sympathetically when they saw the uniformed bodies draped over the horses. A murmur rose among them when they discerned the sagging figure of a white woman. She was still alive! They fell to speculating on what hardships the poor thing must have endured.

Major Buford led his detachment through the heart of the fort, right up to the commander's door. He had quite a lot to report, and all of it would make him look the hero.

"Sergeant, bring the woman," he called, alighting. He was perfectly aware of the palpable curiosity of the onlookers and he contrived to look his most dashing, removing his wide-brimmed hat and beating it against the side of his pants before resettling it on his head. He was the perfect image of a brave officer who'd led his men into combat and returned to face his commander. He even managed to limp a little as he climbed the steps and entered Commander Sanderson's office.

Sergeant Crook gripped Colly's arm, ushering her in behind the major. Inside she was shoved into a chair and told to wait. Major Buford crossed to a door and tapped on it lightly. At a command from within, he opened the door and entered.

Colly sat looking around the rough but sturdy log building. It was the first structure she'd entered in more than a year. She'd forgotten how large and roomy such buildings could be. She noted the wooden floor beneath her moccasins. It felt hard and unyielding. The chair on which she sat was strange and oddly uncomfortable.

The young soldier seated at a desk across the room from her stared at her curiously, and Colly thought she must indeed look strange to him with her painted part and quill-trimmed elk-skin dress. A sound at the window made her turn, and she saw that several people were pressing their faces against the oiled paper, peering around the edges. Self-consciously she smoothed back her hair; then the memory of Lone Wolf falling lifeless from his horse returned to her and she pulled strands of hair over her face and sat rocking herself and sobbing.

At last the door opened and Sergeant Crook called to her. "Hey, you, squaw woman. The commander wants to see you."

Colly stopped rocking, reason returning to her. She calmed herself, pushing her straggly hair back from her dirty face, and slowly rose and walked into the commander's office. She looked so bedraggled that Sanderson immediately felt pity for her, shoving a chair forward so that she might sit again.

"You poor woman," he said. "You need have no fear now. You are safe." He paused, not wanting to be insensitive to her suffering yet needing to hear for himself the full story. "Could you tell me all that has happened to you?"

Slowly Colly nodded and raised her head. Her gaze met that of the commander's. He saw she was not a beautiful woman in the traditional sense, but her eyes were fine and her cheekbones dusted with becoming freckles. There was an air about her that drew him to her. He smiled encouragingly.

"Don't be afraid or ashamed," he coaxed. "We understand that you've been through a terrible ordeal."

"Yes, a terrible ordeal," she echoed. "My husband was killed and lies even now alone in the prairie."

"Did the Indians kill him?"

"No, Commander, your soldiers killed him, shot him down like an animal. But that does not surprise me, for they attacked our village of women and children and slaughtered all who could not escape—but not before they raped the women and committed unspeakable atrocities upon them."

"What are you saying?" Commander Sanderson demanded, drawing back. His stern gaze went to the two officers.

"I told you, sir, her ordeal among the Indians has turned her mad."

"I saw the bodies of the women you tortured," Colly said evenly. "I saw the lodges you burned, the food your men soiled so we could not eat it. You left us, women and children, without robes or food. Some of us froze in the mountains, some died from lack of food."

"They ran off into the woods, sir, and we had no way of gathering them up," Major Buford said.

"Did you burn their tepees and food?"

"Their warriors burned them."

"Liar!" Colly cried scathingly. "Our warriors were away in the hills hunting for food."

The major said nothing, but his face was pale. Colly turned from him back to the commander.

"The soldiers came . . . asking us if we knew of who attacked the wagon train. White Thunder told them our people were innocent of such acts, but your soldiers did not believe us. I have brought you proof that the Sioux attacked the train, not White Thunder's people."

"What is your proof?" the commander asked. He was troubled by all that the woman had said.

Colly repeated the story she'd told Major Buford, explaining how Lone Wolf had rescued her and carried her to his village, how he'd feared coming to the fort, for the white soldiers had already shown great cruelty to the Indians. She told him about the tomahawk and, at last, she sat back in her chair.

"Where is this tomahawk?" Sanderson asked.

"I gave it to Major Buford," she said wearily.

"Major?"

"I have a tomahawk, sir, but it doesn't belong to the Sioux."

"But it does," Colly cried, staring at him with wide eyes.

"I'd like to see the tomahawk for myself, Major," the commander said.

"Yes, sir," the major replied. "I'll get it at once." He wheeled and left the room.

"Private Olson!"

"Yes, sir." The young soldier who'd sat at the desk in the outer office came to the door.

"Get Stone Calf in here immediately."

"Yes, sir."

Colly sagged in her chair, glad it would soon be over. Soon she could return to the prairie and find her husband's body. She would return to the Cheyenne and never gaze upon a white face again.

She did not look at the tomahawk that Major Buford brought. It was placed upon the desk and Stone Calf was asked to examine it. Colly raised her head when the half-breed entered but gave no indication she'd ever seen him before. Stone Calf looked at the tomahawk and stepped back from the desk.

"Well?" Sanderson demanded impatiently. "Whose is it?"

"It is a Cheyenne tomahawk," the scout said.

"No! You're lying," Colly said, springing from her chair. "Why are you doing this?" she demanded, staring into his dark eyes.

Stone Calf nodded his head. "It is a Cheyenne tomahawk," he repeated solemnly, and she knew he had not lied.

Whirling, Colly studied the tomahawk on the desk. "It's not the same," she whispered, raising her wide gray gaze to the commander's. "He's switched tomahawks."

"Why would he do that?" the commander asked.

"I—I don't know," Colly said. "I only know he's trying to make the Cheyenne look guilty, perhaps to justify his own brutality toward them."

Sanderson sighed. His suspicions about his junior officer made him hesitate. Major Buford said nothing in his own defense, but Sergeant Crook stepped forward.

"That ain't so, sir," he blustered. "The major ain't acted bad toward them Injuns. He jus' give 'em what they deserved. Why, this here woman's been livin' among them savages for nearly a year. She's plumb lost her sense."

"I assure you I have my senses about me," Colly began. She was trembling with fatigue and shock. Sanderson saw her condition and made up his mind.

"Whatever the truth is, Miss Mead, it will take some time to figure it out. You need to rest."

"I can't rest," Colly cried. "I must return and find my husband's body. Could you spare a rider or two to go with me?"

"That's quite impossible," the commander said. "Night will be here soon. You'd never be able to find him now."

"But I must," Colly insisted. "Don't you understand what a dishonor it is to a Cheyenne not to be buried properly? His spirit cannot rest."

"Come now, Miss Mead. Surely you have not adopted the mysticism of these heathen savages."

"They're not heathens," Colly said. "I thought as you did once, but I've found they are gentle, good people, as civilized in their own way as you or me."

Though Sanderson prided himself on being a fair man, Colly's claim had offended him deeply. His expression grew cold and he waved his aide into his office.

"Take Miss Mead to the spare quarters," he directed. "Then contact some of the women on the wagon train and see if you can locate some decent clothes for her. Ask the wagon master if he can stop around to see me sometime this evening.''

He turned back to Colly. ''If you're in any condition to travel, Miss Mead, it might be good for you to join this wagon train. They're moving on toward Oregon in a few days.''

Colly had risen when the private entered; now she stood swaying, her stricken gaze fixed on the commander's face. ''I shall never leave here,'' she said hoarsely, and followed the young soldier from the office.

''Like I said, sir,'' Sergeant Crook said, ''she's in a bad way. She talks like she's one of them Cheyenne. She's lost all sense of who she is and who her people are. I don't think I'd put more stock in what she had to say about things.''

''Perhaps you're right, Sergeant. But now I'd like you and Major Buford to tell me again what happened when you came upon the village last winter.''

The young private took her to another cabin that looked like it had once been a supply shed. There was no wooden floor inside it, but a bed had been made up and a chest with a silvery mirror sat at one end. Colly looked around the room, feeling disoriented and uncomfortable. Once she'd lived in a room like this, once in a land called Tennessee, but now she was used to the sloping sides of a skin lodge about her and the smell of smoked furs and campfires.

She thought of Lone Wolf lying on the prairie and prayed that Doll Man and Bear Rope had rescued him and returned his body to his people. Suddenly the enormity of all she'd lost pressed in on her and she sank to the dirt floor, rocking herself while her voice rose in a shrill Cheyenne wail of grief. Her nails tore at her hair and face, bringing runnels of blood to her thin cheeks and arms. She sat singing the hymns of grief she'd heard other Cheyenne women utter when their husbands were taken and she thought of Black Moon closed in her lodge, her mind lost to all but the grief she bore.

Colly longed to be there with her, to share their grief for the loss of the men they'd loved. Now she sat alone in an alien land of her own people and grieved not just for the loss of her husband but for all else that had been taken from her. She was to be sent West, away from the Cheyenne. Her voice droned its sorrow and she rocked herself, while inside a kernel of rebellion grew.

She would not be sent away. The Cheyenne were her people, the people of her son, hers and Lone Wolf's. She would not leave. Some instinct told her she must rise and bathe herself in the tub of water left for her, listen to the white men, and appear to accept their words, for only then would they trust her. She would win their trust as she'd sought to win Lone Wolf's trust so long ago. But this time, she would not run away *from* the Cheyenne. She would flee *to* them.

She rose and used her fingers to comb her hair from her face; then, seeing the water, she stripped away the elk-skin dress and stepped into the water.

"Oh, I didn't know yo' was about yo' bathin'," a voice said from the door.

Colly turned to face two women. She made no move to cover her breasts or genitals. The women glanced at each other, then studiously looked away from her.

"We've brought you some clothes. My name's Sarah Woods and this here's Mary Jo Sinclair. We're with the wagon train on its way to Oregon."

The women waited expectantly for Colly's response. She'd slid down into the water, taking up a piece of soap.

"I'll bet it's been a long time since you seen a piece of soap," said the woman known as Mary Jo Sinclair.

"We use soapwood," Colly answered. "We peel the stalk and inside is a wonderfully fragrant plant that lathers and makes your hair smell clean . . . like the grass in spring."

"Oh." The two women looked at each other again. "We didn't catch your name," Sarah said.

"I am called Spotted Woman," Colly answered serenely, concentrating on scrubbing her feet. A light tap at the door dissuaded the women from any further questions. A plump, beaming woman entered.

"I found some bloomers I thought she could use," she said, advancing into the room.

"Surely not yours," Mary Jo said, and the two women snickered good-naturedly.

"Well, I reckon we can pin them over and tie them, if they're too big," the newcomer said. She smiled at Colly. "I'm Myrtle Woods, Sarah's sister-in-law. Oh, my! What is that?"

Myrtle's eyes had gone large as Colly rose from the water and reached for a towel. She looked at the rope that had captured the other woman's attention.

"It is a chastity belt," she explained. Once she would have asked such questions herself. Suddenly she wanted these women to understand about the Cheyenne and their ways. "All unmarried women wear them—and even married women when they are leaving the safety of their camp. This is to protect them."

"I see," Myrtle said. "No wonder the Indians rape and kill the white women they get when their own women wear such contraptions."

Colly paused in her drying and looked at the women. They were determined to misconstrue the things they learned about the Indians. Wearily she sighed and reached for her elk-skin dress.

"You must wear these," Sarah said quickly. "We insist." Colly hesitated, remembering she wished them to think her cooperative. Taking up the ugly dress, she ran her hands across it as if admiring it.

"You're very kind," she said gruffly, and pulled on the garment. It was too short in the waist and the hem and the seams bunched beneath the arms. She'd forgotten how uncomfortable white women's dresses were—and how unflattering to her tall, awkward figure. She felt even uglier.

"It must have been very hard for you," Sarah said.

"Not as bad as you might think," Colly answered.

"Didn't you miss anything from the white world?" Sarah asked.

Colly thought for a moment. "Apples," she said.

"What?"

"I missed those little pippins that used to grow in the tree down by the creek," she mused. "They were the sweetest, crispest— Well, no matter."

"What did she say?" Myrtle asked loudly.

"She misses apples," Mary Jo said.

"Land, the poor thing. I've got some dried apples left from our Christmas supplies. I was savin' them for a special occasion. I reckon this is special enough."

"You'd do that for her?" Sarah whispered. "Can't you tell she's little more than a savage herself? They say she was married to one of those heathens. I'm surprised the commander lets her stay here at the fort among decent folks."

"Some of us ain't so decent," Myrtle said. "She can't help she was captured by them Injuns, or even that she bedded with one of 'em. Maybe they forced her to it. Them red devils would just naturally want a white woman that way. But I ain't goin' to turn my face from her for doin' what she had to in order to survive—and I am fixin' to bake her an apple pie!"

"*Hmmpf!*" Mary Jo said in outrage.

"*Hmmpf!*" the intrepid Myrtle said in return, and waddled out of the room.

"Please," Colly said to the two women left behind. "I'm very tired."

"Yes, of course. We'll leave you now," they said, and sidled out, never quite turning their back on her. Colly wanted to laugh and to cry.

Once she, too, had thought as these women did, that the Cheyenne Indians were godless pagans with murder and rape on their minds. If they only knew the taboos and strict codes that ruled the Cheyenne people in their daily lives. But they would have to do as she had done, go to live among them, work beside them and laugh with them, learn their fear and courage.

Colly first sat on the bed, but, feeling the uncomfortable softness of the white man's world, she then sat on the dirt floor and thought of what she must do. A knock sounded at her door and there was an offer of food; finally she heard the sound of a tray being left and then silence. Darkness filled the room, and at last she rose and opened the door. She was surprised to find the door unlocked and no one guarding it from the outside. Tentatively she stepped out, and, still hearing no one oppose her, she walked out onto the moonlit parade ground. Feeling closed in by the walled trading post, she climbed to the narrow walkway along the palisade and stood looking at the hills and prairie beyond. Her thoughts went to Lone Wolf. In his last moment of life, he'd tried to come to her and had found death instead. How could she go on without him?

Sorrow welled inside her; she raised her head to the sky and emitted the high-pitched, undulating cry of grief the Cheyenne women used. In the fort below, figures tumbled out onto the parade ground, hands fumbling for weapons.

"Up there!" someone shouted, and heavy-booted feet pounded up the stairs. Rough hands grabbed Colly, cutting off her wild cry. As in a fog, she looked at the soldiers.

"Bring her down here," a voice called, and she was pushed, none too gently, down the steep stairs and shoved forward, until she stood before Major Buford.

"What were you doing up there?" he demanded.

Colly didn't answer at first. How could she tell him she was engaged in something so intimate as grieving for her dead husband?

"What were you doing up there?" he shouted. His hand flashed out, leaving a red welt against her cheek. "You were signaling those devils, weren't you?" he raged.

"That's enough, Major," Sanderson said, coming forward. He had hastily pulled his trousers over his underwear.

He stopped before Colly. "Now suppose you tell us what you were about," he said kindly.

"My dead husband is out there somewhere," Colly said. "I was unable to claim his body, but I can at least grieve for him properly."

Sanderson looked sheepish and stepped back. "See she gets back to her quarters, Major," he said. His face was set when he faced Colly. "Your time among the Indians has ended, Miss Mead. You can return to your own kind. I've spoken with Jim Stratton, the wagon master of the wagon train, and he's willing to let you join them. A good family with children has agreed you can work your way to Oregon with them helping care for their children. That's a mighty generous offer, considering you've been—" He paused.

"Considering I've been living with the heathen Indians," Colly said softly, her gray eyes bright with anger.

Sanderson's jaw tightened. "The wagon train leaves at first light," he said, and didn't have to add how relieved he'd be to have her gone.

"And what if I don't wish to go?"

"I'm responsible for the welfare of the emigrants passing through this country, Miss Mead. That includes you. If you refuse to rejoin your own people, I must assume you have suffered irreparable harm from your horrifying experience and can no longer make decisions for yourself."

"You'd force me to go?" Colly stared at him, unable to believe what she was hearing.

"I think my orders are clear. You will leave with Stratton's wagon train in the morning." He turned away, then hesitated. His face was troubled when he looked at her, and she sensed he was a good man at heart. "Though you may not agree with me now, Miss Mead, I'm trying to do what's best for you. Once you've adjusted to your own people again, you'll thank me for this." He strode away, giving her no chance to protest further.

Major Buford's pale eyes flashed with spiteful triumph. He didn't like this white woman or her arrogant ways. "Sergeant

Crook," he called, without taking his cold gaze from Colly's face. "See that this woman gets back to her quarters and assign a man to stand guard outside her door."

"Yes, sir," the sergeant said, with a sketchy salute.

Colly returned the major's gaze. She felt his hatred for her and she felt elation. He was her enemy, the enemy of her people, the Cheyenne, and she had no fear of him.

"You ordered my husband killed, Major Buford," she said quietly, "and you have caused the death of many of my people. Be forewarned: I will avenge their death."

"Sergeant," the major called. "Make that an armed guard—and if this woman tries to leave her room again, they are instructed to shoot her."

"Yes, sir," Crook said, staring after the departing major's back. He wasn't sure if he should give such a command or not, but others had heard it as well. If something happened to the white woman, he had witnesses to say he'd only acted under orders.

Two soldiers led Colly back to her room. Once inside, she paced back and forth. Obviously she was a prisoner . . . and tomorrow she would be put on a wagon train against her will. She'd done all she could. The commander did not believe the Cheyenne were innocent of attacking the wagon trains. Major Buford had made his lies too convincing. There was nothing left for her but to escape and return to her people. But how? Two men guarded the door outside and there were no windows in this shed.

She paced in the dark, twisting her hands together in agitation. When she was half-mad with despair, there was a sound. At first she flew to the door, thinking someone had come to rescue her. She peered through the tiny square window, but only the soldiers were there. One of them had fallen asleep and was snoring rather loudly. The other stared dully into the dark shadows while he hummed a tuneless melody.

The sound came again, and this time Colly moved to the back of the shed. Placing her mouth near a crack in the boards, she whispered.

"Is anybody there?"

"Spotted Woman?" a voice whispered back.

"Yes, this is Spotted Woman," Colly answered, kneeling so her voice was nearer the one on the other side. "Who's there? Doll Man?"

"Stone Calf!" came the answer. Hope died a little bit.

"What do you want?" she asked listlessly.

"Help Spotted Woman escape."

Colly's heart thudded in her chest. "How?" she asked.

"Have horses outside fort. You come?"

"Yes, but how do I get out of here? The door to the shed is guarded."

"I will take care of guards," he whispered back.

"Don't kill them," Colly said quickly. There was a long silence on the other side of the wall.

"No kill them," he answered; then all was quiet. Leaping up, she looked about the room. There was nothing she wanted. Someone had taken away her elk-skin dress—to burn it, she guessed. She would have to make do in the draping skirts of the white woman's dress. She turned to the door and looked out the tiny window. They sat as before, their heads slumping on their chests as if they'd fallen asleep at their posts. Colly tried the door, knowing before her hand touched the knob that she'd been locked in.

A sound at the back of the shed drew her back. Stone Calf was trying to pull away the planks. Colly lent her weight from inside, but the planks were stronger than they looked. Lying down on the dirt floor, she kicked at them with her feet, hearing the groaning give of nails. The plank was still intact, but there was a space at the bottom, impossibly small. Colly gathered the voluminous skirt around her and stuck her feet through the opening. It was even tighter than she'd expected. She felt the scratch of splintered wood but kept scooting herself out through the hole. Her buttocks stuck. As slim as she was, she couldn't get through.

"Pull!" she whispered frantically, and felt the wood give a little as Stone Calf lent his weight against it. She scooted

downward, feeling the scrapes along her buttocks, the tightness around her abdomen. She pressed backward, trying to
protect her stomach as much as possible. Lone Wolf's child
rested there. She would do all she could to protect it. She
was nearly free. Painful scratches along her ribs and back
marked her progress. Stone Calf took hold of her legs and
began to pull her from the narrow opening, and then she was
free—her body scratched and bleeding in a dozen places, but
free.

"Come," Stone Calf said in a low, urgent voice, and she
followed him.

They crept around buildings, freezing at the sound of
voices, gliding through dark shadows like specters of the
prairie. At last they were at the palisade; Stone Calf climbed
over, reaching back to assist her. It was a long drop to the
ground on the other side, but she didn't hesitate, bending her
knees and rolling with the shock of impact.

Stone Calf motioned her to silence. They pressed themselves to the ground, waiting to see if anyone had heard and
would now pursue. All was quiet.

Stone Calf motioned to her to follow, and she crept along
the fort wall and down a shallow ravine toward the river.

"Halt! Who's out there?" a voice cried from the parapet.

"Run!" Stone Calf whispered hoarsely, and sprinted
ahead.

Colly followed, spurred forward by the whine of bullets
over her head. They made the river and ran along its banks
until they reached a small grove of trees.

"Running Deer?" Stone Calf called, and was answered
by a high whistle. He ran forward and Colly followed, thank-
ful to see the horses. A young girl, not more than twelve or
thirteen, held them.

"Mount up," Stone Calf ordered, but Colly had already
slung herself onto the back of one of the horses.

She did not have to be told to ride. There were shouts from
the fort and a steady barrage of bullets. Digging her heels

into the horse's side, she sprinted away along the riverbank. Stone Calf and the Indian girl followed.

"Major, what's happened?" Lieutenant McKinney asked, running out of his quarters.

"The white squaw has escaped," Buford snapped, taking out his pistol and checking his ammunition.

"And the soldiers are firing at her?" McKinney demanded incredulously. "On whose orders?"

"On mine," Buford snapped. "You haven't forgotten that I'm your superior and may give such orders?"

The young lieutenant stared at the major's angry face. All former refinement seemed distorted by the ugly rage he saw there.

"You wanted her to escape so you could kill her," he said, with sudden understanding.

"Why would I want her dead?" Buford asked, his expression still and watchful.

"Because she knows the truth of your attacks on the Cheyenne village. She can expose you for the monster you are."

"Be careful, Lieutenant," Buford warned. "A man can be killed for helping a prisoner escape."

"You can't scare me, Buford," McKinney said in disgust. "I'm sorry I didn't speak up about you last winter. I'm going to remedy that now. When Commander Sanderson hears the truth, you'll face a court-martial."

He swung around, intending to go immediately to his commander's quarters, but the report of a gun caught him in midstride. The bullet grazed his rib, knocking him to his knees. His pain-stricken gaze turned to the man he'd once idolized.

"Like I said," Buford said, stepping closer. "You shouldn't have helped the woman escape. Once she was free, the poor crazy thing shot you for your troubles." Buford cocked his pistol and aimed. McKinney saw his finger tighten on the trigger and tried to turn away from the bullet. He felt it enter his side before darkness claimed him.

* * *

Bent low over their mounts' necks, they rode hard, leaving the fort behind as they raced through the foothills. They'd made it, Colly thought exultingly. A cry from the Indian girl brought her up short. She looked back to see that Stone Calf had fallen. Quickly she galloped back and dismounted. The girl was already beside the huge Indian scout, her small hands patting his cheeks, her own cheeks wet with tears.

"Stone Calf?" Colly whispered, kneeling beside the half-breed.

"White man's bullets bring much pain," he gasped. "Take away breath."

"Where are you hit?" Colly ran her hands over his chest and sides. When she reached his back, she felt the dampness of blood on his shirt and the ground below. His breath came with the rattle of death in it.

"We'll take you to my village," she said. "Dull Knife, our medicine man, will make you well."

Stone Calf shook his head. "I have walked among the white eyes too long," he said. "Cheyenne medicine will not help me."

"It will. Just hang on," Colly urged. She glanced at the Indian girl, who sat weeping piteously.

"Running Deer, my wife," Stone Calf said. "She is young. Take her to village of White Thunder to live."

"I will," Colly said. "I promise."

"Go now," Stone Calf urged. "White soldiers follow, kill."

"We can't leave you," Colly said. "We will take you back to the village so your bones will rest with your people."

"Go now," Stone Calf said. "Take Running Deer and my spirit will walk freely to the hunting grounds."

Colly looked at the sobbing girl, but she nodded her head and threw herself against Stone Calf's chest.

"Go!" he commanded, shoving her away roughly. The effort ruptured the last shred of tissue to his lungs, and blood bubbled from his nose and mouth. For a moment the half-breed fought death, his throat rigid with his death rattle; then his body went slack and he lay still, his sightless eyes staring into the great unknown where he must walk.

Running Deer's voice rose shrill and piercing in its death cry. She sat rocking herself like a small child who has been abandoned.

"We must go," Colly said. "There is nothing we can do for him." But the girl sat as if she hadn't heard, her cry seemingly without end. Colly leaned across Stone Calf's body and delivered a stinging slap, much as her mother-in-law had done to her once. The girl stopped her lamenting and stared at Colly.

"Get on your horse, quickly," Colly commanded, not caring that her voice sounded harsh. Stone Calf had charged her with the protection of this young girl and she would do so to the best of her ability. She owed him that much.

The sound of horses galloping toward them drew her head up sharply. Grabbing Running Deer's arm, she propelled her toward the waiting horses, shoving her up into her saddle before leaping astride her own. They galloped away, but a shot let her know they'd been spotted.

They rode without letup, but still the soldiers stayed close behind them. Colly was unsure of where to go. She'd become lost in their frantic flight. Suddenly a dark figure on horseback rode beside them. At first Colly thought it was Running Deer, but a glance over her shoulder showed that the girl still lagged behind. A soldier then, Colly thought, prepared to strike at him with her empty hand if necessary, but the rider gave her no chance. He sprinted ahead, leaning from his saddle to take her bridle and lead her horse off the trail and down a steep incline. A glance back told her Running Deer had followed blindly. The strange rider guided them beneath a ledge. They were no sooner concealed than the pursuing riders thundered by overhead. Colly held her breath as if they might even yet be discovered. When at last the soldiers were gone, she turned to the shadowy figure who'd rescued them.

"Who are you?" she demanded.

At first there was silence from the shadows, then a soft chuckle.

"Does Spotted Woman not recognize her own husband?" the disembodied voice asked.

"Lone Wolf!" she whispered. A chill ran up her spine. "Is it really you?"

"Or is it my restless spirit come to save my disobedient wife?"

"You may call me what you wish if you are truly alive," she whispered, tears stinging her eyelids. His hand grasped hers then and he brought his horse beside hers. His dark eyes gleamed with love.

Colly fought back a sob. "I thought the soldiers had killed you. I fought them to go to you and give aid."

"I heard." He chuckled. "I lay in the dust and heard your wailing; it gave me courage."

"I love you," she whispered. "Even if you do not understand this white man's word, I must say it, because my heart is so full."

A shadow crossed his face, and she wasn't sure if it was caused by the moonlight or his own emotions. "We must go," he said. "The soldiers will double back when they see they are chasing shadows."

"I am lost," Colly said.

"Follow me." Lone Wolf's voice was quiet and reassuring.

Colly motioned Running Deer to follow and they continued their journey down the steep slope. With sure instinct Lone Wolf led them through the hills. The sky to the east was stained with a blaze of color heralding the rising sun when Lone Wolf finally drew to a halt. His arm made a sweeping arc.

"The prairie lies there," he said softly. "Do not be afraid of the prairie, Spotted Woman."

"Aren't you traveling with us?" Colly asked. Fear that he might be about to leave them coursed through her.

Lone Wolf nodded. "I will try," he said, and sagged forward against Taro's neck. The muscles in his long legs bulged with the effort to keep his seat. But he fell into a heap in the tall grass.

"Lone Wolf!" Colly cried, flinging herself off her horse. Running Deer sat staring down at the fallen body as if mesmerized.

"Stone Calf?" she whispered, and began her lamenting cry again. It echoed across the vast flatland.

"Shut up," Colly shouted at her, and racing to the girl, yanked her from her horse. She fell into the grass and lay weeping.

Colly hurried to Lone Wolf. He was still breathing. Frantically she looked for his injuries. The knife wounds Little Bear had inflicted had opened and bled profusely. The soft leather was stiff with dried blood. She found two places where the soldiers' bullets had grazed his skin that fateful day and another wound in his shoulder.

The bullet was still there; the wound was becoming putrid. Quickly she gathered dried prairie grass and started a small fire. She must remove the bullet and cauterize the wound if he was to live. Taking the canteens from their horses, she poured water over the knife, then held it over the small, hot flame.

Lone Wolf's eyes were open now, though dulled with pain. He saw the hot blade in her hands and nodded. Colly hesitated only a moment, then put aside all thought of the beloved flesh she must torture. Lone Wolf made no outcry while she dug for the bullet. Sweat lay on his brow and shoulders, but he was silent, his even, white teeth pressed together, his lips tight; otherwise there was no acknowledgment of the pain she must be causing him. When the bullet was out, she gathered special grasses from the prairie and made a poultice, binding the wound with a strip from her skirt.

Lone Wolf watched her work, his dark eyes taking in the blue calico dress. "You look like a white woman," he gasped.

Colly raised her head and glared at him. "I am Cheyenne!'' His smile was thin, but it was a smile nonetheless. She felt better.

Rising, she ripped away the yards of material that formed her skirt. Then, searching along the riverbank, she gathered two long sticks and formed a travois. She prayed the calico would hold. She bullied Running Deer into helping her tug Lone Wolf's body onto the travois. He grunted, and she knelt beside him.

"Do not follow the river," he said. "The soldiers will look for you there. Follow the morning sun, but let the afternoon sun lie at your back."

"I'll find the village," she said, and prayed she spoke the truth.

Mounting her own horse, she looked at Running Deer. The young girl's eyes were fixed on her with complete trust. Lone Wolf had already lapsed into unconsciousness. Once again she faced the prairie with only herself to depend upon. But this time she and the prairie held the life of the man she loved.

Colly stared at the vast flatland sweeping away from her and squared her shoulders.

Chapter 19

FEARLESSLY SHE TRAVERSED the mighty plain, following the early morning sun as Lone Wolf had advised her but taking care that it lay at her back in the late afternoon. They paused once to hide themselves in the tall grasses, pressing their horses down on their sides while soldiers passed close by. They paused a second time to dig roots from the prairie soil and eat them raw as they pressed onward. Three days later they came to a swift-flowing river and Colly said a silent prayer that God had led her to it. They trekked northward, and late on the second day they caught their first glimpse of their village. As they reached the outskirts, a cry went up and the villagers gathered to watch their approach.

"Spotted Woman!" Red Bead Woman cried, running forward. She stopped, her face going stark when she saw Lone Wolf's war horse and the travois.

"He's alive," Colly cried, and relief flooded Red Bead Woman's face. They were close enough now for her to pull the ponies to a halt and dismount. "His knife wounds have opened and he was shot by the soldiers. He needs rest and care, but he'll live." Her face was shining when she looked at Red Bead Woman, and, in spite of the dirt and dishevelment of her daughter-in-law, Red Bead Woman thought she was beautiful.

Colly's gaze lit on the young girl who sat on her pony, shy

and wary of all the strange faces. "*Nah koa*, I have brought you another daughter," she said, nodding at the young girl. Red Bead Woman turned her worried gaze from Lone Wolf's face to look at Running Deer, while Colly quickly related what had happened.

"Welcome, my daughter," Red Bead Woman said, and held out her arms. Running Deer stared at her as if uncomprehending; then she slid off her horse and walked to Red Bead Woman.

"*Nah koa!*" she said, and Red Bead Woman's arms slid around the young shoulders. Willing hands helped carry Lone Wolf to his lodge and settle him on his pallet.

"Is he alive?" Black Moon demanded from her pallet.

Colly went to greet her sister-in-law. "He lives," she said, studying the battered face. Black Moon's once pretty face would carry the scars of Little Bear's knife to her grave, but her unborn child was well.

"And you and your child live. Gentle Horse would be happy for that." Colly pushed the dark strands of hair from Black Moon's cheeks.

The Indian girl sighed. "He would be happy for that," she said, her hand going to her rounded belly. "At least I will have his son."

"Soon," Colly said, bending over to whisper in Black Moon's ear, "soon he will have a friend to play with." She drew back and saw lights break through the dull grief in Black Moon's eyes. She was glad she'd told her sister-in-law before telling Lone Wolf. Black Moon lay back against her pillow, her face luminous despite the ugly wounds.

"They will be great friends," she whispered. "They'll be warriors together."

"They'll be brothers," Colly said softly, squeezing Black Moon's hand. Black Moon leaned back and closed her eyes, the lines of her face more relaxed now. Colly turned her attention to her own husband.

Dull Knife had been summoned and now he burned sweet grasses at the head of his patient. Prayers were sent up, the pipe smoked, and crushed herbs applied to the wounds. Lone Wolf was given a strong tea made of red willow bark and at last he slept easily, the jarring pain of travel behind him, the warmth and love of his family surrounding him. The healing began.

Though she was exhausted, Colly went to White Thunder's lodge, and, at his request, told him of all that had transpired, even of the way Stone Calf had helped her escape. White Thunder sat silent for a long time, remembering the orphaned boy who had shared his tepee for a time before traveling with his father to a different destiny.

"Doll Man returned to the village and told us Lone Wolf was killed and you were taken to the fort. Although he said you fought the white soldiers, you rode with them. We were not sure if you wished to return to us. Doll Man gathered a small war party and has returned to the fort in case you wanted to escape."

"I am sorry you doubted me," she said. "My heart has never wavered in its desire to remain with the Cheyenne. I took the tomahawk to the white soldiers, but it has done little good. I can be of no further use to you against their anger. I do not know if you will cast me out now."

"Spotted Woman has been a worthy Cheyenne woman," White Thunder answered. "She is held in high esteem."

Dull Knife rose and held his hands high over the rising plumes of campfire smoke. "In my vision the white woman was the White Buffalo Woman who saved our tribe. Many times you have struggled to bring peace and safety to our people. You have earned the name of White Buffalo Woman. You are Cheyenne—and you may walk with pride among our people."

"I accept this honor," Colly answered, for she knew it was expected of her, but in her heart she would always be Spotted Woman.

When she left the tent, the villagers paused and smiled at her, welcoming her back. The crier went round the village telling the story of her deeds and of her new name. When he came to the lodge of Lone Wolf, Colly was seated inside beside her husband. He'd awakened from his sleep greatly improved. His dark eyes were clear of fever and pain and he smiled easily.

"I hear the praise heaped upon my wife's shoulders and fear I may never equal her fame," he teased.

"You are the war chief in this family," Colly said. "I am your obedient wife." Her words brought a chuckle to Lone Wolf that quickly ended in a groan of pain.

"Don't make me laugh," he gasped, holding his chest. Colly lay down beside him, running her slim hands over his chest in a soothing stroke that quickly calmed him.

"You are the sunshine on the morning dew," he whispered against her brow, and she knew these were his words of love to her.

"You are the mighty oak that grows in a mountain valley," she whispered.

"You are the prairie wind sweeping across the top of the spring grass."

"You are the sunrise—" His kiss cut off her words. She lost herself in the feel and scent of him. Her heart had been so lonely. She'd never be alone again. She thought of her secret and gently pushed against his chest.

"You are the mighty oak whose acorn grows at his feet," she whispered.

"No more, my wife," he whispered, then went rigid, pulling away to stare into her luminous eyes. His large brown hand settled on her flat stomach.

"Is it so?" he asked wondrously.

"I carry our son," she whispered, and knew her heart would never contain as much joy as it did at this moment.

Lone Wolf cradled her against him as if she were some fragile vessel; again and again his hand went to touch her stomach, and when he slept at last, his large hand rested there as if already caressing the small body of their son.

The villagers waited uneasily for Doll Man and his small war party to return. He'd been instructed not to engage the

white soldiers except in defense. The women busied themselves with tanning hides and drying meat, but their thoughts
were on the war party. The rest of the warriors stayed close
to the village, their war ponies tied nearby, their extra arrows
close at hand.

Late in the afternoon, a warning cry went up. The warriors
sprang to their ponies. The women gathered up their children
and prepared to flee to the riverbanks. A single rider entered
the village.

"The rest of the war party is coming," he declared. "We
have ridden hard to warn you that the soldiers are coming.
They are but an hour or so behind us." By the time he had
gasped out his message, Doll Man and the rest of his party
were at hand.

"Prepare to battle," he cried out. "The soldiers are less
than an hour from our village."

A cry of dismay went up among the villagers as all rushed
to do what was necessary. Colly ran to their lodge. Lone
Wolf was up and pulling on a leather shirt. His knife was
belted at his waist.

"What are you doing? You can't fight. You're wounded.
Come to the riverbank and hide."

"I will never hide with the women while my enemies
threaten my people," he declared.

"Please," Colly whispered. "I don't want the father of
my baby killed as Gentle Horse was."

Lone Wolf paused, gripping Colly's shoulders urgently.
"If I do not fight, then my son will not be proud of me. He
will be shamed that his father hid with the women along the
riverbank rather than meet his enemies."

Colly longed to plead with him. He was too weak to fight,
but she knew it was useless. She must send him out with
courage, not weeping. "Our son will never be ashamed of
his father," she said softly, and reached for his shield. Lone
Wolf took it from her and, after one brief exchange of glances,
ran from the lodge.

Colly stood with her head bowed, her lower lip caught

between her teeth so she would not call him back, and when her moment of weakness had passed, she turned to Black Moon.

"We must go to the river and hide. Can you walk?" she asked.

Black Moon nodded and threw aside her robe. Colly hurried to lend her shoulder. They made their way from the lodge. Red Bead Woman had already made bundles of food and warm furs, as well as ointments and herbs for tending the wounded. Running Deer worked at her side, her young face scared.

Amid a flurry of hoofbeats and high-pitched, defiant cries, the warriors raced from the village. They would ride out onto the prairie to engage the enemy, thus giving the women time to flee.

"Can you walk to the river?" Colly asked Black Moon again, concerned at the white rim around her lips. Black Moon nodded and waddled forward, her arms wrapped around her enlarged belly. Their progress was slow, but Colly hadn't the heart to urge Black Moon to move any faster.

Running Deer clung to Red Bead Woman, her nimble young feet tripping along the path, her wide, scared eyes going time and again to Red Bead Woman's face.

"It's all right, daughter," Red Bead Woman said over and over. "Our warriors will protect us."

In the distance Colly heard the first volley of shots, and her heart seemed to stop beating. She must be brave, she thought, and wanted nothing more than to fling aside the food packets and Black Moon's burdensome dependency on her. She wanted to run across the fields to see if Lone Wolf was still in his saddle

"Aigh," Black Moon said between her teeth.

"Lean on me," Colly said quickly, ashamed of her resentment for the other girl's weakness.

"It is time!" Black Moon moaned, her expression a mixture of fear and excitement. "My son wishes to push into the thick of battle. He will truly be a warrior."

"He can't come now," Colly said, looking around. "We're still in the open."

"He likes the sound of the war cry. He wishes to come and see for himself," Black Moon said, and sat down in the grass. "I cannot go on. I thought I could make the river, but I cannot." She began packing the grass down around her, preparing a place for her child to enter the world.

"Can't you try again?" Colly wheedled, but Black Moon shook her head. Red Bead Woman had paused and was looking back at them. Colly waved her back.

"We'll have to carry Black Moon. The baby is coming," she cried. Red Bead Woman looked at her daughter.

"Do not let him begin the journey yet," she ordered, but again Black Moon shook her head. She was already spreading a robe in the grass. Then, pulling her dress high around her buttocks, she knelt in the grass.

Colly could see the smear of blood high on her inner thigh and knew there was no time left. She knelt before Black Moon, placing the pregnant woman's hands on her shoulders so she might lend support, for there was no stout frame of poles for her to grip. Red Bead Woman began to unpack her pouches, searching for herbs and medicines to help her daughter.

"Go to the river," she told Running Deer. "Bring back water." The girl nodded dumbly and ran away.

Colly hoped in her terror she would return. She thought of the riverbanks and the safety they offered, so close and yet so far. They were exposed here in the open, but nothing could be done about that. She heard the sound of war cries and the explosion of the soldiers' guns. The Cheyenne had few guns, only old pieces that were inaccurate and rusty. Most of the warriors preferred the use of their bows and arrows and lances. But these would be of little use against the soldiers' guns.

The warriors swept over the plains like a tide. Some of the young soldiers had never seen Indians in full war regalia.

They faltered and were cursed by their leader. Major Buford gave little thought to the fact that they were facing a full war party of experienced warriors. On every encounter thus far, he'd engaged women and children and half-drunk, unprepared renegades. His contempt for the Cheyenne was complete, blinding him to the skill and courage of the plains warriors intent on protecting their villages.

The soldiers got off the first volley of shots. Several warriors swayed and slipped from their saddles. Their riderless horses charged forward. The young soldiers took heart at this first success and reloaded, but the warriors were upon them now and the battle became hand-to-hand combat. Those warriors who had seemed to be killed had only clung to the sides of their mounts and now reared up in their saddles, a more frightening visage than before for seeming to have defeated death. The horses danced about, trying to answer their riders' demand for a better stand. The battle shifted closer to the village.

Colly heard it coming closer but dared not look. She knelt before her sister-in-law, her gaze pinned on Black Moon's scarred, sweaty face. Soon she, too, would know this moment.

Black Moon made no outcry as she pushed her baby into the world. Red Bead Woman was there, her face beaming, her broad hands ready to cushion her grandson's entrance and remove him from behind his mother. Running Deer had returned with a pouch of water and sat staring at the baby with fascination.

Black Moon stayed where she was, resting, her body shuddering with the effort she'd made. Her dark eyes rolled to the side, searching out her child's face. When she caught a glimpse of his small round head with its wet black hair, she smiled, her lips drawing back from her teeth, her eyes shining. Colly was wonderstruck that in the midst of war and death and pain there could be the joyous miracle of birth. She marveled at Black Moon's bravery.

Red Bead Woman was back, running her finger into Black

Moon's mouth to tickle the back of her throat. Black Moon gagged, and with the squeezing of muscles she expelled the afterbirth. Quickly Red Bead Woman wrapped it in a bundle. "We must dry this and put it in his medicine pouch," she explained. "It contains some of his spirit and must be kept safe." The baby's umbilical cord was tied and cut and a salve from one of Red Bead Woman's mysterious pouches rubbed on it. Then she greased her grandson, powdered him with a dried and ground mixture, and wrapped him in a soft robe. She passed the squirming body to Black Moon. The love on both women's faces was enough to make Colly weep. She caught a glimpse of a tiny fist pummeling the air and felt laughter well up.

A shot sounded close by, ending their moment of wonder and magic. The women crouched in the grass, Red Bead Woman's chubby arm around Running Deer's slight body, Black Moon's body shielding her baby, and Colly's thin arms wrapped around her stomach.

Lying here in the hot prairie grass, with the smell of earth in her nostrils and the sound of death all about them, she thought of her mother and father. Life and death seemed so relentlessly intermingled. She belonged to this earth beneath them, to the sound and fury of battle, the squall of newborn life. She was part of it and it was part of her. She felt elation at this newfound truth. She would travel many roads before she was an old woman . . . and every step would be filled with living.

A horse passed close by them and she looked up. Assured by her expanded vision of life, she felt no fear. The markings on the horse were Cheyenne. Colly leaped up; then she caught a glimpse of the man on the horse and her courage faltered.

Little Bear glared down at them, his eyes terrible in a face painted black. He spared no glance for Colly. His hatred was directed at Black Moon and the baby she cradled. Colly saw the fear of death cross the once beautiful and now cruelly mutilated face.

"Are you still in need of revenge?" Colly shouted. "See

how your mark will stay on her face forever. Do you wish to bring her more pain?''

"I wish to bring her death,'' Little Bear cried, raising his lance high over his head. "Death to Gentle Horse's whore and his son. He will cease to exist on this earth.'' He drew the lance back.

"No!'' Colly screamed, leaping at the bridle of his horse. The mount shied away, rearing high. The lance flew through the air, landing harmlessly in the grass.

Little Bear took out his knife and slashed at Colly, but she refused to let go of his horse. The horse reared again, his front hooves nearly striking Colly's chest. She sprang back, tumbling in the grass.

With an evil grin Little Bear kicked at his mount, aiming to trample them all. A shot rang out, and a look of surprise crossed his face. He slid out of the saddle, his foot catching in his stirrup. Frightened at the gun blast, his horse reared again and galloped away over the plains, pulling his master behind him.

Colly lay where she'd fallen, then slowly got to her knees to peer over the stalks of grass. Major Buford sat on his horse, a grin splitting his face as he watched her.

"So we meet again, Spotted Woman,'' he said, leisurely checking the chamber of his pistol. When he was sure there were still bullets, he closed it again and aimed it at her. "I will tell my commanding officer that you were killed in the heat of battle and that you tried to kill my men and me.''

Colly pressed backward in the grass. "Why do you wish to kill me?'' she asked. "My skin isn't red.''

"Your heart is, which is worse. Besides, you've told a number of tales that didn't coincide with my telling of events. I can't have you making such accusations against me. You will be quieted; I will give my report of how you murdered one Lieutenant McKinney in your escape. You've turned into a renegade yourself and had to be killed to be stopped.''

"They won't believe you. You'll be stopped sometime. They'll see what you've done to the Indians.''

"I'll be back East and no one will care. I'll tell them about you, about a poor, half-mad creature who had turned so savage herself, she couldn't tell what was real anymore. The ladies will sigh and wonder ever so delicately what horrors you might have endured at the hands of these animals and, finally, we'll all come to the conclusion that you were in the end no better than the Cheyenne themselves."

"You're an evil man," Colly said, angling toward the lance Little Bear had thrown. But Buford was already sighting along the barrel of his gun, his finger tightening on the trigger.

No! Colly wanted to cry out, but she was silent, her hands going automatically to protect her unborn baby. She would never see his face, she thought, never hear his first hungry cry, never feel him suckle at her breast.

She waited to hear the shot, to feel the bullet, to have death claim her after all. Major Buford's hand flew up and the gun spun away. His face registered pain. An arrow shaft protruded from one shoulder.

Colly turned to see Lone Wolf riding toward them, his knees guiding Taro, his empty quiver and bow in one hand. He was weaponless. His last arrow had gone to save her.

With a snarl of rage Major Buford tore the arrow from his shoulder and twisted in his saddle, his good hand digging into his saddlebag. He brought out a tomahawk, the Sioux tomahawk Colly had given him at the fort. He braced himself, waiting for the unarmed warrior.

Colly raced for Little Bear's lance, reaching out with it as Lone Wolf rode by. His long arm shot out and he grasped the lance, bringing it up in one smooth movement. The major's smug grin faded as he saw the warrior was armed.

At Lone Wolf's command, the black war horse raced forward. The tip of the lance was driven deep into the major's heart. He was carried backward off his horse, a look of surprise on his face, his hand still gripping the Sioux tomahawk.

Taro galloped ahead a short distance, then turned as Lone Wolf commanded. Lone Wolf studied the dead body of his enemy, then looked at his wife and the other women crouched in the grass.

"Are you all right?" he asked.

Colly nodded. The sound of a bugle rang out, and the fighting soldiers paused, withdrawing some distance back on the prairie. Doll Man and the rest of the warriors gathered around Lone Wolf.

"What does this mean?" they asked. "Is it some trick of the white soldiers?"

"We have killed their leader," Lone Wolf said. "Maybe they will withdraw." They watched as a small group of riders joined the soldiers.

"That was Commander Sanderson," Colly cried. "They're showing a flag of truce." Indeed the soldiers had tied a white flag to one of their sabers and held it aloft.

"I will go to meet them," Lone Wolf said.

The other warriors lined up, ready to attack if the soldiers' actions should be a trick and Lone Wolf killed. Colly felt the stiffness of her own body as she watched him ride forward alone to meet the soldiers.

Commander Sanderson and a wounded soldier rode out to meet Lone Wolf halfway. When they met, they spoke at some length and, at last, Commander Sanderson waved to his men and they all moved across the prairie toward the place where the warriors and Colly waited. When the commander reached them, he nodded to Colly.

"Miss Mead," he said. His gaze took in the dead bodies of Little Bear and Major Buford. "Can you tell me what happened here?"

"Certainly," Colly said, and gave an accurate description of all that had occurred. "If you look at the tomahawk still clutched in Major Buford's hand, you'll see that it's the Sioux tomahawk I gave him when I came to the fort, the tomahawk I took from one of the bodies of the wagon train they attacked last summer. The warrior lying next to him is Little Bear, a renegade who has attacked our village and your wagon trains this year. Our people are innocent, Commander Sanderson, and undeserving of these attacks by your soldiers.''

"I quite agree, Miss Mead,'' the commander said. "Lieutenant McKinney has told me all about Major Buford's behavior over the past few months. He has treated the Cheyenne abominably. He had no instructions to attack your village.''

"Lieutenant McKinney?'' Colly said. "The major said he was dead. He tried to blame me for killing him.''

"He was the man who did the killing. Lone Wolf's lance has saved us from a hanging.''

White Thunder had come to join them, greeting the commander with solemn courtesy. "It is good this misunderstanding between our nations is cleared up. You are welcome to my village,'' he said.

The commander shook his head and pointed to the prairie, where soldiers were gathering their dead and tending the wounded. "I'll take my men back to the fort, White Thunder. But I'll come again, next time in peace and as a guest of the Cheyenne.''

"So be it!'' White Thunder said.

Commander Sanderson signaled to his men and they prepared to move out. He cast a last glance at Colly.

"Did you want to come to the fort with us, Miss Mead? We'll see you're returned to your people.''

"I am with my people,'' she said. "And my name is no longer Miss Mead. I am called Spotted Woman, also known as White Buffalo Woman.''

"Next time I'll remember that,'' the commander said, and rode away.

The women and children were already returning to the village. Someone came to help Black Moon back to her lodge. Red Bead Woman and Running Deer trailed behind. The smell of cooking fires and roasting meat rose on the evening air. A quietness had fallen over the prairie, a sense that all was once again as it should be, a timelessness to the land that man must learn to accept.

Lone Wolf came to stand beside Spotted Woman. Together they watched the line of soldiers disappear on the dusky horizon.

"Will there be peace now? I wonder . . ." she said softly.

"I do not know," Lone Wolf answered. "The medicine man's vision says there will be days of wailing among our people. The buffalo will come no more, the white men will take over the land, and the Cheyenne will cease to exist."

"There are not that many white men to fill these prairies," Spotted Woman said.

"Their number will grow," he said sadly. "Our Cheyenne Nation will be diminished."

"But it will survive," she insisted.

They walked toward the village fires, and Spotted Woman thought of Lone Wolf's words. There was so much about this land the white men did not know. In their ignorance, would they destroy the Mother Earth? Would they destroy the buffalo, and wild prairie grass, and the people who lived here? She couldn't imagine that kind of cruelty. She thought of Black Moon's son and her own unborn child. They were the future of the Cheyenne Nation.

"The Cheyenne will survive," she whispered fiercely. "They must!"

Author's Note

Though a relatively peace-loving tribe, the Cheyenne were often punished for the more aggressive acts of the Sioux, Kiowa, and Comanche, until they at last joined in the hostilities against the white men, which lasted for more than twenty years, ending in humiliating surrender and removal to reservations. Even friendly Cheyenne villages were attacked, as at the massacres of Ash Hollow in 1855 and Sand Creek in 1864, when women and children, as well as warriors, were slaughtered. The Cheyenne joined forces with the Sioux at the battle of the Little Bighorn against Custer but finally surrendered after the destruction of the camps of Dull Knife and Two Moons in 1877 and 1878.

The northern Cheyenne were placed in reservations in Oklahoma, where disease and starvation and unaccustomed hot weather decimated their numbers. Crooked Indian agents and government representatives often pocketed money intended to buy beef and supplies for the starving, dependent Cheyenne, so that in one last desperate attempt to return to their northern homeland, they marched and fought the thirteen thousand troops who tried to stop them. When they reached their homeland, they laid down their weapons.

In the dead of winter, they were confined in unheated barracks without food and water and eventually were force-marched back to Oklahoma. Many were wounded and killed. An estimated thirty escaped.

Today's Cheyenne have done much to adjust themselves to the white world and yet maintain their old heritage. Restitution by the government has helped protect Cheyenne lands, but no longer are they free to roam over the rolling, endless miles of prairie in search of the white buffalo.

JEAN PLAIDY

THE QUEEN OF HISTORICAL ROMANCE PRESENTS THE QUEENS OF ENGLAND